Queen Bee
and the
Turk

TAKE 1

DAPHNE MACLEOD

Contents

Dedications

To my mother who instilled, in all six of her children, the love of reading.
We love and miss you.

To my dad that always supported my crazy ideas even the goose in the
science fair.

To all the teachers out there just trying to get through the day, it is never
too late to chase a dream even one you didn't know you had.

To my friends, both old and new, who listened to my crazy ideas and
encouraged me to write them down, I can't tell you how much it means
to me that you believed in me and tolerated all my silliness.

To my immediate and extended family...surprise! I wrote a book.

Finally, to my husband. Thank you for sticking by me for the last 25 years.
Alaskan girls aren't easy. (Another book idea!)
Oh and...got you back!

Seni seviyorum.
I love you.

A portion of the proceeds of the sale of this book will be donated to the
charities below. If you would like to donate directly to these charities please
scan the QR codes provided.

Alzheimer's
Association of
America

Teachers Unify
To End Gun
Violence

Turkish
Philanthropy
Fund

Teşekkürler
Thank you.

Introduction

Hello! I just wanted to take a quick moment to explain about the birth of the book you are about to enjoy. I started writing in May of 2022 in reaction to listening to a terrible audiobook in which I naively thought that I could write better. A few other things occurred at the same time but the one that inspired this book, and subsequent books thereafter, was my new addiction to Turkish dramas. Along this journey I realized that writing makes me happy. Really happy. Not only the writing but whole writing community has been so incredibly supportive from online writing support groups to the romance book club at my local independent book store.

Ten years ago, my husband surprised me with the funds to be able to go back to school to earn another teaching credential so I could once again teach. I haven't been able to figure out a way to pay him back then I had the brilliant idea of surprising my husband with the possibility of earning some extra money with my writing to help pay our for our daughter's college. Until the day this book launches, my husband thinks I've been looking for bracelet ideas and reading advance reader copies. In my defense, those tabs were also open on my laptop.

Many people in my life inspired my ideas for the book series as I've been told many time to write what you know. I also wrote who you know. Please understand it is with love and admiration that your essence has found its way into these pages. (please don't be pissed)

I hope you enjoy Beatrice and Ihsan's story. If you would like to support my efforts to continue their story, please consider leaving a review on any platform you'd like. I hope you had just as much fun reading this book as I had writing it.

All this to say, when you feel inspired and the universe gives you opportunities, SAY EVET! (that's "yes" in Turkish)

If you'd like receive my newsletter and keep up to date on future releases, visit www.daphnemacleodauthor.com.

Content Warning – This book refers to issues of school violence, PTSD, and child abuse.

Chapter 1

B EATRICE FREDRICKS

"Three strikes, Matthew, I'm done. I've struck out on life."

The path in the space between my couch and the coffee table has become the stage for my command performance.

"Hold on. What are you talking about? You started in the middle of the second scene, sweetie," Matthew replies from the square on the laptop screen. Living in Hollywood has him using movie set vocabulary. "Start from the top."

"Strike one: my mom doesn't know me. When I visit, she panics as if I'm an intruder in her room. She's barely recognizable. It's more painful to be with her than without her." I turn sharply at the end of my path to emphasize the points on my list. "Strike two: there is no one special holding me here. We both know I'm not dating. Who wants to deal with all of this? I couldn't ask them to. Oh, but wait. Just when I think that's enough the universe says, 'hold my beer, let me show you what I've got.' Which brings me to strike three: I can't teach here anymore. I can't walk into the school and pray that I walk out at the end of the day. Did you know the district is calling the hostage standoff 'the intruder incident'? I can't look my students in the face and know their lives could depend on me," I say, finally voicing all my woes for the first time out loud to anyone. This past week resembles a dumpster fire on top of a train wreck covered in hot mess sauce.

"I know something is wrong if you're making sports references and not movie ones. Have you checked for a fever or rash?" His face gets closer to the screen as if searching for the red skin specks himself.

"Matthew, this is serious," I say, trying to convince him that this is a life-changing moment.

"Rashes are serious."

I continue ignoring his attempts to derail me. "My parents traveled the world twice over by the time they were my age and I have been stuck in the fire swamp barely escaping getting burned."

"There you are, Bee. You were almost unrecognizable. All the panicking and baseball talk. Wait, was it *Bull Durham*, *Moneyball*, or *Field of Dreams*?"

"*A League of Their Own*," I answer sheepishly. "But that's beside the point."

"Shouldn't you be talking to Brandon, I'm usually the Schroeder brother you call for gay comic relief."

He's right, Brandon would have understood a lot better but these days Brandon is occupied. Very happily occupied. How do I tell Matthew that strike two was actually Brandon without telling him it was Brandon? I could handle my mom and stupid Brandon's feelings but strike three, that was it.

But when push came to shove, Matthew was always good for help in desperate situations. And this situation felt like the most desperate of all. I haven't seen him in person since he moved to Los Angeles a year ago to work for a publicist. From the excitement I hear in his voice during our weekly online movie nights, LA has been good for him, and he's been good for LA. He fits in with the LA scene with his six-foot-two, lean, slightly muscular stature, and his short dark brown hair with the perfect amount of wave that is on its best behavior most days.

"Because you're on the outside. You already escaped."

A week ago I spent three hours hunkered down in my classroom calming my frantic students, waiting for the "all clear" without any clue about the emergency. After several texts between my teacher tribe, I was informed a man entered the office with a gun demanding his child be released to him. Immediately, the school nurse ducked into the health office and called 911. The "Mr. Roadrunner is in the building," announcement initiated the lockdown. It escalated into a hostage situation where the enraged man blocked off exits and corralled the front office staff. With the blares of sirens and emergency vehicles racing down the street echoing in my ears, I finally decided it's time to throw in the towel. No amount of training prepares you for the real thing. Three hours is a lot of time to think about all the decisions you've made in your life. It's like riding a hobby horse for years and then they throw you on the back of a thoroughbred and smack it on the ass. So here I am, asking my dearest friend to help me plan my escape.

"Matthew, I need to leave. I can't think about my life a lesson at a time anymore. Hell, I need to have a life. I need to change...everything." I couldn't stop the desperation in my voice. At least I stopped short of whining.

"Woah, Bee. Inhale, sweetie. We got this. I tell people all day long what they should do, and I can do this for you, too," he takes a minute to think. The outline of his lean, muscled arms break into frame as he runs his fingers through the blonde spot above his ear. A not-so-subtle reminder of the beauty in imperfection.

"What is anchoring you there? Is there anything in San Antonio that you can't find somewhere else."

His plain brown eyes gleam of 'up to no good,' which usually sends warning bells but today I trust he has tempered his natural tendency for mischievous antics. The family genes are strong in his straight, severe jawline. With thousands of dollars of orthodontia, perfectly straight teeth create a stunning smile which supports my gut instinct to always be a little suspicious. Teeth that straight aren't right. I don't believe I have ever seen a single chin hair, nor five o'clock shadow, much less fur of any kind on him other than his perfect mane.

I look around my home for any clues to answer his question. The macrame plant hangers that I made with my class and my childhood pictures hanging there since I was little are not keeping me from leaving. This was my childhood home, but this was my mom's house. This was her life, not mine.

"My mom's house."

"You can always live somewhere else. Would you be willing to sell it?" Matthew replies.

Mom won't ever be returning and I don't have the time or know how or really the desire to make major changes in the house. It's filled with her memories and I'm just the caretaker of them. The easiest and most dramatic change would be to scrap it and start from scratch.

"I would."

"Is there anything else?"

"Changing everything includes teaching. That is not my path anymore. I have options, right?" I plead.

"Of course. I just need to know your parameters," he says.

Matthew has always loved using me as a project. He does everything in his power to get me out of the house, out of my head and out of my comfort zone. Sometimes, he was actually successful; dragging me to college parties where I became the drink cup monitor or the potted plant human support person.

"What is your money situation? Do you have savings?"

"I'm a SINK, single income, no kids. So, I'm better off than most."

"We can work with that," he says with hope and confidence in his voice. "If you are serious, you need to take the first step. You need to resign."

A giant gulp involuntarily drains down my throat. That is the r-word.

"I could take a sabbatical," I say, losing confidence in my earlier convictions.

"Stop! You are not giving yourself an out. You just made a big deal about retiring. You even made sports references for God's sake. You can't give yourself a safety net. You are at the contemplation stage of change. It's time for action. Look at that pit and have no idea if there is a net at the bottom. Be divergent or whatever."

He is speaking my love language with the movie reference. Calling Matthew was the right move. Something must have stuck during the three semesters he spent as a psychology major.

"Resigning not retiring. I've only been in the system six years. But you're right. Suck it up because there is no crying in baseball!" I shout, channeling my inner Jimmy Dugan.

After saying our goodbyes, I push Matthew's fading face down to the keyboard, walk into my bedroom, stand with my back toward my bed and fall into the covers à la nineties teen movie style, blindly onto the mattress. My mind wanders to Brandon as it usually does.

Brandon is the founding member of the "'Bee Team," as the group lovingly calls it. The Schroeder brothers were both the love and curse of my collegiate life. I met Schroeder brother number one, Brandon, when he knocked on the piano practice room door one evening. I was trying to work out some accompaniments for my side gig, piano accompanist for my former high school choir director, Mr. Davis. It was the first time in my life I really understood what speechless meant. I opened my mouth and my vocal cords were paralyzed.

How was I supposed to communicate with this incredibly good-looking man when we clearly did not live on the same planet?

He towered over me with the same two inches over six feet as Matthew, his younger brother. With floppy, dark, curly hair, a smooth strong jaw, piercing blue eyes and an almost overly buff body of a rugby player, his casual friendliness and grit he showed to learn the piano endeared him to me. He did not just want to pass the elective class he needed for his degree, he really wanted to play. In most cases, I would have dismissed him but his magic charm seeped into my blood and I was defenseless. It also rubbed my funny bone to watch his giant body sitting over the piano keys and watching them best him. Besides the brown hair, he looked remarkably like the piano player from the "Peanuts" cartoon. The Schroeder name was just a perfect coincidence until Matthew called me Lucy and then it hit too close to home.

The University of San Antonio music building never saw someone so enthralled as Brandon was the day I brought him into the recital hall. His eyes grew to the size of teacup saucers and he shushed me as if he was an old grandma in church. I understood his reverence as the wood acoustic paneling framed the grand floor to ceiling Casavent Fréres organ. It was my church.

Matthew was the free gift with purchase. A gift, as they say, that keeps on giving even into post graduate adulthood. Schroeder brother number two invaded my social circle when I spotted him wearing Elton John glasses at Brandon's class recital, not for attention, but to distract Brandon from a rare case of stage fright. Little did I know that after that recital, Brandon wasn't finished with me. To my surprise, we cultivated a friendship during those lessons. We enjoyed each other's sense of humor, taste in classic movies and retro music. If I had all the typical physical attributes that attracted the opposite sex, I like to think that it could have been more. But my thickness in all the wrong places didn't allow me such privileges. Instead, I fell in love with Brandon and reveled in what attention I was allowed, friendship.

I couldn't have asked for better friends my first semester of college. They made this "townie" participate in everything the university had to offer, from the campus freshman scavenger hunt to building floats for the Dîa en la Sombrilla festival during Fiesta San Antonio. Although he said it was to help all the student organizations on campus, I suspect Matthew was adamant we participate because he wanted to ride the float. I swear, any excuse to wear a boa. I didn't realize how impressionable eighteen was. All over campus, bronze hearts are scattered so passersby can rub them and be granted a miracle. I mapped the path to my classes based on how many hearts I could touch, to increase my chances that Brandon would suddenly realize he's in love with me and come sprinting across campus and lay a giant breath stealing kiss on me. Alas, I remained still breathing with untouched lips. According to my math, the universe owes me. It can start right now, while I'm stuck at home waiting for the next shoe to fall.

After the decision not to return to school for the six weeks left of the academic year, parents were given a few days where students could return books or gather anything from classrooms they needed. It would take a lot more time than six weeks to rebuild the sense of safety in that building. Families were offered to enroll their children in other schools or attend online classes. Either way, it felt weird. The librarian finally gave up empty book boxes she hoarded like a psycho hobbit so I could bring home the things that I truly valued: letters from students, picture frames with images of fun spirit days with my teacher besties and a triangular prism desk decoration of the motto "You Got This" in a skinny font that I got from a Secret Santa. I stared at it a moment and placed it in the box in between a couple of half dead plants that hadn't been watered since the lockdown.

Because of the small amount of stuff I was packing into my car, none of my comrades knew I was leaving for more than just the summer. I left all the classroom supplies I had ever purchased or recycled in my room and decorations I used to inspire slash/annoy my students on the walls. As I turned to say my farewells to my classroom, the sadness I thought I would feel turned to excitement with a giant dollop of apprehension.

Most teachers are still in shock and walk around with tunnel vision just to cope. There is an unspoken understanding that we just aren't ready. For anything. The feeling of dread is almost physically measurable throughout the buildings. Friends that would normally greet each other with smiles and a witty comment, cast their eyes down and avoid conversation.

The principal sent out another email about support for not only students and families but also teachers as well. A Band-Aid for a serrated artery. So many of my teacher friends can't get out. They are too dependent and invested in their careers. For the first time, I am grateful I am not one of them and with Matthew's assistance I can make a clean break.

Since the initial call to assemble, Matthew created an online checklist where he laid out my Texas escape plan, updated daily. Sometimes hourly when he's feeling particularly spunky. He even made boxes next to the items so I could check them off. It started off as a simple list but quickly turned into a full-fledged manifesto. This is what I need though. I need to feel in control, but I also need someone to hold me accountable.

Step 1-Pack up classroom. Check.

Step 2-Send resignation letter to my principal and human resources with my intent not to return for the next school year. Half check.

Step 3-Debrief the "Bee Team."

Step three would be the hardest. This is going to come out of the blue.

The most recent member of the "Bee Team" was Sarah. The most beautiful school psychologist that has ever graced a middle school campus. You never saw so many middle school boys more than happy to go to the office. Sarah and I are the yin and yang of our little microcosm. Where she is tall, I am short. Where her eyes shine pure aquamarine, mine are a mash up of green, brown and gold. Where she is up on all the teacher-gram fashions, I am lucky to leave the house with matching shoes. Where she is fit, I am well...not. Where she resembles a graceful gazelle on the plains of the Serengeti, I bear a striking resemblance to a baby rhinoceros; cute, a bit round and quick on her feet. Where her naturally highlighted brunette hair is shoulder length and always styled without a strand out of place, mine can't decide between brown and blonde and is rarely released from it's tethers lest it gets caught in a drawer, door, or giant laminator.

When I "shipped", as my students say, Brandon and Sarah I wasn't surprised when it turned from fantasy to reality and they became "shipped" for real. When I first heard the term, I thought my students were talking about ,but then one kind girl took pity on me and explained it was a play on the word "relationship." No wonder I didn't get it.

Weirdly enough, Brandon's choice of women often saw me as a threat. When he started dating anyone, I backed off our daily calls or texts. It hurt too much to hear about his new girl and most of the time, I found fault with them. It was too hard not to share my opinions. But I knew Sarah before Brandon did and she checked all of his boxes. Inviting Sarah to our little gatherings and inserting facts about her into our conversations means I can safely take credit for covertly setting them up. He is a different kind of happy with her. A happy I've never made him or ever will.

Closing the door of the back seat of my Honda with the two boxes of things I couldn't leave behind, I take a moment to think of the most inconspicuous path to Sarah's office. I decide on the one that takes me by the vice principal's office but avoids all the front office staff, principal's secretary, and principal's office. I make my way grinch-like, on my tip toes, through the side office door and knock quietly on the small square window insert. The lighting in her office is dim and the air smells of lilacs. She turns to the tiny window and ushers me in. I could see by the unfamiliar dark bags under her eyes and her low energy level that her sympathy tank is running low after the past week and I didn't need to pile it on.

"Hey, it's my favorite math teacher," she looks at me with her perfect smile.

"Hey, it's my favorite head shrinker," I reply. She always laughs at my various mislabelings of her profession.

"Do you have like ten minutes to talk?" I ask. I never say a moment because I'm a talker and it's not right to suck up people's time if they aren't prepared. And likewise, if you ask me a question you better be prepared for the answer.

"Of course."

She turns off her monitor as she always does to avoid distraction.

"I've made a big decision, and I wanted you to know before I tell Brandon, I'm not sure how he'll react," I take a long deep breath. "I've been unhappy for a while."

"I've had my suspicions, but figured I would let you be until you were ready to talk. It's the one time I would approve of enabling."

"I appreciate that. I can't stand people looking at me with pity," I reply.

"Sooooo?! Are you getting a pet or new furniture?" She smiles again trying to help ease me into the conversation.

"I'm changing. Everything."

"What does that mean, specifically?"

"I just sent in my resignation letter. I'm selling my house and I'm moving out of Texas."

Now that I have voiced my plans, they feel more real and my gut wrenches slightly at hearing the words out loud. Until now, Matthew's checklist had just been black and white words on a screen with a few red check marks. The voice of Little Red Riding Hood from *Into the Woods* rings in my head. She really does sing it best as she explains her traumatic experience being eaten by a wolf, "made me feel excited, well, excited and scared." The excitement of a possible pivotal change on the horizon encourages me to continue explaining my thought process.

"Teaching doesn't fill my soul the way it used to. I can't even think about going back into the classroom now. Texas just holds too many bad memories. I'm not too old to make a different path for myself. I've made a few plans, but I've dreaded telling my friends," motioning to the office outside.

"So, where are you looking? What are you going to do? Tell me everything," she says excitedly, her eyes growing larger.

Sarah's reaction settles a few of my nerves. Two out of the three of the most important people are with me. So far, so good.

"I don't know. I've joined a few online groups for teachers transitioning, but I'm waiting for an idea to jump off the screen. Because that's the way it works, you know," I laugh at my faux naivety.

"Aren't you scared?"

"Not as scared as I was," I say, bringing the mood of the room down. "I'm ready for change. The truth is I'm lonely and there isn't any man here that will solve that problem. I put a smile on my face to make you all think I'm happy so you wouldn't feel sorry for me. I never date." I finish with the most humiliating statement of all. Almost as humiliating as Carl.

Carl was Brandon and Matthew's first and only attempt to set me up. We dated for a month back in college but when our relationship became more physical, it stopped being something I looked forward to. After a grand total of four sexual "experiences," I found out he had cheated on me, with a guy. A guy I knew. A guy I saw on a regular basis which apparently, Carl was doing as well. To say that put me off men would be an understatement, it put me off humanity. I couldn't put my finger on why Carl's cheating had a special sting to it. Regardless of who he cheated on me with, it was still cheating. I already had a difficult time believing that Carl would stay with me but to not know my competition doubled, was worse.

Sarah looks at me with slightly squinted eyes and a half smile. That is exactly what I wanted to avoid. This stung deep. I don't need to be pitied; I need to be supported. It's unlikely that she ever felt looked over, put aside, or less than in society's eyes.

Sensing my hurt by my confession, Sarah grabs my hands from across her desk and squeezes.

"What do you need from me? What can I do to help? I'm looking for a distraction anyway."

"First, don't tell Brandon. Not yet. I'll tell him later. He's going to want details that I just don't have yet and he'll be mad at Matthew for not telling him earlier. We'll do a video call. Are you two available tonight?" I ask.

Brandon in the flesh is much harder to deal with than Brandon on a screen. I knew it wasn't fair, to ask her to keep this to herself for more than a day.

"I'll make sure we're available," Sarah says, still squeezing my hands.

"Thank you. Matthew probably wants to show his brother what he actually does for a living. Brandon is always busting his balls calling him Prada like he's the assistant in that movie," I say with a smirk across my face.

They were always busting each other's balls. I'm surprised either have any left.

Feeling the conversation coming to a close and the urgency to get out of the building, I decide the conversation is over for the time being.

"Ok, I'm out. I can hear someone calling the cops on me for leaving my plants in a parked car in the sun without cracking a window."

I slip out the office side door, walk quickly to my car and turn on the ignition. I'm pretty sure it's distracted driving to operate a vehicle like you are seeing underwater. I give myself a moment to look back and let it sink in that I won't be pulling into this parking lot again. I put the car in reverse, but it doesn't move. I still can't take the leap. I already sent my letter of resignation and it's not like I can recall that. The keys jangle from the ignition.

Oh sh...it.

I didn't get to have my "badge and keys" moment, the moment that all teachers dream about. The point where they deposit their keys and ID badge on the school administrative assistant's desk and walk out without any regrets.

I guess I need to adult now.

I return to the office as quietly as I possibly can. The attendance secretary is on the phone, the data processor is busy deciphering paperwork and the principal's secretary isn't at her desk. Screw adulting. I quickly drop my keys and ID badge on the middle of her desk and with all of my ninja skills, I sneak around the corner and quickly push on the long bar on the front office door. No one would know I was there. As I try to push the door open, I realize I had forgotten that I should have used the right-side door. The long bar sticks, hard. I slam my face into the school crest painted on the window, drawing all the attention to the front office entry. Wouldn't it be fitting if I had the school's crest embedded in my face? I should have called that. I quickly move to the right and wave goodbye to the office quickly to avoid any concerns for my face. At least I gave them one good laugh before I left.

As I drive home, I realize that I should have made my escape epic. I should have had a clever message painted on the windows of my car like "peace out, bitches" or "suck it, bitches." It definitely had to end in "bitches." "School's Out for the Summer" should have been blasting as I drove through the neighborhood. Watching my former life shrink in the rear-view mirror gives me a peaceful, cathartic feeling as well as the growing excitement of beginning my new life, whatever form it takes.

IHSAN ZORLU

I've never had to pack for such a long trip. After I repack my third suitcase, I realize I'm about to move to the motion picture capital of the world with one of the highest costs of living. There are several places to buy what I want or things I've forgotten and I'll have time before filming starts to get the lay of the land.

My email inbox is full of applicants to be my personal assistant and none of them meet the requirements I sent to Blaine. All of the potentials include headshots attached to their recommendations and credentials. Not just a picture from their phone but a touched up, air brushed, forward focused headshot I myself have had taken. Asli, my current assistant, is afraid of flying and won't be joining me. I'm not disappointed. She tends to have difficulty going beyond the daily list. She consistently misses the little things that make me happy like checking the tissue box to see if it needs to be refilled or making sure I use the same dry cleaner every time my clothes need special care.

"Blaine, none of these people meet my minimum requirements. If I have to go with a temporary assistant until we find the right one, that is fine," I say into my phone. I click send and the message is sent to my slightly odd American agent.

I only have a few days until I leave for America and I'm trying to stay calm. I've been blessed to have such an amazing career in Türkiye but co-starring in a big Hollywood movie is a dream realized. I need to pinch myself almost hourly to remind myself that I'm awake. Asli is busy looking for new employment, so she hasn't been as accessible as she usually is.

"*Abi*," my sister's familiar voice floats up the stairs followed by two loud barks.

"*Abla*, thank goodness. I'm having a hard time figuring out what I need to pack."

Zeki follows her inside my room and lays down in his favorite corner, where he can stretch his long legs against the wall.

"Where are all the boxes?"

"I'm not taking boxes."

"No, you have tenants, remember? You need to pack up everything so they can move in."

"Asli!" I almost scream in frustration.

"Take your favorite everything and I'll help you find a moving company."

"That's what I was trying to do but I still ended up with more than three suitcases of stuff."

"One suitcase for your workout stuff and then one for casual and one for fancy."

"What am I going to do without you?" I say, bringing her into a hug.

I've always had a supportive family but Farah leads the charge whenever I needed a kick in the pants or shove in the right direction. She might have enjoyed it a little too much. The only sibling rivalry between us was who could get the adults to laugh the hardest. My younger brother, Nadir, joined in as soon as he was able to speak. Our family table was never short of laughter. Now I'm flying to the other side of the world and will have to break in a new set of people. It hasn't been a difficult task in the past but I'm moving to a foreign country and the last thing I need is to say or do something I didn't know wasn't cool. That is why this personal assistant is so crucial. Sometimes I need to be kept in check.

I'm excited about moving up to the next level of my acting career. Not many foreign actors make it in Hollywood and none from Türkiye that I know of. They usually cast someone that Hollywood thinks looks and sounds like they come from my part of the world. Türkiye 's population varies almost as much as the United States. To be cast as one of the lead roles in a film that takes place in both countries is a once in a lifetime chance. So many variables had to be solved and when each one fell into place, I knew my new role was meant to be. I've always listened to my inner voice, or gut feeling as some people say. I think of it as *Allah* whispering to me. I'm ready for the challenge that all these life changes will throw at me. But first, I need to find someone more competent than Asli. I hope she finds other employment in my absence. I shouldn't have hired a friend of a relative.

Chapter 2

BEATRICE

At seven thirty P.M. sharp I click on the icons for the other participants in the video meeting. Sarah and Brandon are right on time and, for pure dramatic effect, Matthew appears a minute late in a rainbow boa which would surprise some but not me. Sarah decided that it was probably better if she was with Brandon when I made my announcement so he has a chance to process this information with her to explain more if he needed it. This is the first time in his adult life that I won't be at his beck and call. I won't be available to him whenever he needs. Besides, he has Sarah now so I'm leaving him in capable hands. I'm not really leaving him. He isn't mine. He never was mine. Not in anything other than friendship. I need new connections. I need a life free of old ties to keep me from trying new things.

Team Bee Assemble!

"Okay, troops, we are meeting today not to enjoy our typical retro movie marathon but to announce the ..." How do I put this cleverly?

"To announce...well, I'm quitting my life," I say abruptly.

Brandon's face falls from a slight smile to a hard look of confusion and back to a slight smile again.

"What does that mean? Mid-life crisis style?" Brandon asks.

"At twenty-eight, Brandon? Rude, much? I'm leaving teaching, I'm leaving Texas. I'm leaving my sorry excuse for a life. I'm trading in my old one for a shiny new one with all the bells, whistles, glitter and rhinestones," I smile excitedly...ok, fake excitedly, mostly nervous.

Brandon had never really been good at reading me, so I hope he buys it.

"I've been working with Matthew on my exit/escape strategy. We have a multi-tier plan outlined for a change in location and change in career. So,

I'm calling this meeting as a brainstorming session. We need to answer a few questions. What do I want in a new living arrangement? What do I want in a new career? What do I want in a relationship? Matthew insisted we put that one in. So, if we skip it, I won't be upset," I say in my official teacher voice.

Brandon's face looks a bit stunned and Sarah's hand brushes his shoulder to comfort him.

"Wait, wait, wait. I need a moment to process," Brandon blurts.

I'm sure you can count to ten, Brandon. Especially in years. That's got to be a world record in pining.

Brandon never made me feel 'less than.' He smiled openly when he saw me and never skimped on platonic affection. Our inside jokes made me feel special. He made me feel special. He would text me when his rugby team was playing. I'd show up and sit with his cheering section and scream louder than anyone else whether I knew what was going on or not. I'd starve if I didn't hear something from him every day. Several times I tried to pull away, not showing up at games or just casual hangouts with Matthew but he wouldn't let that stand and found me hiding in my house or in the practice room building, sucking me right back in. Every now and again, I would show interest in someone else. Usually, it was a ruse to try to throw him off the scent of my utter obsession with him. I wasn't brave enough to ever approach any of my potential partners, so I gradually mentioned them less and less and that seemed to do the trick. I was terrified that if he ever knew how I truly felt that it would sour our friendship and I'd lose what I had with him. I tried, I really did but being with Brandon was easy and agonizing at the same time and that is more than I had ever had with any other man. I had to take what I could get. Besides, I had my imagination and at night I'd lay my head down on my pillow and play out scenarios in my head where he didn't care about my size because he valued who I was and not what I looked like. Fodder for a teen movie for sure. Sleep would overtake me with a smile on my heart, but the next interaction quickly wiped it away.

Unfortunately, Matthew had a front row seat. I appreciated his distance when it came to Brandon. He never tried to make anything happen between us nor did he discourage our friendship. He couldn't disguise his pity though. His eyebrows are his tell. No matter what the rest of his face was doing, his eyebrows told his true feelings. If I needed to cry he held me and listened, but he never tried to fix it. My mom did the same thing. It seemed to be an unspoken rule among my small circle to avoid talking about my feelings about Brandon at all costs, which is why Carl was such a devastating personal disaster. I convinced myself to listen to Brandon and Matthew to try out someone else for the position of boyfriend and turns out he didn't really want the job.

When I discovered Carl's betrayal I became the piano practice building's resident hermit. Brandon found me the evening after I broke up with Carl, crying so hard that my tears wet the keys. He just so happened to want to do the same thing over a break-up and came armed with a bottle of whiskey. I could never bring myself to tell him that Carl played for both teams and I didn't make the cut. The humiliation was more than my already fragile ego could handle. With my mom suffering from early onset Alzheimer's, it was perfectly logical for that to be the reason for my tear downpour. There was no way I was going to tell him that Carl preferred blondes. Male blondes. I used her as the source of my sorrow when in reality it was everything but that. He got me raging piss drunk and having zero fucks left in my wallet, I confessed my undying love to him as he rested his drunk skull on my shoulder. He responded with a long-drawn-out snore. I mustered up all of my bravery in that one moment and bore my soul to Sleeping Beauty. It was then that I pledged to never open my big mouth about romantic feelings again. I put it out of my mind until everyone moved on to someone or somewhere else and I was left holding the bag of crappy feelings. Time to change strategies and here we are.

"No more waiting. I'm tired of waiting to be happy. I've been waiting too long," I say urgently back to the little camera above the screen.

"Bee, you can start over here." Brandon tries again.

"You are missing the point. I am 'Bee-flat' here," I say, hoping he gets my music reference. "I need to go. Do you know I heard someone in the grocery store actually say that we were lucky it was just a hostage situation and that it could have been worse? Is that our baseline now? Survival? I'm not going to be around for the next maniac." My voice starts to shake at the end of the sentence, but everyone's face is stoic in understanding.

"And you shouldn't," Sarah says. "That's why we're here, honey."

"Okay," Matthew says, attempting to break the tension. "Let's start with the plan. I have the basic steps but we need to fill in some details so I can see some more of those cute little red checks on our spreadsheet that make me happy. What kind of weather, what kind of night life, what kind of culture are you looking for?"

"I want to be somewhere central. Where there's a variety of things to do around me. I'm looking to get out of my comfort hole."

"Zone...you mean," Brandon interjected.

"No, you know I pick my words very carefully. I'm in a comfort hole," I say, emphasizing the last word.

Brandon looks as if he's going to interject again, clearly not liking where this conversation is going, so I quickly continue.

"I want sun and sea. I want to walk down to the Saturday farmer's market and haggle with the avocado guy while a little girl sings with her dad and a karaoke machine for tips. Texas churns my stomach now," I continue.

The edges of Matthew's smile spread out wider than normal making the hairs on the back of my neck stand on end, tell tale sign his mind is full of evil thoughts.

"I was hoping you would be this adventurous. Come to LA! I mean, you don't have to be in LA proper, but we have everything. We've got fresh produce and stage dads. I can at least find you a place and a job for the time being until you find your way."

"Don't you have your mom's RV?" Sarah asks.

"Oh no. She's been watching too many van conversion YouTube videos," replies Brandon mockingly.

"No, I'm serious. It would keep your living costs low, leave your options open and you'd always be able to up and leave if you get a bee in your undies," Sarah continues.

"I'm pretty sure that isn't a real saying," Brandon eyes Sarah suspiciously.

"A bee in your underwear is far worse than a bee in your hat," she looks at Brandon and he concedes to her logic.

"That monstrosity from *Christmas Vacation*?" Matthew interrupts to break up the Sarah and Brandon show.

"It's not that bad. It's been in storage since before I moved mom to the home. That's what my parents drove on their Forty-Eight States Tour."

"Will it even start? Is it safe?" Matthew's questions are valid. I also have serious doubts about the functionality of anything in that Frankenmobile.

"That might actually be a good idea. I won't have to couch surf and I'll still have my own space. I can use the money from the sale of the house to fund my adventure."

My mind starts to churn. I think I can feel the neurons firing in my brain.

"Ok, LA RV trip it is!" I exclaim.

Matthew pumps both his fists in the air with an uncharacteristic, "Huzzah!"

"That doesn't work with a rainbow boa, sweetie," I respond.

"Everything works with a rainbow boa," he says, sticking his chin in the air and spinning the feathery scarf around his neck to emphasize his point.

"What about all of your stuff you've accumulated your whole life in the house?" Brandon pleads. Apparently during the few minutes he's had to process, he's turned into the Grouch.

"If Debbie Downer and a wet blanket had a baby, you're it. I think we all just heard the sad trombone riff in the background," Matthew teases.

Matthew always has the best way of describing exactly what I am feeling. Where Brandon knows what I like, Matthew always puts into words how it makes me feel. The later years in college, when spring hit and everyone broke out their skimpier wear, Matthew and I would sit on a blanket on a large grass patch and be super judgy. I know I'm a hypocrite, but it was my coping mechanism to deal with my insecurities. This was another way for me to get some sun on my legs since of course that would make them look less dimply and Matthew could survey the male prospects without looking too suspicious.

We had a secret code for certain things so when we were out in the general population we could say what we were really thinking, but not use words that would offend if overheard. Our favorite was "Did you hear that?" It was code for the sound of panties hitting the floor because the person in view was so hot, so attractive, so unattainable that the moment needed acknowledgement but couldn't be put into other words. It also caught people off guard and defused the situation. Most of the time when that phrase was uttered it was to keep you from opening your mouth and panting or saying something awkward. Our last semester of school, Matthew and I took a geology class together and the first day the teaching assistant walked in with his Nordic self, we both leaned to each other and proclaimed, "Did you hear that?" in which the white Viking replied, "Yeah, those lights make a very annoying hum." We both blushed, nodded and opened our books to some random page to look busy because we certainly weren't lusting after the same man.

"The next step of our plan is to determine my travel route. I need places to stop, places to eat, places to see because if I'm really going to do this I might as well live it up. But I guess I need to find a real estate agent first. I'll call around to my mom's family and see if anyone is interested in the house. I would rather have it go to someone in the family than to a stranger. It would also be nice to know that there'd be someone in town looking out for my mom. Does anyone know if I need to get some kind of special license or training to drive an RV? Do I tow a car? So many questions!" I say as I clutch my head.

"There's a better chance a car tows your mom's RV than the RV towing the car." Matthew says.

His point is valid. The best chance of not breaking down is getting my own rig. Besides, I have some money and I can always sell it if needed.

Brandon raises his hands as if he's going to try to calm me down, so I press on in an attempt to distract him from trying to talk me out of this.

"I should get a three-legged dog."

Sarah's face contorts in confusion.

"Why a three-legged dog?"

Brandon sits up and takes a deep breath before responding.

"Three legged dogs are the happiest creatures on the planet. You can't be mad at a three-legged dog. They only have three legs. They are inspiring and they've overcome so much adversity," he says as if reciting the Pledge of Allegiance.

Sarah laughs and shakes her head. Matthew, not one to be sidetracked while on a mission, takes advantage of the moment to get our planning back on track.

"Focus people," he claps into the camera.

"Should we have some kind of definite moving date or should we just go with the flow?" I ask.

"Let's figure out what Bee is going to do when she gets there and that should help with the timeline," Sarah adds.

"I've made quite a few contacts in this area," Matthew says, his eyes growing large as if the ideas are filling his skull. "Let me do some research and recon. Let's think about your skills."

The excitement in his voice is contagious.

"Well, I'm good with paperwork. I'm good at multitasking. I can simultaneously sort papers, hold a conversation, and return an email. That's got to be good for something."

"Teachers got it down for sure. It's just...do you really wanna step out?" Brandon asks.

"Yes, I do. The profession is leeching the soul out of me. There just isn't enough balance between the happy times and ...well, everything else."

"Well, don't put it out of your mind entirely. We all know about the teacher shortage," Brandon reminds the team.

"And it's not just the difficult kids, it's the difficult parents. And then there is all the other crap."

I take a deep breath to soothe the anxiety as it threatens to hijack the conversation. This is a start of something new, this is exciting. I can do this. I can do exciting. I've been playing it safe for so long, telling myself that I'm here for the kids. That's safe. Or at least it used to be. I need to do something for myself and take a risk even if that means risking it all.

"Well guys, I think we have something to work with. Let's delegate jobs," Matthew says. "I call employment!"

"I'll look into RVs," Brandon volunteers, a little begrudgingly. I can't tell if he is warming up to the idea or accepting that he hasn't won this battle.

"Let's see how much I can get for the house and how much I should save. So, I have finances."

Sarah exclaims, "I'll find the real estate agent I used."

With this group of incredibly capable and committed friends, I feel the love and the confidence they have in me revving up the engines inside. I wasn't planning on sleeping tonight, anyway.

Chapter 3

B EATRICE

The next week turns into a flurry of activity which is exactly what I need to keep my mind off my current state of being. Brandon, Sarah, Matthew and I spend an evening planning out what RV parks I will stop at, where the food stops will occur and how many miles I will be driving per day. When we go to pick up the carefully researched and vetted RV with tow package attached, the dealer sends us over to an empty parking lot where I get to practice. The RV drives, and looks, like a large minivan which is still bigger than anything I have driven before. I didn't kill any orange cones so we are all satisfied that I will be safe or at least random orange cones will be. I decided that I might just want to take along most of my food because driving into strange cities with this rig may stress me out. We figure it should take no more than five days depending on how long I want to drive each day.

Dealing with my mom's house couldn't have been easier. I was more than thrilled at my aunt and uncle's offer to buy it. They were so happy to help that it all seemed serendipitous. My cousin Travis, retired from the military, needed a place of his own. He was having some difficulty returning to civilian life and having a familiar place to heal and rejuvenate would help him enter back into the real world. They had all the paperwork drawn up and I was happy with the price. I suggested he take a shot at seeing if he could get my mom's RV back in shape, to give him something to do in his off time. There were lots of my mom's things to pack up but I only took a few pictures, including my favorite of my mom and dad at Machu Picchu. The framed cross stitch with the phrase "This too shall pass" also made it into the box. The furniture all stayed, and I told Travis that if he didn't like anything he could sell it or give it away. The final walk through with my aunt, uncle and cousin would have been more painful had I not had so many things to look forward to.

One of the last things on my list is to visit with my mom in the memory care facility before I drive off into the proverbial sunset. My aunt and uncle offered to come with me so when I see her I have a buffer to help me keep it together. My aunt is several years younger than my mom and I often wonder if she sees her future when she looks at her.

As we enter her room we hear her humming "Strangers in the Night" in a volume that seemed a bit loud for someone alone.

"Hey, Mom? It's me Beatrice," I call out.

She's having a good day. I can tell because the look of panic I saw from several of my other visits is absent from her face.

"It's time for lunch," she replies and grabs her walker, not acknowledging anyone else in the room.

"I have to go to lunch," she says, pushing her way through the wider than normal walkway.

I cut her off at the doorway to her suite, put my hands over hers on the walker and meet her eyes.

"Mom, I'm going away for a while. But your favorite nephew, Travis, will come by to visit."

She stares at me blankly and I can see as her eyebrows crinkle in the middle, the telltale sign that she is starting to feel unsafe.

"I want to kick people," she says sternly. This is not the Ann Fredricks that I grew up with.

"I'll give you a list." I smile in return. A deep breath pushes into my lungs and I push it back out.

I stand straight, realizing my goodbye didn't mean anything to this version of her and tell her, "Enjoy your lunch, they are having beans."

"I hate beans! They better not give me any beans," I knew her legume hatred was still a thing, so I had to get in a little loving tease before I left just to hear her old self. At this point, it was the only emotional reaction I was going to evoke from her that seemed at all familiar. If the staff finds out I got her riled up after she already expressed interest in hurting others, she may get put into geriatric detention. We walk with her down the hallway to her table and get her situated in her dining chair.

"Ok, you can leave now," she says to me as if I'm the wait staff. I welcome that permission because this is all too much for me. My aunt puts a loving hand on my back and Travis sits down in the dining chair next to her. That was unexpected.

"Well, Cuz," Travis says as he looks up at me with a smirk. "Things are looking up already. I got a job here where Auntie lives. I thought I would surprise you."

My eyes well up and I can't stop them from making a stream down my cheeks. My parents were adventurers before me. It's the only way I can justify leaving my mom. She would never want me to put my life on hold to watch her turn into a shell of herself. She would have cheered me on and sent me with a tin of cookies for the trip. I still struggle with it, but knowing Travis will be here gives me the reassurance I need.

My mom slaps my arm slightly and says, "Oh, stop that."

Showing emotion makes her anxious, so I wipe the tears off my cheeks and turn to walk away.

They probably should have ushered me out the back door. It is quite unsettling for visitors and residents in a care facility seeing an emotional equivalent to Chernobyl complete with vocal bawling and shaking. I had put on a brave face for a long time, so I was due for the dam to break. My aunt and uncle knew there was really no way to console me so we said our tearful goodbyes and I watched their car pull away. I sat in the parking lot for a long while until I deemed myself safe to drive.

Brandon and Sarah organized a going away party for me complete with colleagues, Mr. Davis and their friends who heard alcohol is free. I keep myself to a one drink maximum and mingle through the crowd of supportive friends and excited acquaintances. Matthew is the only one missing and he is the one I really needed.

"My Queen, you've made some pretty big changes," Mr. Davis says, sitting down next to me. "It's so exciting!"

His pitch raises on the last word and instantly my heart swells. He hands me a gift bag with a droopy bottom.

"Don't open it now. Tequila and tasers don't mix."

"D, you didn't!"

"I sure did, honey. There's also pepper spray, brass knuckles, and one of those spikes for your keychain to break out of car windows. I would have included a cattle prod, but I know you and you would have ended up convulsing on the floor, somehow lose a pinky and then there goes your piano career."

"Thank you, D," I say, hugging the only man worthy enough to replace my dad.

"Alright, enough. I wanna show you how I've been workin' on my twerkin'."

I squint in disgust as the tall black man takes my arm and leads me to a sparse area of the bar. Seeing my father figure/former teacher/ mentor dancing with mostly his ass gives me a sour taste in my mouth. Praying for rescuing is an exercise in futility with this crowd. The night ends in lots of goodbye hugs, well wishes and silly care packages thrust into my arms. Tomorrow, my life becomes mobile.

Thor, my Mercedes class B motor coach, holds everything I need to control alt delete my current operating system and load all current updates. I've convinced myself I'm ready to execute our plan. My anxiety is low even though I've never been to any of these places we've entered into the map app. I loaded several hours of podcasts and audiobooks onto my phone so I could keep my mind busy rather than ruminate on what I am leaving behind. Brandon and Sarah strongly requested that I check in with them every time I stop. I have a mental running list of snarky texts or selfies to send.

Breaks. Accelerator. Mirrors, all fifteen hundred of them. Interior items stabilized. Yep, all things check out. This feels too easy. I'm going to take this as the universe giving me what I'm owed although I'm keeping my eyes peeled for potential literal and figurative speed bumps. I look around carefully, making sure there isn't a sex toy hanging from the rear window. Leave it up to the Schroeder brothers to leave a parting gift.

As I lock down Thor for the last night in San Antonio, a quote on a poster from my high school English course sneaks into my thoughts.

"The purpose of life, after all, is to live it, to taste experience to the utmost, to reach out eagerly and without fear for a newer and richer experience."

Thank you, Mrs. Eleanor Roosevelt. Tomorrow, we taste the richness of life.

Ting ting.

My "Brandon Ding" pops in the air as I pull the covers over my shoulders on the last night in my mother's house.

Brandon: **Dreaming yet?**

me: **Everything is a dream.**

The ring of my phone replaces the text notification. "Thor going to work out?"

"It's like a mini mansion on wheels."

"I'm proud of you, Little B. I'm a little hurt you didn't tell me in person."

"You would have tried to give me an excuse to stay."

"It sounds like I would have failed."

"With Matthew in LA this past year and you with Sarah, I felt it was time for me to do something too."

Mostly to get away from the perfect pair. As much as I love them both, they were causing me gastrointestinal tantrums the longer I hung out with them. I'm too old to be living in a nineties teen movie.

"If we're being honest," he starts.

We're not but go ahead.

"I'm not happy about your move. You sprung this on me out of the blue." I haven't heard Brandon mad very often, but his tone was getting dangerously close.

"Brandon, this isn't about you. It's about me."

"I'm sorry we haven't talked very much. Life is so busy now, starting my own firm and everything."

Yeah, everything. That's code for Sarah.

"Brandon, it's all good," I say, not being able to give him any more of myself.

I kept telling myself that it was "all good" after watching Brandon rush to the school after the lockdown and search for Sarah in the crowd. He waited outside the school behind the police barricade which barely kept him from running into the building to take care of the situation himself. When we were released and all the kids were matched with their families, I turned to see Sarah in Brandon's arms. Mr. Davis found me and his long arms wrapped me up tight but the pain of that last rejection was too much. I saw where I really landed on his priority list. As I got into Mr. D's car, I heard Brandon's voice calling but I couldn't turn my eyes to him. The years I had dedicated to him were worthless. I closed the door on him and the last ten years.

"Bee, I-" The tremors in his voice were slight but audible.

"I gotta get to bed. I need to get an early start to tie up some things. Night, Big B."

Just before my eyelids relax into dreamland, my phone chimes and Matthew's name appears on my phone screen. No rest for the wicked.

"Matthew, do you have a sixth sense for disrupting my peace?"

"How open are you to new experiences?" he asks, ignoring my question.

"I'm not doing BBW porn, Matthew," I say dryly.

"Why do you always go there? It's always about sex with you. Anyways, I just sent your information to an agent of a new actor in town who will need support staff at his place that the studio is leasing from Devon Hazlet."

Devon Hazlet. Ho-ly sh...it. That is big.

When it comes to action stars who don't suck at acting, Devon Hazlet is at the top of the list.

"What do you mean by a new actor, like is he young? You better have not gotten me a babysitting gig."

"I mean new to the US movie scene. I heard some whisperings of a position and did some digging, contacted some people and found the agent. They've been looking for a while, lots of disappointed gen Z's. I put your name in and since I know the agent's nephew, voila, they want you."

Oh, please let him be an Aussie.

"How did I meet the job requirements? What is the job description?" I ask, thoroughly confused.

"Well," he starts excitedly. "You'd be his personal assistant, house manager and possibly a tutor."

"Does he need help in math?" I ask dryly.

"Aren't you the funny one this evening," he answers me in my favorite annoyed tone of his. "He has a couple of kids that need to keep up with school when they visit. I think you might need to run lines with him and get him accustomed to the US."

"But I don't know anything about the entertainment industry."

"You've always told me that teaching was daily on the job training. I know some people who know some people. I will hook you up with all my contacts and his agent and rep at the studio. This guy has to be someone pretty valuable if they are going through all of this."

"Which is why it seems strange that I didn't even interview."

"I gave them a brief history of your employment and they made some calls for your references. I didn't want to distract you on the road."

My mind quickly flashes to my face slamming into the glass door and the cartoon walk to the principal's secretary's desk. It was my mission to make at least one admin laugh every day, I just hope that was enough kissing up to provide a good reference.

"And they still want to hire me?"

"That's what I thought, too," he says, attempting to hide a giggle.

"Are you serious, am I really going to do this?"

An unfamiliar nervous feeling starts to set in but then I remind myself that Matthew wouldn't set me up with anything creepy.

"Bee, if anyone can do this, it's you."

Matthew's faith in me shakes off the nerves and excites my pragmatism.

"So, what's the first thing I need to do?"

"Well, first you have to get here safely, not stopping off at those rough truck stops and end up with Large Marge sitting next to you."

"Oh, very nice Pee Wee Herman reference. And you mock me?"

"I will call or text you with more details. Just get here."

"How long do I have?"

"I would say a week so you can get your bearings. You might want to hustle, though."

"When does he need me there?"

"So, you're saying yes?!"

"That is a yes, sweetie. But if I end up in some weird blanket weaving cult because you didn't read the fine print, I'll find you and sacrifice you."

"He's not here yet either. Again, I will send you more details as I know them. Just check the shared doc. Talk to you soon, Bee."

I've got all the butterflies and feels I can handle. But I know how to do things, lots of things. I can make appointments. I can talk to random people. I can order things. I can drive places. Nope. I can call people to drive places. That would be safer for all. I should get a doctorate for my cold calling skills. However, my less than spectacular social media and technology skills were a running joke at my school. As a staff present one year they gave me an actual full-sized abacus.

"Oh wait, do you think he's an Aussie?" I ask as the line goes silent.

Maybe he's a Brit. I wouldn't throw a Brit out of bed.

I obsessively check the shared document for updates every ten minutes. We have come up with a clever system where all the new stuff is red and if I read it, I turn it to black. This works for us, confirming that we're on the same page, at least digitally. I don't have a name yet, but I find out he's Turkish. I know nothing about Turkey. That's a lie, I know about Turkish delight. No, those are just two words I read in *The Lion, the Witch and the Wardrobe.* I don't even think I read the description of what Turkish delight is. I know there's a song with Istanbul and Constantinople in it by

They Might Be Giants. I add the song to my road trip playlist and plan to find the least trafficky time to drive into LA and only use side streets.

Matthew's call came just in time to save me from another downward Brandon spiral. The work of the day tiring my muscles barely overtook all the thoughts racing through my mind to send me to much needed sleep.

The next day I see more red on the Google Doc than black. He is a Turkish actor famous for his dramas who had previously been a model. Okay. Add to that he was a professional athlete.

Fantastic.

I'm starting to feel like Mr. Glass in *Unbreakable*, as if I exist on the planet to balance out the universe. Blaine Rogers, a famous Hollywood agent apparently, scouted him out of Turkey and signed him on as a client. Matthew purposefully didn't include a name or picture of the actor. Sneaky Pete. Scouring the internet for male Turkish movie stars may as well be searching for a sourdough bread recipe: too many hot tasty choices. If I research too much, I might talk myself into turning around and abandoning this adventure altogether.

Blaine Rogers?

That just screams "LA" to me for some reason and a bit from Letterkenny comes to mind and I remind myself to not change the timbre of my voice every time I say "LA".

Too late.

Chapter 4

İHSAN

"I think I found someone," Blaine's voice reeks of excitement and a bit too much energy.

"*Merhaba*, Blaine."

"She is able to start right away and she used to be a teacher."

"Does she have to go back to school in the fall?"

"No, she no longer teaches."

"Did they fire her?" I ask, slightly suspicious.

"No, she decided not to continue to teach. My assistant called her references and I listened to the conversations she recorded, and I think she will work out great."

"What do you know, Blaine?"

"Let's just say they are very sad to see her go and she goes above and beyond."

"Blaine..."

He tends to leave little bits of information out that he doesn't think will be pertinent but then it turns out that they are. When I took this role Blaine neglected to tell me that I would be working with Charlotte Steele. I've had a professional crush on her since I started acting. She is the cause of quite a few of my nerves.

"She has a reputation for her ...antics."

"What does that mean?"

"All I know is that they have the utmost confidence in her and I have a feeling her former school administration is hard to impress."

Blaine wouldn't steer me wrong. He's invested quite a bit of time and energy on my transition to the American film market, so I believe him about this prospective assistant.

"I'm getting slammed here at the office and I'm having a hard time finding qualified, reliable people to do the work right. I'm going to have to fill her plate from the start."

"If she's a teacher, I'm sure she'll be able to handle it."

"She still has to say yes."

"*Neh?* Blaine."

"Don't worry. I have it on good authority she will most likely say yes."

"Do you know if she likes dogs?"

"I didn't ask. I guess I should have. Isa, someone will be there to meet us at the house. I promise."

If Blaine didn't have such a good reputation in Hollywood, I would be panicking. So far this new adventure to the west has gone almost without a hitch. My current management company renegotiated my contract. I have good tenants for my house, my family is supportive, and all my travel documents went through without any extra documentation needed. Asli is to thank for that. Leaving my little boy and girl with Gül has been the most difficult. My mother, aunt and sister gave me the most adamant assurances that they will be taking an active part in making sure they will be well taken care of. Despite everything I've been through with Gül, she is a good mother. We have plans for them to come to visit several times with one extended visit when the film opens.

BEATRICE

The next few days I drive my life wagon to the sunny west coast where I commit to change the very state of my existence. I'm going from serving thirty little humans to one large one. Moving from a career in which I've had several years of experience in to a temporary position at basically an apprentice status has the potential to be terrifying. My years of training will be used to help secure the future of one man in a field where none of my credentials apply.

No need to worry.

Even I don't believe myself. I'm starting to identify with that female astronaut that wore diapers as she drove across the US in her car. I feel like I'm going to pee myself from nerves alone. Until I get up the nerve to call the agent, I'll distract myself with everything but researching this job which is not like me at all. Times they are a changin'.

The day I pull into LA county, I decide to give Blaine a call but just end up getting his voicemail. After years of calling parents I have the introduction and content down, but I have no experience with Blaine and I don't want his first impression of me to be stuttering 'ums' between various nouns and verbs. I quickly hang up and spend twenty minutes rehearsing a semi coherent message. An hour after I leave a flawless performance on his phone, a jovial fast talker returns my call.

"Hello Beatrice, I've heard so much about you. Matthew just raves about you," he chimes into my ear.

I know Matthew well enough to know there might have been a story or two he included so I better feel the waters and see what Blaine really understands about me. If I'm honest, I'm pretty sure my old vice principal was more than eager to share some of my exploits. She was always up for a laugh but she secretly made most of the staff shake in their cowboy boots. Being on her bad side might as well be purgatory. If I ever made a mistake, usually because of my creative verbal sparring, I always came to her with a solution. There was nothing worse than walking into her office feeling as if you disappointed her. At least her office was a safe place for curse words.

"He tells me you are a retired teacher and willing to work like a horse. Are you skilled in social media?"

Retired makes me sound like I put thirty years into the job, years I hadn't earned.

I can find my way around Facebook, I think. Ok, I do know I have an account. Instagram is a button on my phone that once in a while gets pressed when I'm looking for a good recipe. I still don't know the difference between a story, a reel and a post. Pinterest is my jam. Is it sad that I'm a teacher and just want to look at pretty pictures?

"Oh yes, you have to be able to navigate social media teaching kids these days. These kids are sly, but they tend to post incriminating evidence against them, which is why I keep my accounts private," I lie quickly to cover up my lack of an online presence.

Blaine snickers at my first attempt at humor. So far, so good. I'll be spending my nights sequestering myself in my room, learning all of the social media things.

"Yeah, my whole goal was pretty much to not get on the news."

He laughs again at attempt two.

This is going well.

"Yeah, I hear ya. Teachers don't get enough credit. Anyway, Isa and I will meet you at the house at eight A.M. tomorrow. I'll send you the address. We're gonna have to do some shopping to get you two settled."

Isa, huh? That will narrow down my investigation.

"Well, I have Thor...I mean an RV," I say thinking it will make things easier.

"Oh, no honey, you are not sleeping in mobile accommodations. This house has a guest suite to die for that is all yours. He's going to need you twenty-four seven for a while."

Matthew is an angel. Is it weird I want to kiss him on the lips? What did I do to deserve him? Well, I can think about one hundred eighty-seven reasons why I deserve him and this. One hundred eighty-seven minutes locked down with students in my classroom. The endless unrelenting worry engulfed their bodies, concentrated in their eyes. All looking to me for an end to their fear and answers I didn't have. My eyes start to well with tears and I take a deep breath to focus back on Blaine.

"Let's start from there and we'll figure out what to do when we meet," he ends our conversation quickly to let me finish the final leg of my trek.

I take a few minutes to Google as many variations of the name Isa to give me some idea of who this man is. To my chagrin, I'm just as lost as I was before I heard his name. I thought he was supposed to be big time.

As I pull into a campground at Malibu Creek State Park, it's as if the pressure changed like in the cabin of an airplane. Tomorrow I head out to Mandeville Canyon and meet my client.

Holy sh...it.

IHSAN

The flight from Istanbul to Los Angeles would have been grueling if I had taken commercial flights. I've learned that when there is an option for comfort, even if it costs more, you always take it. What is the purpose of making all this money if you are miserable? Zeki would have had a difficult time curling up on his legs to get comfortable, even in first class. Being on the tall side myself, I understand how important leg room is. As it is, he is not a good flyer and rests his giant head on my thighs, almost cutting off circulation. I can't imagine the next step in my career without him beside me. He's been my loyal canine companion since the judge declared my marriage to Gül dissolved.

As we land at the Burbank airport, I look forward to feeling the earth under my feet. Zeki's gate is erratic as he takes in the new sites and smells of California. The first thing I need to do is get my legs moving again. I feel slightly disappointed when I see the large SUV on the tarmac, knowing I'm going to be sitting for at least another hour.

"Isa, my man! The day is finally here. Welcome to L.A.," says the man I met almost a year ago in Antalya on holiday.

He was slightly slimmer than in his swim trunks and with the woman I have come to find out recently is his fourth ex-wife. Helping Blaine Rogers with translating his requests from English to Turkish to the hotel concierge turned out to be a life altering event. I've always taught my children that when someone needs help, you help them no matter what. It is what the Turkish people do, it's in our DNA. Turns out this simple act of kindness sparked a conversation, then dinner, then before I knew it, we had made plans for him to visit the movie set. The several women who stalked me in the lobby to get a photo gave him a clue that I wasn't some random man. By the end of shooting the movie, I had signed a very carefully worded contract with an American talent agent. Two days later I was sent sides for a new movie and the studio sent a troupe for an in-person audition. That little section of script was my ticket to America.

After spending a restless night in a hotel room, I'm looking forward to checking out my accommodations for at least the next six months. After a month of interviews, Blaine feels he has accomplished his mission to find a personal assistant that fulfills all my requirements, the first being the ability to teach the two reasons for my being. He informs me that she is overqualified in that area and that she is available immediately and will meet us at the house. His description feels a little too serendipitous but everything with Blaine seems to work out exactly how he says it will, except his marriages.

"Isa, she said yes!" Blaine says as we drive onto the highway that should be really named the 'slow way'"

"So, you talked to her?"

"We had a brief conversation on the phone. I think you'll like her. She's quick and chirpy."

"Chirpy?"

"You'll see."

"If you hired me an enthusiastic ass kisser I'm going to find a new agent."

"Your English is getting better."

"I'm serious. They just end up using you as a steppingstone for a better gig."

"You won't have to worry about her."

"How do you know?"

"Trust me."

He's gotten me this far without a scrape I should give him the benefit of the doubt. Besides, my success is his success. Deep breath.

As we enter the house I am impressed with the layout and the attention to detail. It is transparent which is a bit concerning as cameras can sometimes get an actor into trouble, but the gate is far enough from the house that I am comfortable with the architecture. I just hope that butt prints are easily removed on the occasion that I bring a woman home. Not that I've had much female company in the last three years but new country, new prospects.

A few moments after I remove my shoes and socks to let my feet breathe, the doorbell rings and I see an outline of a short figure. The young woman on the other side of the door pierces me with her stunning eyes, wide and welcoming. Her long lashes outline the green, brown, and gold specks in her eyes that strike something familiar in me. She is indeed shorter than I am as most people are but the top of her head, sans the fluffy bun, barely reaches my shoulder. Her straight, sweet smile quickly falters and the panic in her multi-hued eyes is obvious when her first words to me don't make sense. When she asks to try again, I am intrigued. Of the three sentences I've heard, I am impressed with her confidence and her willingness to laugh at herself. Along with her short stature, she is, as my mother would put it "kalin," thick. Her plumpness would probably have been the first thing I noticed if it wasn't for her surprisingly delightful demeanor. Even when she shakes my hand, her eye contact conveys strength and a sense of connection.

BEATRICE

A tidal wave of excitement crashes into the air as my Kiwi phone navigation guy gives me directions up a windy street that I'm pretty sure I've seen in a thriller film. He tells me to turn off the curvy road onto another one which ends at the front of a large elaborate iron gate. I search my phone to find where Blaine had texted me the gate code and stretch across with my T-rex arms to type it into the panel.

When I finally pull into the house on Boca Lane, I start counting my blessings after surviving LA traffic. They should sell bumper stickers or commemorative t-shirts celebrating this accomplishment. Pulling in, I'm shocked at the number of windows one house can hold. Large stone pillars hold up the glass panes that serve as walls. This has to be the famous "glass house" in which no one should throw stones or run around naked. Thor slows down to a crawl as I lean forward, trying to get a better view of the whole structure, and from the looks of it I may have bitten off more than I can chew. That's alright, I've got a big mouth. I pull off to the left and park on a strategic patch of concrete. This place actually has its own parking lot. I'm pretty sure that there is a homeowner's association regulation about RVs because there is no way they are going to let Thor be parked on the street over an extended period. I can imagine an elderly Hollywood starlet walking down the driveway yelling about my eyesore with too much makeup and a tiny dog tucked under her arm.

On the opposite side of the parking area, a black Lincoln town car and black Cadillac SUV shine in the morning sunlight. With the official looking cars in the parking lot, I'm starting to think this may be a safe house for the CIA, possibly the worst safe house with its see-through walls. As I take a deep breath and sit in my RV for hopefully the last time for months, I start to think of a theme song. I need to walk in confident, friendly and exuding professionalism. "Eye of the Tiger." "Can't touch this." "I'm too sexy." Yeah, that last one is not making the cut. Since Thor is my getaway vehicle, if anything goes sideways, I should have speakers installed in the wheel wells like those vehicular public address systems in police cars. Who knows what could happen with this new job and I always need a soundtrack like The Dukes of Hazard or Knight Rider. I hear Tesla's have fart sounds. I snicker to myself at the thought of racing down the highway in my pimped-out RV with my hair flying out the rolled down window, cartoon music blaring from the wheel wells after I'm fired for delivering a jelly filled donut when a glazed one was clearly requested.

I open the camera app on my phone and switch to video.

"Hey Mom, I made it to LA. The trip was uneventful. I can see now why you loved 'Old Betsy' so much. Don't worry, Travis thinks he can revive her. You should see the outside of this place. It's like what we thought mansions looked like in elementary school. I just wanted you to know that I'm following in your footsteps and having a grand adventure. I love you, mom."

She always told me she was proud of me but whenever I did something she or my dad personally loved, her smile was different, like it had more calories or something.

I click Travis' number in my phone and attach the video and press send.

I open the door and step out, the sound of threads tearing apart halts my descent. Well, of course I get a giant tear in my butt seam of the pants I carefully curated at my last stop. I go back into the RV and try to figure out some kind of professional wear that won't make me look like a country bumpkin straight off a Texas ranch. I settle on some blue chino pants that will go well with my adorable tan Vans and bright salmon billowy tank top. I can't believe I forgot to even look at my hair. I decide to train the mane into a bun on top of my head, a style my hair can probably do on its own by now. I check out my eyes and spot a big clump of sleep in the corner. Nothing like an eye booger to ruin a first impression. I rummage around in my overnight bag between the seats and find some mascara. That's one more thing I've got in spades, serious eyelashes; boobs and eyelashes.

Luckily, I parked to the left so it didn't take too long for me to figure out that the RV blocks the view of me getting ready. I grab the smartest looking bag I have, fill it with smart things like a pen and paper and walk with purpose to the front door. I press the doorbell a respectable length of time, not too long and not too short and a tall silhouette appears through the smoky glass of the front door. Maybe one could run naked through there, just not me. Ever. As the figure pulls the door handle, I prepare myself for first contact. The door opens revealing a beautiful olive toned face. The sun backlights his head and I'm pretty sure I hear a chorus of angels singing the final chord of a joyous tribute to the Almighty. His hair is just shy of jet black, short with longer lengths on the crown, framing the face staring back at me. His eyes, dark pools of thick tar with a tiny sparkle emanating out of the corner. The strong, straight jawline continues down toward his mouth where his coral-colored lips stretch to reveal his bright white teeth, all the features working together to present the perfect warm welcoming face. When I heard a man described as devastatingly handsome, it seemed a little overkill but now I understand completely. He isn't a visual sensation; he is a full body experience. So, this is lust at first sight. I one hundred percent would have high tailed it north to Alaska if I had image searched this man before this moment. I open my mouth to greet this Adonis.

"Did you hear that?"

Oh, please no. That was inner dialogue, right?

By the confused look on this man's gorgeous face, I can tell it was definitely outer dialogue. My eyes expand beyond normal limits and in my mind Matthew is watching this scene eagerly, eating popcorn and laughing his ass off as I drop our secret code phrase. He had either been up for a while or the five o'clock shadow grew early on his slightly tanned skin. I would guess this celestial being towers over me far beyond six feet two inches. Brandon tends to be my non-standard measuring device for humans and this man would look down on him. His body shows the hours he must spend on machines, with barbells and in the water. The dark short sleeved shirt untucked with black jeans cling to his body, accentuating almost all of his defined muscles and dark drawings along his bicep. I look down to see bare feet, exquisite bare feet.

When did I start to like feet?

The man looks at me quizzically and I quickly overreact and thrust my hand out and say too loudly, "Beatrice at your service."

Nope. If I'm going to have a do over in my life, I'm not going to regret anything.

"Do you mind shutting the door so I can do that again? That didn't come out right," my torso crumbles forward as I take a few steps away from the door, my awkward body language convincing him to oblige.

The tall dark man smiles, steps back and closes the door without a word. I gather myself together and take a deep breath through my nose and out of my mouth, then ring the doorbell again. From farther back in the house I hear, "Open the door already!"

I keep my hands grasping my purse as he opens the door again and this time I use a more cheerful voice instead of one you would expect from a courier.

"Hello, my name is Beatrice Fredricks and I have a meeting with Blaine Rogers." I flash a big smile and the man steps backward to give me space to enter.

I really should have rehearsed, I know better. I give myself permission to take in a big breath through my nose as this is a moment for all my senses.

Oh MY (à la George Takei).

What kind of Turkish magic scent is he wearing? All the synapses in my brain become sluggish and lax. If my panties didn't drop before they were definitely around my knees now. As I take a few more steps forward, I hear loud footfalls coming closer.

"Beatrice. It is so good to meet your face."

I chuckle at his choice of words. Blaine's voice is definitely a tenor with low undertones. His full head of peppered hair is trimmed just above the collar of his beige, button-down long sleeve shirt with blue slacks and seriously fancy brown shoes, tassels, and everything. The man from the door towers over him as well.

"Have you met your charge yet?"

"No, I just stepped in. I kind of embarrassed myself on the first take and he was gracious enough to let me do it again. That's when you walked in and between the two of us, he hasn't gotten a word in edgewise."

"I like your candor!" he exclaims.

I let out a breath. I was hoping that would go over well. Mr. Hottie McHot Hot turns toward me as he closes the glass door. He puts one hand in his pocket and reaches out with his other, offering the first chance to make a human connection I've had in five days.

"Ihsan Zorlu, it's nice to meet you, Beatrice."

Oh, Ihsan. No wonder nothing came up in my search. Isa is his nickname.

I want to look up at the sky and shake my fist at the gods as his low baritone almost bass voice vibrates my whole torso.

Are you kidding me?!

With that Dracula-light accent, I'm doomed. I want to ask him to talk more but again, I must resist the urge to make it weird. I get to touch him. I should be happy with what the universe has given me. People like me don't get to touch people like him, at least on purpose or without consequence. It usually happens "accidentally" with a casual shoulder brush or fake trip. I should have brought in an extra change of underwear in my purse.

After my brain processes all of what has just occurred, I place my hand in his trying to remember to match his pressure. No one enjoys shaking a dead fish. His handshake is everything you would want it to be: warm, firm and somehow kind.

Can a handshake be kind?

The heat from his hand melts all the bones in the lower half of my body as my knees threaten to give out.

"I was thinking of a quick tour and then down to brass tacks," Blaine announces walking ahead of us.

The temptation to respond with humor may come off looking like an idiot or trying too hard. These men don't need to be introduced to "awkward Bee" just yet, it's too early. As I walk into the foyer of the home, or should I say estate, I take note of a beautiful glass railing that runs parallel to the front of the house which I am going to make a concerted effort to not run into. A flashback of my grand exit from school fowls my brain. Blaine extends his arm fully out toward the hallway to the left.

"Let's look at your suite first."

We take a left and go down a long hallway and my inner squeals almost burst through my lips.

"Welcome to the guest wing."

Chapter 5

B EATRICE

I get a whole wing or a room? I don't want to be greedy, so I resign myself to just settle for the room. I laugh inside at my mock humility as these angels escort me into my new temporary residence. I cross the two step distance of a hall, noticing several closed doors adjacent to the door in front of me. I twist the knob, push and am greeted with a half wall of windows on the other side of the room. To the right, I see a beautiful bed surrounded by a bookshelf thoughtfully cluttered with various sized books and stylish knick knacks that you couldn't find at IKEA. The bedding is faux fur with accents of velvet in the ten pillows that lay atop it. In front of the bed sits a gray velvet tufted couch big enough for a serious nap so as to not disturb the pristine bedding. To the left is another bookshelf with a giant TV placed in the middle. It doesn't take up the whole side of the room like the bed and bookcase though. On the left of the TV shelf is a hallway with beautiful black and white woodland photography at eye level. Continuing a few more feet, the door on the right opens up into a giant bathroom taking up more square footage than half the bedroom.

This is architectural pornography. I would feel a little dirty if it wasn't a bathroom. Walking around the perimeter of the white tiled room, I let my fingertips glaze the fixtures. They just scream to be touched. My eyes move to a beautiful pewter clawfoot tub next to a fully enclosed glass block shower with a square rain shower head. The bathtub seems slightly bigger than normal and a little out of place in all this modern design. But what do I know? All my furniture is convertible and nailed to the floor of an RV. As a person of venus-esque proportions, I appreciate the tub's larger capacity. I have a feeling this was the one piece someone insisted on. If Matthew was here, I would climb in fully clothed to check for fit. It's too early for that type of escapade. The vanity's lowered counter hides a round pink tufted stool which I am sure has a weight limit under mine. I smile and act like I'm just getting my bearings but, in my head, I'm having a seventies dance party complete with disco ball and roller-skating cocktail girls.

The boys peek their heads in, clearly not understanding the value of this one room. I saunter out of the bathroom, as one does when trying to keep their excitement from exploding out their eyeballs and continue down the hallway of my super sweet suite. At first glance a second bedroom seems to be down the hall, but as I enter I feel a Maria on the hills of Austria Sound of Music moment coming on. The giant walk-in closet with a section of the wall just for shoes opens up before me. All my Vans will have a place of their own. I take a turn inside the long closet as if I was in a turn of the century promenade. I am getting better at keeping my excitement and glee canned up.

"You realize that from now on, I come with the house," I announce to Blaine.

Blaine lets out a friendly laugh as he appreciates my approval of the accommodations.

"Further down the hall are two more bedrooms and an office," Blaine explains and then ushers us both back to the foyer.

"I know we say we do things bigger in Texas but bigger does NOT mean better. The expression is 'daaaayaaaauum." I look towards Ihsan as if I am teaching him a colloquialism. His quiet observer act is a bit unsettling, but he seems to appreciate the assist.

Down the stairs from the foyer is an inset living room with modern, cream color couches set in the center facing the left. A beautiful live edge resin coffee table is strategically placed in the middle, decorated with large books and a small sculpture resembling a giant toy jack. On the left wall over the fireplace, a giant framed piece of art depicts angels, demons, and cherubs. All completely naked except for the strategically draped white fabric.

That's where the angels came from!

As I walk a little further, the artwork has a strange gleam that I realize is actually a screen.

"Thank goodness that's a TV and we can change the scene. I can't make coherent conversation with naked Archangel Michael and his buddies plotting their hostile takeover of the mansion."

This time Ihsan gives a little chuckle and I delight in the rumble in his chest.

There is hope for you yet, young grasshopper.

I see many movie nights in my future. So many eighties movies to introduce this man to. Let the indoctrination begin!

Continuing through the living room, a ceiling height set of glass doors separates the backyard from this room. Blaine walks over to a control pad in the stone wall next to the fireplace. He presses a keypad and the glass walls retract, revealing a floor of light blue water. I squint, trying to make out the size of the pool. Now I understand why they call them infinity pools, they never end. I should just assume everything is from Architectural Digest. The pool empties into a stone lined barrier before a thick wall of trees. A beautiful fenced in lawn flanks the pool, marked by a continuous iron fence. Got to keep the riff raff out somehow. In front of the pool, closer to the house, chaise lounges, padded chairs and an eating area with a BBQ island complete the outdoor space.

The house has an air of familiarity as the tour continues.

Can you be a real housewife if you haven't been a wife or have your own tits?

I'm so glad that thought stayed inside.

Ihsan walks over to the BBQ and opens the lid as if to analyze its potential. Most of my thoughts toward the opposite sex are more romantic than sexual but this man, he is going to start a forest fire with all the sparks he's giving off.

Walking back through the glass doors and into the living room, off to the left sitting quietly in its own half-moon room waits a glorious matte black parlor grand piano surrounded by dark velvet curtains, masking the instrument from the sunlight. Does the action star, Devon Hazlet, actually play? In the least, he knows not to expose the piano to the sun, so it isn't just for show. I sit down on the bench and run my fingers over the closed fallboard.

So, there is a God.

Ihsan leans onto the curved part of the piano and lays his forearms on the dull black surface.

"Do you play?" he asks with that ridiculously mesmerizing Transylvanian accent.

"I do. I mean, not professionally but I don't embarrass myself."

It's too early in our relationship to let him in on my musical skills. The time I get to play is precious and private.

He smiles and I try my best to stand up without my skin sticking to the bench, dragging it with me, scraping across the floor with an ear-piercing screech. Not that it's happened to me before. I'm wearing pants but that fear is deeply rooted so I'm always second guessing myself even if it is obvious my legs are covered. The highly glossed floors in this room alone probably cost more than Thor outside and scratching them the first day would surely earn me demerits. Moving past the piano, a very large formal dining room opens to an enormous kitchen that looks upon the open living room, making a full circle around the cabinetry of the kitchen. Nestled on the far side of the very large kitchen island, a quaint breakfast nook looks out upon the front of the house making it a good place to see who approaches our castle.

"This seems adequate," I say out loud, hoping Blaine and Ihsan understand my tone.

Everything is so freaking shiny. The appliances, the fixtures, Ihsan.

I noticed an open staircase to the right when we first walked in, as it has no banister for support. I should probably clock how long it takes to drive from the main road to this house for when I fall to my death. It would only be courteous to give the EMTs an ETA.

"Up here is where Ihsan will be staying," Blaine points, clearly not wanting me to go up there.

"No rock, paper, scissors, huh?" I ask Ihsan as I walk toward Satan's stairway.

"Okay, Ihsan I showed you mine, you have to show me yours. Them's the rules in these here parts," I say in my worst Texas longhorn accent.

I'm not sure if the reference was lost on him but Blaine appreciated my humor as I see his face crack a smile behind Ihsan's back. Either that or he realizes what a complete dork he hired. Probably the latter.

Ihsan clicks his bare heels together in an usher sort of fashion, stretching out his arm to direct me to climb the stairs. The two follow behind me and, in retrospect, that was probably not the best move as they both get a face full of my ass and I pray with every step that I don't fart.

When we reach the top of the stairs, I blink in disbelief. I didn't think there was a bed bigger than a king. This says slumber party all over it, the innocent make-over gossip kind, not the orgy kind. Ihsan doesn't seem like the orgy type, but what do I know? The modern chandelier dangles straight crystals with lots of tiny light bulbs reflecting millions of tiny rainbows all over light gray walls when I slightly open the curtains. I realize that I missed the light switch completely, but it gives me a quick giggle thinking about Ihsan dancing around the room with multicolored lights peppering his half naked body.

"So, have you unpacked yet?" I ask Ihsan as I walk into his room, noticing the lack of luggage.

"No, we only arrived a few minutes before you," he says with a bit of a roll to his 'r's. His 'k', 't' and 's' sounds seem exaggerated and from eavesdropping I can hear a lack of 'th' as well. My ears are going to be perked up every time he opens his mouth. I hope I can concentrate on the content of what he is saying and not just the sounds of the words because that is certainly a stupid look for me. If he continues to use that accent with impeccable English vocabulary, I'm going to need one of those southern belle fans just to get through the day.

"Okay, then I won't be invading your space too much if I explore your bathroom?"

"Go ahead, Magellan."

I'm going to like him.

As I move towards the bathroom, hidden behind the wall that's supporting the giant bed, I quickly get a squeeze of his pillow. That will probably be the closest I get to touching his head. The bathroom and closet slash changing room slash sexy clothes dungeon is located behind a pocket door beyond the shower. The double sinks are silver hammered bowls with waterfall faucets and in a tiny room off to the side is a toilet and a bidet. I'd never seen a bidet in person and I think to myself that I may need to find an instructional video. My search history deletion may need to be added to Matthew's list of things to do when I die.

Oh my god...the shower.

A wall of glass blocks curve toward the rear of the room. I slowly step around the curve and a huge shower room reveals itself. My Honda could fit in his shower. Two rainfall shower heads on opposite ends of the tiled area are suspended from the ceiling and several small openings scatter the walls. I'm assuming the sex lotion spurts out and covers him which makes him glisten like Edward in the afternoon sun. That might be hopeful thinking and a bit weird.

What the eff is sex lotion? Wait. I can use cursy words whenever I want now. What the fuck is sex lotion?

The curve of the wall serves as a water barrier for the shower. I notice there are hooks on the glass blocks for towels and a floor grate covered with bamboo slats serves as a bathmat. I continue through the door next to the shower of the gods and find the closet slash panic room. This is where I will hide during a home invasion. In the middle, is a large island with a solid granite top with white drawers underneath and of course, a floor to ceiling shoe rack.

The boys stroll out of the ensuite as I reluctantly leave my new happy place. Too bad it isn't in my room. I could probably move into his closet and he would never know. I'm sure they're talking but my ears couldn't hear over the drops of drool landing on the floor. We make our way back to the bedroom where I now notice the giant artwork across from the bed. This time there is no TV, it really is art. As we leave, I notice the "stairs of death" threatening my existence.

Do not fall on these men, do not fall on these men, do not fall on these men.

I gingerly and purposefully take one step at a time trying to keep each footfall from making more noise than it should as my feet slap the stairs.

As the staircase turns for the landing to the main level, it continues down to a floor below. In my head, I hear "Dance Macabre" as I could be walking down to my demise with two men I just met. I should have had Matthew send me pictures of these guys to confirm their identities. We continue down the stairs which lead to a hallway which I have now convinced myself is a torture room. Blaine opens the door to the best smelling laundry room I've ever experienced. This is where the Snuggle bear was born.

"Can I change rooms to this one?"

They both chuckle, attempting to usher me out into the hallway.

"I've got to find out what detergent they use here," I say and then add a little quieter to myself, "It must be laced with an aphrodisiac."

There were two washers, two dryers and a long marble counter with a silver pole running parallel to hang clothes. I take note that I might need special hangers to use that pole. This is fancy with a capital, italicized, bolded and underlined "F." Whenever my mother had any extra money she would buy clothes for our clothing closet at school and we would spend all weekend laundering them to get rid of the secondhand store smell. This room would have cut that time at least by half.

Across from the laundry room is a linen closet, or so I thought. Being my nosy self, I open the door to find a tall metal rack with shelves. I look down and notice there are channels in the floor. I hurt my brain trying to figure out what this is used for. Blaine interjects.

"This is my second ex-wife's favorite part of the house. It cost twenty thousand dollars to install one in my, I mean, her house."

"What is it exactly?" I ask.

"It's a laundry dumb waiter system. You can move laundry to all levels of the house by loading this up, pushing in the cart until it clicks and pressing the floor button on the side. When you close the door, the laundry elevator takes the items to that floor. You can put other things in here too if you need. The door won't open unless the cart is on that level. The lights here tell you where the cart is." Blaine explains.

I stand there with my mouth agape. This is where I am spending the end of my days.

"There's another one that goes from the garage to the kitchen pantry."

"Of course there is," I add.

I slowly close the panel as if I'm hiding the Ark of the Covenant behind the door.

In the basement, a bar stocked with liquor and stemware of all colors and iterations spans the far wall. A game room larger than my old classroom back home expands throughout the lower level. It is complete with a pool table, a poker table, dart board and plenty of smooth leather couches, loveseats and chairs with several TVs mounted on the walls. The ceiling is much higher than one would expect in a basement game room. I would expect a faint smell of cigar, but all my nose could detect is the leather seating. I start to plan out in my head a Facetime tour with my peeps back home.

"Behind that door is the garage and gym," Blaine points to a single door on the opposite side of the house. I'm not sure why he thinks I will be using either of those rooms but I turn around and see that I was not the focus of his directions.

IHSAN

The smile I am holding inside grows larger as I watch this pint-sized tornado tour the house we will share while I get a foothold on the Hollywood scene. Her unfiltered and blunt attitude is so refreshing that I stand back, watching her reactions to all the amazing amenities available to us and can't help but feel joy. When we sit down and discuss all the details of her new position, I am impressed with her ability to zero in on things that I didn't realize would be important. She is, as the American saying goes, hitting the ground running. My personal assistant in Turkiye took care of my basic needs but this woman is taking charge of my life and for some reason I am perfectly comfortable being in her small, manicured hands.

BEATRICE

We make our way up the stairs and Blaine guides us to the breakfast nook near the front of the house. We sit down and Blaine pulls out official looking paperwork in a leather-bound binder.

"I'm still old school. I like paper and pen," he says as he opens the embossed binder. "Let's talk about expectations."

I pull out a brand-new half sized notebook from my bag and flip it to the front.

"I must admit, I am a pen whore myself," he laughs as I pull out my pink pen with the giant jewel on the end.

For the next half hour, Ihsan sits quietly and nods randomly as Blaine reviews my responsibilities. I am to be the keeper of social media, travel coordinator to sets and auditions, schedule manager of both formal and informal appearances and communication liaison with his agent and the studio rep that brought him here. I am also to provide him with "script support." I think I can gather what that means. I add it to the list with a star next to it because if I add a question mark, they will know that I don't actually know exactly what it means. My last duty is house manager. This personal assistant gig seems more extensive than filling coffee cups and handing him water bottles.

"Just so I am accurate on my resume, what exactly is my title?"

"Until we find the right talent manager, we added those duties to your personal assistant job description. That is why we thought staying here would be best."

"Sooo...?" I say hoping he can give me a more definitive answer.

"Assistant manager would be closest to your duties."

I envision myself with a paper hat and a red apron trying to convince someone to work overtime and mop the floor again.

Great.

Matthew for sure set me up.

"I'd call his Turkish manager as soon as possible."

"Um, you know I don't speak Turkish, right?"

"He speaks English," Ihsan interjects before Blaine can continue. "I am told you are a teacher."

Oh, I will teach you something. Stop, Beatrice. Calm yourself!

Again, I'm thankful for my fleeting superhuman ability to bite my tongue.

"My two children will be coming to visit a few times this year and I don't want them to fall behind on their studies. The past two years have been tough on them, their mother and I are divorced."

My heart hurts a little at his sensitivity.

"I understand. Fortunately, I've had five years working with all kinds of family dynamics. How old are they?"

"Zeyva is nine and her little brother Tariq, is seven."

"Those are fun ages. Can I ask how much English they speak?"

"They have been studying English as long as they have been able to speak."

The more he speaks the more I notice the little changes he makes to con-sonants. We'll have to spend some serious time working on articulation.

"Good job, Mom and Dad," I reply encouragingly and he smiles back at me with a thankful expression, an expression I will be working my ass off to see every day.

"I've got some ideas brewing already," I add.

Helen of Troy has nothing on him. Ihsan's smile could launch a fleet of aircraft carriers. He leans back in his chair with a quiet sigh of relief. The love he has for his children is written all over his face. His relaxed, relieved expression gives me a little feeling of achievement.

Blaine and I go over the staffing for the house which will include a housekeeper, gardener and a cook. All of which I get to hire. I've never been on that side of the table before.

"Well, that should be enough to get you started. I am handing off the reins to you, Beatrice. You are confidence personified," he exclaims as he backs out of the front door and waves. "You have my number."

Turning to my new charge, I muster up the courage to lay it all out on the table.

"Ihsan. So, here's the deal. My previous gig required a couple degrees, a teaching credential, and several background checks. This is new to me, but I want you to know that I never make the same mistake twice and my goal is always to come to my boss with solutions not problems. Since I'm diving in the deep end, I just wanted you to know."

"If Blaine has confidence in you, then so do I."

I've never had a job where I didn't feel like I had to prove my worth.

Ihsan starts to stand up from the table and I look up at him and swallow the lump in my throat.

"So, I have a couple of questions for you before we get our stuff."

He lowers himself back in the chair, ready for the first gut punch.

"This is going to possibly be very personal, but I can see how much you love your children. I need you to be absolutely honest with me. I won't judge. This is important for them."

Ihsan nods his head indicating for me to ask my questions.

"I want you to know that I'm not asking this out of personal curiosity, I'm asking out of respect for your family," I take a deep breath and close my notebook deliberately, careful not to fold the pages.

Please don't regret asking this.

"Was your divorce amicable? Do you still get along?"

He blinks back his shock of the audacity of a person he met an hour ago to ask such an intimate question. He takes a moment to think about what

I had prefaced my question with. This loud American woman has some balls.

"Yes," he says a little curtly.

"I'm sorry, that came out more intrusive than I meant. I don't want to make anything awkward between you two or us. I try my best not to embarrass myself and I really don't want to embarrass you."

"No, it is fine. We were both young when we married," he says as he takes his time thinking about what words to use for the rest of the explanation.

"You don't have to explain." My eyes squish as I realize that maybe I could have waited a day or so to get down to the nitty gritty.

"It is better I tell you than you read it somewhere." His chest expands and he releases the air slowly before he starts. "After I got my first big role I became very busy and she became lonely. Then she started to get more modeling jobs. Both of our schedules got very busy. When we had the children, we were more like friends than a married couple. We wanted to chase our dreams, but they were going in different directions. She went in a different direction. We respect each other as parents," he paused, "and that is what is important."

I didn't realize I was holding my breath while he was talking until he finished and my lungs scream for relief. He chose his words very carefully, revealing just enough to answer my question and deter me from asking any more.

"Thank you for sharing that with me. It will really help with communication with their mom. It's important that she is kept apprised of their activities and progress while they are with you. I want to be able to be a resource for you both and I need to know how to approach her if I need to talk with her for any reason. Like to find out if I need the sheriff on speed dial."

"I very much appreciate that," a small tension breaking chuckle breaks through his smile. "Thank you for understanding," he says, masking a small cough as he stands up from the table fixing his now wrinkled clothes.

I've had more children with single parents in my classes than the traditional nuclear families. Even my situation is out of what is considered the 'norm'. I have given that speech many times. Through the years it has been revised and fine-tuned and I seem to have perfected it on this last delivery. It may seem like none of my business, but one awkward conversation prevents several others later. It's all about avoiding the awkward, like that is remotely possible with me.

IHSAN

When she asks about my divorce, my stunned chest seizes. I feel stupid that I still have this reaction to an event that happened three years ago. In the two years since my divorce was finalized, I've tried to give myself time to connect with someone else, but every time I even think of asking out a woman the press is all over me and my family. The attention Gül and I suffered from the divorce was relentless with outlandish speculation and unfounded rumors. It just compounded the devastation of the ending of my relationship to the mother of my children. It took us a long time to develop a new relationship, but we agreed that the health of our children is the most important. If it weren't for my fans and their outpouring of support I would have stayed in a very dark place. Working out my body has always helped my mind. Years of futball and modeling has trained my body to expect to sweat and I can feel my muscles twitch when it has been too long since they've had a workout. It calmed the inner voices that threaten to eat at my soul and urge me to doubt myself. This new woman that walked in the door an hour ago seems to have left her doubt thousands of miles away in Texas. Until I signed with blue ink on the dotted line with Blaine, doubt seemed to visit daily.

Chapter 6

BEATRICE

"Ihsan? Would you like to move in with me?" I ask, trying to change the mood of our first meeting.

At first, he seemed confused, then a look of understanding washes over his dusky-toned face as we make our way from the table to the front door.

"It's a little soon, isn't it?" he replies, catching my joke.

My grin widens as I start to think that we are going to get along just fine.

He walks out of the front room, through the front door and opens the large black SUV. I follow him out and head toward my mobile safe house. I hadn't noticed that his ride had been running this whole time with a driver in the front. As he opens the door, I hear the sound of pure love. A deep dragged-out bark roars from the rear of the vehicle. I hear the clasping of latches and Ihsan loudly exclaiming *"Gelmek*, Zeki."

No way...he has a dog? Joy of joys!

Zeki stumbles to the end of the tailgate and he is a sight to behold. Ihsan grabs what is possibly the biggest dog I have ever seen under his chest and around the back of his legs and lowers him to the ground with little effort which means those muscles popping through his shirt really do work. His ears droop alongside his jowls and his tail whips back and forth as he love bombs his doggy dad with face licks and body nudges. This giant black, white and grey harlequin Great Dane is the canine version of love at first site.

Ihsan soothes him with a litany of lyrical Turkish words and lots of pets and pats. Being a good dog person, I don't run up to him and give him all the love he deserves. I stand frozen in time, waiting for this massive creature to contain all his energy.

"Don't worry, he's friendly," Ihsan says with a treat dangling over Zeki's nose.

"Oh, I can see that. I'm not worried. I just know better than to greet a new dog with too much excitement. I'm trying to hold back as much as he is. I'm going to walk over to my rig and when you think he is calmed down, bring him over. I need me some of that lovin'."

I immediately regret that last sentence but it left my mouth before I could stop it.

I know a dog that size could easily take me down and I'm no waif. I pride myself on my dog etiquette. My old principal allowed a therapy dog to come in every couple of weeks and work with our population of students that didn't have the best home life. It seemed to draw them out when there was no pressure to perform. I really love dogs and we had several growing up, but it just wasn't fair to the poor pooch if I was gone all day teaching, so I was the dog auntie to at least twelve dogs between my school and my neighborhood. Zeki is easily three times the dog I've ever had so there is plenty of him to share. I open the side door to my RV and sit on the top step, waiting very impatiently for Zeki, The Turkish Wonder Dog.

"Are you ready?"

"Yep," I reply, doing everything in my power to not clap like a two-year-old.

He walks this badass over to me on the leash and I feel like I have my own tail whipping behind me as I try to contain my energy. Zeki pulls on the leash towards me, but Ihsan stops and makes sure that he lets him know they will not continue until he lets Ihsan lead. They arrive at my feet, but I ignore Zeki and then when Ihsan commands him to sit, I put my hand under his muzzle and give him a generous scratch. His coat is so ridiculously velvety it reminds me of a brand-new plush blanket under the Christmas tree. Of course this man's dog feels as good as he looks. When I stop, Zeki scootches forward and puts his monstrous head in my lap. I can't contain my joy as I swipe my hands over his forehead and back to his ears.

"I was hoping you wouldn't mind him," Ihsan says with a warm smile.

"He should have been in the job description with a waiver or an option for hazard pay. As house manager though, I will need to assign poop pick up duty."

I laugh silently in my head since I'm sometimes a seventh-grade boy inside. I don't know if I'll have to explain that joke but I'm certain it will come around again.

"I think the gardener will need a bit of a pay raise if we ask them to do that. Will I need to hire a dog walker?"

"No, I can do that."

"I could too, you know, if you got tired of him," I say shyly with a little hint thrown in for good measure.

I'm hoping my body language surpasses any kind of verbal language barrier.

"The plane ride must have been brutal for a dog his size," I say.

"It is because of him that we chartered a plane," Ihsan explains.

Maybe I should just wear layers of panties.

"Zeke."

"Zeh-kih," he corrects.

"Zeh-kih when he's a good boy," I say, digging my fingers into his chest. "Zeke for when he eats the couch cushions."

Ihsan small laugh would indicate agreement as he unlatches Zeki from his leash and allows him to run around the property. His long legs stretch out at least seven feet long with his ears and tongue flopping in random directions, imitating a dog version of a smile. He calls him back as his driver brings in the last of his luggage. I, on the other hand, climb into Thor and grab a few things for the night.

"You pack simply," Ihsan remarks as he sees me shut the door with an overnight bag.

"I'm a little tired from being on the road so I'm going to freshen up and get the rest later."

"Blaine left food for us, so when you are ready we can eat."

I can't help but feel a bit of affection for this man at this point. He checks all a warm-blooded hetero female's boxes and this endearing offer to dine with him is just the cherry on this sexy sundae, and he's very lickable.

I open a door which I believe is a refrigerator, or freezer, the front of it looks like all the other cabinets. All the paneling in the kitchen is a uniform white. I use my sleuthing skills to find the handle for the freezer. Why I feel the need to provide a meal for this man I don't know. The freezer side of this massive appliance is the same full size as the refrigerator which is the epitome of decadence. The bright lights reflect off the walls of the empty space, causing me to ugly squint. A few brown wrapped brick sized packages labeled 'breakfast burrito' in a slightly fancy font sit on the refrigerator shelf. Just below those are a few pizzas that look to be half baked. I am going to impress the pants off him with my serious warming up skills.

"How's pizza sound?" I ask him as he casually walks into the kitchen, as if we've been doing this for a lot longer than a few hours.

"Do you know anyone who doesn't like pizza?" he replies.

I toy with the idea of playing the game where you only talk in questions but that is a two-week-old friendship game. We are only on hour three.

The instructions on the top of the plastic encasing the pizzas are very clear that I don't even need a pizza tray, definitely not your grocery store's eight thousand ingredient boxed pies. I peer around the kitchen trying to find something that looks like an oven.

"The oven seems to be hiding," I declare.

Ihsan takes a look around and doesn't move. He extends his arm and grabs onto a handle and pulls down. Where a normal oven would be lower, this one is more chest height, at least on me. I avoid looking in his direction because I don't trust my eyes to get stuck on that marble chest of his and release the pizza from its packaging.

"You're so clever," I say, in the most mocking way possible.

Testing his humor limits will determine what I can get away with or if I might need to have a chat with Human Resources.

He smiles at me and extends his other arm for the directions.

"Fahrenheit not Celsius, otherwise we will be having breakfast burritos which I am not against."

"We have the letter 'F' in Türkiye."

"It seems you have smart asses too," I rebut.

It's hard to keep my cheeks from turning bright pink with all this friend-ly banter.

The rest of the meal is quite pleasant after we fumble around the kitchen trying to locate plates, potholders, and a cookie sheet to remove the pizza from the oven. Zeki waits patiently, laying down with his head on top of his crossed paws behind Ihsan's kitchen stool, just waiting for me to drop a morsel. I made a note to myself to make sure to hire staff that also loved dogs because this guy might be a counter surfer.

"So where does Zeki sleep when he's at home?" I ask after wiping red sauce from my lips.

"At home he sleeps in my room, but I do not want him going up and down that staircase," he said as he glances around the room. "I did not think of it when we planned all this."

He really understands the responsibility of a large dog owner. Zeki is not a dog, he's his friend.

Our conversation for the next half hour is light and fluffy. We don't share anything too personal and mainly talk about the house, Zeki and how his country is officially "Türkiye" now not "Turkey" due to association with the stupidest bird on the planet. Now I'll sound super smart for all these Hollywood types. We laugh at each other's jokes and seem to both have the same goal of just trying to figure out how we will get along.

"Now that I have refueled, I think I'll go ahead and grab the rest of my stuff out of Thor and make myself at home."

Hopping off the stool, I make my way to the kitchen and stand in front of the sink on the island.

"I would think they would mark where the trash is. This house makes me feel stupid."

"I'm glad you said it. I thought I was the only one," Ihsan laughs as he rounds the island.

"I thought my first adventure with a movie star would be more glamorous than finding where the trash goes," my tone slightly annoyed.

"I'll work on that." He nods his head as if he is making a mental note.

After we finally discover the trash can extracts itself from the island with a foot swipe from below, we spend a few minutes discovering all the other tricks the kitchen is hiding. The way he is able to switch on that childlike excitement and charm so freely, I realize he has it in him to be just as big of a dork as me. I just need to find ways to bring it out.

"Now I'm going to go get the rest of my crap."

"I'll have the driver bring them in."

"You mean that guy has been sitting out there the whole time?"

"I hired him for the whole day. I figured we would need the help. I asked if he wanted to come in and wait and he said no. I'm not insensitive."

He places his hand on his heart in mock offense.

Adorable. Damn adorable.

"You should really get your money's worth then. Let's go!"

IHSAN

It has been a long time since I have had a friendship with someone where I wasn't suspicious of their sincerity. From our first meeting, this woman earned my respect. She says what's on her mind and doesn't hold back. In my experience, there are only a few people I can truly trust, and Beatrice is about to make the list in record time. Zeki confirms my initial sentiment when he is pulled toward her as if they are opposite sides of an industrial magnet. His track record of seeking out good people is better than mine and I've come to rely on his instincts as mine have been unreliable to say the least. But I don't need to rely on Zeki's intuition when I see the look on her face as he creeps up to her lap. She couldn't get enough of him, stroking his chin and lightly gripping his ears to experience the soft sensation in her palms and between her fingers. Not only does she have a wicked sense of humor, but she is also a dog lover. My last assistant cowered to the farthest corner every time Zeki entered the room, regardless of if he was leashed or free to roam. Beatrice and Zeki, those names sound surprisingly satisfying to my ears.

As we sit, discussing light topics, I am enamored at her ability to make the most mundane topics and activities amusing. The way she uses her whole body to tell a story not only entertains me but leaves me wanting more. I find myself focusing my attention on her just so I don't miss a witty quip or curious observation. I realize that Blaine has succeeded again, providing me with exactly what I need.

"*Hallo, abla,*" I greet my sister with the traditional nickname.

"Isa!"

The timbre of my sister's voice rests sweetly in my ears.

"You sound alive and well. How did Zeki do?"

"He's good."

"And the new assistant?"

"Beatrice? She's ...interesting."

"That does not inspire confidence."

"*Yok.* She just has a lot to say and doesn't call me Mr. Zorlu like I expected."

"Did you tell her to call you Ihsan-bey?" she says with a disappointed low tone.

"No, and I'm ok with that. She doesn't seem to be the type that respects typical workplace boundaries."

"Oh, do tell."

"So far, she treats me more like a partner. And she has no clue who I am."

Farah's laugh is high and fast and lasts too long to be polite.

"That's new for you."

"It's refreshing. In fact, I don't think she really cares about fame."

"Good, it's about time someone brought you down."

"I'm not that bad."

"I had to kick you out of the country."

"I left to get away from you."

"Do me a favor and don't mention to a*nne* that we live in the same house?" My mother has a strong heart but I don't want to be the one to test its limits.

"I won't. This will be good for you. I'm so happy for you. We are all so excited."

"Even Nadir?" I ask knowing the answer. Nadir and I had a hard time agreeing these days and I'm hoping for any speck of our sibling relationship to return.

"Isa, it will take time for him to come around."

Chapter 7

B EATRICE

After a couple hours listening to my favorite eighties and nineties playlist while moving, unpacking, organizing, and editing all the crap I dragged with me to fit into this new life and packing it back into Thor, I decide that workday one must come to an end. After releasing the driver from his service, Ihsan did his best to distract me. He didn't have as much to do, so he decided to read in the living room, occasionally asking if I needed help. I would decline and the cycle would begin all over. Walking out to the kitchen, I see Zeki and Ihsan sprawled out fast asleep on the couch, Zeki's front paws twitching. I should suggest Blaine look into bedding or mattress commercials, because he is just as hot sleeping as he is conscious, his face slack and peaceful. I bet sales would be record breaking.

The volume of the rumbling in my stomach threatens to wake Sleeping Beauty and his dragon so I continue on to the kitchen as quickly as possible. Having pizza twice in one day seems like the easiest and best option. I never understood why people had a problem eating the same thing for consecutive days or meals. Reminding myself of where the oven is, I select all the options for pre-heating. Taking the other pizza out of the refrigerator, I prepare it for the oven. Ihsan's head appears over the back cushions of the couch and a smile instantly washes over my face.

"I will prove to you that I cook more than pre-made pizzas, but this is what we've got for now. Any objections?"

"None."

"Excellent. Your selection this evening is an artisan flatbread topped with a variety of your favorite spring vegetables with an Italian herb tomato-based reduction and fresh hand pulled mozzarella," I say attempting to make it sound fancy with a slightly snotty British accent.

Hearing the ding from the oven, I insert the pizza, doing my best to not impale my boob with the edge of the oven door. I am very aware that Ihsan is watching this whole process and it feels very much like he is just waiting for me to make an ass out of myself. I deny him the pleasure, this time.

"Why don't you find something for us to watch?"

"Anything you have in mind?"

"No reality dating shows and no horror. Wait, aren't those the same thing? Otherwise, I'm good with anything."

Ihsan surfs the streaming services to find something that would satisfy both him and the woman living in his house that he barely knows.

"A friend recommended this show about seven people that share the same birthday awhile back. Try to find that."

Matthew could possibly be setting me up. Since he didn't really mention it again, I can assume it is fairly tame.

"What's it about?"

"No clue. Watching it blindly will be our second adventure."

When the pizza is ready, Ihsan helps me get it out of the oven and we sit to discover a show that we can share together. As the plays on, I'm glad I trusted Matthew. We're both enjoying it and only have to pause a few times to clarify to each other what's happening. I can feel my eyes start to close as it reaches the thirty-minute mark and I bring my hand over possibly the largest yawn I have ever performed. My jaw might have popped out of its socket.

"I'm going to have to call it a night."

Ihsan takes our paper plates to the kitchen and dumps them in the magic trash can. I peel myself off the couch to help him put away the leftovers. I'll look for more rigorous dish cleaning tools in the morning. We say our goodnights for the first time, and I give Zeki a big kiss on the head before making my way down the hallway, trying not to put my fingerprints on everything. This strange situation felt surprisingly normal and familiar.

I place all of my toiletries on the luxurious vanity. Stepping back, I start to feel like something is wrong. It's like putting lipstick on a pig. This is not the type of place where you leave your toothbrush in a cup next to the sink. I look down and find quite a few drawers where I can hide my pit stick and tooth scrubber. I pull out the first drawer and find it's extra deep, with two ceramic cups inside. Perfect for my toothbrush and water cups. There is a separate little spigot next to the waterfall faucet and at first I think it's a soap dispenser but discover that when I run my hand under it, cool water flows out. I stand and think for a moment. Oh, this must be filtered water, for drinking.

This is totally the work of a brilliant woman.

I tuck all of my other products in various cubbies and hidey holes. There's even a drawer in the vanity area that has cylindrical metal holders for styling products with outlets toward the rear. I decide when I have more energy, I'm going to spend an afternoon setting up the perfect Zen getaway in this bathroom.

The shower has a special brass and glass shampoo dispenser which I appreciate as I don't want to sully this beautiful temple of cleanliness with my plastic product bottles. I spy a small red button on the side of the towel rack.

No effing, I mean fucking way. This is a heated towel bar!

The bathmat in front of the shower door is bamboo with a drain built into the floor. I notice when I open the shower door that there are also brass plates on the walls with grids of holes. This must be side spray for when I'm too tired to scrub under my armpit myself, I just have to raise my arm. Deciding that I will have to do more exploring tomorrow, I make my way towards the bed and open my bag that I dumped there earlier. I wrestle around and find the super soft PJs that Brandon and Sarah had given me one night when I had an especially hard visit with my mom. I throw the bag on the floor and proceed to take off my bra. Every time I remove this dreaded contraception, I hear "Release the hounds!" in my head. I'm very grateful that mind reading is not a real thing.

I realize I hadn't checked my phone for messages since this morning and when I opened the home screen a tiny eleven cornered the icon for text messages, all from Matthew. Brandon had tracked my phone a long time ago, so I was pretty sure he was satisfied I was safe. I plop onto the bed and gather up the furriness of the coverlet around me. I find Matthew's number and touch the Facetime option. It rings a few times and then his back teeth pop onto the screen. I appreciate his attempt to shock me. At least it wasn't down his pants this time. That was only funny to one of us.

I laugh into the phone. "Oh, I'm sorry, I was looking for Matthew's uvula."

"Oh, let me go check."

He pulls back the phone and his smiling face appears and fills the screen. "HEEEEYYYY GUUUUURL!" he exclaims.

I repeat the greeting back to him.

"I am calling you to say thank you from the bottom of my heart. I'm going to see this as a week-long working vacation because I'm absolutely going to get fired. They added manager stuff to my duties, and I'm already promoted to assistant manager. But I'm here to live whatever the universe throws at me. Even if I only make it a week, this is worth it."

"You're an ass man?" His laugh leads me to believe he didn't have a clue about my additional duties. "Sorry, not sorry. Spill it, QB."

"First of all, this house. Second, this actor. Third, this dog."

"In that order? Elaborate."

"I'm tired but I want to take you on a tour as soon as you have an hour free. I don't know who or what is prettier, the house, Ihsan or Zeki."

"Which one is the dog and which one is the actor?"

"Who would name a dog 'Ihsan'?" I ask exasperatedly, as if it was totally obvious. "I'm just telling you that whoever found this guy is a hotness bloodhound. I'm going to be totally professional and do some background 'research'," I say using dramatic finger air quotes.

"Yeah, reseeeaaarch," he draws out the word totally getting my drift.

"Tomorrow we're planning on doing some shopping to pick up some stuff for the house. If you have time, you should join us. You know how much I like being the meat in a babe sandwich."

"I'm too busy," he whines.

"I haven't seen you in so long," I whine back. "We have to connect soon. I miss your face. You need to give me a crash course in this celebrity wrangler gig."

"I just googled him. Did you hear that?"

"Those were my first words out of my mouth when I met him."

"No!" Matthew gasps and covers his mouth.

"Yes, and I am holding you responsible for his reaction if or when he asks me why I said that. In fact, I will defer all questions on the matter to you."

"He is the definition of tall, dark and hands down his pants hot."

"Do NOT put him in your spank bank, Matthew. Do not!"

"Are you calling spank bank dibs?"

"Ew! I won't be able to look at him knowing you're looking at him too. You shouldn't be interfering with my work. I'm glad I didn't google him before I met him because I wouldn't have made it inside the city limits."

"Oh, stop being all professional. Promise me when you get a chance you will google him," he says sternly.

"You make that sound gross too. Oh, we started to watch that show about the seven strangers."

"So, you didn't get to the dream orgy."

"Matthew!"

By the sound of him rolling on his bed laughing, I know this dream orgy does, in fact, exist. I hope Ihsan doesn't ask to finish the series. Or maybe I do.

"Ok, I'll text you tomorrow. Make sure you have fresh batteries. Wink, wink. Sweet, sweet, sweet dreams, Honey Bee," he says almost breathless.

The more I think about it, the more I'm convinced Matthew got me hired just so he could get me fired in the most embarrassing way. I still love him, though.

I feel I have a few minutes of consciousness left in me, so I pull up the web browser on my phone and type in 'Ihsan Zorlu' into the search bar and press the spy glass. Hundreds of images pop up on the screen. I don't believe I will be going to sleep any time soon. He went through several different phases of facial hair styles. One hair-tastrophe in particular I will be teasing him about when I get to know him better. His stylist must have had a fixation with Tom Selek.

How am I supposed to work with this man? I'm proud of myself that I'm able to show a little of my personality within the string of words I'm barely able to put together. I've got to figure out a way to bring him down to my level so I can work with him on a daily basis. I think for a moment and it hits me. Why should I shy away from his magnificence? I'll just call him out on it. Why pretend it's not there? If it's out in the universe it won't be racing around in my head and creating friction and heat in my body. It's not like I'll be saying anything he hasn't read or heard before. I'll just put my spin on it and then I'll be able to work without fixating on his hypnotic features. This will totally work. Yep. A well thought out plan for Ihsan's animal magnetism. With exhaustion setting in, I figure no one will judge me if I just fall asleep on top of these super soft covers with an image of Ihsan full screen on my phone. Research, purely research.

IHSAN

"Farah, it will be fine. *anne* will just have to get over it," I try to reassure my sister. My mother is going to find out Beatrice is my live-in assistant. There is no way I can keep it a secret. My mother is a bit of a bloodhound and she'll either hear Beatrice in the background on a phone conversation at a late hour or see a post where something slips. The whole neighborhood is on the lookout as well.

"Isa, she is going to have one of her fits and you are on the other side of the world."

My mother tends to be melodramatic which is where I probably get my penchant for acting. She's always been more concerned with what the neighbors will think than what I do. Most of the time it is out of love, but the divorce was almost as hard on her as it was on me. The neighborhood ladies brought her containers of comfort food which she hated because it meant that she would have to return them full of homemade goodies she didn't want to cook. They treated it more like a death than an end to a marriage. In my neighborhood, my family was royalty thanks to my talent on the field. Farah is right though; she is going to need someone to catch her fall when she finds out a young woman is living with me.

"It's not like that. Beatrice is more like an obnoxious little sister than anything else. You'll love her."

"As long as she is taking care of you, I don't care if she smells like a hot day at the fish cleaning station."

I laugh at my sister's call back to one of the worst smells that has ever entered my olfactory system.

"As far as I can tell, her hygiene is not going to be a problem," I add, remembering the floral smell of her blonde-brown hair when her large poofy bun whizzed by my nose as she climbed up the stairs to my room.

"She seems to have all the skills I need."

"Ihsan, you need to save some luck for the rest of us."

"You know I'll always take care of you."

The hardest part of this move is leaving my family in Türkiye. We've had some seriously hard episodes but my mother, brother and sister have always been there to support me whether it was in the stands during a match or making sure the whole neighborhood was supplied with my latest magazine cover. My father took my uncle to live on a relative's farm near the Black Sea after he wore out his welcome living with us for several years. My father didn't feel like he could kick his brother out and since I was able to support the family, he took his brother away. It was much more peaceful in the house once my uncle had left. When he feels his brother is able to handle being alone for a few days, he comes home and my mother acts as if he had never left.

"Have you seen the kids?"

"Yes, we went to the amusement park today."

My sister is truly Allah's blessing.

"Thank you, Farah. I already miss them."

"I know."

I stop myself from admitting to her that my arms ache from the absence of my children. Zeyva is freakishly intuitive and has a slightly mean streak which she uses to maneuver herself into the most advantageous situations. I already have an account to save up for law school. Tariq will most likely end up as a stunt double as he has no fear. He doesn't allow anything to stop him from what he wants and he will do whatever it takes to accomplish his goal. It has made school a bit of a struggle for both of them. When I entrust them to a nanny, I am more concerned for their safety than my children's wellbeing. Beatrice may be the only one up to the challenge.

BEATRICE

The harsh sound of whining pierces through the hollow door of my bedroom. At first, I think I'm having a student-teacher flashback nightmare of when I did a stint in elementary school. I turn over slowly and hear scratching at the door. If this house has a poltergeist, well...who am I kidding? I would still stay here. I climb over the bed and listen carefully to where this obnoxious ruckus is coming from. I stumble over to the door and turn the knob. Just when the latch releases, a wet nose pushes its way past me and jumps onto the bed.

"You are not the creature of the night I expected," I scratch my head, trying to clear the cobwebs from my brain.

"Ummm. Ok, off the bed," I make a motion with my arm and point with my hand from the bed to the floor. He looks at me with his head tilted like he didn't know what I was saying but, by the look in his eyes, he clearly does. Damn, I need to ask Ihsan how to say "off" in Turkish. I lean over my bed and grab Zeki's collar. It didn't take much to get him to move but he's all legs and he struggles with untangling them. I can't just kick him out of the room and the floor has to be hard on his elbows.

"Ok, I don't sleep with boys on the first date so to the couch with you," I say to this seriously adorable gray pocked face and big sappy eyes and pull him onto the long couch.

Getting settled for the night, I turn and shut the door out of instinct this time listening for the latch. I lay at the foot of my bed as Zeki gets comfortable. His body spans over the entire couch with both his front and back paws dangling off the edge. He looks back at me upside down over the couch as if to say thank you. Since Zeki seems to want a bed buddy, I grab a pillow and make myself a little nest next to the back of the couch and drape my arm over to scratch his head perched on the arm rest. Who needs a security system when you have your own personal guard sleeping in your room?

Chapter 8

BEATRICE

"Zeeehkeeeh!" Ihsan yells from the stairs as he makes his way down to the main floor.

The unfamiliar voice wakes me with a start and a groan. Even when he elongates the name, his accent comes through. Zeki lets out something between a bark and a howl from the couch and with his giant chest acting as an amplifier, there is no sanctity to my morning. I hear the pads of bare feet slapping against the floor tile as Ihsan approaches.

"Um, Beatrice. Is Zeki with you?" he asks after he knocks politely.

Zeki lets out one of his howl barks before I can answer.

"No," I say playfully. I open the door, not realizing how disheveled I was with my bright pink PJs scrunched in all sorts of inappropriate crevices.

"I'm in here with him. He's holding me hostage," I add, trying to wipe my hair out of my face.

I'm not sure he understood my meaning, but I plan on helping him with understanding all of the 'Bee-isms'.

Zeki pushes by me and slams into Ihsan's thighs, pushing him off balance. I finally move the veil of hair from my face as I see Ihsan bend down, grab Zeki's face and plant a kiss on the top of his muzzle. Zeki's love fest spills over to me, his whip-like tail striking me at my waistband. I step back to avoid any further bruising as Ihsan stands up and laughs at our first morning interaction. As he rises, I notice the baggy black jogger style sweatpants and loosely fitting long sleeve white t-shirt with a giant neckline. I guess he needed to make room for those big ass trapezius muscles. His shirt falls slightly down his shoulder and as he pulls it back, the tip of a tattoo peeks through the black fabric.

"I'm sorry. I guess I'll have to find a solution to the stairs soon," he says sympathetically. I almost offered my bed to him right then and there.

Down, girl.

"Did he keep you awake?"

"No, it was nice to have a male want to be in my bed for a change."

He huffs a little uncomfortably, trying to decide if I was actually trying to convey humor or not.

Why can't I keep my mouth shut?

"I'm sorry. The brain to mouth barrier isn't fully operational in the morning."

He smiles back at me with impossibly white teeth. "I'm going to take him outside."

Ihsan turns around and puts his hand on the back of Zeki's head, ushering him out. As they walk down the hallway and turn left into the living room, I lean against the door frame, taking in the view of the titan's cute ass.

Boss, Beatrice. Just say no.

I slowly walk into the bathroom and turn on the lights, avoiding my reflection until I'm directly in front of the mirror. Ok, not too bad. My hair looks tousled, and my face only has one blanket line stretching from ear to nose.

I pull up my hair, twist and tuck it into a makeshift bun. I urge my still asleep legs to take me back into the bedroom and look for my discarded bra because even though I'm in my jammies, these wild ladies need to be caged.

Out of nowhere, the doorbell rings incessantly. Only one person I know rings a doorbell like that. Matthew Schroeder. I stumble out of the room, pulling the back of my pajama shirt down as I stare at him through the shaded glass.

"You bring a new meaning to the words 'You suck!'" I yell through the glass. He then lifts up a cardboard tray of lidded cups and a brown bag of blessings.

"I brought you a survival kit!" he screams back at me through the little slit in between the glass doors.

"How did you get through the gate?"

"You know when I want something, I'm unstoppable."

I'm starting to wonder what he said and did to get me this gig.

"Blaine." I say. His name needs to be said in a low grumbly tone with squinted eyes and tight teeth from now on.

I take a moment to remember how to unlock the door and step aside as he dashes past me. My nose is bombarded with a combination of the smell of hot coffee, warm bagels and Matthew's favorite cologne. He's wearing pink jeans rolled up above his ankles, white plain tennis shoes and a short-sleeved button-down shirt with palm trees and flamingos printed on it. Typical Matthew.

The instant Matthew lets go of his breakfast surprise we turn to each other and, without another word, he bends down to tackle hug me like we did ten years ago when this style of greeting was more socially acceptable. My attempt to keep us upright almost fails but as adults we try to stay off the floor as much as possible, unlike college when we tended to become a Matthew Beatrice fruit roll-up. My eyes start to glaze over as I realize I haven't had an in-person full on Matthew hug in over a year. He had been my rock of Gibraltar through the last few years and when he decided to leave San Antonio, I crumbled. Even though Matthew was irreplaceable, Sarah filled the hole that Matthew left.

We finally release each other, almost breathless from the excessive squeezing.

"Wha.... the.....fuh," he exclaims as his shoe screeches slightly on the floor.

"I know," I say as I entwine my arm into his. I guide him off to the right and try to keep his feet moving toward the kitchen. His sunglassed eyes can't seem to focus on one thing at a time as his head rotates almost three hundred and sixty degrees.

"And it only gets better," I say, opening the bag of circular heaven and taking a deep satisfying breath through my nose. "As happy as you made me when I saw your face through the door, please answer the obvious question, Matthew."

I sternly glance at him while trying to find a plate which resides in a drawer, not a cupboard. At least one previous tenant understood the plight of the short ones.

"Well, I wanted to make sure you had a strong start in your new position and so I brought you a power breakfast."

I glare at him knowingly with my eyebrows low, my head tilted, and my lips pursed. The tempo of his words increased dramatically as he added, "I went down the Turkish rabbit hole last night. I had to see him for myself."

Matthew leans over to place one butt cheek on the kitchen stool and then scoots the other one on with ease. Must be nice to be tall and thin. What I wouldn't do for a few extra vertical inches. It would stretch me out and my Weeble shape would be less noticeable.

"You brought something to wipe up the drool, I hope," I reply. "I haven't been able to do all the 'required reading' yet."

My back stiffens as I hear the back glass doors slide closed on their tracks.

"Be cool, man. Be cool," I warn Matthew.

Zeki bounds into the kitchen with his floppy ears smacking his head. His giant paws slip and slide as they try to gain purchase before he runs into the kitchen island. Matthew pulls his legs up toward his chest and lets out a little yelp that doesn't really fit his elongated body type.

After the initial shock of seeing the enormous hound, Matthew does what Matthew does best.

"Did daddy finally buy you that pony you always wanted?"

Matthew's joyful condescending voice is to be expected and wholeheartedly welcomed.

I don't have a chance to compose a snarky answer when Ihsan walks in with a look of slight surprise, his hair still ruffled from sleep.

"Heeelllllo, daddy," Matthew declares as his eyes grow large and his jaw slackens.

"I'm sorry for him. This is my friend Matthew who helped me get this job. He has appointed himself the one-man welcome wagon."

I walk over to Matthew and put my hands up to his shoulders, close his mouth and utter each word slowly.

"Matthew, this...is...Ee-sahn. He's...my...client. Can...you...say...Ee-sahn?"

By the annoyed look on Matthew's face, he did not appreciate my humor and Ihsan's expression signals confusion. Matthew slides off the kitchen island stool ridiculously gracefully and puts his hand out for Ihsan to shake.

Ihsan offers his palm out to the Clyde to my Bonnie and I realize that if Zeki stands on his hind legs, I'm the shortest person in the house by at least eight inches.

"It's nice to meet you, Matthew."

While still holding Ihsan's hand, Matthew turns to me and fans his face with the other.

"You can let go now, Matthew."

"I'm sorry. I've never met anyone from Turkey before," a nervous laugh accompanying his apology.

"He has a disorder where he involuntarily loses all good sense when he encounters a good-looking man."

Matthew drops Ihsan's hand knowing he has to engage his superpower of saving me from my glitchy mouth filter. I should let Matthew in on my new tactic for interacting with this man.

"I brought black coffee with all sorts of add-ins. As soon as Beatrice stops getting high off the bagel fumes, we can indulge ourselves with the best carbs in LA."

Thank the Lord Almighty in Heaven for Matthew. He knew exactly what to say to draw away Ihsan's attention from my stupid remark about his looks. I will have to do better than that in the future. Ihsan opens the plate drawer and takes out a few and places them on the counter. He pushes his shirt sleeves up a few inches exposing the serpentine veins climbing his wrists. I must have some kind of staring psychosis because every move this man makes I have no choice but to watch intently. If I don't put this creeper behavior in check, Ihsan will for sure fire me on the basis of suspected sinister intentions.

We sit around the kitchen island enjoying our bagels and schmear, explaining the difference between schmear and cream cheese which causes us to giggle as Ihsan struggles to put all those consonants together.

"Don't worry about it. It will make you more endearing to your audience," I say reassuringly and pat my palm on his shoulder.

And it's sexy as hell.

"Besides, I'm counting on you teaching me a little Turkish, so Zeki doesn't look at me like I'm stupid. I know my mouth is going to have a hard time getting around some of your syllables."

Matthew spits out a small spray but plays it off as if the coffee he had been drinking for ten minutes is suddenly hot.

Why can't I just shut up?

"I'll teach you your first lesson then. *Bir fincan kahvenin kirk yil hatiri.*"

The skin on my lower lip stings as I feel my front teeth bear down. I don't think I've ever had an eargasm in person before, certainly not by an accent. And what the hell is going on between my thighs?

Ihsan continues as the blank stares on our faces indicate our level of understanding.

"A single cup of coffee commits one to forty years of friendship," he translates.

"Whoa, I'm not ready for that kind of commitment," I say, placing the cup quickly on the counter. "Matthew's my longest relationship and we barely tolerate each other."

Matthew nods in agreement then takes another sip.

"Um... how about *Kahve cehennem kadar kara, ölüm kadar kuvvetli, sevgi kadar tatlı olmalı*. 'Coffee should be black as hell, strong as death and sweet as love.'?" Ihsan smiles while holding up his up for a toast.

"To strong hell, sweet death, and black love!" I raise my cup in the air and wait for the others to bump in a toast to distract myself from the rush of nerve pulses in my lady bits.

I can tell by the way Ihsan tips his head, flattens lips and squints his eyes that he's not sure if I re-arranged his words on purpose or if I was truly confused.

"You better get used that; Beatrice's brilliant talent at twisting words," Matthew warns.

"Or was it black death, sweet hell and strong love," I continue. "But if we rearrange them again it makes more sense, strong love leads to sweet hell which leads to black death."

"I'm not sure about you," Ihsan says, setting his coffee down but still smiling that thigh gripping smile.

"I'm a mystery," I say, using my deepest Kathleen Turner voice.

"Are you, though?" Matthew interrupts, giving us a brief second to contemplate his question. "Okay, team. Thank the Botox gods for my boss needing a touch up this morning. I might have hinted a little but you gotta do what you gotta do. I couldn't miss the chance to appear in the Queen's court. So, we have the morning to do a little shopping."

Ihsan's eyes squish halfway closed. I can see the tiny little Christmas bulb in Matthew's brain as he remembers that Ihsan is brand spanking new to us and isn't accustomed to our vernacular.

"You, my new foreign friend, presently reside with the ruler of all she surveils, the Majesty of Mayhem, the Sovereign of Sinister, the Potentate of Puerile," he says using his announcer voice complete with widespread arms. "That one I just learned the other day. I have the immense pleasure of presenting to you, Queen Bee of Bexar County," he finishes, rolling his hand over itself and bending his neck almost to the counter.

"My court jester," I roll my eyes.

Ihsan bows his head in appreciation of Matthew's introduction and attending to the faux of it all.

"Just so you know, I didn't name myself. The title was forced upon me by Matthew and his brother."

"Oh, but you earned it," he says, turning toward Ihsan's half-filled cheeks, a speck of cream cheese trying to escape through the corner of his lips.

"You are lucky for scoring a spot in her entourage. There is no doubt she's in charge. Just wait."

"Matthew," my eyes flash a warning for him to tread lightly.

"What? I didn't use the word tyrant," he says with mock innocence, his favorite tone of voice.

"Ok, that was one time I asked you to come help me with a presentation. I was under pressure to impress the professor and there were deadlines and two people dropped the ball. I will admit to being assertive."

"You made us cry."

"You and Brandon should have at least one pair of balls between you," I say without thinking of present company. I turn to look at Ihsan happily watching the two of us bicker like an old married couple to gauge how my new employer would react to my crass sense of humor. Luckily, either he didn't understand or chose to let it slide considering it was early in the morning and I may not be on the clock just yet.

At first, I was annoyed that Matthew showed up unannounced and uninvited but now I am sincerely grateful. He will know everywhere to go and how to get there and be the buffer between me and my instinct to say stupid things with commitment like it's normal. Matthew is a force to be reckoned with when he sets his mind to it.

"Enough," he says firmly and immediately relaxes his body as if to finish the scene. "While you are getting ready, Bee, we can go over some of the info I brought for you."

This is code for we need to dish privately and pick out an outfit on the downlow.

"What will we do about Zeki?" I ask. We couldn't just leave him in a house like this with no supervision.

"The places we are going honey, you could bring in a buffalo and they wouldn't bat an eye. They just want the Benjamins."

I'm pretty sure Ihsan understood most of that.

"We will take the SUV and put him in the crate in the back. Otherwise, he will sit in your lap," Ihsan suggested.

If I ask him to read the dictionary to me, would that be weird?

"Great! Meet at the front door in forty-five minutes?" I ask.

"That's good. Can Zeki stay with you down here until we figure something out?"

Matthew looked confused. "We want to keep him off the stairs so he doesn't hurt himself," I say as if I was part of the decision.

"Yep. We're off to the races, boys!" I say running down the hallway and getting body checked by the gray beast right before I pass the threshold to my room. We get to the room and Zeki jumps on the bed, making himself at home. Matthew didn't seem to mind as he marked his spot on the luxurious couch.

IHSAN

Beatrice doesn't seem to mind appearing in her baggy pajamas in front of me as if this wasn't our first night here. Finding Zeki in her room this morning almost delighted me if it weren't for how bad I felt for her. He's a bed hog and I've woken up with a paw in my groin too many mornings. Seeing her unpolished and barely able to open her eyes, with her hair falling almost to her hips is a sight I have sorely missed. The women I am used to seem to be more concerned with how they are seen than letting people actually see them. Beatrice is almost as transparent as this house. Our first morning together and she answers the door without any hesitation or pretense. It's as if she flips a little switch in my brain that allows me to temporarily forget I'm in a new country, away from my family and about to embark on the most important adventure in my career.

Beatrice seems like the kind of person that doesn't have frivolous friendships which, after meeting Matthew, is confirmed. When he rushes into the house armed with breakfast to welcome her to his turf, I count myself lucky to have the chance to be in her inner circle. I'm almost jealous of Matthew as I watch them reconnect after a year apart, holding each other tightly and their palms or shoulders or arms always touching like twin babies in a crib. My brother is the last person I had that kind of relationship with but now he doesn't speak to me, and I miss the way we laughed and cried together. Beatrice and I are both out of our element, but she at least has Matthew to give her a sense of comradery. They start in right away, teasing and laughing as if they were never apart. I'm not sure if it is envy or sadness collapsing my chest, but I don't like the feeling and purging it from my body will be the first order of business.

Chapter 9

B EATRICE

"I know you want to dish on my big Turkish delight in there, but I really need to shower. Can you keep yourself together that long?"

"This is sooooo haaaaard," Matthew imitates the distinctive elongated whine of one of my old students. I probably shouldn't have repeated that to Matthew as it has become a thing with him to torture me.

I go into the bathroom to strip down and leave my clothes in a pile on the floor. It feels like blasphemy, but I don't have much time. I search for the few items I need to shower that I apparently hid from myself last night. After I get my act together, I carefully step into the shower stall. I took it for granted that I was a college educated woman because it takes me way too long to figure out how to get this water closet working. After finally getting the hot water flowing, I make a mental note to myself to prepare instructions for the next inhabitants of this glass fortress.

"You owe me one, Bee!" Matthew shouts over the waterfall.

"I'm pretty sure you have a name plate in heaven, 'M'," I shout back trying to reach him over the sound of water smacking on the shower walls.

"I made a list of my contacts around town including numbers, names, and emails. This is the holy bible of our industry," he says as he leans against the door jamb of the open bathroom.

"Thou shalt not share," I say back.

"The devil will do anything to get this."

"I bet I could hit it with holy water from here."

"Be careful, this is the only copy. I didn't put it online on purpose. Bitches are vicious vultures out here."

"Oh, write that down as a good band name. Vicious Vultures," I giggle as the water streams down my skin. "But seriously though, I can keep documents confidential."

"Oh yeah, that teachery thing," he mocks back at me. "Anyway, call as many as you can as soon as you can and coordinate with the studio. I know they have a plan for Ihsan, but you need to get his name out there ASAP. We don't want to dye his hair blue if that isn't in the script."

I rinse everything out of my hair and off my body and open the shower door to reach for the warm towel hanging on the horizontal rod.

Oh, hell yes.

I wish I had more time to savor this moment. There are few things in this world that make me happier than a warm, soft, poofy towel.

"The towel is so fluffy I could die!" I scream. Someone had to hear that and appreciate my reference to an animated classic.

As if reading my mind, Matthew dryly says, "Yeah, I got it," knowing how important my movie quote cred is to me.

"We unpacked Thor yesterday, but I think I forgot something."

"Well, you aren't a fashion icon but let's see what we are working with."

I did manage to remember to hang up an outfit last night after the intrusion of Zeki. I walk down the long suite hallway in my towel which falls slightly short of wrapping around my body and grab my dress off the rack. It's a nice criss cross neckline that will show a little cleavage if I choose. The sleeves cut across my biceps but aren't tight. These guns are more like saggy cannons. I'll have to wear a jean jacket over the pretty pink floral motif. The waist cinches under my bust which gives it an empire waist feel then straight down to the floor. I then realize what I had left in Thor, my reliable shapewear. I will have to fake some reason to have to make a quick wardrobe adjustment.

"I know it's not chic but I'm here to work, not walk a runway."

I turn sideways and slide the hem of the dress up one leg.

"Nothing beats a classic," I say as I expose my bare ankle, pointing my toe with my old reliable light pink Vans.

Matthew nods with lying approval. He does that for me because I'm almost helpless when it comes to fashion. This outfit is one of the pre-approved looks. I blow dry my hair straight and add a little wave with a flat iron which I then realize is a mistake because my hair is so long and there is so much of it. It was going to take a bit longer than I wanted but no bell is going to ring and rush me this morning. After the loud noise of the dryer stops, Matthew enters the bathroom and sits on the edge of the tub.

"Okay, girl...it's teatime."

"I know," turning to him, I quietly scream in my best middle school girl voice.

"Matthew, he is ... I can't even begin. The 'Friend Zone' is an international co-ed fraternity. I'm thinking about running for president."

Matthew huffs like I just sucked all the wind out of his sails. He knew it was safer to stay out of my love life since his previous efforts resembled the bombing of Dresden. I rarely broadcast my affections for Brandon to Matthew, but he wasn't blind. But for me, he acted as if he was. Matthew's eyes would pour out the sympathy every time Brandon pushed me aside to spend time with his latest love interest. He was always gentle, which made it infinitely worse. It wasn't fair for me to put Matthew in the middle of my love pickle. So, whenever he could, he tried to call my attention to someone else.

I apply simple make-up as Matthew tries to give me other options.

"They are taking a giant leap of faith with me, and your rep is on the line too. You know I don't do anything half assed. But this is something entirely different."

"Oh, honey there is nothing half assed about that man."

I laugh a little while I realize I may have put an extra coat of mascara on subconsciously. I'm satisfied with the eye shadow blending and the length of the lashes. Like Blaine said, confidence personified or at least fake it till you make it. Now to get my torso torture tube.

Asking Matthew to grab my bag would have been easier but he has a habit of going through things he shouldn't. The chances of him sticking his hand into a bag full of spandex and Lycra without embarrassing me is of course, very unlikely.

I peek out of the edge of my door and sprint to the foyer. I then slow myself down in preparation for the ninety degree turn to go through the glass front doors. Remembering what happened at school, I stop in front of them and made sure they're both unlocked. I run over to Thor like I had just robbed a bank. When I get to the driver's side, I open the door quickly. Crawling over the front driver's chair and into the back, I find the bag I had forgotten to bring in. Shapewear is a necessary evil in the plus size world. They should really be sold as a set with any dress. Some women don't have a problem with their large body and normally I don't, but when I put on shapewear, it's as if I took confidence Adderall. Not to mention chub rub is real. I rummage through the bag, desperate to find what I need as quickly as I can and finally find the tiny tan shorts. I rush to put them on but as always, they make it difficult by gripping onto my skin as I pull them up. I pause for a breath and finish the job pulling them all the way up to the bottom of my boobs. I learned to hold tight and look up when not long ago my grip was a little weak and on the last upward tug, my fingers slipped, and the momentum thrusted my knuckles up resulting in a slight discoloration of my eye socket. I told my colleagues I ran into the side of my car door, which I had also done in the past. I must have rocked Thor quite a bit since Matthew bangs on the side and yells "Everything alright in there" knowing damn well what I'm doing.

Asshole.

I make a mental note to leave time to give him a wedgie before the day is over.

"Yes," I yell back, "just looking for my cross-body bag."

My jean jacket had been in the passenger seat so that made my outfit complete. I jump down out of Thor with catlike confidence, lock him up and stroll out from behind the tow equipment. I haven't had a chance to disconnect Thor from my car. That will take some time on YouTube. I walk by the dirty windows to give myself a final once over. I slide my hands down my stomach and readjust my bra. Luckily my five foot four and a half-ish stature makes it easy to hide my odd-looking body movements behind the small car.

I've never heard of Turkish magic but when Ihsan and Zeki emerge from the house and time slows down and I hear Sting singing romantic stalker music, I'm a believer. With his fitted dark wash jeans, a white v neck t-shirt and white Fendi sneakers, he's the epitome of casual chic. I only know about his shoes because Matthew coveted a pair a few years back. The slight bow to his legs gives his gate that body builder walk when their inner thighs are too thick that they can't properly close their legs.

Down girl.

"You look nice," he says as he greets us in the middle of the small parking lot. I know damn well I am blushing but try to play it off with a friendly nonchalant response.

"You clean up good, too. And with that you've earned shotgun."

He looks at me quizzically.

"It is the seat in the front next to the driver. In the old American west, when they used stagecoaches to carry passengers and goods throughout the new territories, the person not driving had the duty of protecting the coach with a shotgun. These days we yell out 'Shotgun' when the car is in view to make sure we get that seat."

"Always the teacher," Matthew remarks as Ihsan nods his understanding.

"You can take the girl out of the classroom but you ...nevermind, I'll make it bitter," I say.

"Who drives?" Ihsan says as he dangles the keys. I point to Matthew and make a sign of the cross over my body.

Matthew climbs into the front seat and Ihsan opens the door and waves his hand to the seat. I don't know if anyone has ever done that for me. In fact, I know no one has. I usually beat them to the door either to somehow prove I am an independent woman or to not make anyone feel like they had an obligation to be nice to me.

"Aren't you fancy?" I remark trying to break the unintentional tension I seem to have created, at least in my mind.

I grab the "oh shit" handle and hoist myself into the SUV. Ihsan closes the door and goes to the back to make sure Zeki's ride is safe and comfortable. This gives me time to wrangle my seat belt into submission, but I'm sure it looks a lot like alligator wrestling. Matthew derives too much pleasure from watching the struggle in the rear-view mirror as he attempts to stifle his delight. Luckily, Ihsan gets in before Matthew can compose a remark.

As Matthew adjusts all of the variables with temperature, wind speed, and acoustics, he looks in the rear-view mirror and I look at him and say "Engage" with a Picard-like flare of the finger. I see his face cringe and feel slightly embarrassed. Ihsan seems oblivious to the whole exchange. I may have to start going to church just to thank the Lord for the little things like that. Ihsan moves the seat back for his long legs to fit and tilts the seat back slightly, exposing his large muscled arm resting on the middle console. Chiseled, that is the perfect word. I don't think I've ever been so up close and personal to muscles that I could label their proper names with a sharpie. Brandon, even when he went through his Schwarzenegger phase, never had such definition. Ihsan's t-shirt rides up, exposing more of his tattoo and from my brief inspection it looks heavily shaded, wrapping around his biceps.

Oh, dear Lord in Heaven, help keep my fingers from tracing that gorgeous art, Amen.

The white of the shirt contrasts against his slightly tanline-less skin. In the spirit of my new carpe diem lifestyle, my fingers slide his t-shirt up his upper arm.

"Wow, what is this?"

Ihsan turns to me and pulls his sleeve up to his shoulder to reveal a large intricate tattoo of a man with a helmet worn closely to the skull with a curly beard surrounded by elaborate script and flourishes stretching from around his shoulder to just above his elbow. It's as if my hand has a mind of its own and no matter how hard I tell my fingers not to, they lightly trace the portrait. I've said "Keep your hands to yourself" a million times and here I am pawing at a man I met yesterday. My body is going to need a strong talking to if it continues pulling stunts like that.

"His name is Cyrus the Great."

"I've heard of a lot of 'Greats' but Cyrus wasn't one of them."

"He usually doesn't make Western history books."

I sit back and wait for further explanation.

"He was the ruler of the first Persian empire. After he conquered an area he let the people believe and worship as they pleased and respected their customs. He allowed the Israelites to return to Israel after their captivity in Babylon. The bible even makes a reference to him."

"What do the words mean?"

"Goodness in deeds, goodness in thoughts, goodness in words."

Goodness in body, too.

I guess if you're going to have such an enormous elaborate tattoo, it might as well be a kick ass king.

"Do you have any tattoos?" Ihsan asks after I complete my inspection of his arm art.

"I have funky scars, definitely not as cool."

IHSAN

After a few minutes of resisting the urge to lean my ear to Beatrice's door, I head up to my room to get ready for the day. I have a feeling these two may be cooking up plans for me already. As I walk out to meet them at the car, I notice Beatrice has changed into a dress revealing an ample chest I somehow missed yesterday. Her eyes pop and her perfectly plump lips spread out to greet me. I knew before my modeling career that I am one of the lucky ones in the looks department so the expression on her face is familiar. But the way it looks on her is like a little glow of sunshine. I even like the way she explains American phrases to me, even though Matthew can't help giving her crap. She never misses a beat with her remarks but shows the proper respect when I give her a short history lesson of my tattoo. Her small, soft fingers outline the bold lines of Cyrus, and it surprises me that she lets them linger so long. It isn't just how she touches me or how she inspects the art, it's how she holds her breath and how her eyes widen with wonder and innocent delight. I don't know if it is an American thing or a Beatrice thing for her to be so forward. Something else to figure out in this new land.

When Blaine said my new assistant had a reputation for antics I took it with a grain of salt, but watching her with her old friend I can see where the encouragement came from. She includes me right away and I'm not immune or safe from her barbs, which oddly I appreciate. It finally feels like I can relax and be myself, no airs and no acting. Beatrice would fit in at my family table very easily as nothing seems to be off limits which includes my tattoo.

"Funky scars?"

"You know, weird shaped scars or scars with a backstory."

"Ask her how she got the half-moon one on the back of her hand," Matthew turns toward her as if he is either getting her back or doing something she will get back at him for.

"Let's see," I turn slightly and open my hand out toward her over the center console. As she places her small hand in mine, my arm pulls back quickly.

"What did you do that for?" She says as she laughs at the tiny electrical shock that surprises us both.

"I'm flattered you think I have that kind of power," I smile, offering my hand again.

Matthew's eyes quickly dart back to Beatrice's face in the rear-view mirror.

"Sparks already?" he says quietly. I can tell by the look on his face that he knew he shouldn't have said it, but it was impossible to keep that snappy remark inside. By the sound coming from Beatrice's throat, I'm probably right.

"Let's see."

Before she shows me the back of her hand, she rubs it on her thigh to make sure our connection doesn't create an electrical shock again. She places her hand in mine confidently, without hesitation as if she'd done it a hundred times before. I wrap my fingers gently around her palm and rock it slightly trying to get the light to shine on the repaired skin. The half-moon line shows below her first knuckle.

"So?"

"Let's just say swans are the bullies of the waterfowl world and we have a hate-hate relationship."

"Oh no, you missed the funniest part," Matthew says through giggles. "I still can't erase that image from my mind."

I let go of Beatrice's soft hand and wait for Matthew to divulge the rest of the story.

"We thought we would go feed the ducks at my aunt and Uncle's farm. They had asked us to count them and check for injuries after a house flipping storm had come through. Bee borrowed my aunt's long puffy coat since it would freeze off a cow's udders out here. She zipped all the way from the bottom to the top and could barely keep up with her little legs when we walked out to the pond."

"That's when the devil's guard dogs came out from behind the barn and came running at me with their white wings spread out like tiny B-52 bombers and their necks stretched out hissing and spitting avian profanities."

Matthew's ability to hold his laughter back completely implodes as he finishes the story.

"Three geese grab the bottom of the coat and start pulling her down."

"I tripped! They were swans." she corrects with a slight giggle.

"They were geese. Before I knew it, Bee's little feet were kicking out from the coat and I couldn't tell if the honking was coming from her or from the birds."

"I got the scar because you and your brother would rather laugh at me than help me."

Matthew's body convulses with a full body laugh at their shared memory. I can't help but join his contagious joy. I feel a little bad about laughing at her but when I turn to see if she is in the back seat pouting or smiling with us, I'm happy to see she is half giggling and half glaring at the front seat. Her sparkling eyes press the happy mood deeper inside my chest. It's been a long time since I've felt a genuine smile that wasn't from my children.

BEATRICE

Matthew delights himself telling us all the gossip landmarks around the city. I enjoy the drive as it gives me a chance to make fine adjustments to my hair and outfit. I'm spending more time than usual on what I look like than I ever have. Something about this foreigner makes me more self-conscious than I am used to. As we pull into the parking lot of a farmers market, I devise a brilliant idea.

"Hey Ihsan, do you have Instagram or Facebook or Tik Tok or Flap Jack?" That last one I made up.

"My publicist set up an Instagram account for me in Türkiye," he replies.

"Matthew..."

"I get what you're layin' down," he pulls out his phone from his pocket and presses a few icons.

"We are going to do a few videos of you and your first American experiences. I'm thinking the first few will be edited but eventually I'd like to do some live streams," I tell him.

In the back of my mind, I realize I'm going to have to take a crash course in video editing. I may have to hire a high schooler for a private tutor session. No need to tell the others.

We spend the morning at the farmer's market, making Ihsan hold up different produce, taking selfies with booth owners and teaching Zeki more manners. Ihsan tries to pull me into a couple of shots which I soon learn that if I am holding the phone, I physically can't be in.

I may not be the healthiest eater, but I do enjoy fresh produce. We buy several different fruits and vegetables and Ihsan comes in handy when my arms are too short to reach over the larger stands. At one point, he stood directly behind me as he handed the farmer cash in exchange for a bag of peaches over my head. I couldn't stop my body from falling slightly into his chest, and why should I? Matthew, unfortunately, has the evidence of that moment of indulgence tucked away in his photo app. I should be ashamed of myself, but I'm not.

We film some good footage of two beyond middle-aged ladies in a big stall with fresh brown eggs and locally sourced honey. Their adorable cat calls at Ihsan were the deciding factor as to how much I was going to purchase from them. Charm seeped from his pores as he kissed them both on their right and left cheeks. If he hadn't moved quick enough one of them would have gotten a piece of his left cheek as he took a couple of selfies with them. We walk away with a couple dozen eggs and a jar of honey. I can't wait until I'm old enough to get away with shit like that. I'm going to make a kick ass spinster.

Matthew has some great shots in mind for the next stop on Ihsan's first American tour as he calls forth the spirit of an old movie director. A pre video planning session in the SUV of Ihsan and Zeki walking into the pet store will surely capture the hearts of the dogstagrammers. He works that enchanting Turkish smile as he does a camera walk-by, Matthew and I enjoying the rear view of the shot more than we probably should as professionals.

I need to start reminding myself to be professional. At school, the bell rang and all of the staff put our game faces on and returned to the professionals we were hired to be. I'm going to have to figure out a system to code switch so the lack of any audio indicator doesn't cause problems.

Until then, I'm going to enjoy the time I have with my dear friend and my new employer that is making it very difficult to be professional.

We stroll the aisles looking for fun things for Zeki to destroy. Realizing that we are actually going to have to buy some things, Matthew puts his phone in his pocket. Ihsan breaks away from us and looks for practical items while Matthew and I try to embarrass each other with the animal toys. We make a new game figuring out which ones could double as sex toys. It's times like these that I am so happy not to be expected to be an example to young minds anymore. As I stroll down the aisle with the gates and crates, a simple idea for a hack springs forth cranking the cogs in my head.

As if Ihsan wasn't hot enough, Zeki has the whole store wrapped around his finger. He is well behaved, rolling his head through friendly palms as people would stop to ask to pet him. At some point, Matthew steps aside as the crowd forms and captures Ihsan's pet store popularity. It must be so hard to be that shiny. When we were at the farmer's market, I secretly purchased Ihsan's spindly pony some organic homemade bone shaped dog treats that this grungy hippy lady was selling. The pet store supplied the adorable paw print patterned ceramic container to store them. A way to a man's heart is through his dog's stomach, I hear. Not that I want that, I just want us to get along so here I am spoiling a dog that isn't even mine.

"All right, hot stuff, we better head home. We have quite a bit to put away and I've got people to call and videos to edit," I say, feeling more confident in our professional relationship and then realizing calling my boss "hot stuff" is on the "things not to do list."

I try not to reveal my panic as I realize I've got some programs to learn.

"Yeah, I meant you, Ihsan," I clarify.

"I'm pretty sure I heard something," Matthew states while climbing into the front seat of the SUV.

I give him a little smack on the side of the head before buckling in.

Oh, this wedgie is going to be atomic.

IHSAN

Americans are more forward than I remember them being. I was raised by a typical Turkish family where propriety was our utmost concern. We look out for each other; we act appropriately at all times, and we certainly do not pretend that pet toys are adult sexual aids. The older women have no problem putting their hands on me either, but I think that is a perk of old age in all cultures. After getting over the shock of the open attitude of this culture, I let myself enjoy the atmosphere.

Beatrice and Matthew drag me around like a new pet, showing me off while giving me the full tour of the market. Beatrice doesn't seem to have a problem taking my arm to show me something or pushing my back to move me through a crowd. I've never met a woman that manhandled me without reservation, as if we have been friends for years. The familiar sensation as I reach over her head and feel her body lean into mine surprises me. She instinctively knows that the faster I feel comfortable, the smoother my introduction into the American movie market will be. At least that is what I'm telling myself because otherwise she's a groper.

Ting ting.

My phone wakes me out of my thoughts and I read the message.

"Do you two mind if I call them back?"

"Only if we get to listen in," Beatrice answers from the back.

I pick the familiar icon on my phone and wait for an answer.

"*Merhaba,* abla," I say. I decide to talk in my native tongue just to thwart Beatrice's nosiness. "What's going on?"

"*Abi,* you didn't need to call. I just miss poking at you."

"I went to the market with Beatrice and her friend. There was a lot of poking."

"Why aren't you speaking in English?"

"Because she said she is listening."

"*Abi,* be good."

"She is going to grab the phone if I don't get off. Good to hear your voice."

"Ihsan, you are rude," Beatrice says loudly from behind me in a silly childlike voice.

"I told you. Talk to you later, *abla.*"

"I didn't hear my name so I'm pretty sure you weren't talking about me," Beatrice scolds.

"I can still talk in code in Turkish."

"All Turkish is code to me," she says quickly back.

This woman is too quick for her own good.

BEATRICE

After unloading our provisions, I open the giant glass doors to let Zeki out while Ihsan puts away our supplies. Before I can slide my ass to the side, Matthew approaches swiftly and gives it a rather large smack. Just like old times.

"Thanks, I was trying to figure out how I was going to get in my monthly action," I say to him.

We stand watching Zeki stretch out those long legs running across the lawn.

"I'll have to get the grand tour of the Jetson home some other time."

"I think we got a lot of good footage today," I say to him.

"Yeah, we are going to have to brainstorm a name for a video series for the 'Gram. I'm going to head out, I'm sure they are suspicious of my absence by now. Oh, that dog is gold too. Nothing sexier than a man with a dog. I'm going to give you some time to get some work done, become familiar with the client," he says, finger quoting the word familiar.

"Thank you for the jump start," I say sincerely to Matthew. He backs away from me, does a quick turn and fakes a jog out the door yelling "Buh bye, EEE-SAHN" as he leaves.

I hear "*Hoşçakal*" from the kitchen. I'm going to have to create a Turkish language spreadsheet.

When I am ready to come inside, I yell for Zeki. I try a couple variations of call to get his attention. "Yo, big ass dog...time for a treat," I thought that one would definitely take.

Ihsan appears by my side and yells "Zeki, *gelmek*!"

I see the top of the dog's silver head from the back of the pool. He picks up speed up the hill on the side and again tries to slow down when he hits the concrete patio. He's like a Disney dog with his ears flopping, his lips wagging and his long legs uncontrollable. When he reaches Ihsan, he nuzzles his face into the palm of his hand.

"*Oturmak*," Ihsan commands and Zeki's butt slams to the ground.

"We are going to have to carve out some time for Turkish dog commands," I say, craning my neck up to look at his beautiful face. "Do they work on you, too?" I smile.

"*Gelmek*," I say waving him into the house and walk toward the kitchen.

I hear Ihsan giving him the same command, noting he says it much faster....and sexier.

Chapter 10

BEATRICE

Ihsan places the dappled red and yellow apples on the counter. I snap one up and motion for him to sit on one of the stools. With me standing on the other side of the kitchen island, our faces are more at eye level to each other.

"Your friend is..." he starts.

"A lot, I know," I finish.

"I was trying to say nice."

I smile and nod, taking a nibble out of the apple.

"He really is the best. He's been my rock for a long time," I say nostalgically. "Mmmm...good choice," I say, tipping the apple to him. I finish chewing and grab a napkin that Ihsan has put out. I note how down to earth he is for a superstar.

"Since Blaine has given us some time here to set up the Turkish Team, we should sit down and figure out a schedule for you."

"Us," he corrects. I look at him a little confused. "I need you to be with me until I'm more at ease. This is a big...." I can see the gears rotating in his head as he tries to think of the word.

"Transition?" I chime in.

He nods back at me.

"You did a great job today. You looked happy, excited and the camera loves you. At least Matthew's camera loves you," I joke. "I'm not quite sure what you need me for out there."

"It is fun with you. I was relaxed," his words kind of squish together when he speaks and it took me a second to realize what he said. I smile and mentally push back the blood from my face. Damn body betraying me.

You would think that after years of practice, I would be able to control my immediate reactions.

"Well, the raw material is quality and I'm not exactly intimidating."

Coincidentally his reaction seemed to be the same as mine and I make his face crack a smile as well.

"I'm going to change into some work clothes. I'll gather all my crap and meet you in the office in a bit. Bring your phone and laptop," I say, feeling a bit bossy.

I walk down the hall to my room with a long gait and purposeful foot-falls. Taking another bite of the apple, I enter my room. The newness of this room still resonates in my brain. I may be the luckiest ex-teacher ever. And since I've got a new office, I am definitely getting a "Ms. Bossy-Pants" desk name plate.

After changing into my favorite dark jean shorts and Abby Road faded T-shirt, I slip on my ragged trimmed gray Vans, grab all my support tech, turn toward my bedroom door and take a hard left down the hall to the office.

This is a magic space. Toward the back of the room, in front of the giant windows is a long live edge table with routered sides. I note the tie into the living room furniture. The black resin insert of the table is speckled with gold running throughout the surface. Dark wood bookcases with lower cabinets on both sides of the room span from floor to ceiling. Two red leather tufted chairs are placed on either side of the worktable. I'm hoping my legs are the right length that my thighs won't stick to that leather. I walk around to the chair on the opposite side of the table and feel the sun's warmth on the back of my neck as I sit down, making a mental note for indoor sunscreen. I place a few pencils, my half size notebook, my phone, Matthew's bible and my laptop on the table. I line up all the weapons of warfare, straight and parallel to each other, equidistant apart until it looks perfect. Not that it will last long but better to start off looking like you know what you are doing. I sink down in the chair a little and notice that my boobs can easily be placed on the tabletop with no effort from me. I sit up to confirm my suspicion.

That's just awesome.

At least my feet aren't dangling over the floor like in a Lilly Tomlin skit.

Ihsan leans over in the doorway and knocks on the open panel to get my attention.

"Will you walk into my parlor?" I say in my most husky voice as I motion with fingers for him to come in.

He tips his head slightly with his thick eyebrows migrating toward his nose as he takes giants steps into the room.

"Said the spider to the fly," I continue, finishing the first line of the poem.

Noticing there isn't a spark of understanding in his eyes, I explain.

"It's from a poem where basically the spider seduces and manipulates the fly to disguise his true intentions."

Ihsan looks at me suspiciously.

"Sorry, sometimes it's hard to drop old teacher habits," I say apologetically.

I think twice about telling him I'm not going to seduce him because I should get used to boundaries with him and I've never seduced anyone in my life.

"I don't think you would be that obvious with your plan if you really were evil," he says as he lowers himself into the chair in front of me.

"Or would I?" I say, smiling evilly and tapping my fingertips together and leaning back into the chair à la Mr. Burns. I just can't help letting my geek flag fly.

Ihsan lets out a little chuckle. I'm glad my humor translates as intended.

He places a plain white bag on my desk.

"Blaine sent over new phones," he explains.

"Really? Wow." I pick up the bag and inspect the contents. "Oh, work phones. I guess since we are going to be doing so much on social media it would make sense for us to use the same account. We'll just have to be careful with what we share with each other," I say.

I wanted to add "no dick pics" but decided against it, reminding myself that even if I'm not in a classroom I'm still supposed to act like an adult. Ugh.

"Before we dive into all this Hollywood stuff, let's discuss appointments you..."

"We," he interrupts.

"We cannot miss," I say, correcting myself. "You are all about this team thing aren't you?"

"I used to play a lot of football," he replies. I take note of that little snippet of information and how 'ball' sounds like 'bowl.' That accent is going to fuel a lot of dreams. "Did you not look me up?"

"This job is a life change with a quick turnaround for me. I wanted to make sure I had the skills required to help your career be successful here or at least give you a strong start. I haven't had an opportunity to cyber stalk you properly." I don't feel this would be the time to mention the photo stalking from the night before.

There might have been some words in those postings, but I didn't notice them due to all the attention I was giving to the subject of the photos.

"So, let's get some dates in the calendar," I say as I make three columns on the notepad. "You said your children were coming to visit. Do you know the dates?"

Ihsan runs his hand down his face, a little frustrated sigh escaping his lips.

"Ok, trade personal phones with me. I'll put my information in your contacts and you put yours in mine."

Oh my God, what the hell is wrong with my mouth? "Put yours in mine?" Seriously, Beatrice. Sort yourself.

He takes my phone and starts the process. My iPhone mini looks like a toy in his hands and when I try to balance his phone in mine, I feel like a child. I look down at the screen and wonder if my brain farted. All these letters had extra tails and dots over consonants and vowels for no apparent reason. Then I realize his phone is still displaying everything in Turkish. It feels like another personal assistant fail as he navigates mine without a pause. He looks up and sees the momentary look of panic and frozen fingers over his phone.

"You can tell me yours," he smiles but I know he wants to laugh.

"Thanks, my Turkish is a little rusty. I'd like your ex-wife's information, too. Don't worry, I will behave myself. In my experience, one parent usually has a lot more information than the other. It is not a negative. Parents usually take on different roles in their children's lives."

"I see. Should I have Matthew's number?"

"Yeah, since he really is my only family here."

We recite the numbers and solidify our contact lists, his name with a weird looking "M" next to it.

"What is this?" I ask.

"It's the sign for Virgo. What are you?"

"An Aries."

"That explains it," his head nodding as if that little symbol explained my whole being.

"What?"

"Everything."

"We'll see," I glare. I'm not exactly comfortable with his preconceived notions of me. "Let's focus, please."

I get back to my notebook and start writing my to-do list. The last thing I want is for him to try and figure me out with star placement at the time of my birth. Totally sketchy. He moves closer as I start writing on the lines.

"You remembered their names," he says as he leans over the desk.

"It's an important skill for a teacher to have."

I take a look at the screen and scroll down to the end of May.

"Ok, what other obligations do you have?"

Just as I settle in to start taking dictation, Ihsan gets out of his chair, picks it up and moves it next to me.

"This will be better," he says as he sits down and pulls the chair closer to the table.

It's just not fair that they make them so tall. Thinking of the Randy Newman song "Short People," I smile to myself.

"Is there anything I need to schedule regularly? Like waxing, therapy, or quilting club?"

He is going to have to get used to all aspects of my humor.

"*Neh?*" he says.

"*Neh?* What does that mean?

"What."

"What does '*neh*' mean?"

"What."

"Oooooooh '*Neh*" means 'what,'" I say, finally understanding. "That was a natural 'Who's on First' moment. That doesn't happen too often."

"What?" he asks.

"Oy," I say in exasperation. I click another tab on my laptop and open up YouTube and search for "Who's on First."

Turning it to him, I press play.

He watches it with a little smile on his face.

"Aaaah, now I understand. We are funny."

"When you're too old for half naked photos, we should take our act on the road."

For the love of all things holy.

"The typical response is 'Shut up, Beatrice,'" I inform him with a smile. "Ok, back to your, our, schedule."

"I need to get trainers, that will be every week."

"Ok, so I need to find you a trainer and schedule that."

"Trainers," he says emphasizing the "s."

"Seriously. How many?"

He starts to count on his hand. "Strength, yoga, running, swimming, martial arts, boxing..."

"I guess this…" I wave my pencil around his body. "Needs a whole team. I'll just schedule out a block of time daily. I can work on calling people today. Do you prefer men or women trainers?"

"Doesn't matter," he shrugs his shoulders.

"This will definitely take some finagling once your filming schedule comes out."

His face squints toward his nose as he tips his head slightly. I think for a moment at what might have been confusing about my last sentence.

"Finagling, manipulation without the evil intention," I clarify. "When do you prefer to work out?"

"Early morning."

So, I have to get up at the crack of dawn for the show. I'll have to include that in my schedule.

"Ok, I'll check 'Matthew's Bible' to see if he included anything like that in here."

I feel my skin get a little warm but redirect my attention to my first act as his … whatever I am. Personal assistants don't normally live with their clients. Wrangler seems a bit…unprofessional. Maybe I'll go with "My Girl Friday." I'll have to ask him if there is a Turkish title that would sound better. So far, everything sounds better in Turkish. I lean away from him and grab the "bible."

Matthew bound and printed this holy book on heavyweight paper. I open it up and flip through the pages in awe. He had included not only contacts but also a calendar of events around the city, popular exclusive restaurants with names of who to talk to get Ihsan in, and a list of publicists and agents and who their clients are. He wasn't kidding. This is the personal assistant's tome.

"Matthew really does love me," I say, and I lean toward Ihsan to show him the contents of the bible but quickly pull it back to my chest.

"If I show you, I'll have to kill you," my voice low and stern with my eyes squinting for dramatic effect.

Ihsan leans toward me and reaches for the document, putting his index finger on the top of the bound spine, conveniently located between my breasts. Without breaking eye contact with his own sexy squinty eyes, he slowly pulls it away from my chest and toward his.

"I will risk it."

I should probably breathe now.

I laugh nervously and release it without hesitation. Ihsan used his Mediterranean magic on me and I was helpless. He opens the document with the appropriate respect, delicately and with a safe page turning pace.

After a few moments of perusing the pages, Ihsan looks at me and while nodding, says, "I would keep Matthew around."

"Not even medicated ointment would get rid of him," I say, thinking I'm clever except Ihsan has that slightly confused look on his face again.

"Like he's harder to get rid of than a rash," I explain.

He gives me the obligatory huffy laugh. "Oooohhhh."

I turn my notebook to a new page and write "Social Media" at the top.

"I'm going to need a list of all your social media accounts. Like names or handles that you know about and passwords. I'll need the contact information for your agent back home, too," I say, trying to get back on track.

He takes my phone off the table and realizes he can't open it. He turns the screen toward my face to unlock it, a simple gesture giving me the feeling of familiarity I used to have with Brandon. He seems to like helping out and not expecting everyone to do everything for him. We might actually make a pretty good duo.

IHSAN

When Beatrice turns on her business mode, she is a force. Before long, my workout routine is sorted, I have a to do list and we've organized our contacts. The way her face contorts as she tips her head to the side when she attempts to read my Turkish phone etches on my brain. I decide that it will be my mission to see how many times I can make her face crinkle like that. I find myself eagerly waiting for Beatrice's smart quick remarks. It amazes me how all her seemingly random references are on the tip of her tongue. Most I don't understand immediately but then she explains with her own special flair and they make perfect sense. When she pulls the binder against her breasts, I feel my hand involuntarily moving toward her. I wonder if she knows she not only causes mischief, but she invites it as well because I can't think of any other reason why my fingers move the binder so casually. As I look into her considerably bright eyes, I can't help myself from responding to her taunt. She has melted away my inhibitions in just one day. She would make a good special agent. No one would suspect her.

BEATRICE

Looking over several cleaning businesses, independent contractors and social media marketplace postings, I've come up with a few candidates that I like for our house staff. Mildred "Millie" Clemens is a woman in her early sixties that is looking to do something other than sit around the house. She is widowed and wants to cook for a family. I hope she picks us. We aren't exactly a family but at times there will be a houseful.

Millie was so kind on the phone and happy to do whatever we needed. Her only request is that she is in charge of everything in the kitchen including cleaning, organizing, shopping and if necessary, maintenance. That was the part that impressed me. A woman who didn't rely on others to solve her problems, my mother would have liked her.

Thomas Juarez is my favorite for the housekeeper position. He was recommended to me by Blaine's assistant. He is an injured veteran that has been struggling with finding work that will give him the flexibility and patience he needs. If there is one thing I have in abundance, it's patience.

I invited Thomas to come to the house and as soon as I offered he was on the road. I wanted to get a feel for his demeanor and what his physical struggles might be. Ihsan insisted on being there when I met Thomas. I suspect he didn't like me meeting with a stranger alone even though it wasn't that long ago that he was a stranger. Our meeting was longer than I expected but he offered to take care of the grounds as well as the cleaning inside. I warned him about Millie's request for her domain, he laughed and said his grandmother was like that too so avoiding the cooking area won't be a problem. Zeki trotted in and Thomas' face lit up. I explained that Zeki would need a bit of cleaning up too. He was more than happy to take care of that, to our relief.

My only reservation about Thomas was the thought he would be washing my underwear. He is a couple years younger than me and has a quiet demeanor about him. I decide that either I do them myself, or I just get new ones delivered weekly. The idea of someone I just met handling my chonies creeps me out. Thomas' only request is that if we have special instructions for anything that they are written down with a picture if possible. I suspect he may have a brain injury from whatever he went through during his deployment.

After hiring the house staff, I focus the afternoon on Ihsan's internet presence.

"I was thinking that we could start a series of short videos of you in Hollywood, like a tourist show. We could record you experiencing American things and you could introduce Turkish things to us here. That way we can hit both audiences and give some local Turkish businesses a shout out."

Ihsan's smile erupts on his face.

"This is a fantastic idea."

"We'll link them to all your social media accounts and any fan pages you know about. Do you know of any Turkish influencers?"

"I don't think so but Gül will," he replies.

"Gül?" I ask, trying to figure out if he mispronounced 'ghoul.'

"My ex-wife."

"You think she would be willing to help?" I ask.

"Of course," he says confidently.

"I'm going to carve out some time every week to video chat with my mom," I say, letting him know I'll need a chunk of private time for myself.

Travis and I worked out the logistics before I left. I don't know how long this will last but I want to at least try. I'm not sure giving mom a few seconds of joy will be worth the devastating effect all of the other seconds have on me. A day to recover is not uncommon. She probably gets a lot more mentally from Travis being there than me being on a screen.

"That is a good idea. I'd like to set that up as well, for my kids, but make mine daily."

"My other idea might seem a bit strange to you."

Ihsan nods and motions his hand to indicate he would like me to continue.

"We should create a social media account for Zeki. Hear me out. Animal social media is huge here and Zeki is pure gold. Matthew and I will take care of the captions. We are thinking most of the jokes would be at your expense," I cringe and hold my breath as I say the last part.

Ihsan sit's back in the chair, claps his hands together and laughs.

"I love this idea!"

I let out the breath that I was keeping in and smile.

"I'm going to have to give you some homework."

"Are we playing teacher?" he asks, not realizing there is a whole other implication to that question. I laugh a little at my own nasty thoughts and continue.

"I need you to do a Google search of Turkish businesses in a fifty-mile radius. You should give people in the LA Turkish community a shout out. That will give you a good jump start," giving him a command doing my best Law and Order impression.

"Let's order something to eat, then," he says excitedly. "I will find a restaurant and have it delivered."

"We just bought all this food."

"Do you want to cook right now or keep working?" Ihsan asks.

"Good point."

"Don't forget to name drop when you call. Nothing spicy for me. My stomach does not do spice."

"You trust me to choose food for you?" he says, a little astonished.

"This will be your first test," I respond.

"Ok, does anything make you sick? I don't want to kill you on your first day," he asks.

"I would hope that went without saying. Just order the things you like. If I hate it all, I can live on fresh fruits and veggies for a day."

"I'm going to have to ask Matthew for a social media permission form. You can make this your first video from LA," I say sending off a quick text. A few minutes later, I hear a ding from my email app.

"What is the time difference between Türkiye and California?" I ask as he types into his laptop. I lean over to spy what his computer screen looks like.

"Istanbul is ten hours ahead," he replies quickly.

I notice that when he says his hometown, it sounds way better than when I attempt it, something about the way he pronounces the "u."

He pulls out his phone and searches the screen for information. He dials a number and the voice on the other side is a bit loud. I put my pencil down and turn to watch him read the screen, repeat himself a few times and nod to the voice. Catching myself leaning on my palm and halfway to an eargasm, I hear him say his name and something that sounds like our street name. His Turkish sounds like German and French had a baby without that awful back of the throat "ch" consonant combination. He ends up talking to the voice on the other line for a good five minutes. He ends the conversation repeating the same word over and over. I guess getting people off the phone is a universal problem.

"So?" I ask.

"Selim will be happy to provide us lunch," he says, proud of himself. "And he agrees to appear on my social media."

"And you did that all without me," I nod proudly and clap at him.

"I can even feed myself," he retorts.

"Ooooh, funny and good looking. Ladies of America hold on tight to your panties." I exclaim.

Oh, sh...it.

You can't put toothpaste back in the tube. Time for damage control.

"Sorry, that is a joke between Matthew and I," I say, trying to clean up after myself.

Before he has time to ask, I push the big chair back and make my escape.

"I'm going to take a Zeki break," I say as I turn the corner and stop at the turn to the hallway.

"Oh Zeh-kih, *oturmak*," I yell, feeling proud of myself for remembering the Turkish word.

"That means sit," Ihsan says over the top of my head, leaning against the wall.

"That's what I meant. This way he won't go anywhere when I go find him," I say quickly, trying to convince him I meant to say that in the first place.

"Sure, sure."

"You don't know me well enough to be so smart assed," I shout as I walk down the glass hallway to the foyer because now I have to go find this dog.

Thank goodness Zeki was sunning himself in front of the giant glass doors on the other side of the living room.

"See, he listened," I point out to Ihsan as if I accomplished something.

Hearing us enter the living room, Zeki picks up his head and his ears pop forward. I'm glad he has those floppy ears, it's so comforting to hold them and run them between my fingers. He doesn't seem to mind either. I walk over to him, but his gangly body doesn't move. Ungracefully, I lower myself to the floor and snuggle up to him where I am the little spoon, my back to his stomach. I raise his front leg and lay my head down under his chin and put his paw around my neck.

"Oh Zeke, you're the best boyfriend ever," I say in an exaggerated girly tone.

Ihsan stands in the foyer with his arms crossed, his face looking like an overbearing father.

"I made it weird, didn't I?" I say looking up at him.

"Now those words I understand," he says as he skips the steps down to the living room.

I turn to look at Zeki's face and get an eye full of Dane nostril.

"I'm sorry, it's not you, it's me. It's over, Zeke," I say even more dramatically. I look over at Ihsan who has taken a seat on the cream couch, his long muscular arm draping across the back cushion.

"I'm just not girlfriend material," I fake cry as I crawl out from under Zeki's sapling like legs.

"So, no more boyfriend?" Ihsan unsuccessfully contains his laughter as I try to get up just as ungracefully and make my way to the living room. I couldn't tell if he was still playing along or really asking me if I am single. I figure it is as good a time as any to divulge my status.

"I couldn't be more single. I am the Mayor of Singletown. I am the Grand Puba of Singleness, The Queen of Solo," I say with as much dripping sarcasm as I can trying to make this information more palatable.

Ihsan glances at Zeki and flicks his head to invite him over. Zeki clammers up more gracefully than I did and trots toward Ihsan. He puts his arm out and Zeki slides himself under it. I find myself in the throes of Zeki envy.

"Just me and Thor," I motion out to the front of the house.

"Thor?"

"The RV outside. You tend to get lonely on the road, so you personify things, so you don't go crazy," I answer. "Plus, the model is actually called Thor, so it was a no brainer."

"Did you break up with someone and that is why you moved here?" he asks casually, like that's a casual question.

"Nope. I just needed a change," I feel my eyelids start to flicker and I take a deep breath.

"I'm going to get something to drink," I say walking toward the kitchen avoiding his annoying line of questioning as if it is a swarm of locusts.

I know Ihsan is following me because I can hear both Zeki and his footsteps flap on the hard surface. I pull my phone out and furiously text Sarah.

> **me: SOS, call me ASAP!!**

I hope my cryptic message was clear. She is usually good at reading subtext even when they are acronyms.

The glasses are in the upper cabinet next to the refrigerator, I'm pretty sure.

Stupid monochromatic kitchen wall.

I just need to make myself look busy. I find the fridge, open it and pull the water filter pitcher out. With perfect timing, a Facetime ring sings from my pocket.

"Hey guurl!" I exclaim.

"Heeeey. I just wanted to call and check in on you and see how things are going," she says excitedly.

"They are going great. Do you want to meet my giant Turk?" I say as he stands within smacking distance.

"Sarah, this is Ihsan," I say, turning the camera toward his unprepared face. He gives her the million-dollar smile and waves.

"Hello, Sarah," he says, perfectly polite.

"Hi there, Ihsan. Is Beatrice behaving herself? She can be a handful," Sarah says, trying to be friendly and not flirty, but I know what she's thinking.

"She has tried to steal away my dog, but they broke up," he says to her and looks over to me and winks.

Sarah laughs and adds, "Lock up your puppies!"

"Stop flirting with my friends, Ihsan," I say fake annoyed and focus the phone back on my face.

"I'm going to just turn you around and show you our view from the kitchen." Realizing I combined Ihsan and me into "our", I try to quickly think of something else to say to cover up my misstep.

"This is Zeki, my ex-boyfriend," I say as I pan down toward Zeki's big muzzle.

"Oh, now I see why she was so attracted to him, Ihsan," she says loud enough for Ihsan to hear. "Tall, dark and handsome is exactly her type."

Why would she say that?

Her phone will have many disturbing images texted to it she can't unsee in the near future for that last comment. She will also be returning her friend card. I press the button to turn the camera around.

"I'll call you later, we are waiting for lunch to arrive and I'm going to film Ihsan's first social media video."

Sarah eeks loudly into the screen. "That's so exciting. I'm so happy for you, Bee."

"Is that Queen Bee?" I hear Brandon's voice in the background right before his face appears on the screen as Sarah hands him her phone.

"Hey, Brandon," I say a bit excitedly. My stomach always squeezes itself when I haven't seen his face for a while. The pain from years past still hasn't dissipated.

"Have you killed Matthew yet? I won't judge. I'm just offering to help you hide the body."

For some reason I feel the need to show off Ihsan to Brandon. I turn the phone towards him and say "Ihsan, what do you think about Matthew?"

"Matthew is a good man. A strange man but a good man."

Maybe it was just me, but I could have sworn Ihsan laid on the accent a little thick while speaking with Brandon. Ihsan flips his palm up and says "hi" to my phone.

I turn the phone back at me.

"That is Ihsan, my client. Be nice and no stories."

"I like stories," Ihsan chimes loudly.

"I like this guy, Bee," Brandon interjects.

"Like him enough to follow him on all social media platforms? I'll let you go and do that. Be nice to Matthew. He has already saved my ass and it's only the first day," I warn.

"Byeeeeee." Sarah waves goodbye behind Brandon's head.

"I see why you call them the uber couple."

I suspect the expression on my face dropped a little.

"This is hard for you," Ihsan states.

Ihsan steps a little closer with a soft, kind expression on his face.

"No, this is exciting for me," I correct in an annoyingly chipper tone after a deep breath and straightening my spine.

"Do you know much about acting?"

"The art? No. I have made a whole class believe that April Fool's Day was canceled because it caused too many injuries. I have a little experience," I say rather proudly as I walk into the living room.

I have my own personal objections to April Fool's Day which has caused many injuries, just not the physical kind. I love a good prank; I just don't like being the subject.

"Much of it is reacting to the other person's body language."

"Yeah, and?" I really hope he isn't going where I think he is going.

"Your body does not say 'exciting'."

The bottom half of my jaw drops and takes half my face with it.

"*Yok!* That's not what I meant!" he says, almost sprinting after me.

I know that he didn't mean anything rude by what he said but this is one way I know how to make a man squirm and it is too tempting to let slide.

"No, it's fine. I just thought that it would take longer than twenty-four hours for you to be comfortable talking about my body. I guess it is my turn then. You need to see someone about those eyebrows. You've got some serious weeds growing willy nilly, disrupting the whole landscape. The camera picks up everything. I'll just tweeze them for you," I say pretending to walk back to my bedroom before he grabs my arm and hauls me back.

"*Yok, yok.* I meant the tone of your voice doesn't match what your body is doing."

"Ihsan, you are too easy," I say as I fight back my nature to let out something between a full-on laugh and a giggle.

"You are teasing me," he says with a sultry glare.

Yeah, that's a look I'm going to have to be careful with. It could go one of two ways, loss of muscle control or loss of audible reaction. Or worse, both. I can see myself letting out some kind of breathy sigh and my connective tissue completely relaxing and I am reduced to a pile of over sexed flesh spreading across the polished tile.

"Of course, I am," I say, sitting hard on the couch and attempting to put my feet on the coffee table. My toes barely scrape the edge as I stretch out, trying to punctuate my response.

"A little help here?" I motion toward my toes.

With great effort he pushes the heavy accent piece a half a foot toward me. I pat the space next to me, inviting Zeke for a cuddle. He understands my command and, with a bit of effor, he climbs on the couch limb by limb, turns in an awkward circle and plops his bottom down next to me to use my lap as his pet bed. I get in a few good long pets before Ihsan sits down in the corner and I am abandoned and am left with the not as attractive back end facing me.

"You enjoy this 'alpha' thing, don't you?" I say as Zeki's back paws push against my thigh.

"Respect the alpha." His smile is confident and broad.

I'm in so much trouble.

As we wait for Ihsan's food delivery, our conversation steers to how different California is than our former residences. I tell him that Texas and California might as well be the Hatfields and McCoys then re-explain the relationship in Shakespearian terms a la Capulets and Montagues and his eyes flashed understanding.

The doorbell rings and my body jumps slightly at the sudden noise as all the emotion of the past year threatens to bum rush me.

"Get ready!" I say running over to the front door trying to click all the right icons on my phone and stand with my butt against the glass railing.

I give him the signal that I have started recording. Ihsan answers the door with hands wide open, speaking to the delivery guy in foreign words. He takes the bag from him and pulls him into the foyer. The little man is all smiles. Ihsan turns to the camera and says a few more sentences in their common tongue and I almost drop the phone from my sweating palms.

"And for my new American friends, this is Selim, the owner of Ana-tolian Kitchen. He came all the way to my LA house to welcome me to America with this delicious Turkish food. I can't wait!" he says excitedly. "Lezzetli!" he says even more excitedly as he lifts up the bag to the camera with the logo showing off the restaurant. Selim's face didn't stop smiling since he came into the foyer and he adds his own thumbs up to end the video.

Ihsan is not a factor I have to worry about in this social media plan of ours. He is a natural. He knows exactly what he is doing; smiling at the right time, perfect inflection in his voice and his body language is on point. He pauses with the bag in the air with a big smile brightening his already glowing face. I wait a little too long and realize that is the cue to stop recording.

I turn to Selim. "Thank you for doing this. Come with me to sign papers."

I lead him to the office where I have printed out the necessary media release forms. I show him where to sign and he puts pen to paper. This guy is so trusting. I motion for him to leave the office and he shakes my hand rigorously in the foyer. I open the door for him to take his leave, but I have to peel his hands off of mine.

"That guy is adorable," I say as I walk into the kitchen.

"Let's show them the food," Ihsan says as he opens the boxes.

"Great idea!" I put my phone down and help him organize the boxes in a more pleasing arrangement. If the seven boxes of food he ordered taste as good as they smell, I may have to join him in his workouts. Blech. I hope that he doesn't think I eat that much.

"I forgot to say 'Action' last time. 'Action'!" I scream at a slightly louder volume than I needed to.

Ihsan's hands are so expressive as he describes each dish in English. He brings his head down to the food and waves his hand up, moving the scents to his nose, closing his eyes and breathing in all the aromas. He lifts each dish up to the phone so the audience can get the full visual effect and finishes with "Thank you, Selim at Anatolian Kitchen and thank you to my new friends. Now I need to feed the camera lady. Try something new!" He takes a big bite of rice and chews with a satisfying smile.

I click the red stop button and roll my eyes.

IHSAN

I don't know what it is about Beatrice, but I can't help but feel like I need to protect her. Something about her slightly immature sense of humor and the way she is open about everything could be contributing to this instinct. She flutters around as if trying to distract herself and me from something more. She reminds me of a pixie wearing a coat of armor. It's too heavy for her but she is determined to carry it on her own. This strong instinct to keep her safe surprises me. I know that events in my past have hardwired my brain to build a wall around what means the most to me. She must have built a tunnel and crawled right in. My Turkish instincts seem to be rearing their ugly head.

If ever I have a day that I am feeling low, I know that Beatrice will be there to remind me how lucky I am. It's as if she calculates everything she says to get a reaction that will spark joy. When she introduces me to her friends from her hometown, I can see that she uses this technique with everyone. Matthew's brother and his girlfriend were genuine and friendly. I'm getting an inkling why she felt she needed to move so far away. They are a beautiful couple and by the way they tease each other I know they love her but when she saw Brandon, I could see the shape of her eyes change and my heart twinged in sympathy. Brandon is more to her than just a friend. One of my anne's tidbits of wisdom, "that bright face hides the weather", took me a long time to figure out but Beatrice has that bright face, and I can feel the barometric pressure change in the room. My sister was always suspicious of close friendships between men and women and by Beatrice's shallow unsteady breaths while talking, I understand why. The heart doesn't comprehend distance.

Chapter 11

BEATRICE

"Are you done having sex with the food?"

"*Neh*?" his shock at my bluntness will wear off in time.

"You have destroyed your innocent foreigner persona. You know exactly what you are doing."

"You like?" he asks as he puts a variety of foods on a plate.

I'm pretty sure he was asking about the food and not about me liking him.

"Yes, you did a great job. I hope you couldn't hear my stomach rumble toward the end." I take the plate of green rolls, something resembling ravioli, thinly sliced meat, and a variety of pickled vegetables. I bring the plate up to my nose and understand why Ihsan did what he did. This food smells fantastic. I plop my butt on the tall kitchen stool ready to dig into the Turkish feast.

Ihsan swipes the plate from me before my fork has a chance to stab anything.

"No, this is table food not kitchen food."

As he walks away with our plates, I grab the napkins and follow. He puts them down on top of the long, pale, rectangular wooden table and pulls the straight-backed fabric covered chair out for me. He motions for me to sit then sits in the chair across from me.

"You know you are setting the bar pretty high for lunch," I comment.

He smiles and motions toward the plate to start eating. I don't know when the last time was that I sat down with a casual meal alone with a man that wasn't Brandon or Matthew. I put the green leaf roll in my mouth and close my eyes as I chew. I'm savoring the food and the company, both of which were amazing and worthy of the formal dining room. As I take bites of each dish, Ihsan explains in great detail what I am putting in my mouth and some of the variations he likes. He even has me attempt to pronounce the names of them. I laugh as he tries to get me to form different vowel sounds.

"My mouth doesn't do that," I say when I grow frustrated.

Sometimes I ask him to say things slowly just so I can watch his mouth move. He soon picks up on that trick and he thinks I'm only teasing but in reality, I love hearing his accent. It has been a long time since I've had a hint of happiness. The mood is so relaxed with him. No pressure to impress him, no expectation other than to enjoy myself. When our plates are close to being wiped clean, I sit back, place my hands over my stomach, close my eyes and smile.

"That is a happy smile," he says, nodding at the small accomplishment.

"Well, I can't move, so yeah, I am happy. It's been a while since I have felt this way. It must be the food."

"Then my plan worked. Stuff you until you are weak then interrogate you."

Oh, that accent again. I will tell him anything he wants as long as he keeps talking. I smile and let out a little giggle.

"Why did you move here?" he asks.

The smile from the food fades back into my face. There wasn't even a warmup question.

"It was time," I say with a big sigh.

"That does not work for me. More details. You want me to trust you, don't you?"

So many images race through my mind; Brandon, my mom, the scared faces of my students. I take a deep breath and try to summarize my pain to not sound pathetic.

"My mom's brain is so sick she doesn't know me; the love of my life loves my school bestie and..."

How do I finish?

"Take your phone out and search Round Rock, Texas. Look under the news heading. Just keep the volume off of any videos...for me."

I watch him look at his phone and I know he has found the story when his face falls and his hand covers his agape mouth.

"Was that your school?"

"We were in lockdown for hours. I kept expecting to hear gunshots. I used up a lifetime supply of adrenaline."

"*Allah*" he whispers. "I'm--"

"Please don't," I stop him. "This is the most I've ever talked about it, it's still too fresh."

He puts his phone down on the table, honoring my request by clasping his hands together in front of his face, his eyes focusing outside as he remains quiet. Several moments pass in silence and instead of leaving him to create his own narrative with the given information, I elaborate.

"My mother has Alzheimer's. You met Brandon, said love of my life, and Sarah. They are an uber couple. After several nights of serious self-evaluation, I realized I couldn't have protected my kids and I didn't have the confidence to do it in the future if necessary. I was the only adult in that classroom and I'm basically alone all the time. My flight or fight response kicked in in a major way. So, like I said, it was time."

"You are not alone," he says slowly in a low voice as a matter of fact, undebatable.

I want so badly to believe him, and his sincerity almost makes me. I take a giant breath through my nose, hold it and let it out slowly, the tears regressing back into my eyes.

"That would normally be week two information, not day two," I say, closing my eyes and resting my head back on the chair.

Without responding, I can hear him take my plate and utensils and walk to the kitchen. I hear packaging crackling and figure out he's opening something else. When I hear a plate being placed in front of me, I open my eyes. In front of me lies a diamond shaped pastry with a glistening glaze over the top, peppered with chopped nuts next to a pink shaped cubes covered in powdered sugar.

Ihsan points to the pastry and says, "Baklava."

I sit up slowly.

"I could have sworn Baklava was Greek."

He glares and shakes his head and points to the other confection and says, "Lokum, true Turkish Delight."

"You sneaky boy. I didn't see Selim bring these."

He smiles at me with a hint of menace.

"I hid them."

I flatten my lips and eye the dessert with a bit of trepidation. It's layered with pistachios and honey and other things I can't identify.

"Your face isn't using its inside voice."

"Ihsan, that was solid. I'm impressed."

Taking half the pastry in my mouth I bite down, squishing the crispy layers between my teeth and trying to catch the ones falling down off my lips as I take the first bite. Ihsan takes a bite with me and watches my reaction. This dessert tastes as good as Ihsan looks. The light syrupy layers of thin dough spread across my tongue as the nuts give it a light crunch. I set the half-eaten portion on the plate and finish chewing, trying everything in my power not to moan as I lick the remaining sweet goo off my lips.

"Ok, we can only have this in the house on high holidays."

"Yeah? Ok, next."

I pick up the Turkish delight and squeeze it with my fingers. This little cube is more suspicious looking or "sus" as the kids say.

"It's good," he says encouragingly.

"This is where I trust you," I say as I press my teeth down into the jelly cube.

It is sweet and a little tart and I bite down further and find more pistachios. It is not a texture I am used to but after a few chews, I am pleasantly surprised with how the gumminess and crunchiness comes together in my mouth.

"I wouldn't throw you out of my bed for eating this," I say after I swallow, and quickly add, "That's a variation on the saying 'I wouldn't kick him out of bed for eating crackers.' I have to confess that I often have wildly inappropriate thoughts in my head and sometimes they escape through my mouth, especially now that I don't have to worry about little ears."

Ihsan attempts to keep his amusement inside while chewing the last bit of desert.

"I won't take offense if you tell me I've said something that makes you uncomfortable."

"I'm an actor, I have to be comfortable with discomfort," he replies.

We spend the rest of the afternoon catching up on personal communications and continue little tasks of settling into our house together. I add my "You Got This" giant paperweight on my side of the office table and a framed photograph of a bromeliad my dad took on one of his many adventures with my mom. It is my favorite plant as I always saw it on sci-fi shows because they look so exotic with their long tongue like striped leaves and blooms that explode from the middle. I make a mental note to find myself one to decorate the office.

Later that afternoon, I decide I better get to know everything I can about this Ihsan guy. I take a break from getting my house in order, plop onto my bed, cross my legs and open the laptop in front of me. I type his name into the search bar and several pictures show up. I click on his Wiki biography page and scroll past all the Turkish words. He wasn't joking. If you look at the word "understatement" in the dictionary, Ihsan saying "I used to play a lot of football," would be an example. He not only played European football, but he was also selected as the youngest player on the Turkish national team while he was playing for one of Istanbul's super league teams. After that, he became a model and then got into acting. I click on a couple of YouTube excerpts of his dramas. The Rock has nothing on Ihsan's shoulder smolder. He really knows what works on a woman. I quickly shut the laptop screen, feeling a lot more than a little dirty since he is within shouting distance somewhere in this house. I will be doing more research when I can dedicate more time to it and when I'm alone in the house.

IHSAN

My heart falls to the floor as I watch the footage of children crying and running to their parents. The flashes from the police cars and the officers rushing across the screen are embedded in my eyes. Besides dealing with her mother's illness and her heartbreak from Brandon, she's endured one of the scariest things that a teacher could endure. That hopeless feeling is not easy to overcome, and I realize that on some level she needs someone to take care of her while she recovers. The fact that she hasn't barricaded herself in a room shows me she has a strength that is not only rare but should be envied. A huge sigh of relief washes over me when she tells me that after the long standoff, the intruder was captured without injury. I can't imagine trying to hold myself together for that long without any idea of what was going on.

This woman has made my career her first priority in the aftermath of so much trauma. I want to hold her, to tell her she is safe, tell her I see who she is, and I couldn't be prouder to have her in my life. I've never made a connection so quickly and from what I've seen with Matthew and Blaine, that is just what she does. As a teacher, I suppose there really isn't a grace period at the beginning of the year. The best I can do is tell her she is not alone, and I want to kick myself because I know that is not enough.

"Oh, Ihsan," she calls out as she leaves her bedroom.

I haven't seen her for a while and since she has that eighties music blaring, she hasn't heard me either.

"I'm going to have some dinner," she says with the not-really-that-loud sing song voice.

Walking past the tall glass doors outside, she sees the brightness of the outdoor lighting. Zeki is sprawled out with his back legs going one direction and his front legs going the other. She quickly grabs her phone and quietly opens the doors as to not disturb me. The camera loves Zeki, and those photos are going to get all sorts of hearts popping up the screen. I stretch myself out on a chaise lounge wrapped in a black knitted cardigan. She quickly gets a shot of me script studying with an orange highlighter in my mouth and a pencil in my hand.

"That is a gorgeous shot of Zeki." She turns her phone around to me as I put the cap back on the fat marker. "Need me to help with anything?"

"Not right now."

"Millie will be starting soon so you'll have to put up with my cooking until then."

"I already ordered us dinner."

"Personal assistant fail, ouch."

"You seemed busy, and I didn't want to distract you."

The doorbell rings throughout the house and she stands to retrieve our meal. I attempt to do the same until she stops me with sass.

"Oh no, you're trying to put me out of a job already. So, sit your ass down and let me do my job damnit." she stomps off in fake anger. Maybe she can act...sort of.

As she opens the door, the young delivery man hands over a large white bag that smells of hot noodles and soy sauce. I sneak in behind her to hand him a tip and attempt to take the food.

"Oh no, I don't want you to pull a muscle carrying all this food and then what will they do without their action hero?"

I put my hands up in the international sign of hands off and find a few dishes to serve our dinner.

"You ordered for me again. That's pretty confident. You just assumed I'll eat anything you dish out."

"I'm sure most people like chow mein, nothing special."

Picking up the pack of utensils, I say, "Dinner and entertainment I see."

"Neh?"

"Chopsticks or fork?"

"Chopsticks, you?"

"Oh, that is where the entertainment comes in. I have yet in all my twenty-eight years to master those darn things. But I will not let them defeat me!"

We sit down in the fancy dining room with our traditional Chinese food containers across from each other and dig into the pile of thick Asian pasta. I deftly maneuver my chopsticks spilling over with Chinese goodness into his mouth.

"I don't understand what I'm doing wrong. I put my fingers in the right spot and can move these stupid mini stilts around perfectly, but the noodles escape every damn time."

She demonstrates yet another chow mein failure. I smile at her frustration and reaches over the table to move her fingers into the right position.

"You have to keep the tension until you put it in your mouth." Her face immediately changes but I'm not sure if she is laugh at herself or embarrassed about what she just said.

"I'm too hungry to practice." She picks up a noodle with my fingers and dangles it above her mouth.

Letting it fall in between her lips, she chews with satisfaction. "I'm going primitive."

Watching her attempting to conquer chopsticks was exactly what she said, entertaining. When she gives up and opens her mouth while tilting her head back, my groin twinges. It is mesmerizing to watch the thick noodle disappear down her throat. It has been over three years since I've had a woman moaning in my ear. That has to be the reason my body temperature is rising. I can't think of a worse idea than taking a personal assistant to bed and I tend to think she would think the same thing. That would mostly certainly go on the "What Not To Do as a New Actor in Hollywood" list.

I chuckle at her desperation to eat the noodles before they get cold. After a few minutes of silent eating, she pauses and wipes her face with her napkin.

"You have pretty eyes."

A noodle lodges in her upper throat causing her to cough loudly.

"Where did that come from?"

"I noticed them when I first met you. They are a pretty color."

"Thank you. You too, on well, everything," she says, her face twinging at her awkward response.

I smile and my chest jiggles in reaction to her less than tactful response.

"So, tell me more about your family," I say. Beatrice can't hide her prolonged glance at my chest.

"I'm an only child so it's just been me and my mom and Brandon and Matthew, the strays I picked up in college that came around when she decided to cook. I was a townie, a kid that lives in the university town. She was an elementary school teacher, fifth grade. My aunt, uncle and cousin, Travis, were around a lot when I was younger. What about you?" she asks, quickly changing the subject.

"My dad was a mechanic in the army so when he got out, he built his own business. My mom is a glass artist and did a lot of little jobs around town when we were young. My uncle lived with us too, he helped my dad in the shop."

"So how did you end up acting?"

"I played futbol on a pro club team, but I got injured and was approached by a modeling agency. Then a friend said I should try acting and I liked it."

"You held back."

"*Neh*?"

"You were a freaking football prodigy. If I knew anybody that watched soccer, they would pay my yearly salary to switch places with me."

I can feel my shoulders bounce as I laugh. Her tone and the back and forth sway of head proves to me that she is not woefully unaware of my previous career. I've lived such a blessed life. She knows nothing of any of those worlds.

Her phone chimes with a text message but she doesn't answer, being polite to not interrupt our dinner conversation. She continues to ignore it and attempts to keep the noodles on the sticks as she watches me eat dinner so easily. The phone nags her again.

"Are you going to check that?" I ask.

"I didn't want to be rude."

"Go ahead."

All her life, she has adhered to a strict academic calendar. Without a lot of time in the day to let her hair down. I can see why she has let herself relax and behave a little badly. Considering how long she has been in school, that's a lot of down time to make up for.

BEATRICE

Pulling the phone out of my pocket, I see a text from Sarah. I think she has been hiding her concern about me since I told her I was leaving. She tried to mask it because she saw this as a positive change, but I have a feeling she is worried about me venturing out on my own for the very first time in my life.

> Sarah: **I ran into Mr. D at the grocery store.**

> me: **I miss him.**

> Sarah: **We're both worried about you.**

me: **So you are writing it in a text?**

Sarah: **Written evidence so you can't deny it later.**

me: **Damnit.**

Sarah: You need to get a therapist. We all have too much to deal with on our own.

me: **You're right, as always. Mr. D is too far away.**

Sarah: **Exactly. Love you, Queen Bee.**

me: **Love you, too.**

I let out a big sigh as I close the text app.

"Everything ok?"

"I'm sorry, that came out louder than I thought it would. Yes. I figure I may as well be completely honest with you since you'll be stuck here with me in close quarters. Sarah wants me to get a therapist. It just feels like another thing to add to my list right now."

"I agree with her."

"Wow, we've known each other for two days."

He sits back in his chair, not bothering to mask the look of concern on his angelic face.

"You think you can handle what you have been through, what you are going through without help?"

"You're right, Mr. D is right, Sarah's right."

"Who is Mr. D?"

"He's an old friend, like a wise old owl kind of friend."

"Wise old owl?"

"Lots of wisdom."

"I'm right here," he smiles at me.

"Oh yeah, four years my senior, so old."

The next half an hour we sit and tell stories of growing up and answer random questions I found on a website. He answers honestly without reservation where I calculate my answers to not appear as inadequate as I feel around him. My trick of covering up these feelings with humor seems to work on him as it has so many others in the past. His stories are very animated and exciting which shows me how differently we grew up. My most exciting story is when I accidentally set my hair on fire with a candle going to church with a friend in middle school. I should have taken that as some kind of sign.

Compliments are difficult for me to deal with. The secretary in the front office would tell me every so often that I was pretty and describe in detail what I did right that day but when you remain single without prospects you tend to give compliments less merit. I try not to call more attention to the focus of said compliment because of this. Something in me feels like I need to hide it away as if I don't believe it. But I can't exactly cover up my hazel eyeballs.

The two of us and Zeki in a kitchen feels like a three stooges' skit trying to put away leftovers. His attempts to be polite and proper while navigating around me were less than cat-like as I avoid touching him as if he has a raging case of cooties. Zeki just wants to be where all the action is. After we successfully store all the leftovers, throw away the trash and pick up a few things in the kitchen, I let out a giant yawn and stretch my arms over my head. My fingertips don't even reach the top of his head, not that I will need to get up there for any reason.

"Did I exhaust you?"

"Yes, the conversation was mind numbingly boring," I say in my British regency voice I've been working on.

"I will work on that."

"Please do," I continue with the act. "I'm going to retire to my bed-chamber where I will be catching up on the correspondence of the day and reviewing my social engagement calendar."

"Don't forget to review mine too."

"If I must."

I take the path to my new bedroom with grace and nobility to exit the scene I had created. Well, as much as I can while trying to keep a straight face. The past hour has been so normal, so easy, and so what I need. Ihsan makes everything seem effortless and comforting.

"Listen to Sarah," he reminds me from the middle of the stairs.

Damn him.

It's not that I don't agree with therapy, I just have it in my mind that no one wants to hear a fat girl whine. My mental state doesn't stem from how I feel about my weight, it stems from all the other trauma in my life, but it always seems to be the focus of any appointment. No matter what doctor I see for any reason, my weight always comes up. Infection-lose weight, cough-lose weight, IUD-lose weight. Like I don't know I'm a bigger girl. I have been successful in my life at the weight I am, so I don't see the problem. I still fit in airline seats, I can still shop in regular retail stores, and I can go up three flights of stairs without running out of breath. I wish doctors understood that us fatties know we are fat. We are reminded every time we interact with society. We don't need them to remind us. We have to step on the scale every time we see them for God's sake. I pray every time to get a plus size nurse.

Chapter 12

BEATRICE

Looking at the schedule for next week it's packed with online meetings, about ten thousand phone calls, incessant brown nosing to strangers and a lot of online shopping. I am exhausted before I even start the list.

The chime of the doorbell shakes me out of my overwhelmed state. As I approach the front door, I see two large boxes half the size of me and a few smaller ones the size of the large kitchen tiles. I run excitedly to the front door and stop abruptly not giving Zeki time to slow down as he plows into me, pinning me to the door.

"You must know this is for you," I say trying to push the beautiful monster away.

Ihsan appears at the top of the stairs and jogs down to help me drag in Zeki's surprise.

"Deliveries already?"

"It's for Zeki."

I wish I had those recording glasses as I watch Ihsan and Zeki both tilt their head and scrunch their eyebrows. The myth that dogs look like their owners has just been proven to be accurate.

"Can you find some kind of tape measure?" I ask Ihsan, standing there holding the mystery packages.

As I rip the boxes open, Zeki gathers the wrappings around his legs and keeps us safe from the danger that is precut, preformed cardboard. I pull out the long plastic pieces and set them on the ground with Ihsan standing over me still looking confused offering a tape measure.

"I bought a child's slide."

"I think you are old enough for a big kid one by now," Ihsan says smiling over me.

"Oh, Ihsan, aren't you adorable. They're for Zeki. Measure the width for me," I say, removing the remaining clear plastic.

"Are these for the stairs?"

"Yep, and the flat square boxes have peel and stick carpet tiles so we stick them to the slide for traction. They'll prevent him from slipping and secure the slide pieces a bit more. When we move out, you can take it with you."

"That's brilliant." His mouth grows into a large, brilliant white smile.

"You'll get used to it," I say, trying to return the smile but with a bit of wickedness in my eyes.

Ihsan and I spend the afternoon teaching Zeki how to use it, which was really more entertaining for us than training for him. Ihsan insisted on trying it out himself before we stuck on the tiles, but I found the only place where his perfect ass doesn't fit.

Matthew took the time out of his busy schedule to visit us several times in the next few weeks to strategize the least obnoxious ways of getting Ihsan in front of paparazzi. Although Matthew, like me, is attracted to pretty things so ulterior motives could not be ruled out. We planned for Ihsan to go out with his agent to a popular bistro and see if he can work his magic with some influential people. Matthew went over the editing tricks and trained me on some easy software to learn to post all of the videos we'd been doing with all the bells and whistles. Making those videos is my favorite part of the job so far. Ihsan is just so easy on the eyes and watching him for hours while I practice with the software was icing on the Turkish cake. Matthew also gave me a crash course on social media etiquette and manipulation. I took several pages of notes.

I set aside a few hours for manual correspondence. My mom, being the extra one as she was, always wrote handwritten thank you cards. She would occasionally include home baked goods. One of my tasks this week is to find someone who did handmade greeting cards as buying local was also my mother's tradition. The delivery of finely crafted note cards made from recycled paper and pressed flowers arrived early in the morning. Since baked goods would probably get thrown into the dumpster immediately because of well...Hollywood, I sourced a creator of wood flowers. The ugly plastic flowers look cheap and too commercial, but these flowers made from tapioca root were gorgeous and unique and every time someone saw them, they would smile and think of Ihsan. I also added small vials of different floral aromas so they could pick what they'd like them to smell like. Sending them to administrative assistants and office managers to thank them for their help navigating our way around the intricate web that is Hollywood gives them a little reminder of Ihsan every time they look up from their desks. My mom taught me that it's the thoughtful things, no matter how big or small, that people remember and that's my goal; Ihsan in everyone's thoughts, not just mine.

"I thought you were done for the night," Ihsan says as he glides by the desk.

"You don't realize how much I do for you." I turn my head slowly as he sits down.

"And it's only the beginning." The slightly low tone of my evil villain voice breaks through. "John Hancock these."

I slide the pile of thick cards over to his side of the desk. His head tilts sideways as his right eye closes.

After a quick internet search, I enlarge the bottom of the Declaration of Independence on the laptop screen and turn the computer around toward Ihsan.

"What do you notice?" I ask.

"Ah, you know what they say? Big signature, small..." Ihsan smiles slightly and raises and drops his eyebrows quickly.

"Pen?" I say without allowing him to steal a perfectly good joke.

He lays his head down on the cards stacked on the desk in exasperation. "I should warn you now, I rarely pass up an opportunity to crack wise."

"What do they say? It's on." He says, picking his head up while warning me.

Oh, yes it is.

IHSAN

Good food and good friends give me immeasurable joy. Simple things make me happy. Beatrice pulls an easy pet ramp out of her bag of tricks which gives me a glimpse into her forever churning mind. We sit and write beautiful thank you cards which gives me a glimpse into her profoundly tender heart. Spending this bit of time with her not connected to a screen brings me back home. She doesn't seem to be good with silence as the next thirty minutes are spent discussing who the cards will be going to and how connecting with this person will benefit me. The second part of her plan to kill Hollywood with kindness shows me the depths of her humanity. Gifting the office assistants with fragrance infused flowers is a stroke of shrewd creativity. Her skills reach far beyond anything that would be listed on a resume.

I steal a few glances while she gathers the materials so deliberately, its as if each one is made for that specific person it is addressed to. She carefully lays each card slightly askew from the other, creating a little fan of correspondence. As the completed pile is fanned over the desk, a prideful grin and spark in her eye makes my insides warm. It doesn't take much to give her a spark of joy. This is something I will have to commit to memory.

When she invites me to the couch I am more than willing to join her, curious to see what film she has planned for the evening. She's been burning the candle at both ends and dragging me along for the ride. When she attacks me I enjoy our playful physical contact, probably too much. My body naturally reacts to a woman's touch, not because it's Beatrice. Nothing seems to stop her from what she sets her mind to. In fact, I find it admirable.

BEATRICE

After the last conversation of the night of the first official two weeks finishes and Ihsan's name adorns all the fancy cards, I change into my favorite super soft XXL PJ's and return to the living room with the furry comforter from my bed.

"I'm hosting a spontaneous movie night in the living room," I call out to the house.

Ihsan stands at the top of the stairs in his baggy black sweatpants and equally baggy gray t-shirt.

"It's BYOB!" I look up at him. "Bring your own blanket."

"Can't we just share?" he asks. He has already figured out how to make life more difficult for me.

"I suppose," I whine, not putting up much of a fight and allowing myself a little sweetness.

He jogs down the stairs with Zeki tailing him down the ramp.

"What are we watching?" he asks.

"An American classic, *Some Kind of Wonderful.* Eric Stoltz, mmm...tall ginger," I say summoning the worldwide sensation, Homer Simpson. "This movie comes with a high tear rating so be prepared for ugly crying."

Ihsan leans over and takes the box of tissue off the end table and sets it on his lap and sets two glasses of dark red wine on the coffee table

"I am armed and ready," he smiles.

It's like we've been friends for years.

I'm not a fan of wine but for some reason I don't want to tell him. The large glass full of a beautiful liquid looks gorgeous on the table. I don't remember a night where I have spent the evening under the covers drinking wine like fancy people. I can stomach a few gulps of sour grape juice.

I find the streaming service that has my favorite Howard Deutch film and press play.

"This soundtrack is catchy, so there may be some singing too."

Ihsan takes a couple of tissues, balls them up and puts them in the hollows of his ears.

"I am prepared for that too."

"Thems fighting words, son," I say and quickly turn and grab him by the ribs and squeeze. He yelps and grabs my wrists. Little does he know that I have plenty of experience in tickle fighting with Brandon, Matthew and Travis. Their ultimate goal was to make me pee in my pants, so I had to be good just to not give them blackmail material. I twist out of his grip and strike once again. He holds his arms tight against him and leans away from me. I realize if I go in again, I will be grabbing his butt. I stop myself before I go too far.

Not okay to grab your client's butt. Not okay to grab your client's butt.

"Ok, I'll show mercy."

"That's the word I couldn't remember!"

I pull the gray fur comforter back on top of me and Ihsan grabs a side, covers himself and puts his arm on the top of the cushion behind me. Deep inside, I stifle the urge to nestle into his armpit, something I did with Brandon that always salted the wound. I rewind the movie a minute and let it play out. We make it to the end, but my ugly cry didn't really make an appearance, just a few tears at the end when he figures out he loved her all along. I secretly thank the Almighty again considering I've been taking sips from the wine glass faster than Ihsan is. Just as I lean over to grab the remote the video chat ring chimes on my phone. I press the green button when I see Sarah's name appear on the screen.

"Saaaarrraaaaah!" I say jokingly. Brandon's face came into view behind her while she sports a very large smile across her model-like face.

"Sarah," I repeat her name as her fingertips slowly move up the screen. On the fourth one was a large round diamond.

"Sarah!" I scream and cover my mouth. Ihsan leans over and presses his head against mine to see what is causing all the screaming.

"No way! I'm so happy for you two." I fight the bile quickly climbing up my esophagus.

"We wanted you to be the first to know," she says joyously.

I know exactly why, too. I introduced them. I set them up. I supported them and now I suffer the consequences.

"That's fantastic," I say, keeping my eyes wide and a forced smile on my face.

"And since we have you on the phone we want you and Matthew to be the Maid of Honor and Best Man."

I let out an excited laugh to mask the ugly cry that's building up. "Of course, I will!"

I may be the only woman my age closest to being a true 'Maid' of honor. That run for the hills feeling travels down my legs.

"I'm sure you both have so many people to call, and I was about to go to bed. I'll call you tomorrow."

"Love you!" Sarah exclaims and hangs up the phone.

I place the phone face down onto the coffee table with a loud clunk. Both Ihsan's and my glass are at least half full of wine so I take our glasses in both hands and shoot them back, then gag and cough remembering why I don't like wine. After setting the glasses a little too hard on the table, I lean over my lap and put my head in my palms. A minute passes before Ihsan dares to speak.

"You looked like this was happy news."

"The love of my life is marrying my school bestie," I say into my hands.

I stand quickly with my teary head held high and strut into the kitchen, dragging the blanket behind me à la Linus.

"There's booze around here, right?" I desperately open and close all the cabinets I can reach. Sensing the urgency of my actions, Ihsan follows me and opens the rest of them.

"Whiskey?" he asks, holding up a dark bottle.

"Of course, whiskey. That's perfect. Don't bother with glasses." I grab the bottle from his hands, rip off the wrapping, untwist the cap and put it to my mouth. The trail of fire it leaves as it drains down my throat is exactly the distraction I need. Gathering up my blanket from the floor, I blaze a trail to the glass doors leading out to the pool.

I stand in front of the glass doors and scream, "Open Sesame!"

Ihsan knew what I wanted and had already pressed a button on the control panel. He probably thought I was going to attempt to walk through the glass.

"Lights off!" I command as I walk out onto the concrete patio and take another swig, this time quite a big longer.

Ihsan obliges me and in four long strides catches up to me on my warpath. We walk down the soft grassy area in front of the pool. I sit down curtly and pull the blanket around me, hoping the furriness will counteract the sharpness I feel prickling all around me.

Ihsan gingerly sits down next to me, careful not to disturb my misery cocoon. I silently offer the bottle to him and he removes it quickly, probably thinking that it's safer in his hands than in mine.

"Do you see how beautiful it is out here?" My lips start to quiver and the tears quickly run down my cheeks in waves.

Ihsan slowly nods.

"I shouldn't even be able to be in the vicinity of such beauty. I shouldn't have even been friends with Brandon and Sarah," I continue. "They're technicolor and I'm grayscale. We don't live on the same planet."

Moving to my knees and pushing myself up, as if I'm two I stand in front of Ihsan with my arm outstretched. It's time to pace. He leans forward and hands me the bottle and I take another long drink, swallow it, and concentrate on keeping it from repeating on me. I shove it back at him and wipe any left on my lips off with the back of my hand.

"What do you mean by ... technicolor?" he asks.

"Wizard of Oz? When Dorothy opens the door and it goes from ugly dustbowl to vivid...ness," I finish with a slight hiccup.

"Vividness?"

"You are technicolor," I retort sharply. Trying to start my steps in a straight line is proving to be difficult as the whiskey starts to take effect.

"You are colorful. Shiny. People notice you and want to be with you," I say, pointing to him. I hit my upper chest with the palm of my hand. "I am grayscale. I am bleh. I am passed over and no one has ever—" I start to cry so hard that my words are blubbering through my lips. I take a breath and finish my sentence, "wanted me. You know I set them up? I wanted them to be happier more than I wanted to be happy. Who the fuck does that?" I shout.

"Fucking pathetic," I say softer. "And you! You looking at me with your beautiful fucking face with so much pity in your eyes. Do you know how often I see that? Do you know how technicolor people make us grayscalers feel? You show us kindness and friendship and we take it and twist it into a sick version of love. We starve for every touch, every glance, every tiny instant of affection. That 'love' that we so desperately want is a fantasy. We want to believe it's real so badly that we give it a place to live in our soul but it doesn't live, it consumes it leaving a big gaping black hole. But we are so stupid that we convince ourselves there's hope."

The dam is broken, and I can't stop all the feels from gushing out. I collapse into the grass and cover my face with my blanket covered hands. I feel Ihsan's arm as it wraps around my shoulder.

I shrug his arm off, pleading, "Please.... don't."

Ignoring me, he pulls me into his chest, squeezes me gently, and lays his head on top of mine.

"Turns out moving thirteen hundred and fifty miles away wasn't far enough. Fucking meatloaf."

"Meatloaf?"

"I can't explain."

I cry so hard my body shakes until there are no more tears left. As I start to lean away, he releases his arms. He pulls me off the ground and wraps the furry blanket around my shoulders. Slowly taking deliberate steps toward the house, I grasp the blanket at my neck like it's an emotional life jacket. Ihsan follows behind me until we reach my room. Crawling into my bed on all fours, I try to find my pillow and let my body melt into the mattress. Ihsan sits on the edge of my bed and straightens the comforter over me, his large hand sliding down my skull.

IHSAN

Everything changes when Brandon and Sarah called to share the news of their engagement. Everything that I knew of Beatrice leaks out of her when Sarah reveals her ring. Her confidence, her excitement, her zest for everything leaves her body, slumping into her hands. I want so badly to help her, but I know from experiences with my sister that the best I can do is just listen. Whiskey is probably not the best idea after two glasses of wine shooters. Her pain is so much deeper than I realized. I want to tell her that she is desirable, but she is in no place to listen to a "technicolor." I can't relate to the kind of rejection she describes, what she has lived through for so long.

She has been in love with Brandon for almost ten years. Ten years of feeling not good enough for the one person she wanted in the world. I've had my share of heartbreak, Gül being the most recent, but I was able to recover and move on, at least partially. To be dedicated to one man who didn't reciprocate your feelings almost seems as if she might have been in love with the idea of Brandon, not Brandon himself. But as her tears soak my shirt, I decide what she needs from me is to wrap my arms around her shaking body and keep my amateur therapist's opinions to myself.

When she pulls herself together enough to walk to bed I follow behind, ready to catch her if she face plants in the grass. I make sure she is secure in her bed but seeing her lying flat out, I can't leave her room. I want to cradle her in my arms until she is fast asleep but instead I sit on her bed, stroking her long silky hair, hoping it is giving her some comfort.

"One of these days, Beatrice," I start as the tears dry on her red cheeks. "You are going to find a person who can't think of living one minute without you. Someone who'll understand all your jokes and know all the same lyrics to the songs older than you. He'll take you on trips, teach you new things and make you laugh as hard as you make me." By the end of my last thought, all my hopes for her sounded more like a prayer. This woman has chosen to help me fulfill my dreams when hers have fallen apart. This is the least I can do.

Chapter 13

B EATRICE

The sun is bright in my room, and it feels like Kryptonite. Zeki attempts to wake me up by licking the soles of my feet, leaving them slimy. Maybe my face is too salty for his fancy dog pallet. My eyes barely peek open as I look around at the covers around me and find Ihsan leaning up against the nook between my bed and the bookcase, fast asleep. He's so pretty, I fear if I look at him too long I may turn to ashes. I push his thick, hard thigh to rouse him awake. His eyelids crack as he attempts to shade his face from the light.

"I'm ruining my reputation by waking up with a strange man in my bed," I say as I sit up. He chuckles as he leans over, his feet finding the floor.

I put my hand on his forearm. "I'm so, so, so, very sorry. I remember bits and pieces and what I do remember...well, I was an asshole. You don't have an eff..fucking face."

He leans forward slightly and turns his chin toward me with a slight smile. The empathy and kindness in his eyes are just not fair for us mere mortals. This shoulder smolder is real and magic at the same time.

"I forgot you insulted my face. I told you, you are not alone."

I point to the door dramatically.

"You can't stay here if you are just going to make me cry again."

He takes the hint peeling himself off my bed and slowly strolls out my door, rubbing the back of his neck. I always take a moment to enjoy the view of him walking away, but this time I don't deserve it.

After I visit the bathroom, I zombie walk to the kitchen, my legs heavy as my toes drag across the floor. Ihsan starts the coffee maker and puts out cups and sliced up fruit. I would usually whine about the pounding in my head, but I accept the penance for my bad behavior without a word. Ihsan makes his way through the kitchen but remains speechless. When he finally decides to grace me with his words of wisdom, he leans against the kitchen island with a cup in his hand and looks at me until I meet his eyes.

"I wasn't pitying you last night, I was watching your pain."

"Yeah, it's pretty gory, isn't it?"

"Well, it is certainly loud," we chuckle in unison.

"You really love him," his voice low.

"In my own sick way," I admit, staring down at my cup.

"It's not sick, just ..."

"Pathetic is the word."

"Unrequited," he corrects.

"Dumb ass me thought moving here would distract me."

"A broken heart is a deep wound; it takes the longest to heal."

"What did I say about making me cry?"

Ihsan slides around the corner of the island and tips me to his chest. His arms wrap around me, and I let out a shuddering breath, giving into his kindness. After a few soft pets on my head, he releases me to put his mug in the sink.

"Do you mind if I lay low today? I need a day to recover from...well, all the things."

"Of course."

He gives me a half smile and walks upstairs with Zeki obediently following up the ramp.

After I clean up my coffee banana breakfast, I walk towards the piano and sit on the bench. I don't even have the urge to open the keyboard cover. The one thing in my life that has always made me happy doesn't hold any power for me right now.

I did this to myself.

I jump at the ring from my phone on the kitchen island. I peek at the number and let out all the air in my lungs. Matthew. Might as well rip off the Band-Aid.

"I'm here, barely," I answer.

"Oh, honey," he answers back.

"Please don't ask me how I am doing. Ihsan had to put me to bed after a drunken diatribe detailing my relationship theory. It was ugly."

"Ouch," he replies.

"We'll debrief later."

He hangs up the phone, leaving me to recover.

I decide changing into clean clothes is going to be a waste. If any day called for an all-day PJ Day, today is the day. I create a nest of pillows and blankets on my bed, a safe comfortable place to be miserable. Instead of sitting here with a box of tissues, I escape to my go to activity. The movie selection for today should be curated carefully. Netflix is my standard go to and I decide to start there. Beside me is a bowl of grapes, a half bag of fish shaped crackers, two acetaminophen pills, and a giant glass of ice water that Ihsan insists on refilling. Simple food to give my brain a break and absorb whatever is left in my stomach. As I scroll down the list of potential brain numbing entertainment, I see the selections recommended based on previous searches. From the suggestions, I determine that I might watch more than my fair share of rom coms. I continue to search and then realize I have research to do. No better time than now.

I type Ihsan's name into the search bar and two selections pop up: The Web and Mentor. Ihsan's handsome tuxedo clad torso appears on "The Web" thumbnail.

Oh, this is the distraction I need.

It's a drama with three seasons, but is it binge worthy is the question. I wiggle my body to the perfect angle and press play. I have two options, Turkish with English Subtitles or English voice over. Whenever there is a voice over, it feels like I'm viewing the generic version rather than the name brand. I go with the subtitles. I love hearing the lyrical sounds of Turkish anyway. Ihsan speaking it is just a bonus.

After about an hour, I realize each episode is practically a full-length movie. Not sure I like this format, but I am grateful for how much plot there is in one episode. I can see why the studio has dedicated so many resources to this guy. This particular show has very little kissing, obnoxiously so. Ihsan makes up for it with his skilled facial expressions. The scenes where he has a lot of dialogue or very little dialogue, convey the same amount of emotion and plot information. I am transfixed by every scene he was in. At one point, I realized I had my mouth open, holding a grape in front of my lips for at least a minute. The story is riveting with unforeseen plot twists and all the new Turkish cultural norms I needed to learn. The female lead of the drama was beautiful, sweet and clever. I want to be her.

IHSAN

"Matthew?"

"Ihsan?"

"I don't think I am qualified to give Beatrice the help she needs."

"How bad was it?"

"I think the words are 'epic meltdown'. She got her hands on some whiskey and said something about meatloaf."

"Oh, dear Lord, I'll be there in a bit."

"I owe you big."

"I got you, big daddy."

I'm thankful that Beatrice has someone like Matthew. He drops everything for her and after the last few months of her life, she needs that support. I know when I am out of my league, but I wish I could give her the same comfort. She has done so much for me in the weeks we've known each other, I feel inadequate in my ability and it's killing me. I've heard of finding your kindred spirit, but never would I have thought they would be on the opposite hemisphere. That can be the only explanation for how Beatrice has infected my life. I wish I could tell her how amazing she is, but I know she won't believe me. She's had too many experiences that tell her the exact opposite. A voice inside me tells me it would be a bad idea to call Brandon and tell him what a fucking dick he is.

"*Abla?*"

"Hey Isa, it's late. Everything ok?"

"*Evet*, I am fine, but Beatrice is in a bad way."

"What happened?"

The next five minutes I try to explain what I saw last night. How hurt Beatrice is, what she went through at school and what is going on with her mom. Farah has always given me the best advice and I'm hoping she can help me now.

"You did the right thing. Let her know you are there and that what she is feeling is valid. She's got a long road ahead of her."

"I just wish she knew how amazing she is."

"Ihsan?"

Her voice sounds suspicious.

"It isn't like that. She's been well...you've seen my socials."

"Sometimes I can't tell if she likes you or not."

"Exactly. She keeps me on my toes. But don't worry, no one can replace you."

We say our goodbyes and the air races out of my lungs.

I feel less heavy after talking with Farah. I pace the living room trying to think of something I can do for Beatrice. My immediate thought is to make her soup, but I don't think my mother's soup is the best medicine for what ails her. After last night, I'm not sure giving her a bowl of hot liquid would be the best idea. As if right on cue, Matthew rings the doorbell, saving me from myself.

"I'm not sure how she is going to react to my help," he says, putting down his messenger bag.

"You're the only person I could think of."

"Her Brandon feelings are the only thing we both tried to avoid talking about."

"You can't avoid it now."

"I figured. I feel like I should have some kind of protective gear before going in there. You got hockey goalie padding lying around?"

Matthew and Beatrice's connection is enviable to say the least. It's hard to swallow that I can't do for her what he can.

BEATRICE

Around the middle of the second episode, Ihsan taps on the door. I pause the TV and click back to the menu. I didn't need him to know that I had become so invested in a show he stars in even if it was for research.

He opens the door and slides his head through.

"Are you still breathing?"

Heavy breathing.

I smile at my clever self.

"Yeah, I'm just checking out," I say, trying to focus my eyes in the same direction.

"You have a visitor," he says as the last syllable has a Turkish flavor.

I look at him, piercing a hole through his chest.

"A stripper, you say? You shouldn't have," I say, trying to lighten the mood a little.

Ihsan lets out a husky laugh then raises his arm as Matthew pushes past.

"He sent up the 'Matt Signal' and I answered the call."

Matthew sits hard on my bed. Following Matthew claiming his stake on the bed, Zeki jumps and grinds his knees and elbows into the soft tissue of our legs. After all the groans and bed territory is full, Matthew places a sympathetic hand on mine. Ihsan picks up on the cue and starts to back out of the doorway.

"Oh no you don't, big man," Matthew commands. "You are the co-president of the 'B' team now. You sit down right here."

Ihsan's expression tells me he didn't realize he was going to be a part of this meeting of the minds. As he sat down on the gray sofa he brought his long, tanned ridiculously defined muscular legs up and looks at us over the back. I try to push my hair back away from my face with my fingers and realize that, as usual, only a bun will suffice.

"Clearly, you still hold a torch," Matthew starts.

"I put the torch in the water barrel last night," I reply. "I let the balloon go and today I was just watching the wind take it away."

Matthew turns to Ihsan. "Don't be afraid to raise your hand if you don't understand something."

"That's usually my line," I say, remembering back to six months ago.

"Not anymore, sugar. On the ride over here I was thinking it's time for you to get back on the horse."

"You realize I was bucked off that horse in college, turns out it ran for the other team."

I turn to Ihsan and turn on my professional voice. "Matthew is saying that I need to start dating again. He forgets that the last guy I dated cheated on me with a man."

Ihsan wasn't very good at hiding his thoughts in casual nonprofessional settings. His eyebrows said everything. Now that is a pity.

"I'm concentrating on work right now. Keeping my mind busy."

"To distract you from how lonely you are," Matthew interrupts.

Stabbing me with a dagger directly into my stomach and twisting would have caused less pain than that sentence. For the past few years I thought I was good at hiding it. It's a good thing I don't have any tears left. I take a giant breath into my chest.

"I have a weighted blanket and heating pad. It's like a warm hug every night without all the drama. Matthew, working here makes me happy. I get enough satisfaction with a job well done, you know that."

"When you are doing things for others. And that is not the satisfaction I'm talking about. Do you give anyone a chance to do things for you?" Matthew starts as Ihsan sit's back quietly, knowing his place.

"Who is going to do things for me? Who?" My volume and my hands raise.

"Give someone a chance," Ihsan breaks his silence.

"Who?" I glare at him.

"Stop lashing out," Matthew says. "You do that to discourage people from helping you."

"You've spent too much time in therapy, Matthew."

"You just proved my point," Matthew says sternly.

"Go out, meet people," Ihsan chimes in again.

"Go out, meet people," I say mockingly back to him too quickly to stop myself.

He stares at me straight in the eyes, with no humor or sympathy.

"Sus."

That one-word sentence shut me up immediately. Rarely, does anyone say something to me in that tone. I look at him with slight shock on my face.

"Damn, Ihsan. You got skills," Matthew says, trying to break the tension.

"It means, shut up," Ihsan says flatly even though I figured it out with context clues. "You work hard for me. For Blaine. For everyone else. Put that energy toward yourself and what you want," he says sternly.

He gets up off the couch and avoids making eye contact as he walks out the door.

Oh no, pretty boy. This is my pity party and I'll decide when it's over.

My angry energy as I jump off my bed forces Zeki to follow me out of my room. I stomp on the tile as fast as my short legs will go without running as I search for Ihsan.

"Because it is just that easy!" I yell into the wide-open air of the main floor.

I hear scurrying in the kitchen, trying her best to get away from all the morning theatrics. Most of the time she is the heard but not seen kind of person but its more like smell/eat but not seen.

Ihsan is halfway up the stairs before turning around with his response. "It is."

"For you! You are a human super magnet," I say pointing at him with my palm up, so I don't look like an old lady.

Ihsan rolls his eyes and starts to walk back down the stairs. "So are you. Everyone you talk to walks away happier."

"Exactly! They walk away. That doesn't exactly translate to jumping my bones."

"Is that what you want?" he asks sternly back.

Matthew stands back, leaning against the staircase, watching the show with eager delight plastered across his flawless face.

"I'll show you what I want," I storm up the stairs, grab his hand sharply and drag him down the steps into the hallway and back into my bedroom.

"Oh, damn girl. Go get him."

"Not now, Matthew," I say as I march past him with steam piping out of my ears.

I push Ihsan onto the gray couch and grab the remote control. He remains speechless waiting for an explanation. Scanning through Netflix to find a specific scene, I click and let it play. Ihsan's back is turned away from the camera with his face tilted over his shoulder to the lead actress and press pause.

"That is what I want."

Matthew stands in the doorway with his jaw dropped as far as I have ever seen it.

Damn.

"I want someone to look at me like that," I quickly clarify and lean forward toward both of them to emphasize my point.

"Now, do you two understand?" I toss the remote gently onto the bed, cross my arms and stare at them challenging them to speak.

"How are you supposed to see that if you don't want to meet people?" Ihsan asks, not understanding the word rhetorical.

"Where am I going to go? An LA club? An LA bar? I wouldn't get past the bouncer even if I was dressed in drag," I slap back.

Pausing to breathe out all of the air I had inhaled to fuel my rant, I realize I'm lashing out at two people that genuinely care about me and pull my posture away. They don't deserve my wrath. I'm not sure who does. I just don't know if these two gifts from God understand. Taking a moment to calm all the pent-up feelings that blasted out of my face, I muster up the courage to apologize to my audience.

"I'm sorry. I know you are both just trying to help."

"We know, the wound is still fresh," Matthew says sympathetically.

Ihsan looks at Matthew, seemingly not knowing what to say next.

"I don't think I could be more emotionally naked right now. Sorry to scare you, boys. I'm going to take a shower and attempt to feel like a functioning human being again. This pity party is officially over."

Ihsan's eyes squint a little with the four letter "p" word said aloud.

"I'm getting naked and if you don't want your eyes to burn out of their sockets, you should leave."

Matthew grabs Zeki by the collar, ushering him out the door. "That means you too, big boy. No one likes a dog staring at their nether regions."

Ihsan pushes himself off the couch, takes a few easy strides to face me, places his large palms on my shoulders, leans over and presses his lips on my forehead, his aroma steaming up my face. My official Friend Zone badge. I savor this precious moment as a gesture of kindness and support, wishing from a tiny little spot deep in my soul that it was more.

IHSAN

It's worse than I thought. I didn't know my heart could break any more for her until she revealed that her only boyfriend in college betrayed her. In the minute I let that fact sink in, my heartbreak turns to anger. I can't keep my disdain to myself any longer but what escapes my mouth is not exactly helpful. But I stick with it because it is all I have and I can't sit here and offer nothing. Sadly, I agree with her that the world is not kind to people who don't measure up to societal expectations. She is bigger but in the two weeks I've spent with her, she has proven to be better. I spend so much time working on my physical appearance because that is what it takes in my business, but she isn't in the business.

Yes, she was cheated on and that kind humiliation is gut wrenching but the being cheated on with a man, that is just another thorn. To then admit that out loud to me, must have brought her to a new low. It was at that time that I realized pain is contagious too. When she drags me down the stairs to show me in a way she thinks I will understand I am taken aback by my picture on the screen. I've seen that look a few times and she is right. We all want someone to look at us that way.

She has this amazing ability to pull herself together after an outburst, but I still feel the need to help her pick up the pieces. Before I can stop myself, my palms cover her shoulders and my lips attempt to push some of my confidence through her skull. I wish with everything I have that it would work.

"You're a brave man, Ihsan," Matthew says as I walk into the kitchen reassuring Millie everyone is fine.

"Millie, we are going to go out. Do you mind putting it in the freezer?"

"Sure, that girl needs to leave the house," she says in her slightly growly voice and pats me on the shoulder.

"I just wish I could do more," I say picking up the conversation with Matthew again.

"The fact that you risked your life means a lot."

"*Neh*?"

"I've been on the receiving end of Bee's wrath. She doesn't take kindly to messing with her personal life. That's why you don't see me getting involved. You see, Brandon and I had the bright idea that we would play cupid and set her up with our friend, Carl. We call it the 'set up that shall not be named' for a reason. Boy was our aim off. After Carl, she not only didn't talk to us for two months, but she also changed the passwords to her streaming services, blocked our numbers and even changed the passcode to her house. We tried to send her flowers to one of her classes and she went to the science department and used the Bunsen burners to singe them and sent the briquet skewers back."

"*Vay.*"

"Yep. When she finally let us back in, we never talked about it again. She answered our texts, and she acted as if nothing ever happened."

"You never talked with her about Brandon?"

"How on earth could I walk the tightrope that is my friendship with Bee and my relationship with my brother? When she accepted he would never feel the same way, she never said a word about it to me again. But I saw it. She couldn't turn off that switch as much as she wanted me to believe she did. Bee doesn't hold a torch; she makes a bonfire, and nothing was going to put out that blaze."

"What about Brandon? He never said anything to you?"

"Once. He was fresh off getting dumped and I found them asleep on a bench on the top of the music building. She had her crying face on. He told me she told him she loved him, and he faked being asleep so he wouldn't have to reject her to her face. He said it was more humane that way."

"*Hayir.* I mean, no."

"Yep. I lost a lot of respect for him that night but then I realized it was the only thing he could do to not break her heart. He tried to be more careful about what he said to her after that to spare her feelings, but the damage was already done. She tried to back away from us, but Brandon wouldn't let her. I accused him of keeping her in his back pocket. He punched me so hard he broke a tooth. He continued to act as if she said nothing."

As if her feelings didn't exist. My brain brought up Beatrice's previous night's speech and I had to fight back the urge to rush in and squeeze her until there was nothing left of the heartbreak. She could truly start over. Adding this to everything else she has told me and I'm understanding everything she is avoiding, everything she is trying to save herself from.

"She lives in a lot of fear."

"Ihsan, my brother, I couldn't have said it better myself."

"Amen," I hear Millie whisper under her breath.

Chapter 14

B EATRICE

    After scrubbing the salt off my face, the gunk out of my eyes and spending extra time lathering the shampoo and conditioner into my hair, I quietly stand, letting the water wash away all the ugly feels. The past sixteen hours wreaked havoc on my emotional self-control. It felt good to get that all out but as I dry off from the shower and make my clothing selections, I feel like my mind is in a war movie with small smoke plumes and fading fires among the concrete rebar debris the day after the battle. I walk through trying to figure out what can be salvaged. My dignity isn't among the wreckage.

    Picking my phone off the bed I see a text notification from Sarah.

> Sarah: **I'm going to leave the style of the brides-maid's dresses to you. I don't really care about the style, just the color.**

> me: **What color are you going with?**

> Sarah: **Something in the red family.**

> me: **Any other factors I should think about?**

> Sarah: **I like a softer texture like velvet.**

This is perfect timing for a distraction like this.

> **me: Keep sending me details as you finalize them.**

Sarah sends me a thumbs up emoji and I press the poop emoji but then decide that I don't want to explain it. I send her back a kissy face because this wedding should be the best day of her life, regardless of my emotional trials.

> **Sarah: Did you find someone?**

> **me: For?**

> **Sarah: Therapy**

> **me: I'm working on it. I was thinking about the online kind.**

Everything I said was true, I just didn't tell her that I wasn't dedicating a lot of time to the search.

Feeling closer to the human species again, I walk out of my room in my finest athleisure gear. Ihsan sits in the breakfast nook, his phone updating him on the current goings on while Matthew camps out on the living room couch with his feet on the coffee table, staring at his phone.

"You are an Instagram savant, Bee!" he says excitedly.

"I just post what I would be interested in seeing."

"Your instincts are spot on. Ihsan and Zeki are gaining a significant number of followers daily."

"I had another quick idea. I had to scroll pretty far down to find Ihsan's Turkish dramas. We need to promote them to pique interest." I turn toward Ihsan and shout at him like a whiny kid, "Ihsan, I neeeed you."

I turn on the TV and look for Ihsan's shows as he trots into the living room, game time ready. I find the perfect shot of his stern and sultry look and finagle around with the commands to get rid of all the other crap on the screen.

"Okay, I want to get a shot with you and your face from one of your dramas."

"Oh yes, great!" he says quickly and walks over to the screen. He strikes several poses: serious, fun and, to my surprise, inappropriate. Matthew and I have become a bad influence on the well-mannered Turkish heartthrob. Between the three of us, Ihsan has quite a variety to choose from. The mood of the house returns to being comfortable and relaxed.

"We should go out and look for more 'Gram worthy footage," Matthew suggests. "Go pretty yourself up and we'll go out for lunch, I'll buy."

"Ugh. Give me four hours," I reply.

Matthew rolls his eyes and pushes me toward my room, leaving him alone with Ihsan. Probably not my best move allowing them the opportunity to conspire against me.

My hair air dries in a non-committal wave and my face lacks all color and accents. I change into a floral peasant shirt with green cargo shorts and my red Vans. I pick my most flattering bra that uplifts the ladies but has a comfort half-life of six hours. Sliding large silver filigree drop earrings in my ears classes up the outfit. My standard nude and natural eyeshadow combination and carefully applied mascara maximizes the fabulous lashes and accents the gold and green in my eyes. I top off the outfit with my pink cross body thin strapped bag that conveniently falls right between my breasts. Maybe if I distract people with the way I look on the outside, they won't realize how shitty I feel on the inside.

The house is strangely quiet, so I make my way out the front door. Ihsan and Matthew wait by the black SUV, gossiping about me I'm sure. Matthew climbs into the back seat as Ihsan opens the front passenger door for me. I traverse my way into the front seat like a confident goat and watch Ihsan walk around the front of the car and get into the driver's seat with ease. A perfectly acceptable time to stare at him without worrying about looking conspicuous.

"I don't know if I'm paid up on my life insurance."

"Ha ha," he replies, not appreciating my humor as he usually does.

As we drive through the winding roads, I can see how much he loves speed. He drives confidently, skillfully and, to my dismay, swiftly. The conversation is easy in the cab with the three of us taking little jabs at each other. I almost feel normal again save my whisky-slapped brain.

Ihsan pulls up in front of a restaurant and a valet opens the door for me. I slide out and take in my surroundings. The sidewalk is busy with flashy people and a buzz of excitement fills the air. This is not my scene at all. Matthew takes the lead and walks under the restaurant awning like he owns the place. He greets the host and another man approaches Matthew like they are old friends, his arms outstretched and his smile wide and happy. Matthew is in his element. He introduces us to Kevin, the owner, who walks us to a table outside near the sidewalk. I'm happy to be in a place where I can people watch to distract me. Kevin ushers a waiter over and hands him his phone. He pulls up a chair next to Ihsan and they put their arms around each other and smile like they've known each other for years. Damn, Ihsan is charisma personified. Both flash their million-dollar smiles for a 'gram worthy photograph. I hand the waiter my phone for him to take a shot for me. Before I realize it, I am caught up in the activity when Ihsan's arm suddenly snakes around my shoulders. I grow more conscious of the warmth coming from his arm around me and the spiciness emanating from his neck.

Nope, nope, nope...not again.

I pull away from him and hastily ask for the waiter to return my phone. I scroll through the pictures and each one of Ihsan is just perfect. Don't have to worry about him, so I focus on finding the best one of Kevin. I tag the restaurant, Ihsan's fan groups and Ihsan's ex-wife's account too. I've done this every time and she hasn't reacted negatively, at least to me. I post the best of the pictures and close my phone. Ihsan and Matthew have had a whole conversation that I wasn't a part of while I was updating posts.

"Yeah, let's stick a pin in it and circle round to that at a later date," I add as if I was paying attention at all to the subject at hand.

Matthew gives me a knowing smirk.

"Hey, a girl's gotta strike while the iron is hot," I say to Matthew, wiggling my phone.

We order lunch and Ihsan takes pictures of his food before he digs in. He even writes it up and posts it himself which I shouldn't be surprised he can do. I take a moment to look at these two men, so different and yet both so important to me.

Why can't this be enough?

I feel my heart twinge a little.

Ihsan's phone chimes as he receives a text. His face breaks out into a smile as he reads and replies back.

"We are going to have a couple visitors."

"Oh?" I reply.

"Gül will be bringing my children in a few days."

"That's great!" I say, not really sure how great it actually is. "Do you mind if I give her a call later?"

"Please, I'm relying on you." This statement is just what I need. "The kids have seen all the posts and they are missing me," he says, clearly feeling loved.

"Since we are in such a good mood, I have something to pitch to you." Matthew leans in. "I wouldn't suggest this to anyone in my arsenal of clients, so you should feel privileged. There is a fun series with Tyrone Fox where he takes a celebrity and does something fitness-y with them."

"I've seen it! You really think we could get Ihsan on that show?" I asked excitedly. "You are doing this, this will happen," I say with all the confidence I've ever had. "First things first, we need to plan for your kids' visit."

The rest of the lunch was crackling with excitement. The only time we had to bite into our meals was when one of the others were talking. But then we had to be careful not to spit out food since that seemed to be the secondary goal of the luncheon. I live for these moments.

As Matthew and Ihsan bond over making fun of me, I ignore them and scroll through the photo app on my phone. Here I am smiling with Ihsan's arm around me like I belonged there. I quickly delete all of the pictures of us together as a pre-emptive move to prevent future late night pinings.

On the way home, I suddenly remember the message from Sarah.

"Matthew, Sarah wants me to pick out the style of the bridesmaid's dresses."

Matthew covers his mouth in joy.

"She said she is partial to softer textures," I add.

"Contact!" we scream in unison.

IHSAN

"Does that word mean something else than I think it means?" I ask.

"No." She turns her body toward Matthew and continues. "In the movie 'Contact' Jody Foster wears the most beautiful, gray and burgundy neo-regency dress. Matthew and I have been obsessed for years with that dress."

"If ever you had a reason to wear that dress, this is it," Matthew says.

"I'm not sure how we'll find it but I'm sure we can get help in this town," Beatrice says as her eyes get wider.

"I'm afraid I'm going to be of no help," I say.

"You don't mind if we ignore you until we get home?" she asks.

She pulls out a notebook from her bag and quickly sketches on the paper. The car ride makes it slightly difficult, but she takes advantage of the new energy around the idea of this event. Matthew adds his notes from the back seat and by the time we reached the house they had a pretty good sketch about what Beatrice wanted in the dress.

"So, if you're in the wedding, are you going together?" I ask.

"Oh no, honey. I'm going to get me a fine man to escort me," Matthew responds.

Beatrice stays silent and looks out the window as if the question blows the air out of her lungs.

As if on cue Matthew continues, "I'll wait until closer to the date to finalize plans. I'm sure they are going to get married in San Antonio, which means wedding week!"

"I hadn't thought about that," she says in a more looming tone.

"We'll have to carve out some time to plan all the events." Matthew's excitement grows a little more as we get closer to the house.

"Events?" I ask.

"Yes, since this is kind of a destination wedding for us, we'll take the whole week before, assuming Bee can get the time off, to plan things for the bridal party to do. Everything is bigger in Texas, including weddings." Matthew sit's back and claps to himself. "All the fun things!"

Beatrice's expression looks as if she is cussing inside her brain but doesn't want to shock the rest of us.

Matthew is good for Beatrice. He's a dedicated friend and always knows what will pull her out of the dark place her mind has wandered off to. I almost feel like an intruder at lunch with the two talking so fast and finishing each other's sentences. But they both bring me in as if I've been with them since the beginning of their friendship, as if it has always been the three of us. I've had a few friendships like that from the old neighborhood but when my football career skyrocketed, it was difficult to maintain.

When Beatrice excuses herself to use the restroom, I take the chance to have a serious conversation with Matthew in the middle of the restaurant.

"I have to tell you Matthew, I'm a little nervous."

"About what?"

"Beatrice's mood changed pretty quickly."

"I have found that it is a blessing. She tends to explode but then comes to her senses. She doesn't see the value in focusing on anything she can't change. Except when it came to Brandon. I get what you're saying though. She has a lot more emotions to keep in check than she ever has. But don't let that scare you, she'll work her fingers down to the bone to make sure you are taken care of."

Maybe that's what I'm afraid of.

"She is a force of nature that is for sure." The last thing I need is to break an assistant, or worse bring Beatrice to that point. From what I've seen she's a bit like a grumpy dog with their favorite toy when she's set her mind on something, vicious and territorial.

Matthew's phone pings, giving me a minute to think before Beatrice returns. An unexpected message from Gül catches me off guard. Seeing her name on the screen elicits strong feelings I'm still struggling with. Marriage is important to me and the fact that we couldn't make it work, as fortunate as we both are, reminds me that some things are out of my control no matter how hard I work. Gül ripped my heart out but I won't let my broken marriage affect my children. That is the one thing that Gül and I agree on; Zeyva and Tariq come first.

Seeing Beatrice so invested in making sure that their visit goes smoothly is a huge weight off my shoulders. I have never seen someone dive so deeply into a task besides maybe me. If I asked her to rebuild an engine, I am confident she would have it done within the week with the car's tires rotated, the interior freshly detailed and a lemon scented air freshener dangling from the rear-view mirror. The thought of grease smudged over her puffy cheeks and across her cute nose with that bun in disarray brings a smile to my face. Her dedication is admirable and fierce, which reminds me to always stay on her good side. She is an open book so when I inquire about the wedding, she does a terrible job disguising her pain. Farah has taught me better, that was stupid of me.

Chapter 15

BEATRICE

The next day I'm feeling a little lighter thanks to my crew. I sit down and do some quick math to figure out if it's a good time to call Gül. I take a moment to google her, and find that she is the female equivalent of Ihsan. Her skin is a little more olive, and her eyes are lighter in color, but they did in fact on the surface make the perfect couple. Many of the results that popp up have the word 'model.' Why is this a surprise to me? It will be about eight p.m. if I call now. I push in all the international numbers on my phone and wait patiently for an answer.

"*Merhaba*," says the voice on the other line.

"Hello, Gül?" I greet her hoping I pronounced her name correctly.

"*Evet?*" she says cautiously.

"This is Ihsan's personal assistant, Beatrice."

"Oh, *hallo!*" Her accent is just as sexy as Ihsan's.

"I understand you will be bringing your children for a visit, and I want to make sure I can provide everything they need to be comfortable."

"Oh, that is great," she replies.

"I am going to text you some questions, if you could answer them as soon as you can, I'd really appreciate it. This way I won't miss anything important. Not that Ihsan couldn't tell me but boys miss stuff."

Boys miss big stuff.

"Of course! How is Ihsan?" she asks.

"I believe he is doing very well, no major problems."

"Oh fantastic. He says you have been invaluable to him."

My heart swells just a little and I know she can tell I am smiling.

"He's easy to work with or at least easier than thirty seventh graders."

"I agree."

"Ok, I have a day to start and you have a day to finish. I'll text you soon."

"Ok, Beatrice. Stay strong."

What does that mean? Something must have been lost in translation.

"I will," I say back to her.

Ihsan strolls in casually just as I click the round red button.

"Just got off the phone with your ex. She had a lot to say," I tease.

He doesn't bite.

"You've been a bad boy," I try again.

Crickets.

"You know other people would react to someone gossiping with their ex." I follow him into the kitchen.

"I know you are trying to bait me," he responds coyly.

"I'm trying to toughen you up for all those obnoxious reporters soon to stalk you."

"I've already been through that," he answers.

"Not American ones."

"They have nothing on Turkish futball reporters. I have little to be ashamed of so they don't bother me."

"Damn, you are freaking endearing. The cougar crowd can be particularly hard core and they are going to love you."

"What does 'cougar crowd' mean?"

"They are older ladies that go after younger men. They are usually rich and always on the prowl," I emphasize by showing him my claw fingers.

He lets a small laugh escape.

"Tough room, that was hilarious," I say through a snarky scow. "Anyway, I wanted to ask you if there was anything you wanted to do with the prince and princess while they are here that I can set up ahead of time."

"I told them that I would take them to Disneyland if they came to visit. Gül is coming too. Man to man defense."

I smile at the sports reference I actually understand.

"Trying for 'Father of the Year'?" I explain when I see those confused eyes. "It's a fake award. I'm sure I can set up a guide or something for you all. Give you the gold star treatment."

"Yes, please. But you aren't coming with us? You are always welcome, you know."

"Yeah, no. That is family time. I wouldn't want to intrude. Besides, if I'm going to Disneyland I don't want to be working."

"You wouldn't be working."

"I'd be concerned if you all were having a good time the whole day. I think it's best I let you all go by yourselves. Just make sure you take a lot of selfies."

I need to leave now before he puts me in a trance by Turk-merizing me with those eyebrows and I accept being a fifth wheel on this trip.

"I'm going to take Zeki for a walk," I announce.

"You sure?"

"Yeah, did you put his saddle in the tack room?"

Ihsan opens a far kitchen drawer and pulls out a complicated looking leash.

"He pulls a little," he says as he hands it to me.

"This really is a bridle."

"This way he won't pull you," he explains. "And just so you know, Great Dane owners are tired of hearing horse references."

"Ah I get it, being named Bee and all," I say, trying to untangle the clump of cords. I shove it back into his chest. "You get him situated, I'm going to put on my shoes."

I should really do this more often. Get some exercise. Trim down before the wedding. Zeki will be my personal gym. I put on my rarely used tennis shoes, sweat shorts, sports-ish bra and my Pink Floyd t-shirt. I put my phone in the pocket of the shorts and put my hair up in a ponytail. Ihsan waits at the door with Zeki wearing what looks a little like bondage gear.

"Does this come with a ball gag too?"

I have absolutely no control.

My comment struck him as particularly funny, resulting in a resounding laugh I can be proud of. Thank goodness Ihsan understands and appreciates my sense of humor. With that and my struggles with keeping my thoughts from escaping through my mouth, he often graces me with his laughter. Whether he thinks I'm actually funny is yet to be determined.

"Ball gag, you know, huh? I'll just make a mental note of that," I say, taking the leash. Ihsan bends down and whispers something Turkish in Zeki's ear as he pats him goodbye.

I see why this head harness works. The second Zeki gets a little excited and wants to pull, the harness keeps him from darting off. I decide to head toward a house a little ways up the road that has beautiful roses climbing the front wall that I've been wanting to check out. I pull out my phone and select my murder podcast, thinking this would be the perfect place to listen to it. Zeki and I set off with gusto.

The path we choose is worn and serves as a sidewalk and bike trail. Luckily, it seems that traffic along the trail is pretty light for our trek. The only other people I see are a couple walking ahead of us, Zeki's presence probably encouraging them to pick up their pace. It's a bit of a hill and I kind of wish Zeki would pull me. As we approach the rose house, I plan my strategy to check out all the flowers yet not look like I'm casing the place. I figure I'll keep a safe distance, make a few passes and then start my approach. If there are security cameras, there is no way I look like a threat. It's not like my big booty could scale the wall.

Oh, but all the flowers are soooo beautiful.

When we walk up to the stone wall covered in climbing roses, I completely ditch the plan. In front of the walls are rose bushes slash hedges covered in not only rose blooms but also long red flowers that seem to have legs. I push Zeki behind me as I smell the flowers to prevent him from stepping into anything thorny. I can feel him rub up against me and stand up to see what he's interested in. I turn and look around but nothing catches my eye. In a typical Zeki move, he takes a step back and hockey hip checks me toward the foliage. I feel my balance fail and attempt to grab onto anything to keep me upright. Everything I reach for has tiny little death spikes. I land with my ass between two of the bottom stalks of the bushes with my back, arms and head stuck deep within the stems. My legs stick up and out, resting on several branches. As I look up, Zeki's giant nostrils stare down at me through my knees as if he is celebrating the success of his evil plan.

Assessing the situation from the ground up I concede that I have no way of getting up by myself. Everywhere I try to put my arms to push myself up it seems as if the thorny branches are moving purposely in my way and I can't bring my legs down to gain any kind of ground without painful repercussions. I sit still and can think of only one thing to do. It's the worst. I call loudly into the air "Siri, call Ihsan." Thank goodness Siri did not mishear me. "Calling EE-SAHN." That sweet kiwi voice is going to save me. I silently plead to the heavens as the phone rings. Ihsan's voice answers in his easy casual way.

ISHAN

Beatrice is in her element when I ask her to help with the Disneyland trip. I was sincere that I wanted to bring her along. I think she would be good company and it would be nice to have a buffer between Gül and me. We have a custody arrangement that accommodates both our schedules but when I landed the job in America we had to make adjustments. Previously, I only had to see her for a few minutes when I picked them up or dropped them off. This new arrangement requires more time spent in her presence and I'm still struggling with seeing her. I thought she would be bearable after two years. Claiming I didn't have anything to be ashamed of wasn't exactly truthful. Defending your honor and not risking the welfare of everyone who works with you is a delicate balance.

I can see Beatrice starting to become uncomfortable the more I press her about joining us on our day trip. One of her many talents is her ability to turn on a dime. I have a feeling it is part of a fight-or-flight response when she feels ill at ease. I like to watch her eyes as she composes her quips while simultaneously strategizing her escape route. The way her forehead wrinkles and her eyebrows raise a millimeter is her tell. Before I send her away with Zeki, I bend down and whisper in his ear to make sure she comes back safe.

Apparently, Zeki didn't hear me.

My phone rings, interrupting a spontaneous nap.

"I don't want to alarm you, but Zeki and I got into a little accident. Zeki is fine. If you could just drive over to the Beauty and the Beast house and lend me a hand, I'd really appreciate it."

"Are you okay?" I ask urgently.

"Yep, just dandy. If you could come ASAP, I'd really appreciate it," she asks dryly.

I can hear her struggling to keep her emotions in check and as with most things with Beatrice, she resorts to humor.

"*Tamam*, I'll go now." I hang up quickly and rush to gather my keys and wallet.

I pull up to see Zeki's head inside the brush and his tail wagging ferociously. I fail to see Beatrice and slam on the brake, barely pulling the key out of the ignition before jumping out onto the gravel.

"Zeki! Where's Beatrice?"

"I'm behind Zeki," I hear her respond from the ground near Zeki.

I approach Zeki and hold onto his head. When I finally see her being eaten by the rose bush, I gasp and cover my mouth. Her eyes try to hide her pain and embarrassment at the same time, but I see a tear slide down her cheek as she blinks rapidly. It's adorable.

"I literally just need your hand before Audrey Two digests me. I know it is going to hurt but just grab on and give me a good yank. We'll deal with the damage later."

"Oh *yok, yok, yok*," I reply, hoping she feels my sympathy.

I grasp her hands, dig my heels into the ground and pull her up with cautious speed. She lets out a bit of a screech as the thorns scrape her skin on several breaking branches as I lift her up. Her half crumbled-over body cannot fully stand after she is free from the devil flora. She releases my arms gingerly and waits for the next stage of my rescue. To ascertain the scope of the injuries, I walk around to her back and pull a giant breath through my teeth.

"I don't feel any thorns in my butt but my back and arms sting like hell," she starts to cry a little, I'm assuming partly from pain, partly from embarrassment.

I knew if I laughed at her when I saw her head and legs poking out of the bush that she would kick my ass as soon as she was physically able. Her quivering voice when I attempt to clean her off hurts the inside of my chest. I can't imagine how much she had to suck up her pride to call me for help. I use delicate movements as I remove any loose leaves and thorns that are stuck in her skin on my first pass. She poorly resists the urge to yelp every time I pull a tiny Satan spear. I hope she feels a bit of relief with every piece out of her hair.

"Do you think you can sit in the car?" I ask.

"I think the only thing I can do is sit," she answers meekly.

I guide her to the front seat and help her climb up the long thin footing. She leans forward to put her hands on the passenger side airbag label and lets her forehead fall forward. Zeki's excited tail beats against the upholstery as he realizes he gets to sit in the backseat and splits the front two seats with his enormous muzzle.

Beatrice's face shows me exactly how much she appreciates his enthusiasm.

Parking as close to the house as I can, I jump out and jog around the front of the SUV. She opens the car door slowly, trying not to disturb all the little bits still stuck in her skin. She slides slowly off the leather seat and waits for her toes to touch the pavement before she grabs a hold of my outstretched hand. My dad instincts kick in as I help her out of the car and into the house. I want to take away her pain, but I also know how hard it is for her to accept help. She really has no choice as I inspect her skin and clothes.

"Moving wasn't hard an hour ago," she manages to utter through a tense face.

I open the door and guide her to the kitchen as if she were a hospital patient attached to an IV pole. She places her hands on the cool counter, slowly leaning forward and hoisting herself onto the stool, hissing through the whole maneuver.

"There's a first aid kit in one of the lower cabinets by the sink," she tells me through strained facial muscles.

"I didn't know we had one."

"I ordered one the day you told me your kids were coming."

"That is what was in the box. I thought it was adult toys," I say with a giant smile on my face, hoping I will see one on her face as well.

"Ihsan!" she says in mock shock then grunts in pain.

Beatrice fell in a particularly evil plant with very tiny spines. Death by a thousand tiny cuts would be the closest description I can think of to the damage to her body. There are pieces of the bush in her tied back hair and stuck to her clothes. The rose prickles are large but she is covered in those thorns and attempting to pick them all out by hand is almost impossible. I fear with her luck that she might have fallen into a plant with toxic sap. I made sure when I had children and a dog that I knew what could make them sick and what was safe.

Of course, she has supplied the house with first aid supplies. I didn't even think about that when we moved in. The look of shock on her face when I decided to show my inappropriate thoughts served its purpose to distract her from her pain. I hope I provide her a little entertainment to cheer her up when the plastic on the kit puts up a serious fight. It feels good to be myself around her.

BEATRICE

"Why now with the inappropriate jokes?"

"Taking advantage of your weakness."

"Dastardly."

His large fingers struggle with the plastic wrapping. It is really the universe trying to right itself by giving me this little moment of glee, watching this manly man be bested by a small piece of cellophane. Finally, the impossible wrapping rips apart and he throws it across the counter dramatically.

"There should be some kind of alcohol wipes."

"This isn't my first circus," he replies.

"This isn't your first rodeo," I correct. "Never mind, this is definitely a circus."

He walks over to me with a few wipes in his hands and sympathy on his face.

"I know, doc, it's bad."

"This will not be pain free. We are going to have to pull your shirt up to get at the wounds. Your arms are bad, too."

"What is going to hurt more, you seeing me half naked or the wipes?" I ask.

"Let's just do it," he says, pushing my scraggly hair over my shoulder and pulling up the back of my shirt to expose my very supportive bra.

"It might be easier if you pull it over your head instead of holding it."

I know he is right. I reach back and let out an enormous gasp from the pain shooting through my body.

"Here, I'll do it."

"Oh Jesus, this just keeps getting better," I say with no more fucks to give.

I grab the front hem of my shirt to keep it from sliding up as he lifts my shirt gently over my head, trying not to rip out my hair. I am leery of exposing too much of myself and keep the fabric bunched up just under my chin with my arms tight at my sides.

He carefully unlatches each hook of my bra and pushes the clasping fabric away from my back. I hear him gasp loudly and imagine the gag-me-with-a-spoon face he is making behind my back.

"Well, that really does wonders for my self-esteem."

"Your back looks ... angry."

"There was a different flower planted between the roses. I got a good view while I was trapped. All those tiny spikes have to be from it. I better not have poisoned myself."

"I'll see if I can find out, but I need to get the thorns out first."

He opens the little package with almost as much grace as he did the big kit. He presses it gently onto the red specks that still may have a prick in them. I close my eyes and try not to hiss after every application. At some point I feel his fingers on my back, lightly gliding over my punctured skin and scanning for tiny thorns.

"We should really wash this off thoroughly. These little serviettes aren't working very well."

"What did you say, Mr. Fancy pants?"

"These," he dangles a used wipe in front of my face. I take note to ask him about that word later.

"What do you suggest?"

"You should soak and then wash your back."

He's going to see my scar. Great, another can of worms.

"That will be fun with my gnarly arms."

"I'll help you."

"Take a bath?" I say with honest shock in my voice. Nothing sounds more horrifying to me than having him help me bathe.

"Yes. You wanted to try out your tub, anyway."

"How do you know I wanted to try the tub?"

"I saw how you looked at it when we moved in."

Was I that obvious or is his ability to recall insignificant information freakish?

"I'll help you to your closet and you can unclothe there. I'll take care of the rest."

"Unclothe?" I laugh at his adorable use of English. "Just so you know, this plan sucks but I'm in no condition to put up a fight."

"Wait, let me cut your hair tie," he says opening drawers looking for something to cut.

"You think I'm going to let you near my hair with scissors?"

He pulls out a small kitchen knife and I immediately laugh.

"Neh?"

I can't help myself. It's my mom's fault.

"That's not a knife." Everyone can say that line in a decent Australian accent but me. "Don't roll your yes at me, that was a perfect pitch and I hit it out of the park."

I make a mental note to add *Crocodile Dundee* to the "Bee Goes to the Movies" watch list.

When he pulls out the scissors, I am relieved. Although, his Turkish dramas would lead one to believe he would be carrying a knife at all times.

"If you give me a bald spot, I'll retaliate in kind," I warn as he tries to separate the hair tie and avoid cutting my hair.

I feel my hair fall down my back and squint as whatever got stuck in it, is now scratching attacking my back.

"Git," he commands, helping me off the stool. I love it when English and Turkish sound the same.

Waves of mental nausea crash over me. If it weren't for the fact that I can barely move without thousands of pain receptors announcing themselves, I would do this on my own. I would have eaten glass before letting Brandon see me this humiliated. Not so much with Ihsan. As Mille so often likes to say, "he could give a rat's ass."

Chapter 16

B EATRICE

Intellectually, a hard stream of water pounding on my back sounds incredibly painful, but all I want to do is wash everything away, so a bath it is. Emotionally, nothing sounds better than a bath in my condition but Ihsan giving me said bath feels like humiliation on a whole other level.

The dignity at which I walk down the hallway with my back exposed and my shirt half on is at an all-time low. With each sleeve or bra strap I remove, I unsuccessfully hold back a hiss and a yelp. The gray robe I purchased as a special treat for myself still sits in the package on the closet shelf. Without patience I rip open the clear plastic, unfold it with malice and gingerly slide my arms in the sleeves, causing me even more pain. I loosely tie it around my waist. The whole reason I purchased this particular robe was giant pockets to put things in like snacks.

The sound of the water hitting the pool in the bottom of the tub invades my entire suite. Peeking around the door to the bathroom, I see Ihsan sitting on my pink tufted vanity stool looking ridiculous, bubbles rising above the rim of the tub. He turns and sees my fluffy robe and smiles. Any warm-blooded heterosexual adult woman wishes she was me right now. He takes two large stealthy steps towards me and takes my hands into his as guides me to the tub.

"Can you get in okay?"

"Ummm...do you mind turning around? The last man to see me naked delivered me."

Which was true. Carl, the cheating bastard, always had the lights off. That should have been a clue.

"Of course," he says as he turns around like a five-year-old sent to the corner. I delicately remove the robe from my body, taking care not to let it brush my skin too harshly and throw the robe on top of Ihsan's head. It was worth the slight tinge of pain radiating over my arms and shoulders.

"Hey!" he struggles to free himself from the fluffy fabric.

Nice shot, me.

"Big baby," I tell him.

"Just get in," he commands.

I look at the tub, trying to figure out the least painful and most dignified way to get my body into the water. I decide on the classic "hold on and slide down" technique was my only feasible option. It was a little sloshy, but it did the job. It is hard to judge the depth of the water with all the bubbles. The level of the water came to the middle of my back and my maneuvering caused all the bubbles to be pushed toward my feet and cover my face to my eyebrows. The hissing doesn't stop when the warm water crashes over my skin, the soapy bubbles were probably a mistake.

Knowing my whole front is covered, I turn my bubbly face to Ihsan.

"All right big boy, it's your lucky day."

He turns around to see nothing but a body shaped pile of tiny bubbles. The loud guffaw he lets escape reverberates against the tiles.

"Can you hand me a washcloth or something?"

"Or what?" he asks in a playful tone.

"Take off your sassy pants and hand me something to wipe this off my face."

"Did you just tell me to take off my pants?"

Did I?

"No, it was an expression. I meant for you to stop being silly and just do as I say. What happened to all those famous Turkish manners? Take your pants off, the nerve!"

"That is bossy pants, no?"

The bubbles bobble around as I laugh at his purposefully thick accent.

I try to use my hands, but they are no use as they are also covered in the fluffy white stuff. Suddenly, I feel his hand on mine as he places a wet cloth in my palm. Before he pulls his hand away, I give it a gentle squeeze and he squeezes back then releases my grip. It was a silent thank you that I hope he understood. My shoulders drop and a release of tension flows over me in a soft wave from my skull to my toes.

"I use a bucket when I give my children a bath but all I could find was this plastic bowl."

Before I could question what he was talking about, a gush of water lands on my head.

"That should help with the bubbles."

I wipe away the water from my eyes.

"Ok, enough of that. I'm not three," I say protesting. I need to keep the bubbles covering the big chest floaties.

He sits down on the stool he has set up next to the tub. Handing him the wet washcloth, I start to take in what is happening here. The gasp I hold in from feeling his fingertips move my hair over my shoulder almost escapes which would absolutely embarrass me. A snicker radiates across my face at the juxtaposition of it all.

"Does this tickle you?" he asks in surprise.

"No, just thought of something funny."

"*Neh?*"

"You really want to know?"

"*Evet,*" he answers in what I have learned is Turkish for yes.

"I just think it is unbelievable that I'm sitting in a tub full of luxurious bubbles with a gorgeous man washing me. All I need is someone feeding me peeled grapes and fanning me with a giant palm frond and I would be Elizabeth Taylor."

"You think it is unbelievable that someone would want to take care of you?"

I walked right into that one. Damn him.

"Can't I just enjoy this moment, as painful as it is?"

He takes the cue and leaves the subject alone, examining my back to figure out where to start his treatment.

"I found a piece of what attacked you in the car and looked it up. It's called a California Fuchsia or goo...seberry," he says struggling with reading the last word as if it doesn't make sense.

"Oh, hell no. I am not going to be taken out by a gooseberry. I'm sticking with killer roses."

Staring at the front of the tub, I feel the washcloth rub gently across the thousand tiny scratches littering my back. Only a few hisses make their way through my teeth when I feel the tiny little bastards burrow their way further into my skin. The temperature of the water easily hides the crimson hue radiating over my body. He picks off as many miniscule prickles as he can see as the washcloth washes them away. The warmth of his breath grazes my skin. I pull up my knees as close as I can to my chest and wrap my arms under them to hide my body's involuntary response. Then I feel the small cloth travel across my shoulders and over my arms which, despite the warm water having betrayed me, has me developing millions of little bumps.

"Are you cold?" he asks.

"A little," I lie. "But it's fine," I lie again.

It's a hell of a lot more than fine.

He suddenly stops and drops the washcloth in the water. I quickly attempt to retrieve it before he does but again, my skin fights me with every movement.

"Wait, I have mood music."

Don't you dare.

This will put me over the top. He dries his hands off on a nearby towel and pulls out his phone. He presses the screen a few times and then smiles at me. The sound of acoustic guitar fills the room.

After a few strums I hear the male singer "We both lie silently still."

I slowly turn my head back to his giant white toothy smile.

"You sure are proud of yourself, aren't you?"

He nods vigorously as the lyrics to "Every Rose Has Its Thorn" play out.

I let the song continue as I sit thinking that I would have probably done the same thing.

Clever boy.

He continues to remove the tiny spines from my back and squeezes the warm water out of the washcloth to soothe my skin. If I had a spank bank, this would be a large deposit.

I look down and I realize that the bubbles have almost all dissipated.

Don't panic.

The mounds of bubbles are reduced to a frothy film on the top of the opaque water as Ihsan continues to clean all the tiny wounds speckling my skin.

"I think I'm sufficiently basted. So, skedaddle so I can get out of this tub without an audience for my humiliation."

"Since I'm here, do you want me to wash your hair?"

"Oh my god, no. That's way too much," the words barely intelligible through the laugh.

"If I don't then you're more than likely not going to shower for a few days and I won't be able to stand the stench or your complaining," he says as he walks out of my shower, his palm full of shampoo.

Who am I to say "yok"?

Sweet fancy, Moses. Dear Lord, forgive me for what I am about to let him do.

"Move to the back of the tub, it will be easier for me to reach."

"I'm losing my bubbles, could you give me something bigger than a coaster? You know, to protect my modesty."

He hands me a large bath towel and I sink it under the surface. It seems a little strange to cover my body in the water with what I'm supposed to dry it with.

"Never in a million years," I whisper to myself and the absurdity of this whole event.

"You said something?"

"It's nothing. Just try not to tangle it too much."

"I've washed my girl's hair many times. I think I've got this."

The cold, thick liquid lands on the crown of my head followed by his immense hands wiping the goo over my waist length hair. This is the part in the salon when I close my eyes and enjoy the inadvertent head massage that happens in the bowl. Closing my eyes is just asking for trouble as the internal struggle to keep my eyes wide rages behind said eyes. Tiny bubbles build and pop as his fingertips scrub my scalp. The rose and gooseberry bushes left a few deposits deep in my locks and I feel a few tugs and a quick apology from behind me.

"It's fine. Would you believe I have a hard head?"

"No doubt about it."

I'm pretty sure he can't see my side glare complete with flat sideways lip action.

The way he massages the shampoo all the way down to the ends confirms his claim. He is gentle and thorough, being careful to not pull too hard but also scrubbing the base of my skull. My eyes threaten to droop once again.

"You can relax," his low voice rumbles.

"Yeah, no I can't," I reply, slightly panicked. As much as I would love to indulge in the moment, I have to be careful not to tempt the universe. I will certainly not allow myself to enjoy something that was never meant to happen.

"You think too much."

"I'd rather be known for thinking too much than not thinking enough."

"Ah," he says, taking the bath wand and turning the water to warm to rinse the lather down my back.

Naturally, I tip my head back to avoid getting soap in my eyes. As if a jet stream of air passed down my back, the muscles in my body relax and I succumb to this Mediterranean man's bathing ritual. He drapes the freshly cleaned mane over my shoulder and a moment later I feel another round of product glide over my head.

"Wow, I'm getting the spa package. Does this count as a Turkish bath?"

"I would not let you go to a Turkish bath in your condition," he says through a loud chuckle, his fingers raking the conditioner to the ends of the strands. "I'll show you on the computer later."

As the second round of rinsing begins, I'm starting to think I'm not the first woman he has washed. Forgetting my back resembles a freshly tilled field, I start to lay backward against the tall end of the tub.

"*Yok*!" Ihsan warns, holding the edges of my shoulders.

A sharp hiss escapes my mouth. His unintentional manhandling shocks my mind and my body back into reality.

"*Üzgünüm*."

"Bless you."

"It means, 'I'm sorry', Be."

"I should commit that one to memory. I have a feeling there is going to be a lot of apologizing."

Again, he humors me with a snicker but when he bends down by my toes I realize he's reaching for the drain.

"Woah! You can go now. I got this."

"You might fall," he stands to his full height and dries his hand on an extra towel.

"Ihsan, I'll be fine."

"You could really hurt yourself. You seem to be good at it."

My eyes scan from his knees all the way up to his overly concerned pupils and I let out a quiet throaty growl. It seems like the only appropriate response.

"There is only one way I'm going to get out of this tub with you in the room." I pause for dramatic effect. "Blindfolded."

"Me or you?"

"Ihsan, I'm not sure this is going to work out if you continue to joke at my expense."

"That's the best part," he smiles, searching through the linen closet. "Ah-ha!"

"What? Oh no, seriously?"

"You said blindfolded," his muffled voice coming from inside a dark blue pillowcase.

"If you weren't so big, I would mistake you for a kidnapping victim."

As he baby steps his way back to the tub, I release the drain plug. His plan isn't as bad as I let on. He'll be right there if I faceplant and I won't bleed out with my ass in the air. The visual in my head is almost as painful as the tiny thorns that tore up my back.

"I brought the antibiotic ointment, too."

"Seriously, now how am I supposed to use that?" I say hissing as I maneuver my body into a lifting position.

Oh sh...it.

Isn't it enough that he is bathing me, now he's going to rub slimy smelly crap all over me? I thought walking down the hallway half naked was bad, this is actual rock bottom.

"I'll be fine. I just want to get dressed."

"No, you need to rinse off and use the ointment."

"Listen, Nurse Ravishing, you are not putting that on me. Just smear some on the wall and I'll rub against it."

"Let me know when you are ready," he says as he holds up a large towel spread out in front of him.

"Give me a second to rinse all this crap off. You are lucky I'm in too much pain to make more fun of you."

"After everything I've done and that is how you repay me?"

"You may have a point."

We stand listening to the playlist of my humiliation and wait until the last gurgle of the drain. I grab the removable water wand and turn on the faucet to a gentle flow. As the water drains out I spray myself off, letting the water both rinse me and cool me down at the same time. It isn't any less painful when I run the water down my body than when Ihsan attempted.

He extends his arms and I swiftly grab the towel as I am not confident that the thread count of his pillowcase is high enough. Thankfully he grabbed a bath sheet instead of just a regular towel, I wrap it loosely around my back and tight under my arms, wishing I wouldn't involuntarily gasp and hiss so much but it is better than the yelping from earlier.

"Ok, I'm decent-ish."

He removes the headcover and offers his hand to support my arm as I try to lift my leg over, brace myself and keep myself covered. After clearing the edge I finally stand to my full height, somehow feeling lower than I usually am. As I start to walk to my closet, I feel another towel on my head.

"Thanks, Ihsan. I'm good now."

"I'll wait in your bedroom."

Jesus, Mary, and Joseph.

Patting down my hair is about the best I can do as my arms are still rebelling against any large movements. I figure that putting my arms all the way through the sleeves of the robe would be a waste since he has to get at my back, so I put on my favorite comfortable panties and a pair of loose shorts, trying not to make any quick movements. I wrap the robe around my waist, letting the sleeves dangle in front of me to cover up my chest. As

I walk down the two stairs, Ihsan opens the medicated slime and motions for me to sit next to him.

IHSAN

She is letting me bathe her. The shock of this needs to be pushed as low into my gut as possible or she will turn it into a tragedy, like she always does. I dig deep in my acting tool bag to not reveal to her how watching the water flow down her hair onto her back is causing my body to tighten in the most inconvenient place. The instinct to touch her takes over, but moving her hair over to her shoulder makes sense in this instance. She can't help the self-deprecating comments and I can't help pressing her just a little and predictably she pushes back. The need to lift her up seems to constantly enter my thoughts.

I hope she doesn't notice my deep breaths as I try as delicately as possible to remove anything causing her pain. She is curled up as tightly as her body will allow in an attempt to hide from me. I don't want her to feel like she needs to withhold anything from me. It's not as if clothes hide the fact that her body doesn't fall in the model category. She picks outfits that complement the parts of her body that she should be proud of, her muscular calves, round ass and those amazing breasts. I am not brave enough to tell her that. I can jump through fire onto a moving car, but I will not risk telling Beatrice she is attractive. She wouldn't believe me and I do not want to hear her contradict it. It is striking how much Beatrice resembles the goddess in Titian's "Venus with a Mirror", with her long hair pulled up on her head, her thick supple body and the blush on her cheeks. Paintings have always fascinated me and this one in particular stuck in my memory. Venus, however, was not as blessed in the breast department as Beatrice.

It tickles me as intriguing how we can have a conversation so casually and openly in this very odd situation. My mother wouldn't know how to react. I am doing everything I can to help her, but I am also sitting next to Beatrice naked in a tub. I'm pretty sure I would get a few smacks of her slipper. I will be leaving this event out of our weekly check-ins.

While she undresses in her closet, I try to think of ways to make this experience less excruciating. What would Beatrice do? She would find the humor in it and what better way than to do that than good music. After selecting a few songs to brighten up her mood, I execute my plan. Beatrice is predictable in that I know she will react but also unpredictable in her exact wording. I never know if she will be offended or find the whimsy in my shenanigans. Lucky for me, she appreciates my efforts to amuse her with my farce.

I listen quietly as I finish cleaning off her skin, the sound of the water hitting the pool breaking up the background music. I can't help myself. All that beautiful, gleaming hair draped down her scarred back is a siren song to me. I almost feel bad taking advantage of the situation when I insist on washing her hair but this instinct to ease her pain and offer her comfort weaves into my desire to dig my fingers in and I'm helpless to resist. The water traces the lines of her red face as she tips her head. Yes, despite what she thinks, someone would find her very attractive, especially like this.

When the water starts to clear, I notice the muscles on her back contract. More of her skin is exposed and I take note of a few small birthmarks down her ribs. I can feel the slight panic in the air when she realizes I'm going to get a pretty good view of most of her body. What she needs is to feel safe, to feel accepted, and to feel cared for. It's difficult to convey these to her when she makes everything a joke. But I continue to try because at some point I'm going to break through. At some point, she will listen.

When she is finally plucked and cleaned, I insist on continuing the treatment. The last thing she needs is an infection to remind her of the flower fiasco. For a few moments, I doubt she will meet me in her bedroom. While she undoubtedly is trying to come up with an excuse to stay sequestered in her closet, I run to the laundry room to see if Thomas left some clothes for her to put on but all I find is a basket of mine and I grab the biggest shirt I can find. She already feels humiliated and any attempts to convince her that her body isn't as repulsive as she believes will just push her back into her closet.

Her hesitant approach to the couch warns me to keep my demeanor serious.

"*Hadi,*" I say, trying to get her accustomed to my home language.

"Come or sit? Wait, do you use those words with Zeki too?"

"Come on," I say, patting the couch, not allowing her to retreat.

The fluffy gray robe she previously used as armor drapes loosely over her red, speckled shoulders. Her full lips squish in the middle of her face with her gemstone eyes semi glaring at me.

"I tried to pull my hair up, but it just didn't seem worth the pain."

Having a little girl does come with some perks, like knowing how to deal with long hair.

"I can do it, or at least put it in a pile on top."

She hands me the soft fabric hair tie slowly over her shoulder as she gingerly sits on the couch, nestling into the space between my bent leg so

I can easily apply the ointment. I gather her thick, wet hair, wrapping it around my hand and securing it to the top of her head. This close to the nape of her bare neck is nothing new but when my eyes wander down her exposed spine I'm drawn again to the curious scar. My fingers instinctively trace the four-inch straight line near her shoulder blade.

Venus, for sure.

"What is this?"

Like before, her muscles contract but this time, she relaxes almost immediately.

"My angel wing scar?"

"*Neh?*"

"It sounds much better than telling people I had a touch of cancer."

"*Neh?*" I didn't expect that answer.

"Skin cancer. Mine was like the fender bender of cancers."

"It's still cancer, Beatrice."

I'm shocked she has never mentioned cancer in all the late night talks we've had.

"I know. That thing in my bag is not a vibrator, it's sunscreen. Why do you think I insist your skin products have SPF and I always have a hat for you?"

Everything in my body stiffens when a quick flash of Beatrice with a vibrator overwhelms my thoughts. I try to shake it off without making it completely obvious to her that she just made every cell in my body reverberate.

Beatrice's chin hovers over her shoulder, my make-shift bun flopping to the other side of her head.

"Ihsan, I take care of it. I get checked twice a year."

"You better," I say, starting to apply tiny swipes of clear goop on the small cuts. I'll have to remind her she needs to find someone here in LA to take a look.

"Do you use anything for the scar?"

"For what?"

"To make it go away, I'm already back here."

"No, I just keep it covered. I'm pretty sure if someone saw me this naked, they'd turn to stone."

"I'm still flesh and bone," I remind her.

"It doesn't apply to gods."

"*Vay.*"

This woman has an answer for everything.

"Medusa was a beautiful maiden before she was punished by Athena," I say, trying to beat her at her own game.

"Yeah, but she was caught doin' it with Poseidon at Athena's house and the bitch got what she deserved."

"I don't think it happened quite like that."

"That's how I tell it."

Beatrice's animosity for a mythic beauty is a bit disturbing but the infidelity theme hits us both. She tends to do that though, turn the subject around to serve her viewpoint. A good skill to have when she is out there representing my interests, but it's hard to have a genuine conversation when her defenses seem to be on high alert.

"Why didn't you tell me you've had cancer?"

"Because it's one of the few scars that I'm not reminded of on a daily basis."

By the harshness of her reply, I can tell she is losing patience with my line of questioning and I wish I could take that as a cue to put off my inquisition until a more appropriate and less naked time.

As I continue to treat the rest of her back, my eyes stray back to the 'angel wing' scar and the slightly discolored skin that surrounds it and my mind drifts to what life was like for her before she came to work for me.

"How long ago?"

"Did I have cancer?"

"*Evet.*"

"About four years now, I think. Honestly it was so long ago, I don't think about it."

"How bad was it?"

"Surgery, then radiation treatments. I wasn't out of school that long. Like I said, it could have been worse."

Beatrice's nonchalant attitude leaves an uneasy feeling in my stomach. The evidence that she spends more time on my health and safety than her own is piling up. She has inadvertently placed herself in the role of caretaker and if she weren't so good at it and I didn't need her help, I would point it out to her.

"Put your arm out."

"Are you going to send me a bill for this?" she asks.

"Oh yes, and every complaint is another charge."

"So, this isn't out of the kindness of your heart?"

"You think I have a kind heart?"

She doesn't answer the question as she adjusts her robe to cover up her chest, giving me access to her upper arms. Suddenly, her posture droops dramatically, and her head falls forward as she cups her face in her palms.

"Woah, Beatrice."

Her breath becomes faster and deeper as I attempt to calm her but both her back and my fingers are covered with the ointment. She raises her face out of her hands and even though there are no tears, her eyes are red and wet.

"Beatrice, wha--"

"Yes, you have a kind heart. Too kind. I'm sorry, I just couldn't hold it together anymore."

"Beatrice, I'm..."

She gingerly pushes her arms quickly through the sleeves before I can finish, squinching from the obvious pain. From her reaction at the scene and the way she just melted in front of me, I realize this incident and the subsequent treatment is affecting her deeper than what she is letting on.

"Give me the tube, I can do the rest myself."

"*Yok*, sit."

"Ihs--"

"Stop running and just let me do this for you."

I slide the sleeve of her robe down her arm and the instant my fingertips touch her skin, tiny bumps flush down to her wrist. She leans sideways and lets me help pull her arms up and out, being careful not to reveal her ample bosom. She doesn't speak another word as I finish covering her wounds and when I turn my eyes toward her face she focuses her attention away, hiding her expression.

"Here, I brought you one of my big t-shirts," I say cautiously, extending my arm around her torso.

She takes the large black shirt from me and lays it on her lap, quietly waiting.

"Beatrice, what's wrong?"

I can't let her stew her in her own misery. She takes a long deep breath, straightens her back slowly and wipes away the wetness in her eyes.

"When I was going through treatment, Brandon never left my side. He drove me to appointments, picked up meds and even made sure my fridge was packed. I had to put mom in a home because I couldn't take care of her anymore while undergoing treatment and teaching. When I got cancer, it wasn't the hardest part of my life. The hardest part was being taken care of by someone who doesn't love you as much as you love them while losing the one person who did. Those are the scars you can't see. That's what it was like with him, so many painful invisible wounds. Your kindness feels like you're back there poking at every one of them. See why I distract myself with movies?"

Brandon left Beatrice with a lot of damage. Ten years of friendship. This woman would have moved mountains for him. When Beatrice drunkenly explains that she set up Sarah and Brandon, I deduce that it is so she could have a reason to cut him out of her life and logically move on. Her reaction to their engagement announcement demonstrates she never made that step. She isn't the first person to fail applying logic to emotions. Damn, this girl was in deep.

"It's called '*kara sevda*'," I say quietly.

"What is that?"

"What you are going through. The closest translation in English is 'black love.' It's the kind of deep unrequited love that leaves you ...broken."

"Any cure for this black love disease?" she sniffles through the question.

"*Yok*."

"Tell Kara Sevda, she can fuck off."

BEATRICE

Is it too early for PJs? Eleven am seems like athleisure-o'clock to me. I search for Ms. Lifty Lift and consider if the pain is worth it. Then I look down and realize there is no choice and put her on in record slow time, biting my lip to keep me from screaming and causing Ihsan to rush in, getting blinded for his chivalry. After taking a long drag of Ihsan's large black t-shirt into my nose, I put it on and add a pair of soft black capri leggings. I may steal this shirt when I leave just to bring his scent with me. Black Vans complete the outfit. Wrapping my hair in a bun was a lot more painful than usual as my scrapes and scratches on my arm rub against the shirt. I am tempted to ask Ihsan to do my bun again, but I think better of it. The bath helped but my bra straps rubbing against the fresh scratches were still very painful. As much as I want to just chuck this day in the trash, there is work left to do. Stepping down into my bedroom, I cringe.

Is that Seal?

Pulling my phone from my side pocket I find a Turkish to English dictionary.

I walk to the kitchen where Ihsan has rid the counter of all the first aid wrappings.

"Really?"

I look at him as "Kiss from a Rose" plays in the background.

"What? I like Batman," he smiles at me with a not so innocent grin.

Taking his phone off the counter I press the stop button and look him straight in the face.

"*Igrencsin*," I scorn in my best Turkish.

His face lights up.

"So good!" he says back to me excitedly as I put my nose in the air and walk over to my laptop to finish the day's work. I'm going to have to integrate the Turkish version of "you suck" on a daily basis. I sit down hesitantly, turn to look at him, blow him a raspberry and calmly return to work like the last two hours didn't happen. Because maybe if I don't believe it happened, I won't think about it every night as I fall asleep as Chris Isaak serenades me with "Wicked Games."

Cue my internal jukebox and sick feeling in my gut.

If Chris and Meatloaf ever collaborated on a song, I wouldn't leave my bedroom as my face would be permanently in a state of wet, sloppy, swollen grotesqueness. Once again, I'm thankful for small miracles.

Leaning forward on the couch, I set my laptop on the coffee table in front of me. On the black screen, I see Ihsan sitting at the kitchen island, clueless that I can see   the over-concerned expression on his face in the reflection. I didn't think so much pain could feel so good.

Chapter 17

BEATRICE

I spend the next few days on phone calls and video chats with various people in the industry introducing myself, re-introducing myself, re-re-introducing myself and I realize that this is a lot harder than I thought. Especially when I need to do most of it laying on my stomach for the first week after "the incident." Now I know why Matthew has all these columns in the spreadsheets. Taking notes with even the smallest details has been my lifesaver. When I finally figure out that using Blaine's name is the golden ticket in Hollywood, suddenly the person on the other line remembers who I am and bends over backwards to help me.

My goal for the day is to find an available recommended stylist and someone to hose and shine Ihsan up. A hair stylist to help me with my hair sounds like something I deserve as well. The recurring bun look is getting old and since I don't have any parents to impress or admin expectations of decency, the thought of doing something risky with my hair crosses my mind.

The comfort nest that I built in the living room has been my spot for the past hour as I check on Ihsan's social media. Resisting going down my own digital rabbit hole has become more of a problem since I started this job. The doorbell rings and Zeki bolts up off the couch and barks like a cat burglar is trying to break into our house. Ihsan jogs up to the front door and pulls apart the glass doors.

"Isa, you sexy thing," I hear Blaine's voice shout loudly from the foyer.

"Oh, thank goodness. I needed a break. This is good timing. I need a line on a good stylist that you use, all of Matthew's are booked up. Maybe if I throw your name around then I can make some headway," I say.

"Oh yes, I'll have Shelley send you a copy of our team list. Isa, I am parched, what have you got?" Blaine puts his arm around Ihsan's shoulders and walks him into the kitchen as if they were old drinking buddies. As he spies my command center I have made from the couch, his face cringes.

"You know this place has an office, right?"

"Yes, but this has direct access to the kitchen," I reply. "I can't throw ice cubes at Ihsan if he's on the other side of the house."

"Are you two fighting already?" he continues the ruse.

"Blaine, he is impossible to work with. I have never met such a prima donna in my life. It's like he's never had a bad hair or ugly face day in his life. He doesn't understand what it's like for the little people."

Ihsan's face slowly turns from surprise to a slight glare as he looks over at Blaine.

"Where did you find this one? She barely knows how to turn that on," he points to the laptop, "and who doesn't know how to walk a dog?"

"*Igrencsin*" I say.

"Is he teaching you cuss words?" Blaine asks.

"No, he doesn't want me to use them against him." I smile and look at Ihsan opening a beer with a bottle opener.

I wiggle my phone at him. "But Google is."

"Okay you two, this is not an audition for a sitcom. I came by to check in and see how things are going."

"Which ex-wife is hunting you?" I ask with a silly smirk.

"Aren't you cute?" Blaine says.

"I am all about cute."

I flip my hair with dramatic flair, looking at Ihsan for a reaction. He rolls his eyes dramatically back into his sockets then laughs as he sees me cringe from my shrubbery injuries that have taken longer than normal to heal.

"Your American online presence is impressive in such a short time. As you know, shooting starts in two weeks and the table read is next week. Isa, your schedule is going to be packed so everything needs to be solidified by then."

"Yeah, I saw that. If anybody can get anything done in two weeks, it's a teacher," I say with pride, reminding him why he hired me.

"So, you're going to have to consult the production team about his look for the movie."

"I know what good-looking is, I'm not blind."

"They may have a specific look they want for him."

"I think gorgeous pretty much covers everything. It's like he fell out of the sexy Sycamore and hit every branch on the way down," I explain.

"Check with them anyway. But she's got you there, Ihsan."

"He squirms every time I call attention to his Adonis-ness. It's nice to know I can make a man do that."

In the back of my head, I hear Matthew's voice say "Oh, you nasty girl."

Blaine laughs as I walk away, overemphasizing my terrible hip and butt waggle and keeping my pained face away from the both of them.

"I wouldn't piss that one off," he gleefully reminds Ihsan as he follows me into the kitchen.

"I'm not sure what teacher attire is like in Texas, but I think you're gonna have to go get yourself some new threads."

I turn around and look at him wryly.

"Late twenties school marm casual isn't good enough for you Hollywood types?"

I mentally peruse my closet and I know my wardrobe was the best that Target, TJ Maxx and Nordstrom Rack clearance has to offer. Even with the less than couture fashion, I felt like I'd put together some cute outfits. However, I've had a few interesting stares from co-workers in the past and I do remember a para educator calling it "What Are You Wearing Wednesdays." In my defense, one of those days was a spirit day. Perhaps Blaine's thinking is correct.

"You're going to have to go out and find some professional outfits for meetings."

I look at both of them with a sultry smile and wave my hand from my head down to my toes.

"Where do you suggest I find outfits to complement this Venus-esque look I've worked so hard for?" Not wanting them to even attempt to answer that question, I continue.

"Nevermind, I'm sure Matthew's Bible has the answer."

Why I thought a gay man had information to find plus size LA couture, I don't know.

"Oh, she'll just flirt her way into a free stylist," Ihsan says casually, moving down to his elbows on the island.

"Excuse me?" I turn and put my palm on my hips.

Ihsan's eyes condense toward his nose while his flattened lips migrate to the right side of his face.

"Flirt?" I say in disbelief of his accusation.

"*Evet*, flirt," he sits on the kitchen stool and takes a large bite of an apple, a bit of juice dripping down his chin.

"I don't flirt. I don't have a flirt game. My flirting wheelhouse is an abandoned shed on the edge of town said to be haunted."

Ihsan and Blaine look at each other, hoping that one of them under-stood me.

Blaine sneaks over to the couch, wishing he had a bowl of popcorn I'm sure.

"You do flirt. You are the captain of the flirting team, and I don't know what a wheelhouse is but I'm sure it is the size of a mansion."

"Explain yourself," I say, crossing my arms.

"Ok, you always compliment the person you are talking to. You mention their appearance or something special about their clothes."

"It's called being nice."

"But don't you want something from them?"

"Well, yeah...but it isn't sexual," I reply, almost in a whine.

"No, but you use body language too."

"Not when I'm on the phone."

"No, you laugh at everything the other person says. Especially when it isn't funny."

"Again, just being friendly."

"Beatrice, you put on more of a show than I do."

"You don't think it's genuine?" I ask as if he doesn't have me pegged.

"Are you?"

"Most of the time. But that isn't flirting. It is more like kissing up."

"It's the same."

"You are telling me, Beatrice Katherina Fredricks, that I am a flirt?"

"A brilliant flirt," he corrects, continuing to casually nibble his fruit.

"If it gets the job done, I don't care if she flashes her shirt," Blaine adds.

"Oh, that's just awesome. So, you're telling me that all these years of being nice so I can get what I want is flirting?" I ask in disbelief.

"Yep."

"Nope. That's what I did all day at school. Ew. And that would mean I flirt with you all day. Ew...ew," I say pointing to Ihsan.

"*Evet*. Wait, that's you being nice?"

"Why did no one explain this to me? I thought people thought of me as Bubbly Beatrice but really I was Flirty Fredricks?"

"*Evet*," he answers loudly, biting off a big chunk and slurping up the juices just to irritate me.

"Excuse me while I go reevaluate my life choices," I say as I leave the room palming my forehead.

"It's worked for you so far," Ihsan belts down the hall, his voice muffled with apple pieces in his cheeks.

"I'm stuck here with God's gift to women, so has it though?" I yell back.

Sitting down firmly on my bedroom couch being careful to keep from scraping my back, I stare at the black TV screen reflecting my image back at me.

He can't be right. Being nice and kind to people and making them feel good about themselves isn't flirting. There is no way. I don't bend over, exposing my cleavage. Ok, maybe once or twice, but not in LA. At least not on purpose. I don't smile unnecessarily when someone is polite to me. I don't overlaugh when it isn't warranted, not consciously.

Oh God.

Unbeknownst to me, I have been flirting my whole life and still end up empty handed. That's just fabulous, absolutely fucking fabulous. Perhaps, I'm subconsciously overcompensating for my fear of ending up in a stinky basement apartment wearing three days worth of coffee down the front of my shirt, surrounded by a sea of cats and a blind dog eating raw ramen noodles out of the package.

me: **I need to ask you a serious question.**

Matthew: **Two lines means you're pregnant.**

me: **Too soon and how do you know this?**

Matthew: **Go ahead.**

me: **Am I a flirt?**

My phone abruptly rings, causing me to juggle it in my hands so it can't escape to the floor.

"What?"

"Am I a flirt? Blaine and Ihsan say I flirt to get what I want."

"Weeell," he draws out his response.

"Matthew!"

"I wouldn't call it flirting but you are...substantially...cordial," he says, proud of his choice of words.

"It's called killing them with kindness."

"Then you've got an exceedingly hefty body count. But, on the other hand you also slaughter with sarcasm."

"That isn't helpful."

"Bee, are you sure they weren't teasing you?"

The thought never crossed my mind. Could the two of them have tele-pathically spawned a plan to get a rise out of me by choosing the one thing I know for a fact I cannot do.

"It's possible they may have been colluding. They think they will pull one over on me. This will not stand."

"Bee, I can hear your gears grinding through the phone. Don't do any-thing you'll regret later."

"Oh, Matthew. You don't know me at all. Besides, you attract more bees with honey than with vinegar."

IHSAN

It still amazes me all the ways Beatrice uses humor to her advantage. I catch myself listening to her phone conversations and feel empathy for the oblivious people on the other end of the call. They have no chance resisting her calculating magnetism. Her natural instincts to put people at ease and her slightly self-deprecating comments compel others to not only help her but deeply desire to do so. I wonder if she knows she practices professional witchcraft.

When Blaine pops in to check-in and calls her cute, she actually accepts the compliment in her roundabout way, verging on mockery. The way she moves her hips to emphasize her thick-set body attracts my attention. Even if she does not fit all the typical criteria for hot, she knows how to move what she's got. For a woman who has such a low opinion of her looks, she has confidence in spades but any attempt at a positive remark is usually returned with a backhanded compliment I have to Google.

Blaine and I should probably have let Beatrice off the hook but it is deli-cious to watch her squirm while accusing her of using her feminine wiles to get what she wants. She gave me that technicolor speech but I'm learning that Beatrice is a symphonic experience. Her depth of emotion and residual feeling of kinship is discordant with any other involvement I've had with a co-worker, let alone a woman. The quality I'm most attracted to in a woman is confidence. The typical physically attractive woman is confident by default, but Beatrice's confidence comes from somewhere more sub-stantial. Whether born with it or it was learned, no one doubts her. She could convince you the grass is red and you would stand on a barrel in the middle of town and announce the fields are crimson. Maybe because she is unaware of her unique power she doesn't wield it maliciously. Beatrice's spell entwines itself in everything she touches, in everyone she touches. It must have been a handy skill in her classroom. I would have loved to see her in her natural habitat.

BEATRICE

I look forward to spending time with my screening partner. Even though his movie choices tend to be on the more award-winning side where mine are more pop culture. My mother and I picked movies that didn't make us think too much. Ihsan's worst choice was a Spielberg movie about a truck stalking a guy in a red car. I will sometimes follow him around the house and stay five feet from him to remind him how he tortured me. Tonight, I'm hoping he's refined his search and selected something more palatable. As I wait, I click around his socials to see what is happening to give me an idea of what I will need to focus on tomorrow. At some point, he's going to have to learn one of those TikTok dances and when he does, it might be the highlight of my life.

Suddenly, what at first I believe is a giant flat brick lands on my lap, dropping my phone to the floor.

"Hey!" I protest.

"Two birds, one stone," he says sitting down in the opposite corner.

"What is this?"

"*Kitap*, a book."

"Are we doing Turkish lessons?"

"No, you're going to read to me," he says, pushing pillows behind his head.

"Isn't that what audiobooks are for?"

"Yes, but you'll fall asleep. You're almost...um, narcotic."

"Narcoleptic," I correct.

"That. If you are the one reading, then you won't fall asleep."

"What is this all about?" I eye him with a significant amount of trepidation.

"I thought we could do something different tonight and I thought reading the same book would be fun."

"Like a celebrity book club?"

He looks at me with a flat gaze.

"Just two people reading the same book."

"I don't see your book."

"I want us to read at the same time in case we want to talk about something. I'm just guessing that a teacher and native English speaker reads faster than I do."

Brandon and Matthew never wanted to read with me. Probably because our taste in books was not only polar opposite but also because I had to save all of my books for the summer and they got to read whenever they wanted. I wanted to escape, and they wanted to learn something. Learning got in the way of a lot of things.

"Do I get to charge by the page or…"

"Beatrice, just two friends reading and talking."

"This is weird."

He stands up and reaches his hand out for mine. Without any clue to what his intention is, I'm a little leery but I take it anyway.

"Then let's make it fun."

He leads me out to the patio and escorts me to a chaise lounge, propping up the back. Turning off the lights of the house and flipping on the string lights that outline the patio, he creates a soft welcoming mood. He brings out a couple blankets from the living room and places one on me and one on himself as he sits on the lounger beside me.

"This is still weird."

"The air is sweet; the lights are dim and not a bug to be seen. Beatrice, it is a beautiful night and I want to enjoy it."

With me?

"Can you lean back yet?" he asks.

I test the waters cautiously and find my back will allow me to take advantage of this lovely night.

"Look at me," I say proudly.

"I knew you could do it."

"Ok, what are we reading?" I say indulging his Mary Poppins fetish. I turn the book over in my hand hoping the cover will give me some clue. "The Alchemist? This isn't a 'do it yourself' meth lab manual is it?"

"Just start reading."

I open the hardback book and immediately tingle at the sound of the small binding cracking. A few sounds on this earth are more beautiful, but not many.

IHSAN

Our movie nights have become a bit routine and tonight I want to do something different. I love books but I don't enjoy reading. Listening to my mom read to us at night was something I always looked forward to and when she missed a night, I had a difficult time falling asleep. It was as if she gave us a template for our dreams and when we finally closed our eyes, all we thought of was the adventures our minds would take us on. Sometimes

Farah, Nadir and I would share what we thought would happen next in the story. Farah was always the creative one and Nadir was confident that he knew where the story was going. Most of the time he was right. When we grew older, we would start a fire in the round pit in our courtyard and I would listen to them read stories as I let my imagination build the setting and characters in my mind. For some reason, I was homesick tonight. It seems silly to be homesick at my age but an ache was building and listening to someone reading a book is the only relief I could think of.

When Beatrice isn't harping on me her voice is pleasant and keeps me entertained. It only makes sense to ask her to read to me. I hope she believes my excuse for not having a novel of my own to follow along. I want to enjoy the words, not wound them.

After giving her something to snuggle, which she seems to always need, I create a mood with the lighting. When I walk out to where I plan to sit, I notice how the small bulbs shine bright enough to give her face a gentle glow, turning her eyes almost sage. I start to open my mouth to tell her but quickly shut it, knowing I'd only receive even more scorn. Pulling the blanket over my legs, I prepare myself for what I'm hoping will be at least thirty minutes of blissful literary escape.

She hadn't even finished the first few pages before she threw in her own commentary.

"Well, now I can't call you Narcissus anymore. This Paulo guy ruined a perfectly good nickname."

"Beatrice, just read. We can talk about it later."

"But I'll forget my witty responses."

"You are killing the vibe."

"Ok. I'll stop. That was a pretty damn good introduction. You might have a winner here."

As she presses on, I'm finding it hard to concentrate on the words of the story because Beatrice's precise delivery of the script is captivating. For as much as she protests, she knows how to draw me in. The sweet smell of jasmine and the slight shaking of the leaves from the bushes behind us transports me away. Away from this hectic life, the residual heartache, and the constant pressure to perform. Being in the moment is rare and Beatrice, a rarity herself, doesn't fail to perform.

"Well, sh...it," she says with that twinge of drawl.

I sit up slightly in confusion.

"Neh?"

"This book is sick. You look good, you smell good, you sound good and now I know you think good too. We need to get you a woman before I jump your bones."

My eyes grow wide as she marks where she stopped after an hour of entertaining me and drops the book at my feet, wrapping her blanket around her arm and walking into the house. I follow not far behind, closing up the house behind her.

"Don't look so shocked. It's after dark, you know I turn."

She may transform into a dangerous creature some nights when she is starved for sleep, but she has never said anything so forward. Her humor is blunt, obvious and on point, and honestly sorely needed.

"We should do this more often," she says in a deep, sultry voice.

"I told you you're a flirt," I say, knowing full well one of the couch pillows is bound for my head.

"Ok, I see your point."

Ihsan for the win.

Chapter 18

B EATRICE

The calendar for the next couple weeks still needs tweaking. Several emails from various companies, casting agents, studios, and charities are on today's docket. As my eyes skim down the inbox, I search for particularly important names and always look for Blaine's agency. With my short stature, I often sit on my calf to bring me up to a more productive level or at least to where my boobs are an inch above the working surface. This morning it's the breakfast nook. Looking intently at the screen, I barely notice Ihsan setting down a glass of ice water and pulling up a chair next to me. The scent of him wafts up into my nostrils, tiny hairs all standing at attention.

"My checklist for today is to set aside time for script study, update the calendar around your newly booked TV interviews and check out some charities," I say, trying to distract myself from that highly infectious scent. "I've transferred Matthew's information into a more functional document for our needs. Each category has its own tab and is organized according to what is most likely to be used. It includes columns for all contact information, socials, passwords, last time contacted and a column for notes. Matthew likes to write things that will help remember something personal about who he talked to. It's what makes him such a good brown-noser. I added a column for links for any documents, pictures, screenshots, or scans that might need to be referenced too."

Ihsan listens intently, sipping his coffee and nodding. I click around and point to tabs that he might need to access on his own. I push the laptop more toward the middle of the table and lean towards him. For a brief moment, I look down at my shirt and realize I've got some serious award-winning cleavage screaming for attention.

Okay, ladies, I hear ya.

"My 'If I die' folder. So if something happens to me, you would still be able to function."

As he looks over the screen with my fingers pointing in various places, he glances at his coffee again. Out of the corner of my eye, I spy him slyly taking a peek at the ladies. Sometimes there are little victories that you need to celebrate. I can't keep the smile from my face.

Why not give him a little bit more?

Stretching over into his personal space, I reach for a pencil next to him. Sometimes I can't help myself. My evil streak is something that I'm proud of. It's how I coped with all the small, irritating things when I was teaching. Like providing golf pencils without erasers when students didn't bring some of their own. I try to play it off but sometimes, when my patience is empty, I can be vicious.

"We also still need to find something for all of this," I say, waving my hand in front of his face and torso. "I can't deal with this. We need to include a clothing stylist on team Ihsan and someone who knows what to do with your hair."

I reach over and pull a few strands of hair to emphasize my point. He is so, so close. Again, I take the opportunity to take a deep breath of his scent. His signature citrusy, earthy, spicy almost incense fragrance transports me off this mortal plane for a millisecond. After not being able to take it anymore, I look him straight in the eyes.

"What is that scent that makes you smell so good? Is that your natural aroma? Screw acting, we need to bottle that up."

"Oud."

"You mean like the alien that holds their brains in their hands?"

He looks at me and it's like he doesn't understand English all of a sudden.

"On Doctor Who there is an alien called an 'Ood'. And that would be gross if you were wearing 'Ood.'"

"*Yok, yok, yok!* It is also called agarwood. It's already bottled up."

"Well, it's giving me some lady wood. I can't stand being so close to you right now, it's too much."

"What are you talking about?"

"There are some animals that give off pheromones to attract the opposite sex. It's like you're wearing your own brand of pheromone. I can't sit this close, move over," I command as I try to push the anchored chair.

His mischievous look concerns me. I glare back at him, feeling a little sassy pants myself.

"It's simply not nice. In fact, it is incredibly unfair, cruel even for someone to be walking around looking like you, sounding like you and smelling like you. You don't give any other guys in the city a chance. But I suppose that's why you're here. I think the picture of the alien holding their brain will help counteract the effects of your oud perfume."

He pulls the laptop over to himself.

"How do you spell oooood?"

"Oh, oh, dee," I say slowly as he types it into the search engine.

"I do not believe I want to look like that." His face compresses in on itself.

"Right?! So, if someone asks you what scent you are, do not say oud. Agarwood or whatever else you come up with but don't say ood."

Curious about the bottled stuff, I type a different spelling into the search engine.

"It's expensive being you! This stuff costs more than my car payment." My face in no way masks my slight disgust at the price of his scent. At least I know that there won't be many people that smell like him.

I fall off the chair slightly as my calf has fallen asleep.

"Hey, so I was clicking around on YouTube and saw a program called Hollywood Reporter and I looked through Matthew's Bible and found a contact that knows someone who works for that show. Why not shoot for the moon? Maybe we can get some roundtables on actors from foreign countries. But I also watched some of your interviews. You can be a bit harsh to the host."

Ihsan looks at me with my favorite confused face.

"No really, you cut off one host and told them that you were doing exactly what they asked you to do. That seemed weird and awkward. I need you to kiss up and be charming pants, Mr. Fancy pants."

"Who is this 'charming pants'?" he asks as if he has been confused for a while.

"Sometimes, I can't tell if you're serious or trying to be funny. You already don't laugh at half the jokes I make."

"No, I think you are funny."

"Funny looking," I tease.

"Why do you do that?"

"Do what?"

"Say mean things about yourself."

"I'm just trying to keep the mood light and funny. It's leftover from high school, I guess. I make fun of myself before someone else does."

"I don't like it."

"I'm just joking."

"I don't like it."

I roll my eyes and quickly change the subject so as not to endure the "stop putting yourself down" talk from yet another clueless technicolor.

"I was thinking about doing something fun for the kids, but I wanted to run it by you first. My mom used to do an exotic fruit tasting with her students every year."

"That sounds fun."

"Of course, it is. I'm Ms. Smarty Fun Pants," I say, straightening my posture and feeling proud of myself. "I'm gonna have to really work some contacts but I'll see what I can do. Some fruits may be difficult to get my hands on. I may have to kiss up to some farmers."

"Then wear that shirt," he says. My eyes grow wider involuntarily.

"Ihsan, what has happened to your manners?" I push his shoulder hard, knowing that he knew exactly what he did.

"You put them out there."

"I can't be held accountable! They have a mind of their own."

Ihsan leans back in his chair, holds his belly, and laughs as his whole body shakes. Leaning against the kitchen counter, I laugh at him laughing at me. I thought his shoulder smolder was his most attractive look but seeing his face light up with happiness is by far the best he's ever looked, and I caused that. It makes me feel so much joy but then there's always that shadow of pain when the laughter dies down.

"Is it a good time to run some lines for an audition with me?" he asks, holding up a thick script and walking over to the couch.

"Sure, am I the bad guy or the good guy?"

"I'm the good guy, which makes you bad."

Oh, yes I am.

"In this scene, you are my uncle and you've been hiding a secret from me. You know you can't talk about any of this, right?"

"I'm a diaper," I say assuredly.

"*Neh*?" His head tilts like Zeki. He knows how much that makes me laugh.

"You know, diapers don't leak."

"Ah, add that to our list," he says.

He takes my shoulders and sets me in the corner of the couch and moves the wood and resin coffee monolith table over by the fireplace. My suspicion of Superman DNA is confirmed by how easily he is able to rearrange the living room. He unfolds the script and finds the page he wants to rehearse and hands it over to me. Several highlights and strange markings distract me from the text on the page, but I've deciphered penmanship that resembles early hieroglyphs rather than modern English letters before.

"Do you want me to do a man's voice or anything?"

"No, just read it over and try to say the lines with sincerity."

"So, the exact opposite of me," I smile.

He turns away from me, shaking out his hands and rolling his head around his shoulders as I read over the page.

"Ok, I think I have it."

"Go ahead," he says.

I clear my throat a little because it seems like the professional thing to do.

"Kerem, what are you doing here? I thought you were in Bozcaada," I read aloud but decide that I can remember the text and actually look at him.

"Really *Mehmet-amce*, you always know where I am." His tone is accusatory with a hint of anger.

"Kerem, I'm not quite sure what you are alluding to."

"I know you are tracking me," he says, the growing anger in his voice peeking through.

"That is ridi—" I start but he quickly turns toward me, pointing outside.

"I see your men in cars parked outside, hiding around corners, sitting in restaurants, I am not oblivious," he says, strutting around the room, flailing his arms about.

"It is for your protection," I say, trying to sound empathetic.

"What about my phone? I know you've been listening. How does that protect me?"

I take note that he is improving his "th" and "w" sounds.

"Kerem, there is so much you don't know."

"Oh, I know plenty, Uncle. I've been listening to you, too."

I turn the page; I hadn't read this far, and the scene is becoming very intriguing.

"What?!" I say angrily, since I'm thinking Uncle Mehmet would not like that one bit.

"Oh yes, Uncle." His face grows redder. "Or should I call you 'brother'?"

I gasp out loud, both as Uncle Mehmet and as Beatrice.

"All this time you've lied to me." The anger in his voice and body starts to boil over as the veins become more visible along the sides of his neck. He moves toward me with heavy steps.

"How many others know? Is Dephne even my sister?" His arms open wide as his eyes become larger. "Your manipulation of me and my daughter is over. You'll never see either of us again."

His angry strides feel threatening as he comes closer. He puts his hands on either side of my head on the back and side of the couch. The rage in his eyes burrows a hole into my brain. His lips stretch across his teeth, the hate seething with a fine mist of saliva spraying into my face as the final words erupt from his crimson mask.

"You are dead to me. Dead!"

My heart races with every syllable, air no longer filling my lungs, my mouth is frozen open. He may be acting but I am feeling real fear. He pushes himself upright and walks out of the living room as part of the scene. Nothing in my body is listening to my brain. I'm stuck in the corner of the couch.

"Beatrice," Ihsan's voice calls to me from a mile away.

"Beatrice!" His hand on my shoulder shakes me back to earth.

My lungs suck in a huge breath, and I look around as if my soul returned to my physical body. My eyes blink rapidly looking for his face.

"Holy sh...it, Ihsan. I...um...damn."

My eyes are wet and a tear threatens to fall.

"Are you ok?"

"I don't think so," I pause, trying to think of a way to explain what is happening to me. "You are...amazing." Suddenly, I realize that every part of my body is tingling. Prickles are forming every inch of my skin including places on my chest I have never felt before. To say this man has talent is like saying the Beatles were a good band.

What the eff...fuck was that?

"I need to um...cool down I think," I push myself off the couch and quickly step to the kitchen. With the faucet on the coldest setting, I fill my cupped hands and splash my face. Rubbing a cold hand to the back of my neck then past my collar bones, almost sliding my fingers between my breasts.

"Beatrice...are you?"

"Ihsan, just shut up!" I point my finger in the air in warning.

His face returns to a close to normal shade but with him stifling back a small laugh, the red makes a comeback.

"Really?!" he asks in disbelief.

He can't hold his amusement back anymore, his hand covering the beautiful smile he's trying to hide.

"How did I know this was going to happen?" I fan my hand in front of my face. "Ridiculously gorgeous man two inches from my face breathing hot air onto my skin. For a second, I forgot who you were. I warned you about lady wood," I try to explain by adding more cool water to my skin.

He takes a few steps toward the kitchen, not knowing how serious the situation is.

"Do not take another step!" I take the dish brush from the side of the kitchen sink.

"Go over there and pick your nose or something else gross." I point the long cleaning utensil at the other side of the living room.

"*Neh*?"

"To counteract whatever you just did, freaking Turkish sorcerer."

Hell yeah, he is.

Ihsan walks over to the fireplace and leans his back against the bricks trying hard to regain a straight face, unsuccessfully. That didn't help since no matter what he does, his sexual aura permeates everything, but proximity seems to affect my current situation.

I take my phone and desperately look at my music app, flipping through classical composers.

Bolero-nope, Mars-nope, Wagner-winner! Ride of the Valkyrie should do it.

"I'm going to go outside and have a moment. If you breathe one word of this to anyone or reference it to me in any way, my resignation letter will be on your desk before you can flex your pecs," I say, standing in front of the large glass doors. As I walk toward the chaise lounges, I can hear Ihsan laughing, sweeping away any dignity I attempt to retain.

IHSAN

Any red-blooded male would look. I do not apologize for peeking at Beatrice's large breasts, and I am actually proud of her that she showed them off a little. When she complains about my cologne, I want her to bury her head in my neck. I want to tell her that whatever scent she is wearing revs my engine up as well. It's a clean, slightly floral scent that reminds me of walking through the clothes hanging to dry in the courtyard of my childhood house. She smells like home.

I almost wish someone would smack her upside the head to knock some sense into her when she makes comments about her looks. There are men out there that are attracted to women like her but either she steered clear of where she might find them, or she didn't see them at all because of her tunnel vision with Brandon. Even if she did, no one will ever measure up to Brandon. From the moment I saw him on a tiny screen, I could see why she fell for him. He seems shorter than I am but classically handsome with everything proportional to fit the mold of an attractive man. I'm not sure if Beatrice had an influence on his sense of humor but he has charisma for sure. Sarah is absolutely gorgeous, making them a very attractive couple. I can see why Beatrice set them up, but I can also see why it broke her. In finding someone worthy of him, she cemented how little he thought of her.

Watching Beatrice's face flush bright pink as I lean over and stare her down is quite possibly one of the best moments of my life. Actors want to elicit emotional responses from their audience but when you can cause a physical reaction you know you've reached them on a deeper, carnal level. To actually turn her on is a fabulous bonus but I didn't think it would make her angry. After thinking about it more I realize she isn't angry, she's embarrassed. The state of her after escaping from the couch will be etched in my memory for the rest of my days. I rarely get to witness the reactions of my audience in real time, and it is absolutely thrilling. Her rosy skin transforming into a wine color before my eyes is at first concerning because she isn't breathing but when the light returns to her eyes, her expression is...intoxicating.

I let her sit outside alone for a good ten minutes before I attempt to make contact with her. Who knows what damage she could have done with a dish brush.

"So, Beatrice," I approach slowly, being careful that my movements are non-threatening. "All clear?"

"Approach with caution," her voice a low rumble causing a bit of a stir in my belly.

"I'm sorry for laughing at you. I've just never seen you like that." I sit down next to her knees in the little room she's given me on the chaise.

"It's an unexplained phenomenon, like the Northern Lights."

"Those are actually caused by particles smashed into gasses in the upper atmosphere," I say before I can stop myself.

"Ok, maybe NOT like the Northern Lights."

"But just as beautiful."

Beatrice's cheek immediately floods with red and pink dots. She grabs onto her face as a look of horror locks into her eyes and then a flurry of smacks and pushes descend upon me as punishment.

"You can't go around saying sh...it like that," she yells, or at least that is what I think she yells as I continue to laugh as her small, not so delicate hands pummel my arms, shoulders and upper back.

"*Tamam, tamam*, okay. I've learned my lesson. No more random facts." I put up my hands hoping she understands the international sign for surrender.

"You are grounded until you think about what you've done," she says, putting her arms over her chest and crisscrossing them, squishing them up right where I like them.

Oh, I will think a lot about what I've done.

Chapter 19

BEATRICE

From the other side of the tinted glass, I see two sets of squashed palms pushing each other out of the way for attention, their tiny knocks getting more aggressive the longer it takes Ihsan to let them in.

Now it's one thing to be gorgeous, another thing to be gorgeous and marry gorgeous. It's quite another thing to have gorgeous offspring. I can't believe they let these little jewels out in the open.

Of course, the math adds up; two beautiful people equals two beautiful babies. Duh. I should have known better. I am a math teacher, well I was a math teacher.

Behind the two small figures is a rather tall slight hourglass figure. Ihsan walks sternly to the door and pretends that he doesn't know who could possibly be there. Of course, he's a damn adorable father too. He has officially strummed every heartstring the little invisible cupid was playing above my head. The feeling I didn't expect was longing for paternal attention or perhaps it was jealousy.

I stay in the living room and let them have their perfect, beautiful family moment. The little green monster could not feel more real. The two Tasmanian love devils push through the door and take Ihsan down to the tile floor. Zeki barks relentlessly in reaction to all the excited energy. My attention is drawn up to the Turkish goddess that strolls silently through the door. Her perfectly wavy chestnut hair falls just below her shoulders which frames her glowing olive skin. Her face looks completely natural, as if she was born with perfect make up. She probably had a make-up artist on call. The feeling of complete inadequacy overwhelms me as I wait for the mob to settle down.

I'm not worthy to breathe the same air as this family.

Alone in the living room, I stand waiting to be noticed but don't want to interrupt. The human ball of arms, legs and laughter finally calms down and when Ihsan is able to get to his feet, he kisses the woman on both cheeks, the little ones still grabbing at his chest. Zeki tries to nudge his head in between them in all the excitement but the tall woman pushes him away. Ihsan turns towards me and waves at me to come closer. Walking with trepidation, I take a few steps into the foyer. Ihsan tries to keep his balance as his children have taken up purchase on each side of him, pushing and pulling him as if he has ropes tied to strategic parts of his body.

"Gül, this is Beatrice my...boss," he smiles.

"His bossy personal assistant," I correct.

I offer my hand out and with a long sweeping movement, she takes it, shaking it slightly. For some reason I feel like I should kiss her hand and bow, but I resist.

"We've spoken on the phone. It's nice to finally meet you. Thank you for all the information you gave me on Ihsan. He's much more manageable now."

I look at her and wink. She picks up on my ploy and winks back.

"Happy to help."

Her accent seems more natural and her voice more lyrical than Ihsan's.

I bend down a little to greet the kids and stick out my hand. The little girl approaches me first.

"You must be Tariq," I say, smiling.

She laughs and corrects me.

"I'm Zeyva."

The little boy jumps out from behind Ihsan's backside.

"I'm Tariq," he yells, very close to my face.

We may need a conversation about personal space.

"Oh, I hope I remember that. You two will have to help me. Have you been to America before?"

"*Yok,*" they say together.

"Does it look different from home?" For the next couple minutes, they chit chat and argue like siblings do, each trying to be smarter than the other. I am a glutton for punishment, even with his children.

"How would you like to see where you are sleeping? Your da...I mean *baba* can bring your bags."

I take them each by their tiny energetic hands and walk them down the hallway as if I'm the California version of Nanny McPhee.

"Let's go, Lurch!" I say over my shoulder.

As we walk by, I point out my room and then I turn right and walk them past the office to the other smaller guest room.

"If you guys want to share, I thought we could make a fort and it will be like camping inside!" They both look at me a little strangely as if I was speaking in tongues.

"Trust me, you'll love it."

Ihsan appears at the door, carrying all of their bags like a pack mule. Gül walks, more like floats, behind like Morticia.

How do her shoes not make any noise?

Making a big deal out of putting all the luggage down, Ihsan yells "Let's go see the pool!" as he runs down the hallway, the two little ones running clumsily behind him.

"All doors for the backyard are locked so they can't get to the pool. And we've activated the proximity alarm. Poor Zeki didn't like that one bit."

Gül looks at me kindly. "You read my mind."

"It's safety first around here." I laugh a little to myself.

My phone suddenly chimes with a text. Removing it from my pocket, I look at the words, thankful for an out.

"I'll be in the office if you all need something," I say, walking down the hall while texting a lead on a TV appearance. Trying to compose small talk is much harder with adults when children are around so I'm glad for the interruption.

Sitting down in the red chair I have claimed as mine, I try to think of any reason why this family is no longer intact. Ihsan's explanation left a lot of questions. They both seem to love their children so much and still respect each other. If they can't make it work, I don't know how anyone expects any of us lower beings to have a chance. Seeing the way Ihsan held his children and let them love on him makes my heart not only swell but makes the hole that much more obvious. I never wished I had a different father. Mine, from what I gathered, was perfect. I do wish I knew him the way Zeyva and Tariq know theirs. Thoughts of my dad were often fleeting but boy did they pack a punch when they snuck into my consciousness.

The scene from the kitchen was sickly sweet and since jealousy and I are old friends, I keep to the office until I hear a huge eruption of laughter. Not one for missing a good joke, I decide it's time to leave the bat cave and return to our guests. As I enter the kitchen, I see them crowded around Ihsan's phone.

"I looked up 'Lurch'," Ihsan scowls at me while Gül laughs into her long-fingered hands.

"Well, you both are tall and talk funny," I say innocently.

"And they both look funny, too," Zeyva adds with the most adorable accent. I look at her in shock. She's scoring big points with me.

"Your English is perfect," I say to Zeyva.

Ihsan lunges at Zeyva for the expected tickle revenge.

Watching them interact with each other makes my heart warm and break at the same time. My mom became morose whenever I would try to talk about my dad. Her heart was still broken after so many years. So many kids didn't have dads around growing up that it didn't seem strange to me. What was strange was I knew my dad loved me and I knew he loved my mom, but he just wasn't there.

Breaking up the cutest Turkish Hallmark commercial ever, I clear my throat, partly to get their attention but also to stave off the bit of emotion about to break the surface.

"Gül, could I talk to you for a second? Don't worry, Pops, it's nothing about you."

"Sure," she answers with that damn sultry accent. We sit at the round breakfast nook table so I can bring her in on my plan.

"I know we've only talked on the phone, and I hope you don't think I'm too forward but you seem to have your fashion act together, and I need a little help. Apparently, Blaine thinks I'm memorable in the wrong way."

I look at her pleadingly with my best large anime eyes.

"I do not know what would help me stand out and look good on me in this new position. I'm a bit nervous because my first concern has always been comforting so my instincts are all off," I continue.

Her eyes light up more than they already are.

"Not too forward at all. I will be very happy to help."

I let out a huge audible sigh of relief. I knew it was a risk asking her after just meeting her in the flesh but maybe this is a way we can bond and get to know each other. We've been texting a bit but mostly about the kids. I have found that if you allow people to help you using their strengths, they are more than amenable and I need doctorate level of support.

She makes eye contact with Ihsan and glances over at the kids with a "could you please" expression.

"But they are MONSTERS!" he growls, raising his hands like claws. They both shriek and run into the living room with werewolf dad stalking them all the way.

"I also have another small thing," I say sheepishly, hoping I'm not asking too much. "I have a wedding and I need to pick the dress. I've always loved this one specific dress from a movie."

I pull up a few screenshots I've saved on my phone.

"The problem is, it doesn't really exist like a pattern or anything. I'm not sure where to start."

"Hmmm, I can help with clothes for you easily but let me think about the wedding dress."

"No, I'm not getting married," I laugh way too hard at her innocent mistake. "I'm the Maid of Honor."

"Oooh. That makes more sense with the color."

I'm glad she clarified about the color and not because she thought that me getting married made little sense.

She points to the laptop. "May I?"

"Yes, please," I say excitedly and push the laptop toward her.

Her eyes scan the screen and her fingers type eagerly over the keyboard. It's like watching Data on an Enterprise console. Watching her work is mesmerizing.

"Here is your look board."

"I know you are speaking English but I'm not sure those words go together."

She turns the screen around, showing me large thumbnails of several outfits complete with shoes, scarves, purses and even jewelry.

"Wow, I can't. Wow."

"You like these?"

"I love them! That took you less than five minutes. Daaaayum."

The board is filled with smart looking suits and separates to dresses that she has selected that will accentuate my neckline and slightly muscular calves. For some reason my calves have always looked fit. More than likely buffed up from walking up and down those stairs in the piano practice room building in college.

She rubs her curved fist over her heart, the international sign of badassery.

Now that I have a look board I can sync it to my phone and impress my friends and neighbors. Matthew would be so proud of me. This might actually be fun.

"Text me this dress. I will find it for you."

I have a Jedi of curated clothing on my team. The burden of having to handle Ihsan's career and trying to get my own act together feels significantly lightened. I desperately want to throw my fists and my arms in the air but this is not the time to out myself as a complete twit.

The rest of the afternoon I spend trying to fill the carts for several online stores with the same styles that Gül had selected. I think I'll treat Matthew to a curvaceous fashion show once the clothes arrive.

The echoes of splashing and screaming emanate from the pool patio as "The Fabulous Family" enjoy the afternoon sun. Standing, holding my closed laptop just before the giant windows leading to the outside, I take a moment to enjoy the scene before me. My eyes start to well up both from seeing something so beautiful and from the emptiness in my life. I have stifled this feeling so many times. But this time, it feels deeper. Before my great life change, it was easy to quell the gut punch that accompanied the tears. I would consume my time in schoolwork, spending time researching new classroom management techniques and strategies or hours on Pinterest before the feeling consumed me. Now I live with the source twenty-four seven with few chances for respite. I knew I wasn't prepared for this job, but I didn't realize there would be all this emotional crap too.

I turn away and wipe the tears the best I can.

"Beatrice!" I hear Ihsan calling me from the pool.

"What!" I call back in the style of Miracle Max's wife. I'm glad he gets my humor otherwise that would have sounded super bitchy. I continue to wipe my sadness from my cheeks before I am ready to face the Fab Four. I walk out with deliberate steps, hoping my false confidence will distract them from my red face.

"Gül, could you look at my picks on the tabs? Just delete the items you don't like. I trust you but I will out you as my stylist if these fashionistas give me the evil eye."

She knows exactly what I'm talking about.

I pass the laptop to her and she accepts it eagerly as I invite her into her happy place.

"Come in with us," Ihsan says, laughing and splashing with the littles.

My first instinct is to laugh out loud at the ridiculousness of that request. If he thinks I am going to put on a bathing suit and trounce around with the first family of Olympus, he has less of a clue than I thought.

"I have too much to do."

I'd hoped Gül would be quicker, but she seems to really be studying my choices. I didn't think I would have that much to scrutinize.

"I'm not quite healed up and I'm already behind on RSVPs."

The amount of kissing up, brown nosing and general feigned interest in the most mundane things I've done in the past few weeks has made me realize how much of my soft teaching skills I retained. Ihsan, via me, procured invitations to a few Hollywood parties, a fashion show for a designer that Gül knows, and a formal dinner at the Turkish embassy.

The formal dinner I am particularly proud of because I used a few Turkish words I knew to open a dialogue with the embassy. It's in celebration of some meeting with some guy of some foreign country. I was so happy to have secured an invitation that I didn't listen to the rest of the details of the event. But Caan is my new best friend after I said that I was the personal assistant to *the* Ihsan Zorlu. I'm sure he wouldn't mind having another conversation considering he mentioned that he followed both Ihsan and Zeki.

"Oh, come on, you need a break," he urges.

"Seriously, I have your life to run. There are a lot of spinning plates. Oh ouch, my back," I finish with just the right amount of fake whine.

Just in time, Gül delicately passes me the laptop.

"All done for you."

"Thanks so much." I take the laptop from her and move my legs as quickly as I can without an obvious full out run through the giant glass doors. Deciding to work in the actual office will limit Ihsan's ability to include me in activities that would expose more than fifty percent of my skin to the innocent public, blinding them in the process.

Getting settled into my big red chair, I check out what adjustments Gül has made to my selections. I click on the 'orders' button and see she's added accessories, but she didn't delete my choices. Clicking on the shipping information, I notice that my credit card information isn't right. I click around and it looks like Gül has not only paid for expedited shipping, but she has paid for the whole order. All the other tabs from stores I had filled carts had the same shipping and payment information. Taking a big breath and sitting back in the chair I let my shoulders fall.

Gül is a sly one. I know it's futile to resist her generosity and they are kajillionaires so I'm not going to make a big deal out of it and make everyone uncomfortable. Somehow, I will show my gratitude, but I have no immediate ideas. I still don't understand how these two are not together.

Is "shipping" exes allowed?

I still need to iron out the logistical details for all the events I spent the past week procuring. The next hour I book cars, drivers, stylists, and update social media postings with the standard five hashtags. This week has been kind of lean on posts, so I take my phone and click on the camera app and head out to the pool to get a few shots. Stopping at the entrance to the pool patio I take a few pictures of Gül on the chaise lounge and Ihsan in the pool playing games with Zeyva and Tariq. As I'm looking through the screen on the phone, Ihsan rises out of the water like Bo Derek, in slow motion even. The water is like a glaze dripping down a tattooed muscle donut. He is completely edible. I have seen him shirtless on one of his dramas, but he must be hitting the gym more than I know. He has that inguinal crease going on in a serious way right above the droopy waistband of his suit. Thanks to Matthew I know that part of the male torso that makes that "V" shape right above his waistline. The definition of a "Did you hear that?" moment. Almost on creeper instinct, I change the setting to video and press record. The phone falls slightly as I feel myself mesmerized by the scene before me. Returning the phone upright to fix the shot, I pray I can edit what I just shot while paralyzed with lust.

I might as well make the best of the situation. The kids are trying to knock each other off their giant pink pool floaties as I approach. Noticing my filming, Ihsan walks over to me, drying his torso and head with a beach towel.

"Is it cool to film the kids?" I say, trying to shake off his influence over my body temperature. He nods back and I press the record button.

"What's going on today?" I prompt him.

He turns on his charm and smiles at my phone camera.

"Gül has brought my two beautiful children for a visit, and we are enjoying the gorgeous day in the pool. It would be a shame to not take advantage of the weather today." He outstretches his arms to the sky as if thanking the sun god for granting his request. "We have the flamingo war going on to give us parents a break. Even Zeki wants in on it."

Zeki took up a position on the sun shelf area of the pool, not understanding the kids weren't exactly getting attacked by enormous neon birds.

Ihsan doesn't refer to Gül as anything other than her first name. Which means she might possibly be the Cher of Türkiye, Cherkiye if you will. I am not quite sure what to make of that snippet of information, so I file it away in the back of my brain marked "random info on Ihsan."

Putting the phone in my pocket, I quickly turn away from the pool party and try to make my getaway.

"Beatrice!" Ihsan calls out.

I can feel my face and shoulders cringe. Why does he insist on torturing me?

"You need something?" I turn around, flashing my biggest smile.

He rolls his eyes and walks towards me. I make a concerted effort to not drool with each step he takes. He is unadulterated, hand pulled gourmet eye candy.

"I would like to barbeque tonight for dinner. Can you put an order in for groceries?"

"Birds or bovine?" I ask.

He looks at me quizzically.

"Chicken or beef?"

"Both," he smiles.

"Is there anything specific you want? Are we doing an American barbecue or Turkish style?"

"Let's do an American barbecue, you pick the food."

I figure charring meat is the same all over the world.

"Are there any special requests from you, Gül?" I ask, thinking that she will probably be grazing on wheat grass.

"No, I'm actually going to leave in a few minutes for the hotel. This is a holiday for me too."

IHSAN

For the sake of my children, I will never show them how much I loathe this woman. Gül may be a model but she has been acting her whole life. I greet her with the traditional kiss of her cheeks but even brushing up against her churns my stomach. Luckily Zeyva and Tariq provide a valid distraction and I am able to focus all my attention on them. Beatrice doesn't need to know why or how it ended with Gül and I plan on keeping it that way. We worked very hard to keep everything out of the press and the fact that I haven't had a serious relationship since Gül has the internet trolls waiting to pounce on any rumor or picture. The cost of fame is privacy.

me: **Gül is here.**

Farah: **Unclench your fists.**

me: **I'm handling it better.**

Farah: **That's because Z and T are there.**

me: **Beatrice is helping too. I won't be left alone in the same room with her.**

Farah: **That's smart.**

me: **I'd probably throw up and then Beatrice will get out the first aid kit and you can guess where she will insist on sticking the thermometer.**

Farah: **She's not Asli, that's for sure.**

me: **She is unique.**

Farah: **Exactly what you need.**

me: *Sou, abla.*

Just like everyone else, Beatrice has charmed my children as well. Watching how they take to her warms my heart. Zeyva is normally stand off-ish with strangers, but Beatrice knocked down that wall fairly quickly. It's nice to see my little girl accepting another woman so easily. Tariq loves everyone so I'm not as worried about him.

Even though exposing Beatrice to Gül is the last thing I want, she does really know fashion and Beatrice needs her help or at least she thinks she does. Gül has no problem throwing around money but we both have been successful, so when she wants to treat Beatrice to some new clothes, it doesn't surprise me. She will do right by Beatrice, even if she didn't do right by me.

Since I expect Beatrice and my children to spend a significant amount of time together while they are here, I thought it would only be right to invite her to go swimming. And there it is, her fear. It isn't that she's afraid of me seeing her in a bathing suit, it's the fear that I would judge her. Her outward persona exudes strength but her fear of getting hurt drives her decisions no matter how small. I wish I could tell her I understand. I have been forced to face fear head on in my home in Türkiye and that isn't something you can just tell someone stop feeling. But I won't let her get off easy.

Chapter 20

BEATRICE

It's the kids, Ihsan, and me, for dinner; my cute little borrowed family. I get on the phone with a butcher, grocery store, and deli that I spied a few times driving around. All are very helpful in helping procure the ingredients for a perfect all-American BBQ. I plan for everything to be delivered within two hours. In that time, Ihsan checks out the grill, making sure it's clean, functional and fueled up. I'm happy that he is as concerned as I am about losing eyebrows to random flames

"Send me pictures when you get all the clothes. I want to see," Gül says.

"Don't worry, Matthew will insist on a fashion show. I can't thank you enough. It's going to save me so much time."

"I will find the other dress."

"Even if we can just get a pattern, that would work."

Hugging Gül is more like hugging a fat broomstick rather than a thin human. She whisps out the door as if the wind picked her up and helped her into her waiting car.

I don't even know when this wedding is but the only way I've found to cope is to become numb to the feelings and only focus on what needs to be done. I want to be happy for two of my dearest friends, but this is going to be the ultimate exercise in emotional control. I should probably figure out this therapist situation and see if I can get some kind of medication, otherwise the drunk Maid of Honor will be the featured entertainment at the reception. I'm hoping we plan plenty of activities before the wedding to distract me from the main event.

While we are collecting the groceries from the foyer, I tell Ihsan of the invitation to the embassy dinner I scored. I figure the more we can get him in the limelight, the better. Matthew and I will have to strategize about ways to get him a suitable date.

"I can't wait to dress you up and send you out like a debutante. My personal life size Mediterranean Ken doll. Don't tell people I said that last part, it sounds super bad."

"No life size dolls for you," he smiles at me but I'm not sure he understood the subtext of my last comment.

We start separating the vegetables and put the salads in the refrigerator. Setting up the rest of the sides, I remember I included chips because there is no barbecue without plain salted potato chips. The butcher includes some marinated meats as well. During the time the kids and I were setting up all the cold items in the fridge, Ihsan had the grill blazing. We had found the grilling utensils under the island, so he was armed and ready. He dressed himself in dry clothes consisting of a t-shirt, cargo shorts and flip flops. I could easily mistake him for a seasoned barbecue pit veteran. The debate over which is hotter, the grill or Ihsan rambles in my brain. I feel a little Holly Homemaker walking out with a plate of raw meat to him. Maybe I should have ordered an apron with a strawberry motif to complete the All-American BBQ experience.

"Remember, grilled not charred."

"Charred, got it."

I deserve that.

While he is grilling up the meat, the kids and I make fruit kebabs accompanied by a honey and yogurt dip, a Turkish recipe I scouted online for a taste of home. At least I know the kids would eat it and I'm curious about Turkish cuisine. Why not start there? I should have known better than to give siblings sharp sticks. After focusing the two back on their job of spearing fruit instead of each other, I set about laying out the quintessential American BBQ side dishes: potato salad, broccoli salad and corn on the cob. To compliment the chicken and beef, I also lay out sweet Hawaiian dinner rolls so the islands are represented.

I head outside to check out the meat situation with a clean plate. The heat of the grill gives Ihsan a sweaty brow as he concentrates on the perfect done-ness of the meat. Droplets trickle down his face as he tries to keep them at bay with his forearm. I see that he has used the time-honored technique of the sacrificial first piece of meat. Zeki will appreciate that. This man's got it all figured out.

"I've got a surprise for your visit but only if you both help carry everything outside. We earn our keep around here!" I say with my best Texas accent as I walk back into the house. I can't stand the heat in that outdoor kitchen, that's for sure. They scurry over to the kitchen and I hurry after them to make sure they don't make a mess of everything I have carefully set up.

Ihsan's ability to simultaneously keep both children happy while dishing up their plates is quite impressive. I can't bring myself to pitch in because watching him is entertaining but also I'm not part of this family unit and I don't want to overstep. When they sit and look longingly at their plates, I hand out utensils and napkins so they can start eating through their first American barbeque.

"I think you can add grill master and kid wrangler to your CV," I say, attempting casual conversation.

"Quite a compliment from a professional kid wrangler."

"From one pro to another, it's all about bribing."

Ihsan drapes his arm around the back of Zeyva's chair, leans over and kisses her on the side of her head.

"And that one is going to cost you an arm and a leg," I warn as Zeyva smiles with a little devil in her lips.

"You better save up." He motions toward me with his fork full of potato salad.

"For?"

"Bribing your little ones."

If I had been drinking anything, I would have sprayed it all over the table.

"Oh no way, I've done my time."

"*Neb*?"

"I've already raised enough kids. I'm good."

"What about kids of your own?"

"I'm the end of my line," I say, my tone unintentionally quiet.

As if on cue, Tariq launches a giant chunk of potato across the table and onto the patio where Zeki barely lets it touch the ground before he woofs it down into one of his stomachs. And with that comic relief the table returns to making merry and enjoying Ihsan's grilling skills. I try the best I can to mask how much that conversation hurts. I may have shared a lot with Ihsan but that was not a place I am willing to go.

As Zeyva and Tariq help clear the table of all the outside mess, I hear Zeyva humming a haunting tune.

"It's very pretty," I say to her, smiling.

I start to hum a few notes and she turns to me and smiles. She repeats the same first strain to me and I hum it back. As I walk in with my arms full of bowls and plates, I see the piano out of the corner of my eye. I set everything down gently onto the counter and throw the paper plates away.

Zeyva walks in behind me and I help her with her load and then take her by the hand and walk over to the piano.

I play a few of the notes of the melody on the piano. I nod at her to keep humming the melody and work out the rest of the notes.

"Does it have lyrics? Words?"

While she sings the melody, I follow her and then add a bit of harmony under her notes. The longer she sings the song, the more accompaniment I improvise. The smile on her face as she sings and I play is absolute magic, with her eyes large and bright. I'm not versed on Turkish music, but my rendition of the song seems to be adequate.

I didn't notice that she was looking over the top of the piano. When we near the end, she looks at me as we finish the last note and I add a little flourish. I reach around her back and pull her in for a hug. As she grabs around my neck, I see Ihsan out of the corner of my eye with his phone focusing on us. At first, I feel annoyed. I never want to be in any picture that I am not in full control of. Then I realize that I get to be a part of a moment in this girl's life and of course her father is going to want to document it.

She can barely see him over the top of the piano, but I can hear him applauding. He crouches down and opens his arms as she runs around the side of the piano and plunges herself into them. He picks her up and covers her face in kisses. The ache in my heart pangs in my chest again and my stomach churns. I can't help it when my eyes fill a little. I quickly stand up and walk into the kitchen to busy myself with picking up little pieces of trash and rearranging items in the already organized refrigerator.

Wiping down all the counters slowly and meticulously keeps me from having to talk to Ihsan. I don't want to have a conversation about the impromptu recital. It makes me uncomfortable discussing anything about my music.

Ihsan calls his two little cherubs over to him as if they are the eighth and ninth Von Trapp children.

"I want you to go pick out your clothes for tomorrow. Ready. Set. Go!" They both run off giggling with excitement.

As he rises to his full height, a huge smile claims his face as he turns his head toward me.

"That was amazing what you did."

"Thank you," I say and quickly try to get rid of all the debris on the counter.

"No, I mean absolutely awesome. You are incredibly talented."

"Well, I am compared to some but not compared to others. I don't know if I would get paid for that, but it's certainly something I miss."

"Zeyva really loved it, thank you."

"There are a few things I can do, teaching and playing the piano are a couple."

"You never thought of combining them?"

"No, no, the best way to kill your love of music is to teach music. I don't mind playing along, I just really don't like teaching it."

I didn't want to reveal that the last time I taught someone piano, I fell immeasurably in love with him.

"Well, that took my breath away."

"Wow, that's very nice of you to say. I think it was just because your daughter was singing."

"No, it was a beautiful moment. I'm just so glad I got to watch."

I smile and finish my chores. I'm trying to be gracious, but this is just unbearable.

"So, tomorrow I set up a private VIP tour for Disneyland. That will give me a chance to prepare the RV because I realized that my surprise for them will need a little time. Thor is a little worse for wear."

"That sounds like a good idea."

"Alright, get those little monsters to bed. We can do a fort sometime too. This is just a lot for one day. With all the travel and then the swimming and then the barbecue, I'm spent, and I didn't even swim."

"Yeah, why didn't you come and join us?"

"You were having a family moment and I didn't want to intrude."

"It would've been fun for the kids to get to know you more."

"Yeah, I'm uncomfortable being in a bathing suit in front of strangers. I think any average woman would feel that way being out there with you two. Let's not go over this again, I ended up half naked last time."

"I think that's the real reason you didn't come out."

"The pool was crowded," I try to funny my way out of this conversation.

"You really miss out on a lot of things based on your insecurities."

"Wow, are we really having this conversation?"

"I'm just saying, I notice that you miss out on fun when you might be the only one who notices what keeps you away from it."

I lay down my cleaning rag a little harder than I mean to. He asked for this. I'm pretty good at opening both the can of worms and a can of whoop ass. I usually try to go light on the can of whoop ass.

"Look." I take a deep breath in. "You and Gül live in a world where appearances are everything, so you both look otherworldly amazing. I don't."

I can feel my face get red. The pain from the earlier conversation adding fuel to my irritation.

"I have become a pro at cropping the video window, so I look the least Gollum-like. I can't even dress myself. Why do you think I asked Gül for help? Look, Ihsan, I will admit I am a victim of my own body shaming, but I am also an observer of human nature. I can't rest on my looks. Please don't think that I am disrespecting everything you do to make yourself into a living Adonis. I see how hard you work. You do have pretty damn good raw material."

I figure if I can turn this around and focus on him, I can weasel my way out of the conversation that I got myself into.

"Please understand, I'm still trying to figure out how I can represent you the best I can but again, I've got to work that much harder so that how I look doesn't impact you negatively. I didn't think about that part when I took this job. Everyone notices what keeps me away, my insecurities are valid."

He sat and listened to every word I said. It was hard to read his reaction, his blank face watching every hand movement and gesture. I hope I didn't break him with this reality check.

"*Tamam*, I will keep all this in mind."

He walks away from the table without any banter or any kind of emotion. I let my head fall to my chest. His energy is off. Our energy is off.

"Let's go, kids. Off to bed. We have an exciting day tomorrow...Disneyland!" he screams as if he can turn his mood off like a light switch.

They run up to him and he easily picks them up and bounces them on his hips as he carries them to the guest room. The next twenty minutes I hear him corral them through their nightly routine, a quick shower, brushing teeth, getting into PJs and telling them a story. Zeki nudges my hand and so I let him out through the back doors and urge him to come back as soon as I think he is done with his business. I just want to go into my room and be alone.

My stomach is spending the evening twisting itself into the Naval library of knots. Zeki took a little longer than I would have liked so I hurry to my room, trying not to fall with my socks slipping on the polished tile floor. Ihsan shuts the door to the kids' room just as I start to open mine. It would be super weird if I said nothing.

"I let Zeki out already," I say quietly to him.

"Thank you, see you in the morning" he says, looking at his feet as he passes by me to turn to go to the living room.

IHSAN

Beatrice is like my personal genie. I ask and it appears as if in a puff of smoke. She organizes a feast for our first night with the kids and even has them assist. Once again, she astonishes me. It feels so natural, all of us sitting together, sharing a meal as if this is the way it's always been. I can't imagine her without children of her own, but I've also never met a woman who doesn't want them. Another little distinction between Turkish and American women.

When she treats me to a spontaneous recital from my girl, I don't think Beatrice could impress me even more. Not only could she play piano, but she can also improvise on the spot. I should expect the unexpected by now. I can't stop myself from pressing her though and I know I shouldn't. She lays it all out for me in precise, clear language and it makes me ill. I am what people want to see and she is what people want to hide. My very existence is why she feels inadequate. Her admission catches me off guard and as much as I want to hide my disdain, it wouldn't be honest. As much as I want to argue with her, this is the wrong city and the wrong career to try to make my point. It is just so frustrating to listen to her accept what she thinks she cannot change.

BEATRICE

Maybe I should spend tomorrow packing my things back into Thor. What the heck did I just do? Admit that I'm having a hard time doing my job because of the way I look?

This is a new low, Beatrice.

This is a Z-quil night. I spend the next hour until the medicine kicks in trying to think of what other kind of work I am qualified to do. I contemplate starting a LinkedIn profile but decide it's too late to start something like that. My eyelids start to drift lower on my eyes and I surrender to sleep.

My brain would not let me sleep in. At five a.m., after finishing Zeki's morning routine, I prepare a color-coded schedule for the Turks Take Disneyland with arrival time, suggested restaurants and tips from the theme park savvy gurus I discovered while planning this trip for them. I add the contact information for the VIP office and the name of the guide that has been assigned to them. I also suggest the tip she should receive after they finish the day. All the information is coded with icons that relate to the subject, this way it's easy to scan for information without having to look for words. Teacher tricks translate well.

I pack a care package for them including containers of fruit, small crackers, small maze books with little pencils, hardback coloring books with crayons and small first aid kits for all four. The kids left their carry-on backpacks in the foyer, so I clean them out and pack them up, adding socks, cleaning wipes and a small water bottle. I leave the items for Ihsan and Gül, including acetaminophen, on the counter in neat little piles.

After packing up their park bags, I cook up some scrambled eggs with cheese and cut up sausage, toast and fruit. Since it would just be me today, I let Millie have the day off. At six thirty, Zeki announces Ihsan's arrival onto the main level of the house. He has showered, shaved and dressed like a rich dad; running shoes with no show socks, cargo shorts and a black graphic t-shirt with a heart earth with the words "Love Me" outlining it. I'll have to look that one up later.

He bounces into the kitchen and his eyes open wide as he sees the spread I have laid out. The urge to kiss up to him to keep my job was a bit overwhelming this morning. I'm hoping a good night's sleep will have erased whatever mood I put him in last night. By the smile on his face, I feel successful.

"I will go wake the kids up," he says as he turns and starts to half jog to their room.

He quickly discovers that they weren't asleep at all as they run out of their room almost fully dressed minus socks, shoes, and combed hair. I start to make up their breakfast plates as they climb up onto the bar stools.

"You have to start a Disney day with a good meal, so you aren't hungry when you get there. That way you can start the fun right away," I tell them.

They start eating eagerly, barely chewing.

"Another very important tip is to not eat too many sweets. They will all look very good, but you don't want to get sick on a ride and throw up everywhere," I say with an exaggerated, pinched up face.

"Eeeeewwwww!" We all scream together, causing Zeki to bark incessantly.

"Water only until dinner. I packed some things in your backpacks. Nothing exciting but it should keep you from being bored while waiting in lines." I wasn't sure of the access they would have to all the rides.

I pull out my phone and send Ihsan and Gül a text with all the information I assembled this morning. His phone chimes, indicating the text was received. He pulls it out and taps the screen.

"I just sent you all the information for your trip today. It is in an attachment so you can view it easier."

He taps the screen a few more times, scanning each page.

"Wow. This ...is—"

"My job," I cut him off. "Finish up, Disney fans! The car will be coming soon."

I help them off the kitchen stools and gather up their backpacks.

"I'm sending you two on a mission," I kneel down and look them square in the eyes. "I need you to remind your daddy...baba.. like a hundred times to take pictures and do little videos. If you complete your mission, I'll have a surprise for you at the end of your day."

"*Evet, evet*, yes," they both jump up and down.

Ihsan looks at me curiously and I smile at him.

"You'll find out when they do."

Just as I finish my mysterious statement, a large black Cadillac SUV pulls into the small parking lot with a "DIZ ONE" on the vanity plate. The large mouse head painted in matte paint on the shiny hood looks super classy. The driver comes out with his black chauffeur uniform and opens the side door. Like out of a ZZ top video, Gül's leg emerges from behind the door but instead of high heels she has white sneakers with the signature gold Gucci bee logo on the side.

"I have necessities for your packs as well. Their backpacks have a theme park survival kit for them and room for souvenirs. Now get out of here and give me some peace," I say as I put the packs on my little henchmen.

They slip their wiggly little arms through the straps and run to the door. Opening the glass door, they push each other to get to their mom waiting with open arms. Ihsan gathers all of the reusable grocery bags I packed into his backpack and slids one arm into a strap, like an all-American super dad.

"Beatrice." He grasps my hand, looks into my eyes and says with that sincere look I've seen so many times on the TV screen, "Thank you."

He even said the "th" right, just for me.

He walks away to his perfect beautiful family as the driver takes their bags and puts them in the back. He climbs into the front seat and waves goodbye to me as I stand on the doorstep, leaning against the frame. The driver closes the door and walks around to his side. The sound of the door closing echoes in my ears. I don't know why that sound affects me so much. Ihsan rolls down the windows and I hear the little ones yelling goodbye. There is one more little surprise I have for them. I look through my contacts on my phone and text the guide that they're on their way.

Passing the time when they are all gone is not too hard. I clean up all the breakfast plates and place them into the dishwasher, knowing Millie will probably wash and stack them again. After picking up the kitchen and wiping everything down, I pull my phone out of my pocket and find the number for my partner in crime.

"Matthew, I need to find Ihsan a date for this Turkish embassy dinner. I know you know how to find him a fancy date but I don't want it to be like a first date kind of thing. We should set up a lunch or something so they can meet beforehand."

"You are getting good at this young grasshopper."

"Oh, thank you. I just want to make sure he's comfortable. This is a great opportunity for him."

"Have you talked to him about this?"

"Kinda. I'll tell him tomorrow when he's recovered from Disneyland."

"That's right, you sent them on a Disney dream tour."

"Yes, thank you so much for all your help on that. The kids were so excited."

"It's just too bad that you don't get to see all the fruit of your labor."

"I have that covered. Ihsan will be bombarded by his kids taking lots of pictures and videos. He's going to send me a few to post, I'm sure."

"That isn't what I meant. You don't get to be there when they enjoy everything."

"It's a job, Matthew. He asked me to plan this day for them and I did. And it will be the same for all the upcoming events."

"Bee." I hate it when Matthew uses the "Don't try to bullshit me" tone.

"Matthew," I interrupt. "Please help me brainstorm the embassy thing."

I hear a long sigh in my ear.

"Okay, there are a few people that come to mind. I'll reach out."

"Thank you so much. Text me with the details. I'm going to have a couple shots and give Sarah a call. We haven't talked in a while and I'm sure there's a lot to catch up on."

"You sure know how to torture yourself."

"It will be painless thanks to Disaronno," I laugh.

That was only partly true. Alcohol doesn't really dull the pain, but it makes talking to Sarah more bearable.

"I gotta go. Places to see, people to do and all that."

"Ok, Bee. Be a good girl today."

"No fun in that," I reply and end the call.

Chapter 21

B EATRICE

I wasn't really going to drink before calling Sarah, but it will take me a moment to gather my thoughts before I can stomach hearing about all the wedding plans.

I stare at the phone for a good ten minutes before finding her in my contacts.

"Hey, Sarah!" I say when she answers.

"Bee! How are things?"

"Everything is going great."

I became a slimy drunk snot monster in front of my new client the last time we talked.

"I called to find out if you have any more wedding plans."

"Yes, yes. We just put a deposit down for the Royal Inn. Remember, it has those amazing grounds, and the rooms are fabulous. We have it rented for the week of the wedding."

That was a big ass chunk of change.

"We have to get married sooner than we were originally thinking but this way we'll get the whole place and the weather should be great. We are getting married the first week of December. And why wait? We don't have too many people coming in from out of town, mostly just the wedding party and everything will be decorated for Christmas."

Sarah did love Christmas, like really loved Christmas. Her office was always decorated before we left for Thanksgiving break. She even dressed her car in antlers and a big red nose. You could always look forward to "Christmas Sweater December" where every day she would model a new

Christmas themed knitted sweater. She even figured out how to sync her house lights with Christmas music.

"That sounds perfect!"

Sh..it.

I have six months to figure out this dress thing and to tackle all these stupid feelings. These stupid, stupid, stupid Brandon feelings.

Shit!

And I have six months to find a date for this damn thing. The last thing I need is wedding pity. I will not show up to this wedding without a date. Standing up quickly, I walk over to the glass doors, do a one eighty and increase my stride and speed back to the couch. My heart starts to beat faster and the thoughts in my head don't last longer than two seconds.

Shit, shit, shit.

"Matthew!" I panic yell into the phone.

"What happened?" he asks, his voice panicky.

"Their wedding is in six months! How am I supposed to find a date I know well enough to take to this? We will be spending the whole week together. I don't even know anyone in Round Rock I would do that with. I cannot go without a date. Matthew, I don't know if I can do this," my voice shakes.

I thought my feelings about Sarah and Brandon getting married had waned a little.

"Shit, shit, shit!"

"Bee. You have me, we'll figure it out. We can put you on every dating app, change your status on social media."

"From sadly single to desperately available, all applicants accepted?" I ask in an obvious panic.

"We can do this. I know people who know people who know people."

"Screw it. I'll rent a guy. I can do that, right? That's a thing. I think I saw it on YouTube. If I rent a guy there is no judgment, no rejection, no expectation other than to hang out with me."

"Bee." he pauses where I am sure he is giving me a stern face. "You are not hiring a date."

"Why not? It solves all the problems, and I don't have to get all nervous. It's a business arrangement. There isn't enough time to get someone to like me enough to spend a week with me. Just find a date for Ihsan for next week."

"Bee—" I press the hang up button and spin to the top of my contacts. I tap and wait for an answer.

"Blaine! How are you?"

"Beatrice, it's quite early. Everything ok?"

"Yes, Sleeping Beauty. Ihsan is off to Disneyland with the fam. Blaine, this isn't a business call. I need a personal favor. I'm hoping you can help me. This is kind of embarrassing but ... I need a date."

"Oh, really?" Blaine laughs a little to himself.

"Listen, I have this wedding in Texas in six months. I don't have time to date around, find someone who will spend a week with me and do this job at the same time. I am looking to hire someone. This is purely business. I just can't go to this wedding alone. It would just be too humiliating. I'm the Maid of Honor so I have to go. This is like fifty percent of the plots to the holiday Hallmark movies but without any kind of romantic intention at all. Blaine? Are you still there?"

"Yes, I'm trying to process all of that."

"I have no idea where to start. I figured since you've been married four times you'd know what's what around here."

"I think I can help you. I'll have Shelley send any information she can find."

"Are you laughing at me?" I can hear some snickering. "I wouldn't blame you. This is a ridiculous situation."

"No, I'm not laughing at you. I'm just amused by how pragmatic you are. It's early, hon and I haven't sacrificed any baby goats for my blood facial yet, so I need to go."

Blaine is weird.

"Thank you, Blaine. I just couldn't take that on too. Save the goatlets!" I mini shout into the phone and hang up on him.

With that taken care of, I feel more relaxed. I get to work emailing and calling to help set up his trailer for the movie set and take a look at his contract riders for the movie. I'm no lawyer so I spend quite a bit of time researching the ins and outs of the contract. Only a couple things were questionable, but it seemed pretty standard from what I gathered. Blaine is the real expert but looking through contracts is an interesting distraction. Maybe one day I might want to pursue being an agent, but that would require me behaving myself. Still haven't gotten the hang of that.

> Matthew: **I'm still working on a date for you, Bee.**

> me: **I actually got it covered. No worries.**

Shelley's name dings my inbox. It's a list of three companies that look like they aren't slimy escort services. Not that I would know how to spot one.

> me: **No, really I'm all set.**

> Matthew: **You better dish, girl!**

> me: **Matthew, a girl doesn't kiss and tell.**

I don't kiss at all.

> Matthew: **My "to-do" list needs to turn into a "to-done" list, so I gotta go. We'll catch up later.**

This conversation feels like it's tabled, for now.

After packing and organizing Thor, I go through the list of important contacts in Matthew's bible and find the casting agents. I have been working on old school paper portfolios as kind of a template for what I want in Ihsan's page of Blaine's talent agency. I hired a fetus to create an amazing webpage with links to his recent streaming service movies, fan sites and all his social media. The poor little guy filmed a special video with in depth instructions on how to add and delete items from the page. I think he did it so he wouldn't have to answer all my newbie questions. What a trooper. For a second, I debate whether to add YouTube links. I decide to go through a few of my favorites and link them. If I enjoyed them, I should share them with the world. It will make it easier for the casting agents. Since he was a model, there are plenty of pictures I can get a hold of to add to the portfolio. I considered filming him as he walked past the door after his workouts and do a montage for his fans but I think he would realize that project is really for me. Maybe I just don't publish it.

How would you explain that to a therapist, Bee?

It's time to put boots on the ground and get him some more work after this movie is finished. He is going to need some audition videos which I will be hiring a stand-in for since we both know I can't be trusted with his scenes. All his dramas were in Turkish, and I need these casting directors to know he is able to play a character that speaks English. And how sexy that damn Turkish accent is. Ihsan may be a gateway drug.

A few scripts have landed on our doorstep in the past few weeks, so I spend an hour or so perusing the pages for any story that would be a good fit for Ihsan. I really don't know what the hell I am doing but I do know Ihsan's acting strengths and I think I can find something that will show off his chops. He has them marked up with different colored highlighters and scribbles that I am assuming are Turkish. I have seen many a manuscript for thesis papers, but I'm not familiar with his style of annotation or note taking.

His modeling photos make great additions to his acting portfolio and I take a minute to order a bound hard copy to have on hand. After creating the graphics, organized with different sections and creating a business card for me, I'm exhausted but the night is still young. I am all alone in this big house, well me and Zeki. I click through a few movie choices on the TV and settle on "Pretty in Pink." I get the movie set up to the first scene. My favorite PJs were freshly washed today so those were a given, now to find the perfect snack. I investigate the fridge and find leftovers from the barbeque from the night before. Perfect. I make myself a plate with cold chicken, potato salad, Hawaiian roll and chips.

Oh, that is some good sh...it right there.

It's then that I realized I had skipped lunch altogether. I grab my favorite movie blanket that Ihsan and I have shared plenty of times and instinctively put it to the tip of my nose and breathe deep. It doesn't really smell like him anymore, disappointing.

I didn't realize I had fallen asleep until I heard the slamming of a car door. Every time Ducky pines for Andie I lose it and rip through five tissues. I must look like a single woman version of a dumpster fire. With the horror of that image in my mind, I quickly clean up the couch of all the tissues, grab my plate and move towards the sink.

The driver opens the glass doors and Gül walks in holding Tariq. I don't know how she doesn't fall over as he must weigh half of what she does. Following right behind is Ihsan carrying Zeyva. Ihsan leads Gül down the hall to the guest room wing of the house. I run into the living room and fold the blanket up and turn off the TV. I then run back to the kitchen and look at myself on any shiny surface I can find, mostly trying to calm my hair down. I quickly pull it all up and twirl it around into a bun on top of my head. This look always works for me.

Gül walks slowly toward me, clearly tired as I try to catch my breath from sprint cleaning.

"Do you have a second?"

"Yes, of course."

"The bride just told me today that the wedding is in six months. I need to figure out the bridesmaid's dress thing as soon as possible."

"I will talk to my stylist tomorrow and see if I can find someone."

"Thank you so much. Since you are a queen of fashion, I figured I would ask you. I just wouldn't know where to start." I figure this will give us a jumping off point and I really do need the help. Look at me, using all my resources. I walk her over to the front door and watch her climb into the back of the black SUV. Ihsan walks slowly down the hallway, rubbing his hands through his hair and over his face. He looks like sexy hell.

IHSAN

I struggle with a strategy of keeping the existence of Beatrice a secret. I'm sure at some point she is going to get noticed and someone far more impressive than me will try to steal her away. Waking up and seeing the work she had already put in before I was in REM sleep once again elevates her to another league. She puts all other personal assistants to shame. She may not have children of her own but can still anticipate with close to perfect accuracy anything that could possibly put a wrench in our plans. Before I can stop myself, her hand is in mine and I'm staring into those brilliantly kind eyes remembering how I left her last night.

I find myself waiting to hear Beatrice's take on various activities and sites in the park but when I look for her I remember she is at home and I am standing next to Gül, trying my best to keep my face from snarling every time I look at her. Luckily, I have several ways to keep myself distracted. Once again, thanks to Beatrice. My mind wanders, wondering what attractions Beatrice would like best, what food she would go for, and if she would laugh at or mock the guide on the Jungle Cruise.

When our guide ushers us into the exclusive club overlooking the park, I know she most definitely has mystical powers. Even Gül broke her stoic face to crack a smile of admiration. Unfortunately, the amazing experience was wasted on her. I know this face. The smile without the honest feeling behind it. Beatrice would have looked around in awe and sucked in all the energy from the space. Beatrice would have done what you are supposed to do in this restaurant, enjoyed every second. She would have appreciated all the attention to detail and craftsmanship that went into making this place magical. Gül almost negates it.

When we return home, Gül and I put the children to bed. I drag my body toward the stairs to my room as I see Beatrice closing down the house. I can't go to bed without showing her proper gratitude and when her chest slams into mine, my arms instinctively fold around her, and my head falls in the mess of hair always on top of her head. I cover up the deep inhale of her scent by exhaling a quiet thank you. Reminding myself that she is more than off limits, I give her bun a tussle before going up to bed.

I can't be sure if what I'm feeling is from my lack of sexual release with a woman or because she has set a record for needling under my skin like one of those tiny thorns I pulled out of her back. Either way I need to watch myself. She told me herself she mistakes kind, innocent gestures for something more intimate. Of course when she told me that she was raging drunk but it is her truth and I don't want to cause her more pain.

"Hey," I say and turn toward the staircase.

Before she escapes I wrap my arms around her, smashing her face into my chest. She turns her head and just like one of Tariq's brick toys, she fits against me seamlessly. I savor every second, but I don't want to make it strange as we exceed the normal amount of time allocated for an appropriate hug between co-workers.

"Thank you. That was amazing," I whisper into her ear. She pulls away slightly and I smile down at her. "I don't know how you got us into--".

"Sh! Don't say it. They have spies everywhere. Just doing my job," she says, knowing full well I wouldn't believe her. "Ok, I'm too tired. Go stink up some sheets." Her fingertips press into my chest muscles as she pushes me gently away.

It is difficult sometimes to keep myself from touching her. My arms miss her and she shouldn't feel so familiar or good in them. I take every step up the stairs deliberately just to spend a few more seconds with her.

This isn't right. She's my assistant/assistant manager/...friend. Best friend. There should be a professional line. There are rules. There used to be rules.

I'm not good at the rules of the Friend Zone.

BEATRICE

When the kids finally wake up, Millie has breakfast wraps with melon prepared for them. I had been planning next week and reading scripts before the little terrors woke from their well-deserved sleep. By the look on Ihsan's face as he makes his way down the stairs, I can tell he fell asleep hard. His hair is pushed back on his head as he walks into the kitchen rubbing his stiff neck and barely opening his eyes. Zeki took a moment at the bottom of the stairs to stretch his front paws and stick his butt high in the air.

"You survived."

"That is very accurate," he says, sitting down next to Tariq on the island.

"This is why I scheduled a recovery day. The dreaded Disney hangover."

Millie hands him his breakfast and Ihsan nods his head in gratitude as if speaking was too difficult without some fuel. Tariq and Zeyva pick apart their burritos and decide that playing with Zeki is more interesting.

"Let's let him out and you two can play with him outside." I herd the troupe to the outside, giving Ihsan some respite.

Ihsan takes his plate and walks toward the large glass windows where I am watching them watch Zeki poop.

"Dogs pooping is universally entertaining apparently."

Every morning I look forward to the fresh Ihsan scent which I subtly breathe in as he eats standing next to me. We watch his two fabulous children and his fabulous dog play in the morning sunshine.

"Ihsan, can I ask you a question?"

"*Evet.*"

"Any question?"

"*Tamam.*"

"Do you have trouble reading?"

He puts his burrito down on his plate slowly and turns towards me.

"How did you know?"

"I just noticed how you process the information I give you and your scripts looks like a game board with all the little drawings. I'm not sure others would pick up on it, but I've had a few students that learn that way. You do a great job masking it. You and Tariq are a lot alike."

His face grows sullen and sad.

"Do you suspect he has dyslexia?"

His face asks even if his lips don't. "I just figured since you wanted a credentialed teacher and not just a tutor for both of you then that is how I scored this amazing gig. Am I close?"

"*Evet.*"

"You are so lucky you found me," I say with as much cock as I can muster. "He's wicked smart, you both are. He just needs information given to him in a different way. It's very common for it to run in families. The kid speaks two languages, so he's already ahead of me. He has a lot of fun showing you what he knows rather than reading it, right? I bet if I showed him a song on a piano, he would be able to play it very quickly. If I showed him how to read the sheet music he would really struggle, if he didn't shut down completely. I suspect it's the same with you. It's all about hitting all the senses: listening, feeling, and watching. Most kids learn better that way. I don't recommend smelling and tasting the piano, that wouldn't be appropriate."

I was hoping that last comment would help pull him out of the mood I put him in.

"He struggles more than I did. I don't know how to help him. He gets so frustrated with me. Gül does all of that and I shouldn't rely on her anymore. I need to do more for him."

"First of all, you are already doing a great job by being an amazing example. He thinks he's different, but he really isn't. He is the same as you, brilliant. Dyslexia doesn't seem to hold you back. Don't hide how you learn, show him."

I've seen the look on his face so many times. Parents see too far into the future and miss what their children are doing right now. The worry is almost insurmountable.

"I know you don't want him to suffer like you did."

"How do you know that I suffered?"

"I can see it on your face. You got this, big daddy."

I can't help but put my hand on his shoulder, trying to reassure him that everything will be alright, something I wish I could have done to all the other parents with that same expression.

"What were you like in school?" I ask, already knowing the answer.

"I went to the soccer academy, but I was a...punk." He smiles at me when he remembers the word.

"And let me guess, you charmed your way out of trouble?"

He nods sheepishly.

"I got into a lot of fights, but they weren't my fault."

"I would have hated you in school."

The kids have moved on to chasing Zeki around the grass, his long legs tripping all three of them.

"Can you show me how to help him?"

"I was going to even if you didn't ask. I hope you like the sound of my voice."

"Why?"

"Because you'll be listening to me read your lines even when I'm not there." He furrows his brows, so I continue, "If I record your lines, it should help you learn them a lot faster. But you should call a doctor if I become the voice in your head."

Silent seconds pass and I give him one more nugget of information that I hope will quell his worried spirit.

"They have schools for kids with dyslexia here."

"I don't want to send him to a special school."

"I didn't say it was special. I said it was school. Like med school, law school, mechanic school, or electrician school. For the kids that go there it's just school, everyone just has one more thing in common that they struggle with."

Ihsan's torso droops as if the air has been let out of his body. He shakes his head as his eyes partially close and he smiles on only one side of his mouth.

The day is spent watching cartoons and playing card games. We play my favorite card game of all, Uno, and I fake a lot of ignorance so that Tariq will remind me what the different colored cards mean. Ihsan seems to be understanding all my sly little techniques of bringing him out of his shell so that he will try the things that he avoids. At some point, Tariq decides that my lap is his new lounging spot and I let him help me play my cards as well. He fits so nicely on my legs that I hate to have to move him to use the restroom. The little stinker waits for me outside the door and drags me back into the living room to play our fifth round. Maybe when this is all over, Ihsan will grant me visitation with his kids.

IHSAN

She's done it, she actually rips out my heart from my chest. It doesn't take her long to deduce that I've had trouble reading my whole life and the fact that she has already devised a plan to help me with Tariq has me completely wrecked. My acting skills help me cover up how I mask my disability, but she figures it out using her teacher sleuthing skills. It makes me uneasy that someone knows my weakness, but Beatrice doesn't see it that way. She sees it as a way to help Tariq and that is all I want in this world, for my children to be able to do whatever they work hard for.

Damn, this little woman has me all up in knots.

In sports, we use others' weaknesses against them but Beatrice wants to show me how to turn it around for Tariq, to show him how to find his strength. It takes everything I have to keep my heart in my chest when I see my son sitting in her lap as if he made a home there. She playfully tickles him and kisses his head, and he obnoxiously does it back while Zeyva rolls her eyes in impatience.

"Zeyva, how about we make some popcorn and leave these two to take each other out."

"Yeah, someone is going to end up with a black eye and I'm not going to be blamed this time," she says, scurrying up and over the couch.

"We only have a bag of kernels in there," Beatrice says between Tariq's fingers.

"You know they had popcorn before microwaves right?"

"It doesn't taste right without radiation," she says, pulling Tariq's shirt over his head and covering his face.

"Have you never made popcorn on the stove?"

Her soft lips flatten together as she looks up with one eye, squinting.

"Really? Tariq, I need to educate Beatrice on how to properly make popcorn. You can play your video game until it is done."

"Can I watch the...what do they call it, dumpster fire?" Zeyva asks, climbing up a stool as Beatrice rounds the island.

Beatrice's look of admiration and astonishment at Zeyva's comment makes me proud.

"It may end up in the dumpster," she says, laughing at herself. "What are we working with here?"

"We need a big pot with a lid, some oil and popcorn."

"And butter and salt," Zeyva adds.

Between the two of us, we gather the required items and set up our popcorn making station.

I put my hands on Beatrice's shoulders and move her to the stove, standing behind her, ready to instruct and assist.

"Pot," I say into her head.

"Pot," Beatrice repeats, placing the large silver pot on the stove and turning the burner on.

"Oil."

"Oil," she says, turning the bottle of vegetable oil on end. I quickly grasp her hand as my chest presses into her back.

"*Yok*, not too much. We aren't deep frying."

"Your teaching technique needs work. You need to be explicit."

"*Tamam*. Pour oil up to 3 millimeters up the side of the pan."

"Do I look like a metric girl to you?" she says with a playful glare.

"Pour, and I'll tell you when to stop," I say, leaning over her shoulder and enjoying her hair on my cheek.

"Stop. Now add the popcorn and cover." I take away the bottle and hand her the bag of yellow kernels. She pours a small amount into the pot and I look down to inspect the oil to popcorn ratio and laugh.

"What now?" she asks, shifting her weight to her other hip so her face moves away from mine.

Zeyva crawls up onto the counter and looks into the pot.

"What are the rest of you going to eat?" Zeyva says looking up at me.

"I don't need this," Beatrice says as she starts to walk away, which I know by now is just for show.

"Zeyva, go color or something. You are making her nervous."

"I'm not nervous, I just don't need Wednesday's good twin criticizing me."

"So does that make me Thursday?" she smiles, proud of herself.

"Oh my God, I love you," Beatrice says, leaning over the counter and grabbing Zeyva by the cheeks. "Can I keep her Ihsan, puuuleeease."

Zeyva wiggles out of her fingers and jumps off the stool, clearly done with us.

"Ok, back to the lab," Beatrice says, moving back into position in front of the pot, the oil starting to sizzle.

"Put enough popcorn to make one layer on the bottom."

On Zeyva's recommendation, I add more popcorn into the pot, and I hand her the lid.

"Cover it up and shake the pot."

Without hesitation she does what she is told but only shakes the pot once.

"You have to keep shaking it. Like this." I take her hands in mine and place them on either side of the pot. Leaning over her brings me closer to her than I should be. I slide the pot over the burner and pull it back quickly.

"You keep pushing up on me like that you're going to torch my nips."

I let go immediately and take a step back, Beatrice's candor once again shocking my system but this time I needed it.

"That almost turned into an alternate universe Patrick Swayze situation." Yet another reference I don't understand. "The pottery scene in 'Ghost'?"

And then I do.

"Hey, keep shaking it," I say, reminding Beatrice that we have a pot on the stove.

"That's what he said," Beatrice responds.

"*Neh?*"

"Who said what?" Tariq asks from the couch.

Beatrice moves the pot back and forth while laughing hysterically and I'm still a little confused by what just happened.

A pop from inside of the pot breaks up the scene and Beatrice lets out a loud yelp.

"Keep going," I remind her. "We don't want anything to burn."

"Yeah, it's pretty hot in here."

"*Allah, Allah,*" I say as if her comments are really that shocking. I didn't know what I expect hovering over her like this, but it feels good. It feels...comfortable.

I find a smaller saucepan to melt the butter and make sure that Beatrice holds onto the lid tight while we listen for the frenzy of exploding corn to die down.

"Mmmm...that smells good," Tariq says, occupying the stool Zeyva vacated.

"Do you know why popcorn pops?" Beatrice asks Tariq as I take the pot away from her before she lets it burn. "You know how water boils when it gets hot enough? Well, there's a little bit of water in every tiny kernel and the heat from the pan gets that water all excited and when it can't handle it anymore, it explodes."

I quickly turn my head to Beatrice, which from the look on her face I can tell she has even mortified herself.

"You're fired," I say with all seriousness.

"Good call," she says exiting the kitchen, her eyes downcast trying to stifle a laugh.

I fill a large bowl with the little white eruptions as Tariq chases after Beatrice.

"No, you can't leave," Tariq pleads.

"She isn't leaving. We are just joking. She hasn't even tried it with the melted butter on it yet," I say, drizzling it slowly with my most seductive smile just to get my favorite reaction.

She stumbles back into the kitchen, Tariq's hands creating red marks on her skin.

"You are going to all the hells."

Chapter 22

B EATRICE

"Maybe your little minions might have fun sleeping out in the RV. Thor probably feels neglected." I suggest after a day of juvenile alligator wrestling which is the only activity that even comes close to spending time with Tariq.

"They would be very excited about that."

"Have you ever seen anyone that lives out of their car?" I ask the kids, realizing when it comes out of my mouth that that probably wasn't the best way to phrase the question. Both look at me doe eyed. "Like someone is taking their house with them. That's how I got all the way over here from Texas. Instead of taking a plane, I drove."

I explain to them that camping is a big deal in America and tell them that the RV is the van looking thing outside. From the look on Zeyva's face, I'm explaining something she already knew. This girl is what we call in the biz "challenging", too smart for her own good.

"Would you guys like to sleep in the RV?"

Both run to the front of the house to take a look out the windows at Thor. They jump up and down with hands in the air like they just don't care screaming "Yeah!"

"Ok, help me pick up the mess your dad made and then we'll get ready for bed."

The two mini-Turks scurry about the living room, replacing the pillows from the couch and the cards in their now smashed box. Ihsan stuffs a pillow in his shirt and walks around making a big deal about how much he ate. After everything has been returned to its rightful place, I send the Korlu family off to get ready for bed. As I open the door to my room, Tariq the Terror bursts in and tackles my legs. I pick him up and set him on top of the bed and sit down on the edge.

"Climb on, buckaroo. I'll give you a piggyback ride."

"*Neb?*"

"Wrap your arms around my neck and I'll carry you outside."

When the light turns on in his adorable brain, it's one of the sweetest things I've ever seen. His thin, skinny, tanned arms cling onto my neck and I stand and grab his legs at the same time. Ihsan and Zeyva are waiting at the door with armfuls of pillows as Queen Bee and the tiny Turk make their grand entrance. When we reach Thor, Ihsan peels off Tariq and drops him inside.

When the kids are burrito wrapped into the blankets in the sleeping nook above the driver's seat, Ihsan gives them a gentle kiss on the forehead and a last little tickle while they are incapacitated. I give them a shaggy hair toss and pull the curtain closed.

Ihsan looks around for a place to sit but I spent yesterday morning organizing my belongings, cleaning all the surfaces and rearranging my bags to get ready for this little "camp out." I made the kids a little staircase out of coolers and bags so they could climb down if they wanted to use the bathroom. So, there isn't really anywhere to sit in the front of the RV.

"What movie are we watching tonight?"

"I was actually watching a pretty good series. I'll fill you in. Go make the popcorn and I'll set it up."

"Haven't you had enough popcorn?"

"You're right, go grab some chips from inside."

I don't know if he's going to like this or not, but it is true that I am watching a series. He just doesn't know I'm watching his series. I quickly arrange the blankets to give me the most nest material. He squeezes through the bedroom doorway and ducks a little to clear the top of the door.

Every time he walks into a room, the baby butterflies wake up in my stomach. Even if it is just a tiny RV hallway.

"Sorry this RV wasn't exactly built for the Jolly Green Giant."

I quickly call up a picture up on my screen and lift my phone up to show him.

He laughs his common laugh that is sincere and honest. "I thought that was the Hulk."

"I didn't even think of them both being big green men."

I scootch to the back of the bed in the rear of the RV and push the pillows up against the windows. Ihsan climbs over the bottom of the bed and next to me. I have the screen darkened so he doesn't have a hint of what is in store for him. When he is settled, I brighten the screen and it takes him a second to figure out what I have queued up.

"Woah, what is that?"

"I told you I was watching a series. Do I need to catch you up?" I say through infectious laughter.

He reaches over me to get to the remote. I pull it away from him as a cheeky sister would.

"Are you auditioning for the next Dr. Reed Richardson with your long stretchy arms?"

"Ha ha, give it up!"

"Just one little episode....please?"

Ihsan leans back onto the bed in a huff. I should have thought more about what scene I was going to be watching. I press play and I hear a giant "Uuuuugh!" from the occupant next to me. I start the video from the scene where he and the female lead are in a heated discussion where he declares he is still in love with her and she is trying with all her energy to resist him. The tension in the scene is palpable.

"Wow, this is the best acting I've seen you do. I really am pulling for him."

"What do you mean?"

"I want her to leave her husband and go with you...I mean him."

"I knew you were a bad girl."

"Ha... ha... ha," I overemphasize the onomatopoeia. "You are just so intense in this scene. Your eyes...I believe every word you are saying to her."

"Thank you. That is the best compliment."

"Out of all the things I've watched you in, this is my favorite."

"That sweater was the worst; it was like being strangled by a hairy snake. How much have you watched?"

"Only three shows, some are hard to find. I didn't look that hard, I'm not a stalker... It was pure research. I swear!"

"Yeah.... sure."

I didn't want to tell him that it was three full two hour an episode dramas. I've looked up plenty of clips of him as well. But again, research.

"Okay, I have an idea...let's watch a classic and very quotable movie, The Princess Bride."

"I think I have seen it in Turkish."

"Well, you are in for a treat. Now you'll be able to understand so much more of what I say."

I usually never talk during a movie but there are just so many places that have significance in my life. I can't help but add personal commentary. We sit with the chip bowl between us and only a few times do our hands meet in the bowl. I want so badly for him to touch my hand and feel something. I know I would. I'm making myself sick thinking about it. I try to shake these stupid thoughts away, but they continue to creep in.

Damn chips.

On the screen, Wesley and Princess Buttercup kiss on horseback and I mouth the words the grandpa reads from the book as I clutch a pillow to my chest.

"You are a...sap?" he says trying to remember the correct word.

"I've always been a romantic. I have never denied that," I answer proudly.

He moves the chip bowl to the table by his side of the bed and rolls back over as the horses on the screen ride off into the sunset.

I fall backwards onto the bed, clutching my pillow as a large breathy sigh escapes my lungs.

"Timeless. That is what it should be like."

"What should be like?"

"Falling in love, kissing, the six-fingered man."

Ihsan looks at me with the all too familiar confused face with his classic 'I'll figure it out later' look.

"Falling in love I can do. Kissing is few and far between. And the six-fingered man was just a joke. Actually, the kissing is a joke too."

"Why is that?"

I turn to look at him like I'm a middle school girl about to talk to my crush in PE class. A bit of my hair falls down my cheek and in an unexpected move he reaches over and slowly tucks my loose lock behind my ear, inadvertently caressing my cheek. I didn't even realize I had closed my eyes until I opened them.

Damn, I wish I hadn't done that.

He's an actor and reads body language for a living.

I'm so screwed.

"To be honest, I'm just not that experienced. I'm so afraid that I will be bad at it, so I don't put myself out there. With you kissing people in all your TV shows and movies and me with a total I can count on one hand, we probably average out to a normal person."

I chuckle to myself. The universe finds yet another way to balance itself.

"What makes you afraid?"

I take a moment to consider if this is a road I want to go down tonight and against my brain's better judgment, I answer. "I guess I don't want it to be so bad that whoever the victim is, doesn't want to do it again. I'm still in recovery from my last round of rejections, remember? You may use kissing as much as you use toilet paper but I don't. Me getting snogged and a total solar eclipse happens at the same rate for me so when it happens, it's a big deal. They should both be treated with the same kind of awe. It's very personal. I'm not good at being vulnerable so when I do it, I'm entrusting them with my heart and all the ugliness that goes with it. That is a lot to put on someone and I'm not sure that high is worth it."

"The actual physical kiss is not where that feeling starts."

"What do you mean?"

"The moment when you are inhaling each other's warm breath before your lips touch, if you are breathing at all." The pace of his speech slows. "Where your mind cannot settle on focusing on their lips or their eyes, your bodies push and pull against each other like magnets. When you can't decide if they will lean in first or you will. That is when the kiss begins. When your lips finally touch, you are not focusing on what is physically happening, you just want that primal connection with someone. The kiss is just a way for the passion to move from your body to theirs. The kiss happens in your mind," he says as he taps his fore finger on his temple.

His elaborate description involuntarily stops my breath.

Inhale, Beatrice!

"No wonder you get so much action," I say, trying to break up the palpable tension he created with his exotically accented monologue.

I have to escape. My body is doing things I have only read about in those scandalous vampire romance novels which end in extravagant circus performer sex that always leave me hot and bothered.

"Well, enough of that. I'm going to go inside."

"Wait," he takes a hold of my arm, sending the hot and bothered chills up my arm.

"I'm sorry, I didn't mean to make you uncomfortable. *Gitme*...stay. I don't know how Thor works. Look at all these buttons and switches, I would make it a low rider."

I laugh at the thought of Ihsan sitting in the driver's seat of a low riding RV.

He had me at 'gitme.'

I roll my eyes. "You didn't make me uncomfortable, it's just a lot to think about. You're a smart man. I'm sure you can figure out Thor all by yourself."

"What if I get scared?" He gives me giant puppy eyes. Damn him and his acting. He should only use it in a professional capacity.

I laugh a little. "Ok, but only to protect you from the big bad mosquitos."

I know I gave in too easily but I deserve this, even if it is purely platonic. I deserve to sleep next to a vampire erotica book cover model.

He pats the spot next to him as if I need another invitation.

"I get hazard pay for this, right?"

Ihsan always smiles at my jabbing remarks. I reach into the storage cabinet above and grab an extra blanket and pillows. Of course I have to throw them hard in his face, it was expected after he made such a big deal of the operation of Thor. After laying the blanket on top of my side of the bed, I slip under the covers and pull them up over my shoulders.

"Here are the ground rules. Since I'm not a dude, it doesn't matter the whole sleeping hole to hole or pole to pole thing." I give him a second to think about what I said, and the small rear cabin is filled with his bass laugh.

Oh God, that laugh. That speech. I really should go inside.

"No snoring. Don't freak me out with your face. Oh and no farting."

"That goes for you, too," he points to me.

"I would die before I farted in front of you! How many personal assistants have said that to their bosses? Or discuss the ins and outs of kissing? Our professional relationship is weird."

"It stopped being professional when I bathed you."

"Of this we will not speak." I point and glare at him and of course he laughs in my face. Again, with that laugh. Sometimes I feel like I live for that laugh. It isn't lost on me that I get to sleep next to this fine specimen of a human, at least this time I'm sober.

Thank you, universe, for this little nugget of generosity.

"What do you mean about not freaking you out with my face?"

"I don't want to wake up with your face right in front of mine. I'm not used to sleeping with anyone else in my bed. Matthew slept in my bed once and he stuck his face where it didn't belong, and I may have slapped the crap out of him. This is for your safety."

"You are risky to sleep with."

"You are sooooo funny. You survived the first time," I say mockingly.

In any other case I probably would have taken what he said badly but Ihsan doesn't seem to have a mean bone in his body. He's a truly beautiful, good man. Curling a pillow under my arm, I lay on my stomach away from him but then I feel him sit up slightly in bed. Turning slightly over my shoulder, I glimpse part of his tattooed shoulder as he takes his shirt off.

Oh, sweet Jesus, take the wheel.

I quickly turn back over and hope he didn't see me spying on him. He lays back down, reaches over my head and closes the curtains on the long skinny window behind us, making the back of the RV just short of pitch black. Sneaking a peak at him while he is sleeping isn't going to be easy.

Drat.

Throughout the night, I find myself opening my eyes and smiling to his thick muscled back. I don't know why exactly other than this just makes me happy, lying next to him. This is something I never would have thought would make me happy, probably because I never would have imagined me lying next to the likes of him. But how could it not? He is kind, funny, smart, empathetic, talented and of course a looker. I just hope whoever he falls for is worthy of him. Because if she isn't, there will be fisticuffs.

IHSAN

Beatrice's RV campout doesn't seem like a potential landmine, but it is. After securing the kids in their blanket cave, we settle in on the bed in the rear. When I see the screen lighten to my face I can't hold my groan. I know she's been watching my old work and she is really enjoying it which of course gives me more than just a little satisfaction.

Watching her enjoy *The Princess Bride* felt like I was back in Türkiye, sitting in the courtyard with Nadir and Zeyva fighting over a bowl of popcorn while a movie plays on a sheet hung up by nails against the brick wall. She is exactly why I act. For a brief moment of her life, I can provide a respite, an escape. But this time it is provided by a young Cary Elwes and Robin Wright.

At the outset, Beatrice is the least intimidating woman I have ever met which is why I don't think twice before reaching to move a lock of her beautiful hair from blocking my view of her eyes. As I brush it away, her eyes reflexively shut but I swear I see them shutter. I wonder if any other man has made her eyes quiver like that. It creates a flicker and in Beatrice's case where her eyes already sparkle without help, it's wondrous.

The expression on Beatrice's face as she describes what a kiss means to her is nothing short of ethereal. She's right, it should be all of those things. But it is so much more, and I want her to know how much more. I know I shouldn't, but the words flow too easily out of my mouth as I describe how it would be with her. With every sentence, I see her lids subtly grow wider and I can't stop myself. She is hanging on every word and when I finish, there's a moment where neither of us dares breathe. I should have predicted that would freak her out and when she tries to escape I plead with her to stay. I need her with me. Even if I can't explain it to her now, I need her by my side tonight.

At some point in the night, we find each other face to face. Her body has taken up some kind of defensive position as it resembles a sort of hurdling posture with one knee at the same level as her waist. Maybe subconsciously she's preventing me from touching her again. I won't as much as I enjoy the feel of her soft cheeks and silken hair on the skin of my fingertips. So much beauty and kindness inside this shell of sarcasm and spunk. How did I get so lucky? She's not afraid of my dog, of my children or even me. Every woman I've given a second thought to doesn't check all three of those boxes and yet this American woman does it as if it's second nature.

"Oof," I say quietly as I turn over. "Oof."

BEATRICE

Little laughs pepper the sounds of the morning. Nails scratch my toes just before Zeyva and Tariq jump into the bed and tackle Ihsan while he fakes sleeping. I quickly move down to the bottom of the bed, so I don't get an elbow or a knee to the eye.

Is it weird for his kids to see us in bed together? They don't seem to be bothered by it.

"How about we go into the big house and have breakfast?" I say, trying to get the loud mob out of Thor.

Ihsan herds his little morning breakers out the front door and I don't know if it's maternal instinct or my lack of a father but there is something so endearing about watching a man with his children. I even thought that as a teacher. The troupe rushes into the house and disappears into the kitchen.

As soon as Thor is cleared out, I take the opportunity to straighten up the bunk after the littles tore it up last night. After ripping off the sheets, blankets, and pillows, I make a pile to take into the house for laundry later. Going to the back of the RV, I take a second to look at the bed where I spent the night sleeping next to Ihsan. I walk around to the side of the bed he slept on. Picking up his pillow, I take a moment to decide if smelling it would make me pathetic. I decide it doesn't so I cover my face where he laid his head and take a long deep drag from the fabric.

Yep...oud.

It would be creepy to keep the pillowcase out of the wash and hide it in my bed and make a doll out of it. I strip down the rest of the bed and gather up all the bedding and bring it down the almost too tiny stairs. I shut the side door with a thrust of my hip as Ihsan walks out of the house.

"I can help you." He reaches out and takes the pile from me.

"Thank you, gotta get your stench out of the sheets. It acts a bit like chloroform." I smile at him, hoping he gets my little joke. For some reason, that knockout chemical seems to be readily available in Türkiye if I'm to believe the dramas.

"You didn't mind last night," he teases back.

"Don't let that get around, people will think I'm easy."

"Easy, you are not," he says with more authority than he should have.

"Nope," I say proudly, walking by him into the house with my nose slightly in the air.

I kinda wish I was.

Chapter 23

BEATRICE

    I'm surprised at my feeling of loss as I watch Ihsan help his children into the car to take them to the airport to board a plane and travel back across the Atlantic, away from their father. To my surprise, I enjoyed every minute I was granted with his children. They forced my face to smile and my heart to laugh in a way my students never did. Ihsan's hyperfocus on them was not something I've witnessed before. Making sure he was always braced against Tariq's chair so that he doesn't go flying onto the floor and squishing Zeyva's cheek to get her to smile at him even when she was determined not to instead of leaving her be. He must know he only has a few years until she becomes a snarling beast. But, no matter what I think of to distract him, it seems fruitless. To see a man so crushed by the absence of his children pains my heart to say the least.

    Perhaps this week's busy schedule will help. My personal assistant to the stars gig is about to get real as this week starts the serious stages of filming. It is nothing short of surreal that I get to see where all the magic happens behind the screen after spending years in front of it.

    My fondest memories I have with my mom were the movie nights we had almost every weekend in college. When BM, my nickname for Brandon and Matthew, weren't too busy painting the town they would join us, bringing way too much grape soda for four people to consume in one night. Brandon was the first one to have the guts to tell me something I already knew in my heart. My mom was deteriorating. He put the pieces together when they argued about a movie we had seen the previous week. They came over more frequently after that. Matthew claimed that I would ruin the popcorn if he weren't there to monitor the microwave. It was a lame excuse, but I appreciated his lightheartedness. Here I was about to see behind the curtain.

My first experience with filmmaking is one of the last stages of pre-production on a movie, the table read. The whole cast, no matter how big a part or small, sits facing each other, often at several tables, and reads every line of the movie, stage direction and added content. It's the first time the actors get to interact with each other and recite the lines they have been working on for months. I am almost as giddy as Ihsan is about meeting his co-stars in the flesh. There have been several video chats and phone calls and even a text chain, but there is something to be said for personal contact. The composer has even sent some preliminary music to play for the cast.

"Ihsanbaby!" I scream from the bottom of the stairs.

Yeah, that's right. Beatrice is speaking Turkish today.

"Sus! I'm coming," he says, slinging his messenger bag over his shoulder. "And it's just 'bey', 'Ihsanbey'."

"You really think I didn't know that?"

"So, you just did that to annoy me?" He says from his landing outside his bedroom.

I flash him my toothiest smile so he can see it from his precipice.

I'm not sure who is more excited about his first day at work, me or Ihsan. The thought of standing at the front door handing him his briefcase, lunch and coffee in kitten heels before he leaves for the daily grind makes my heart warm. But I have been a bit cooped up getting an overdose of Ihsan. I need to get out today and seeing what all of the other personal assistants do will give me an idea if I measure up or am a complete fake.

He descends the stairs with a weathered brown bag over his shoulder, looking radiant in all his normalness. I should have expected that even his white t-shirt, light jacket, gray cargo shorts and seemingly generic athletic shoes would be Armani and Prada. He had been a model after all, maybe he still had some benefits I didn't know about. I take note that I should look into getting him some kind of deal with Vans. Mama needs a few dozen new pairs of shoes.

"No way, whatever you have in there I can put in my bag. Sherpa is the bare minimum of my job."

"Beatrice, it's fine."

"Why do you insist on fighting battles you know you will lose?" I say, reaching up for the strap on his shoulders.

With a large brown eye roll he reluctantly passes me his bag.

"Look at us Don Quixote and Sancho Panza," I laugh as I watch my knight stride through the door to go pretend to be someone else. And here

I am, his faithful friend, making sure he doesn't get himself into too much trouble. I wonder who his Dulcinea will be.

As we drive to the location sent to me by the studio, I rearrange my bag to accommodate Ihsan's annotated script and various writing utensils. I've already packed his favorite water, lip balm, light jacket and ginger candy for nausea. That was mostly for me. I'm about to go into the lion's den and I'm going to need to be prepared for any side effects of my body reacting to all the new stimuli. I'd always had a bit of a nervous stomach when there was a lot of pressure and these table reads were serious business. If there isn't chemistry or something doesn't feel right, they could recast Ihsan and all his preparation and the major life decisions would be thrown into chaos, and I'd end up on Hollywood Boulevard dressed up like fat Bo Peep trolling for pictures. Watching him sit on the way to the venue without a care in the world, I'm almost annoyed but this is what a professional actor does. The best way to build chemistry is for him to be relaxed and himself. The car pulls up to a building that doesn't give any clue that it is about to be filled with some of Hollywood's biggest stars.

I show our security passes to the guard at the base of the elevators as Ihsan waits behind me and then ushers me to the silver double doors. As soon as the doors close, I grab his shoulders and turn him to face me.

"Teeth," I command.

"*Neh?*"

"I need to give you a quick once over. Quick, teeth, fingernails, nose, collar."

I inspect his face, hands, and the back of his shirt for any stray things that would give someone a poor first impression.

"Blow in my face."

He rolls his eyes, and a whiff of minty freshness fills the tiny space.

"Fly and shoelaces."

He runs his fingertips over the groin of his pants and looks at me curiously.

"Shoelaces?"

"I can't stand when shoelaces are different lengths."

"Who looks at that?"

"You're right, no one is going to look down when they could be looking at your smile." I pretend to stick my finger down my throat and gag.

"You're the worst at compliments," he says, making a few adjustments of his own.

The doors open to a long hallway with printed signs directing us to the large conference room. Before he gets a chance to take a step down toward the reserved room, I push him toward the sign and he poses for a quick shot to post. His dorky excited smile is exactly what his fans want to see and I get to see it all the time. Add that to the lucky column.

"You're skipping," he says, grabbing my arm.

"No, I'm not. I'm walking energetically."

"As you say. Take about twenty percent off that."

"You're right, you got this. Why am I being a freak?"

"You're nervous. It's your first time. Everyone is nervous for the first time." He smiles with a devilish red twinkle in his eye.

"You are a bad, bad boy." I shake my head at his play on words.

"Just getting into the part."

We arrive at the door and I stand in front of him as if I'm his personal door man.

"I can open it myself."

"You can, but should you? Should I? Is it my jo..." he opens the door, places a giant palm in the middle of my back and pushes me into the room, interrupting my slight panic. I stumble over my feet in front of three men looking a little confused by my face. I quickly raise my hand in greeting as Ihsan follows behind and the men's expressions suddenly change to recognition.

"There's a little bump in the carpet there," I say pointing and give Ihsan a bit of an elbow as he walks past to greet his new colleagues.

He shakes their hands and grabs their elbows as if they have met before as I assess the layout of the room. Twelve long rectangular tables fill the space in a giant "U" shape with a large gap in the center where they have set up several cameras. A place card is set at every rolling chair with the name of the actor and their character in large print in front of a microphone on a small tabletop stand. The walls are lined with the same rolling chairs which I assume is for support staff like me. Ihsan's paper placard stands next to Devon Hazlet, the headliner, the man everyone is going to come to the movie to see. Until they get a load of Ihsan, I'm sure. On the other side, the name Charlotte Steele, the bombshell, adorns the large name tag. Seeing their names written so casually catches me slightly off guard. They are real people, who would have known? Another name, Riley Foster, appears on a card and I wrack my brain trying to remember who she is. In the far corner is a table full of fruit, crispy snacks and a large tub full of ice and bottles of water along with rows of water for those who like it room temperature.

I spent half the night thinking about what made a successful profession-al development session during the school year and applied that knowledge to this seating area. Taking my place in the chair behind Ihsan's name, I set up my support station. The prefilled stainless steel water bottles line up under my chair waiting for a request for refreshment. I packed his favorite health bar into a food storage container and threw some pre-opened sug-ar-free hard candies to keep him from getting a dry mouth. No one wants to listen to plastic unwrapping in the middle of dialogue. His favorite wood pre-sharpened pencils, pens and highlighters were packed in a felt bottomed cup to prevent them from making too much noise when he drops them in along with small colored tags for additional annotation. I place the jacket on the back of the chair, his pencil cup on his right side of the microphone and his water bottle on the left. His well-worn script, carefully posed, completes the set up.

As I stand back to admire my work, I realize the room is much busier than when I started arranging Ihsan's tools. I hear his deep bellowed laugh as I scan the room to find where he wandered to. Suddenly, my movie world and the real world collide in front of me, and I can barely breathe or blink. As the actors take their seats and the business of pre-production resumes, I take a moment to savor where I am and who I'm with. So much talent in one room and I am blessed to watch the magic brew and boil to create a beautiful spell to transport the minds of millions.

I did it. I'm sitting here in an entirely different state, in an entirely different career in an entirely different environment, completely foreign to me and I am still upright. Not melting into a large puddle on the floor.

Oh, Jesus, is that a tear?

I wipe away any evidence of emotional overload and sit and wait for the actors to begin, hoping no one notices my slightly red eyes.

The first order of business is introductions. All the actors read their names and how their character is related to anyone else's. I take a few notes for my own reference because not knowing someone you should know is the worst. If I must remind Ihsan, I want to be ready with more than enough information. Once the last actor finishes Miles Walton, the director, addresses the cast.

"Our production assistant that was going to read with us just called out sick," he says, clicking his pen.

"Beatrice, I can do it," Ihsan interrupts quickly, turning around and baring his teeth and nodding as if he is threatening to fire me without verbalizing it.

I had hoped I would go through my whole life without making the "Not a fart," face, the panicked look on a student's face when they attempt to fart but something far more serious occurs. Ihsan managed to ruin that streak for me with his terrible spontaneous idea. After the initial shock, my eyes pinch almost completely shut as I consider a suitable punishment.

"*Carpe Diem, hadi,*" he whispers, reaching out his arm as if offering me an assist.

Latin and Turkish. Wow, dude.

He is right. I'm never going to have this chance again and I'm here to do just that, make changes and take chances. If nothing else it'll make a good story when I'm old and gray, sitting on my front porch spinning yarns to the stray dogs I feed.

The empty chair reserved for the person telling the story between the dialogue is two seats away from Ihsan's. That's probably the safest for him.

Charlotte and another actor stand to move chairs, but I quickly refuse their kindness.

"Oh no, it's better if he is out of my arm span. I hear black eyes are hard to cover up with makeup."

Charlotte chuckles.

Charlotte Steele actually chuckles at a comment I made.

"If you sit next to me, you can use all my...stuff," Ihsan says, helping Charlotte move her things down the table. He quickly realizes that a few of his most intense scenes are with her and switches me to the other side, next to the Devon Hazlet.

Oh, what fresh hell is this?

"You shouldn't feel comfortable sitting next to me with a dozen freshly sharpened mini spears within reach," I say, taking my new spot between the two lead male actors.

He takes the white cardstock name plate and writes "Bee" on the other side in big bold lettering then places it on the edge of the table in front of the microphone.

"There, now everyone will know who you are," he smiles as everyone gets settled.

"This is not how I thought my day was going to go."

"Go ahead, introduce yourself," Miles says.

I clear my throat just to give myself time to think.

"I'm Beatrice Fredricks, Ihsan's personal assistant, and it's been four days since my last humiliation."

Ihsan rolls his eyes as his co-stars welcome me with a hearty appreciation of my annoyance.

"Thank you for this opportunity. You all are a lot prettier than the last group I read for, to be fair reading word problems to middle schoolers is the stuff of nightmares." The crowd responds as I'd hoped, and I feel a small sense of relief.

I can do this.

"Thank you for stepping up. Let's get her a script," Miles says to one of the minions.

"We can share, we're used to it," Ihsan says, moving the marked-up pages between us and forcing me to lean toward him, breathing him in.

Even though it would have been nice to smell the freshly copied paper and listen to the pages turn over the spiral binding, the familiarity of his pencil marks, highlights and small coffee stains on his dialogue pages would make this novel experience much more tolerable.

A fresh pile of bound scenes appears in front of me, but Ihsan takes it away and places it on the floor.

"Yeah, we better have a backup plan. We haven't been very good at sharing. You ask for one grape and someone has a hissy fit."

Another round of chuckling pings against the fabric covered walls as I open the script and Miles cues to start with a nod of his shaggy peppered head. I take a deep breath and start to read the description of the opening scene. The captive audience is more attentive than my old students, but I can tell they are concentrating less on me and more on their lines which takes a significant weight off my shoulders. After the first page of mostly setting up the opening scene, I feel Ihsan's large hand on my knee under the table. He gives it a slight squeeze and I turn to look at him staring down at the pages. Removing his hand from my knee, I lean over and whisper into his ear.

"You're making it worse."

His kindness always seems to make everything inside me tighten.

A large grin spreads across his face as the dialogue starts. After a few pages, Ihsan's first lines appear and instead of reading them off the script he turns to his scene partner and recites his lines with intense sincerity.

"Pause," Miles interjects. "I'd like to hear you read with a few levels of accent. Read it again but with a thicker accent."

"Oh, he knows how to lay it on thick," I say to myself but hear it amplified throughout the room. I couldn't hold back my look of shock at my misstep, and neither could Ihsan. As we try to bring back the attention onto the task at hand, I look around the room to see several people giggling into their palms.

I tap the paper in front of him, slightly too aggressively, to redirect his attention. He breathes in loudly through his nose and restarts his line with a much heavier, sexier, accent. The temperature on my skin starts to rise. I grab a water bottle and bring it to my neck forgetting I'm sitting in a room of people watching and listening to the man next to me and I just gave them a huge clue that his accent makes my insides simmer.

Awesome.

Suddenly, I wish I was sitting behind him, curled up in a ball scribbling in my notebook. For the first time, I wish he would lay it down thin.

IHSAN

I may need to rent a room at a hotel for a week. Beatrice's glare is reliably brutal on a casual day but after the stunt I pulled, she's bringing it like she has never brought it before. But I couldn't think of anyone better to introduce the cast to the story. The nights she reads to me by the pool are nothing short of bewitching. There is something in the way she presses some words more than others that brings to life the world within the pages. When she read to my children, she transported them to exactly where the author wanted them to go. The crescendos at the exciting scenes and soft murmurs at the more sensitive parts were captivating. Our conversations are a mixture of humor and hostility but when she uses her voice as a tool for good and not evil, I am entranced.

She protests in her own way, but I am the only one that picks up on it as she blunts all the pencils under the table and places them back into the cup, keeping the only sharp one for herself, probably to keep her revenge plan at the ready.

By the time we reach the first break, we hit a rhythm. With everyone intensely engaged and invested in the process, I am once again affirmed that this is the right move for my life. For as long as it lasts with Beatrice plotting next to me, that is. I know she secretly loves being part of the process. The actors dovetailing onto her energy after she finishes her description is more than pleasing to watch, making this table read something special, something extraordinary.

I stand to stretch my arms over my head knowing that Beatrice is holding back from punching my kidneys only because she has a room full of witnesses. She shoves her chair back to give her room to straighten up my space. For someone who has never had children, she sure is good at momming me.

Devon drags me over to the snack table, leaving Beatrice on her own to fuss and keep herself busy. From the moment I volun-told her to narrate, I knew I was going to keep a wide berth, or the cast was going to get a front row seat to the Beatrice and Ihsan show. Unlike at home, I would have to let her win because this wasn't her gig and if I embarrass her in front of all these people, I'd end up on a missing person's billboard. As we make small talk, I keep my body turned toward her so I can swoop in if I see trouble. I don't know what I'm afraid of, she's a grown woman and so far she's performed magnificently, but I threw her into the deep end and who knows how long she can tread water. I pick up a clump of grapes and add them to my plate.

"How are you liking the states?" Devon asks, clicking the cap open on a warm water bottle.

"I really like it. Cleaner air, slower traffic and everything is so new."

"I see you've been out to a few clubs."

"Beatrice kicks me out to a different club every other night. I don't think she likes me." I smile as I take a grape and pop it in my mouth.

"Oh, I think she likes you. But after today's stunt, I'd be careful."

"What? I think she's doing a great job."

"I mean, she is doing great but that was pretty ballsy putting your PA out there without a heads up."

"I'm sure I'll pay in some way. The scary part is not knowing how."

"How is the house working out?"

"It's great. You might have a plaque on it when we leave. Beatrice insists it should have a name."

"When I bought it, it was already notorious. The game room went under a lot of renovation."

Devin's eyebrows crinkle above his nose indicating there is more to this story he isn't revealing.

"What happened?"

"From the looks of it everything happened. It was a different kind of game room."

Just as I start to ask him to be more specific, I suddenly understand and stop myself. Under where we have been living our lives is a room that hosted sex parties. Beatrice is going to lose her mind. I hope she is mature enough to be okay with continuing to live there but then I remember who lives downstairs from me and know that this will have to be a closely guarded secret. If I don't tell her she won't find out. It isn't like she runs in those kinds of circles where this would come up in casual conversation. I look around the room for possible leaks and realize I don't know any of these people well enough to know if they had been a visitor to my basement.

"Promise me you won't tell Beatrice. You'll cost me a PA."

He huffs out a laugh and slaps his grip on my shoulder.

"I don't need that getting out as much as you don't." he says and makes his way to Charlotte.

I scan the room for the exit to make my way to the restroom. The amount of liquid Beatrice is forcing me to drink is inhumane and my bladder is at critical mass. I walk back to the table and place the plate of grapes in front of her, a few missing.

"Thanks for the table scraps, Boss Man," she snarls over a heavily scribbled notebook.

Oh yes, we will be driving in separate cars on the way home.

As I return from the restroom, a few of the second-tier actresses gather around my seat holding their scripts and attempting to look business like. I've seen this before, a ruse to make a meet-up more casual. They are all beautiful in different ways and my face can't help but to flash them a smile as I approach and start up a meaningless conversation. As if someone turned up the background noise on an audio file, I hear Beatrice's disapproving harrumphs and lip smacks from table level. I turn my back toward her and sit on the back of her chair, forcing her to lean forward slightly so I don't sit on her giant bun. I'm playing with fire, but I can't help myself, it's so easy and I live to experience her reaction. Suddenly my support from under me vanishes and I half fall to the floor.

"Oh, I'm sorry, I didn't see you there," she says, covering her mouth in mock embarrassment.

The room's attention is on us, concern for my safety is abundant, making Beatrice's snicker even more annoying.

Miles' hands slap together, causing everyone to return to their seats and continue the first rehearsal.

Getting myself settled, I search for the one pencil that still has usable lead. She sharpened them all again, and I take that as a sign of forgiveness. When I turn to her to address the seat stumble, she holds a grape in her hand and smiles evilly.

"Either amuse me or lose me. I'm hungry, peel me a grape," she says, handing me a small purple globe and I return her look with confusion.

"Dianna Krall? Seriously? Oh, *Ihsanbey*, I just wasted a perfectly good lyric on you."

I should tell her she doesn't have to use "bey" at the end of my name. As familiar as we are with each other, we are past formal titles. Way past. Yet there is something about the way she says it with such pride and accomplishment with a hint of mischief that I can't help but enjoy.

Someone on the other side of me hums the sultry melody to the song and my mouth parts.

"See, not an obscure reference," Beatrice says, pointing her thumb in the direction of the humming.

"Oh, you're obscure," I say, getting comfortable in my place once again.

"Your face is obscure," she says, her sassy switch turned to the high position.

My eyes grow large, and eyebrows run away from my face as we hear her voice once again echoing against the walls.

"Seriously, is anyone going to give me a heads up with the mic? Is this some kind of initiation?"

I can feel my face flash bright crimson with stifled laughter, annoying her even more.

"You're supposed to be a professional," she scolds, shielding the puffy mic cover.

I lean back away from the table, turn to her and wave my arms in a signal of truce.

The second half of the table read is even better than the first. Beatrice is more relaxed as she becomes more accustomed to the pace of the lines. When the romance scene comes up, her tone is smooth and breathy. The whole room hangs on every sweet syllable. A few sniffles were audible, but no one picked up their head or looked to see who couldn't hold in their emotion. My chest swells with pride as my little Beatrice brings the cast to their emotional knees. Quite surprising for an action movie. The actual sex scene is eventually "fade to black" but only after a few sentences where Beatrice has to describe heavy kissing and where my hands will eventually land on my co-star. I almost feel bad but then I feel a little turned on and then I want to laugh. I'm not sure that is the appropriate order those feelings should be in but I can help it.

The only time I notice her falter is during the shootout scene. She reads it flawlessly but I hear a faint waiver in her voice and a subtle squeeze of the outside corner of her eyes that, if I wasn't sitting next to her, I wouldn't have noticed. I lean into her arm as if I'm reading over her shoulder and press a little harder against her to give her something to brace herself against. Her demeanor returns to normal and she continues like she's a hired professional.

When she reaches the scene that had thrown her hormones into overdrive in our living room, she breezes through it without even a hitch in her breath. I, on the other hand, had to pinch my thigh in order to keep an encore of my reaction from interrupting the flow. As the afternoon carries on, I am taken aback by the high level of acting skills I am witnessing. It has been a long time since I have felt I am the weakest link. Glancing around the tables, I wonder if anyone else is feeling the same electricity I feel coursing through my muscles. From the concentration level on their scripts, it seems everyone is as captivated as I am. When Beatrice reads the final few words finishing with "The End," the room erupts in applause and laughter. Exactly what I was praying for. All my hopes and dreams have a serious shot at becoming reality.

"That was orgasmic," she says excitedly.

I cover her mic quickly but bow my head as I am too slow and it picks up her outburst.

"Well, now I'm giving myself a reputation," she says, laughing in my face as I find the switch on the handle to prevent any more announcements.

BEATRICE

That might have been the most fun I've had with a crowd in my life. The only thing close was a vocal concert where the all-men's group finished the most beautiful version of Danny Boy and the audience hadn't dared to clap in fear of breaking some unspoken promise. I felt the nervous energy convert in my body to fuel, the meaning behind the words flowing out of my mouth. All the actors are brilliant in the delivery of their lines. Some cast members bow their heads as if they are sleeping but I soon realize they are visualizing the scene. When they raise their heads it's as if they are finishing a fine dessert.

"*Ihsanbey*, is it always like that?"

"No, this is the first time for me too. Miles didn't even stop for line changes or stage direction corrections," he says quietly into my shoulder.

"Now what?"

"We wait for him to give us notes."

"Ladies and gentlemen, I have no words. You said them all. You left me speechless," Miles says.

"Can we thank Beatrice for stepping in?" Devon interrupts.

There is nothing I can do to stop my smile. Devon freaking Hazlet remembered my name.

"That was my next credit. Beatrice, you were amazing,"

Ihsan starts clapping, leading the charge which I'm sure he thinks will get him off the hook for pushing me into this.

"I didn't throw up, so I'll put that in the win column," I reply, giving him a thumbs up.

"You're lucky she didn't 'pew pew' during the shootout," Ihsan adds, cracking up his fellow actors.

"I would smack you but it's true."

"The schedule is in your email. Call times are sharp," the assistant director announces.

The room packs up and I see the young ladies from earlier practically climb over the office equipment to get to Ihsan who looks oblivious that they are on the prowl for him.

"Hey, Ihsan, a bunch of us are going out tonight. We'd love to show you around," says the tall robust brunette.

"Oh, I'd love to, but I have an early morning appointment with..." he says looking to me for the assist.

"A laser wart removal service. They come right to your house. Isn't that convenient?" I finish, quite happy with myself. "*Ihsanbey*, we'd better head out. You have to put that smelly ointment on to get them all softened up."

I grab his arm and push him out the conference room door and wait until we get into the elevator before exploding.

A robust dark haired woman closer to Ihsan's height walks with us and I recognize her as his love interest. I was wondering when I was going to meet her face to face. I just listened to her have a whole relationship with him, I mean his character, and I almost needed a bit of ginger myself. The urge to sneer is almost overwhelming but then she turns to me and smiles. It isn't typical for a Amazon-ish woman to be cast in a leading role but she is remarkable, matching Ihsan's acting skills word for word.

"Hey, Ihsan," she calls out to him.

"Hello, Riley," Ihsan responds, a little formally for someone who is going to do some serious lip locking in the near future.

"It is nice to finally put a face with a name. Sorry, I didn't get a chance to talk with you sooner."

"Yes, I look forward to working with you," Ihsan says smiling too much for my liking.

"I need to get back to talk with the wardrobe coordinator. See you soon and good job, Bee."

I put my hand in the air and wave so I don't do the snotty mocking voice "Good job, Bee" that my mind is screaming for me to let out.

"See you soon." I spit out and with that she disappears down the hall.

I shake out my head and turn to my charge.

"So glad that is over. I did like the opportunity to put you in your place, though."

"Hey, that was amazing," he smiles.

"You should've seen your face with the girls and the ointment!"

Ihsan stands still in the elevator, clearly trying not to react to my triumph as he watches the circular numbers turn off and on as we descend.

"Thou art a ragged wart," I prod. His lips twinge so I continue my Shakespearean insults, "You have a February face so full of frost, of storm and cloudiness."

"I must tell you friendly in your ear, sell when you can, you are not for all markets," he says slow and low as if he's a tall guard in front of a castle. My mouth drops open at his quick wit and ability to quote back my beloved bard to me.

The elevator doors open and just when I think he's done, he rains down the killing shot. "Away, you three-inch fool."

I stand in shock as he strides out of the metal doors purposefully, knowing he has bested me at my own game. With my head lowered in defeat, I follow my master out to the waiting car and climb in as if I am a little kid that got into trouble at the grocery store.

As the sun falls below the horizon line, I turn to watch him for a moment. Just a brief blink in time to admire the man who got me to speak to a room full of strangers, trusting that I would succeed. My eyes return to watching the day come to a close and I feel a deep sense of contentment and, dare I say, purpose. I may have to start thinking about my future and not just Ihsan's, but that might be tempting fate a little too much.

Chapter 24

BEATRICE

The night of the Embassy dinner is relaxing considering all the effort I put into making it easy on Ihsan. He can bathe himself, dress himself and accessorize with the best of them. He only asks me to help with last minute hair style advice to which I almost lie and set him up for embarrassment. With his luck, he would set a new fashion trend. After that, I just have to make sure the car arrives on time to pick him up and then pick up Sonja. That name brings bile up in my throat. Matthew's mission to find her rather than me doing the scouting is a success. I tend to find him dates that would get him noticed by paparazzi. He found a woman noticed by dignitaries. Matthew set up lunch and they got along, so Ihsan asked her to the dinner. It was that easy. It was that eff...fucking easy.

Must be nice.

From the description of the event, it sounds awful. Fancy people, fancy dresses, fancy food, maybe even fancy dancing. Even with that, I still have a little jealous princess inside. 007 starts his descent down the stairs, clasping his cuffs to finish clipping the links. His face is clean shaven, each hair on his head is perfectly blow dried on top of his head to give him a little poof and the suit is bespoke. Even his gait is confident, his feet practically floating down the steps like a secret agent Fred Astaire. When he reaches the bottom, I swear I hear the movie music. The tuxedo jacket is black velvet with black satin lapels with a red square peeking out of the jacket pocket. I can't help but stand up when I see him. My lungs won't even fill with air, he has sucked it all out of the room.

"So?" he asks.

I gasp slightly and quickly blink my eyes as the air races out of my chest. If I don't answer him with my usual mockery, he'll know how breathless he makes me, especially when the black suit covers his muscled body so perfectly.

"I thought you were going to get cleaned up," I smile, walking over to him. "You know damn well you look spectacular."

This calls for a full evaluation of the goods. After a slow stroll around his presentation of finery, I stand in front of him as if inspecting the suit for flaws. I stretch my arm up to pick off fake lint, brush the top of his shoulders and pretend to straighten the little red square. For a moment, I imagine that I am the one who gets to stand next to him all night looking this good. But I know better than to linger on thoughts like these and shake it out of my brain. I stand back and give him a final once over. It's as if I'm staring into the sun.

"Flawless," my breathy whisper breaks the silence as my eyes start to burn. The sweet lyrics from a classic song, "Darling, you look wonderful tonight" leak into my thoughts.

Not tonight, Eric!

"Did you just give me a non-sarcastic compliment?"

My first instinct is to give him a snarky remark, but I can't. It would stain this moment. My mouth is too dry to answer anyway.

He bends down slightly to meet my eyes.

"*Neb*, nothing?"

My eyes start to betray me as my throat swallows. I slap both his shoulders twice and quickly walk toward the direction of my room.

"Have fun storming the castle," I shout from the hallway. Finally, getting to my bedroom, I grab the door and close it quietly. Placing my forehead on the edge of the frame, the last of my resolve whisps away and the tears breach my lower lid and make a thick trail down my red cheek. I'm not exactly sure what these tears are for, but ever since I moved here they seem to appear whenever they want without regard of timing. I didn't hear any response from him after my theatrical send off. A few minutes later I hear the doorbell ring, Zeki's bark and then finally the closing of a car door from the front of the house. As I turn to go to my bed, I see my reflection in the large windows.

This is why I can't have nice things.

To torture myself further, I open Instagram and wait. He did what he was supposed to. He takes lots of pictures of himself posing with several dignitaries and sometimes their wives. A photo of him standing in front of the house with Zeki standing next to him pops up. He must have done that when he left. This one makes me smile the most. This one is the most like him, sophisticated and yet down to earth. I skim through several more and notice he hasn't posted any with his date. I switch to her Instagram. She has posted pictures of them standing close together with his arm around her waist. She's wearing a beautiful red dress adorned with strings of crystals crisscrossing the low cut back. Sitting back against my headboard I turn the phone over and lay it down next to me. He is smart, photos of him alone make him look more available but then again, it doesn't help his profile.

If You Leave from "Pretty in Pink" starts to play in my head as I'm feeling very Ducky. The faithful friend who only wants the best for his love, even if it means living without her. I am the Duckmeister.

My phone chimes several times with Ihsan's perfect smile filling the screen. Nope, I'm not going to get caught up in reading all his texts while he is supposed to be on a date with Miss Universal Beauty.

To distract myself, I go to my computer and click on the email from Blaine's assistant, Shelley. The email includes several links for the sites to help me find a date for Brandon and Sarah's wedding. Scrolling through the photos, I look for someone that people would believe I'm dating. After clicking through what felt like hundreds of profiles, I settle on trying to find the ugly brother of all the men I clicked on. This is not going to be easy. The next hour or so I continue clicking and closing, clicking and closing, clicking and closing.

"Ugh!" I scream to no one.

Zeki gallops in, concerned for my safety.

Maybe I should take him to Texas.

Walking into the bathroom, I decide to attempt to shock myself out of my mood. I turn on the faucet, cup my hands, lean over the sink, and push the cold water onto my face. I fumble around the drawers and find the bottle I was looking for, sleep aid. If I don't fall asleep soon, I'm going to drive myself crazy. I know one pill does a pretty good job but two will guarantee that my consciousness will be out of commission. The problem is I'm less than my best the next day. That's not my concern at this moment, though. I just need to give my mind a break.

Grabbing my phone, I select a true crime podcast and set the sleep timer. The hosts are smart, funny and women I would want to have weekly lunch with. This is the perfect listening selection to keep my mind busy. After the segment of witty banter, the sleep aid starts to suck me in and I'm gone.

IHSAN

The woman that Beatrice set me up with meets all the traditional criteria. She is tall, smart, beautiful, elegant and has a body that would send any man into a tailspin. Our first date went well and I am very attracted to her, so asking her out for dinner at the embassy felt like a natural next step. Of course, I didn't realize that was all part of Beatrice's plan.

Shaving my face with a new razor, using just the right amount of product in my hair paired with meticulously and methodically acquiring one of my favorite designer tuxedos, I'm satisfied that I am adequately prepared for the night. When Beatrice conducts her final inspection, I can't help but notice the extra time she takes running her hands across my shoulders. I'm thankful she doesn't see the tiny bumps on my forearms. When her face falls and her posture stiffens, I can feel the distance between us grow as she straightens my crimson pocket square, lifting herself slightly on her toes. When she power walks down the hallway, I know something I missed triggers her hasty retreat.

The evening progresses as expected. Many of the attendees are familiar with my movies and television programs and I never mind taking photos with fans. Sonja's slight almond shaped blue eyes create an exotic air about her. The red dress, that I'm sure was made especially for her, drapes perfectly over her ass while exposing the milky skin of her back. She's very comfortable on my arm. Our conversation is pleasant and she stands next to me posing perfectly for the cameras, instinctively knowing how to move. It should be a perfect date but everything else in the room seems to distract me. As per Beatrice's instructions, I post several pictures with me looking as if I'm having a wonderful time with strangers. I decide against posting any with Sonja because the press doesn't need any more fodder for their shit rags.

Beatrice is radio silent all night. I attempt to entice her with my version of wit, but she still isn't responding. I find myself thinking of things that would amuse her but when I turn to tell her, she isn't there. I can't deny I'm disappointed. The same void was there at Disneyland.

When I meet the ambassador and his wife, I notice the bracelet on her wrist has a beautiful jeweled *nazur* on a delicate silver chain. I imagine it on Beatrice's wrist and when the ambassador's wife notices my longer than normal stare, I let it slip that I think my assistant would like it since she is getting into everything Turkish. Before we leave for the car, a velvet box arrives in my hand delivered by a sweet middle-aged woman with a warm smile.

Sonja doesn't have anything to say that holds more than two seconds of my interest and our driver drops her off without any plans to meet in the future. I can't even bring myself to casually flirt and spend most of the ride on my phone which, as Beatrice would say, makes me Mr. Asshat. When I remove my tie and start to unbutton my dress shirt as I enter the house, what I normally would expect to see waiting for me on the couch already in dreamland, is absent. This hint of disappointment gives me a slight pause. I know she's here, she just isn't waiting up for me. I never thought the lack of Beatrice's mockery would bother me.

BEATRICE

The smell of Millie's amazing food does a fantastic job of waking me up. Laying there on my bed with little slits for eyes, I debate if I should even be seen today. I'd rather be doing yard duty for second graders than talk to Ihsan about his fancy night at the embassy. He would know something is up with me if I stayed in my room all day and that would just bring up more questions, painful questions with painful answers.

"Beatrice?" says the deep voice on the other side of my door. There is no way of escaping now. I'm trapped. I could possibly go out the window and make a break for it. Keep running until this feeling goes away. Until the wrenching in my stomach is bearable.

"Beatrice, are you ok?" The honest answer to that question would completely ruin our friendship, not to mention my job.

"I'll live," is the best reply I can give him. I have never lied to him except for in the tub, that was different. "Come in."

"You weren't awake when I got home," he says, walking in.

Sitting up slowly, I realize the sleep aid must still be in my system because I almost do my best Richard Marx impression and sing the chorus to "Waiting for You." I'm wondering if I should tell him that I had to take something to sleep so I could stop thinking about him. That I had to take a pill to deal with the ache in my stomach from seeing him with another beautiful stranger.

"I wasn't feeling quite right."

Which is true.

"You didn't text me to remind me to post, I was worried."

"You're pretty good at remembering now, it's like you're all grown up." I have to poke a little to disguise this sickness.

"Have you seen them?" he asks, sitting on the side of my bed. Trying to sit up in my bed is proving difficult as I desperately want to avoid this conversation.

"I took a look at some before I went to bed."

All true.

"Good, I haven't grown up too much. I wanted your approval."

Do you want me to tell you that you shined so bright I couldn't bear to look at you?

"I didn't see any nasty boogers in the pictures I saw so I think you're good."

"I have something for you."

He removes a black velvet square flat box from his shorts pocket and slowly hands it to me.

"It's a very nice box, Ihsan, thank you."

His face does not show the amusement I deserve for that.

Opening the lid, I find a beautiful silver chain bracelet with a sparkling pendant of concentric light blue, dark blue and white circles.

"This is beautiful, Ihsan," I say, pulling the bracelet from the velvet interior.

"It's handmade from Izmir. It is called *Nazar Boncuk*. People call it the 'evil eye.' It absorbs any negative energy focused on you from others."

"Ihsan, you don't need to waste your charm on me."

"*Hayir,* Beatrice, it's not a waste."

Yes, it is. I'm already under your spell.

"Wow, thank you so much. Where did you get it?"

"The 'evil eye' was given to me by the ambassador's wife."

"This is way too fancy for me."

He reaches over and takes it from my hand to help me clasp it around my wrist.

"What did I do to deserve this?" I ask, admiring the bracelet.

"Nothing. I told her that I thought you would like it so she gave it to me."

"Holy crap. It's like royal jewels. Your date didn't mind you giving me jewelry?"

"I didn't tell her."

"Does it absorb bad vibes coming from me?"

"Let's not test that."

"It kinda makes me feel like I'm wearing a Wonder Woman bracelet." I wave my arm as if I'm deflecting bullets.

Admiring the first jewelry a man has ever given me that wasn't made of carnival plastic, I try to mask how deeply I love his kind expression of his appreciation. Again, I realize that my heart is making more of this sweet gesture than it is, and my brain needs to punch it in the face.

"Did you fall asleep while working?"

He notices my laptop among the blankets on my bed. Thank goodness all the tissue had been disposed of prior to my passing out.

"Are you surprised?"

I cross my legs and lean over, looking at him with what I can only guess is a very long and droopy face.

"You need a break." He swipes up my laptop and tucks it under his arm. There is no resistance in me thanks to the medicine and last night's unexpected emotional blow.

"I'm too tired to argue."

He walks around my bed to my nightstand where I at some point in the night had put the remote to the TV.

"Here, you are going to watch TV and think of nothing. You will eat in bed. There is no reason to leave. I can even get you a diaper."

"Your jokes are improving. I'm so proud."

"So, no diaper?" he smiles.

"I better stretch my legs so my muscles don't atrophy, walking to the bathroom will be as far as I go. In fact, nature calls."

"I'm sure you can handle it by yourself," he says as he walks out of my room, closing the door behind him.

Walking into the bathroom, my memory flashes as I see the beautiful tub sitting there. Another punch in my stomach. At least my eyes aren't acting up today. My feet take me to the little toilet room and I close the door. After finishing my business, I shuffle my lead feet to the sink. Washing my hands seems to also take deliberate effort as a glint of sparkle catches my eyes from the gorgeous bracelet hanging from my wrist, a reminder of his limitless kindness. Leaning over the sink, I catch my hands on either side of the bowl. My body instinctively inhales deeply. It's time for me to put in a subscription delivery for big girl panties.

This eff...fucking sucks.

Since I'm being forced to spend the day in bed I'll catch up on my duties for the wedding. It's not work if I'm not getting paid. Turning the TV on, I decide that watching funny wedding movies would inspire me and I'm still abiding by Ihsan's rules. I have Maid of Honor duties to perform. Sarah's wedding week must be the stuff of legends. This is the perfect distraction. I reach for my laptop but instead all I feel is soft blankets.

Thwarted.

He did leave my phone.

Critical mistake.

There are a lot of fun things to do in San Antonio. I just have to think of something fun to do that isn't too boozy, at least for me. Searching through the various pub crawls, multi pedal bike bars and pasta making classes, I find they don't seem exciting. A river cruise looks promising, but it's just too hard to see on this tiny screen. I realize that I'm going to have to leave my room to get my laptop. This is going to take some conniving.

He will not beat me.

"Eeeee-saaaaahn!" I call out.

Nothing. He's actually going to make me leave the bed. Brat.

Removing the covers and escaping the confines of the bed, I wrap myself in the fluffy gray robe that reminds me every time of Ihsan bathing me. At some point he's going to really piss me off, I should probably save it for kindling when I have to burn everything that reminds me of him. Walking through the glass walkway to the kitchen, I don't see him or hear him. Looking through the glass doors to the pool, the water is still and the furniture, empty. The tiny parking lot is full. Thinking he might have gone for a run, I walk toward my room and stop at the doorway listening to Zeki's nails clicking on the floor coming out of the office.

Ihsan must be working on something. He does like those big red chairs. Probably makes him feel like a sultan. I turn the corner and into the office. Ihsan sits behind my laptop with an unrecognizable expression. As he turns the computer toward me, my stomach falls as I realize he has seen my man shopping from last night. Hurt and humiliation overwhelm my body.

"You don't owe me an explanation," he says, still expressionless.

Blink. Don't forget to blink. Blink, dammit!

Nothing hurts more than the truth and I might as well rip off the bandage over my invisible gaping wound.

"The wedding is only six months away. I just can't go alone. There's no time to find a date and get to know them enough to spend the week with me out of town. Blaine's assistant sent me some websites of boyfriends for hire."

When I say it out loud, it sounds like a reasonable business arrangement. I stand with my best matter-of-fact posture, not being able to stop my body from the tiny shakes in my fingertips.

Please don't laugh. Please don't laugh. Please don't laugh. It's too quiet. He isn't saying anything. Why isn't he saying anything?

"Well?" I break the silence. "You don't have anything clever to say?" I can't stop the nerves in my voice as his eyes stay glued to mine.

"No."

Why didn't he just laugh at me? Pity. You don't laugh when you pity someone, that would be cruel.

He's right, I don't owe him an explanation. But if Ihsan thought I hired someone for any other reason than a date for the wedding, it would destroy me. Pity is bad enough but that is sad and pathetic. His gaze draws away from me as he stands slowly and walks around the table. His stoic and expressionless face screams of disappointment. Not being able to let this go, I slide my hand through his arm before he passes by.

"That's it?" I crane my neck to see his face.

"What do you want me to say?"

"I don't know. Maybe a pep talk about how I don't need to do this? Something to make me feel less pathetic."

Feeling a little out of my league, I release my fingers from around his bicep.

"I don't think you are pathetic," he says to the floor, my shoulder against his arm. He can't even stand to look at me. His reaction is confusing, and I just want to get down to the nuts and bolts.

"Then what? You must be thinking something. I'm not hiring a prostitute."

Ihsan turns to show me his flat affect which guts me more than his inability to look at me.

"Did you see if I clicked on anyone?" My frustration fuels the volume of my voice. "No one would believe any of those guys would date me, much less spend the week with me. So even if I pick one, people will question why they were there with me anyway. I'm back to square one."

Every word causes me more pain than the last. He focuses his eyes away to the door, as if ashamed of what he sees. I watch him go in the direction of the living room without another word.

I'm not going to cry.

I'm tired of explaining how different life is for me. He couldn't understand without experiencing it. Unless there is some Freaky Friday magic accident, he never will. I'm torn between risking another emotional outburst, leaving me raw, or letting this heavy cloud drape over the house. My life here is too important for me to hold all this emotional shit. Ihsan is too important to me.

Adults usually don't wear PJs and a robe to do adult things, but I'm a different kind of adult. I don't even know where to start but I can't leave this ickiness in the air. Big girl panty time again. I want to take care of this now so we can move on, so I can move on. Tying the knot of the robe belt tighter around my waist, I set my mind to get this over with as soon as possible.

"Millie," I call out to her walking into the kitchen.

"Yes?"

"Did you see where Ihsan went?"

"I saw him go up the stairs to his room. Will you two be eating dinner at home tonight?"

"I will, I'll ask Ihsan. He's a bit foul right now."

"He told me to call him when I had finished making your lunch. Will you eat it out here or in your room?"

"I'll eat in the breakfast nook."

He was going to bring lunch to my room. I may need some kind of stomach acid reducer.

Turning to go make the climb up his stairs, I feel that damn pit again. It can't give me a break just once. I'm trying to do the right thing, but some unknown force is doing everything to keep me from taking that first step.

I stand at the bottom of the endless stairway. The steps feel farther apart than they did when I first climbed them. Well, the journey of a thousand steps and all.

Let's do this.

When I finally reach the top, I can feel the tension pounding in my ears. Not knowing what is going on with him behind those doors is eroding my initial bravado. I raise my fist up to the door and it suspends in the air. My arm feels too heavy to move yet I urge it forward to knock on his door.

"Ihsan?"

"*Evet?*"

Taking a deep breath, I turn the knob and peer into his room, watching him wipe a towel across his face.

"Can I come in?"

"*Hadi.*"

"Can we talk?"

"I thought you were done."

He walks past me, his eyes down as he sits on his bed, leaning over with his arms set his knees.

"But you didn't say anything."

"You don't want to hear what I have to say," he says with a low vocal fry that causes my neck to twitch.

"It seems like you didn't want to hear what I had to say either, so go ahead, it's only fair." I clench my teeth together as I wait for his response.

"I don't like that you feel you have to hire someone to be with you."

"I'm sure it's hard to see the real world from way up there but us minions have to be creative. Who do you think invented all those dating apps?"

I sit down delicately on the soft navy sheets, far enough from him to avoid feeling the stewing heat from his body.

"I feel like we've had this conversation before," I say to the floor.

"It seems to be a theme."

"Ihsan, we...ugh. You live on a different plane of existence. I'm not sure you could ever understand how it feels. I live in a constant state of envy, and you live in a constant state of being envied."

"Beatrice."

I usually love that he uses my full name but his tone indicates that he's about to bring it down heavy. But I'm not finished and continue before he can start the predictable lecture on what life should be and I argue about what life actually is.

"Look, I never have dates for events like these. I prefer it. I don't have to worry about anybody else having a good time. I'm a professional place holder. I can leave whenever I want and inevitably someone needs a ride home. So, really, I'm saving lives," I say, trying to lighten the mood but his scowl remains. "It's just *this* wedding."

I couldn't have said those words more pathetically, fighting back tears yet again. All my energy rushing out of my body as I slump heavily, my lifeless arms laying across my thighs. He has to be sick of seeing me like this.

"I just can't be alone at this wedding. It would be shitty of me to say I'm going then not go but if I told them I'm not going now, it would be six months of interrogation. Who doesn't go to their best friend's wedding because they're in love with the groom? I'm going to be a blubbering mess and I need someone to save me from myself. Besides, would it be too much to ask the universe for a single date on possibly the worst day of my life? Just this once?"

"Why didn't you ask me?" His head turns sideways, his eyelids half blinking as he connects his gaze to mine.

Oh damn, the shoulder smolder.

"What?"

"Why didn't you think of asking me to go with you?" His back straightens and my mind races. I heard him the first time, but I needed time to process this thought.

Because I never get what my heart truly desires, so why risk it?

"It didn't occur to me, you're my boss. And have you seen you?" I say followed by a big sucky silence. And then...light bulb.

"But I think this might work. You could go with me as my client to experience Texas as a Turk. That way I will have a friend there to distract me from all the shit in my head and no one would even think how mismatched we are because it's a business arrangement. We could do a whole bunch of videos."

I stand up and start to pace across his room to get all my thinking juices flowing.

"You should be done with all the master filming by then. This is a brilliant idea! I'm going to call the studio and Blaine."

"You were supposed to take a break today," he yells out as I navigate my way as quickly as I can down the stairs.

"Idyl hands are the devil's playthings!" I yell as I hit the bottom stair.

IHSAN

There is something serene about watching a woman sleep. Beatrice is no exception and when I see that she is awake when I sit on her bed the next morning, I'm disappointed I don't get to watch her silent and still. This morning, her face looks like invisible figures are pulling the skin down and her eyes only open halfway. I couldn't wait for her to dress and come out to give her the bracelet. Her tired eyes can't hide how much this small trinket means to her. It's refreshing to see someone sincerely grateful, as if I am watching Dobby hold up a sock. She would be proud I made that internal movie reference. But when she pretends the bracelet is the cuff of her favorite superhero, I can't help but cringe and smile at the same time. When I see how she can barely hold herself together, I can't bring myself to ask her to work. I wish she had let me know she wasn't feeling well.

After confiscating her laptop and arranging a meal for her, I sit in the office and try to get the day started on my own.

"Neh?" The images that appear shock me back against my seat. Thumbnails of good-looking men with pull down menus for a selection of services are neatly arranged on the desktop.

Is she trying to hire a date?

I look at her choices and notice the date is for the first week of December and realize what she had been doing most of the night. It dawns on me that the sickness she feels isn't the physical kind. The excessive air my lungs take in should take some of these feelings with them as they leave my body, but they have attached to my insides like parasites.

Is it really that bad for her? Does she want to attempt to navigate the emotional minefield that will be Brandon and Sarah's wedding with a stranger? Does she really think so little of herself that she thinks she needs to employ someone for a date?

She shouldn't have to do this. She shouldn't have to pay someone to be by her side. I can hear the pulse of my blood pumping louder in my ears. Beatrice deserves better than this. The wrenching feeling in my gut can only be described as a storm of guilt, pain and jealousy.

The look of shock, mixed with pain and indignity on her face when she finds me looking on her laptop stuns me frozen. Every word she uses to explain herself pains me more and more because what she's saying is true. I can't deny it and I don't have a right to. Every woman I have ever asked out has said yes. Every move I have ever made has been reciprocated.

I leave her alone in the office because anything I say won't hold any weight. When I reach my room, I head to the bathroom to attempt to shock my face with cold water, something to wash away the ugliness of the morning.

She sits next to me, completely defeated. I take a chance of spooking her and ask her why she didn't consider me. To my surprise, when the words leave my lips, I want to be her date. I want to escort her and be by her side to help her through the wedding, but she doesn't quite understand what I'm saying. She runs downstairs, celebrating the fact that I have provided her with a platonic business arrangement. The role of placeholder does not settle well with me. Silly me for thinking she would consider me for anything else.

> me: **Farah, I volunteered to take Beatrice to her friend's wedding.**

> Farah: **Did you volunteer like "doing her a favor" or did you two come up with it together?**

> me: **Both?**

> Farah: **Oh, abi.**

> me: **What?**

> Farah: **How are you so handsome and so clueless at the same time?**

me: **This is not help.**

Farah: **It is, you are just too clueless to figure it out.**

Chapter 25

B EATRICE

I've been waiting for a few days to hear from Gül so seeing her name on my phone makes me jump a little in my bed.

"I have news!" She greets me.

"Oh, please tell me it's good," I plead.

"It's good! I found a costume designer from a film. She will meet with you."

"No way! Gül, if you were here, I would kiss you."

"You did so much for our Disneyland trip, I had to do it for you. I will send you her number."

"You are the best! I'm going to call right now."

"Ok, *fantastik*."

The news of being able to meet the actual designer of the dress is incredible.

"Eee-saaahn!!" I shout from my room. "Hey, Wonder Boy!"

I get up from my bed and march toward my door. As soon as I step into the hallway, I am pushed back in by Ihsan.

He's lost his balance and slips in his socks on the tile floor. Attempting to hold him up, my arms fumble around his chest and arms. He finally steadies himself in my arms.

"Is there a revival of Risky Business or something? You know better than to run on these floors with socks."

"You screamed for me. I was putting on my basketball shoes."

"We should come up with a better system. I was excited."

"So you're not bleeding to death?"

I look at him as if the answer is obvious.

"I'm sorry but I have exciting news and no one else is here to share it with."

"What is so exciting?" he asks.

"Gül got me in touch with the actual designer of the Contact dress. She's a freaking godsend. This might actually work, Ihsan!"

He turns away to walk back to the living room, no words, nothing. His apathy stings. Following him down the slick hallway in my bare feet, I attempt to get his attention again.

"You can be kind of a jerk sometimes. This is important to me."

Stopping in the middle of the hallway and realizing he isn't listening, I throw an invisible spear at him.

"Sorry, this wasn't about you. I didn't mean to waste your time!"

Stomping back to my room, I realize that I overreacted and I don't know why. The sound of his car door closing doesn't make me feel better. He said he was on his way to play basketball so maybe basketball was more important than me. Whatever. Calling the costume designer is my top priority today. I dial the number Gül sent me and can barely hold in my excitement.

"Hello," a woman says on the other line.

"Hello, I'm looking for Carolyn Masters. I'm a friend of Gül Korlu."

"Oh yes, she told me you are looking for a certain dress."

"I've been in love with the Contact dress since the moment I saw it on the screen. I have an opportunity to wear the design in my best friend's wedding. I don't even know if it is possible, but it can't hurt to ask."

"I hope I can help you."

"First, I'm not built like Jody Foster. I am a big girl and so I'm going to have to have it made special. Fortunately, all the other bridesmaids are closer to her size so if there is a pattern of the dress or a pattern close to the dress, we can somehow work with that. I hope that all makes sense."

"Yes, it does. I would love it if you could come down to my studio and we can see what we can do."

"Wow. I'm speechless. This is beyond my wildest dreams."

"Are you available today?"

"Even if I wasn't, I would drop everything."

"Ok, how about two PM?"

"Perfect! I can't thank you enough. Can you text me the address?"

"Yes, I'll do that now."

My phone dings with the address and excitement erupts in my brain.

After spending the rest of the morning on the phone with Matthew, girling-out on this situation, I get myself ready, showering as quickly as possible and skipping makeup altogether.

I decide to call a car service since the costume warehouse is somewhere I've never been and parking is always a nightmare. I'm dropped off just outside her workspace and I practically dance to the front door. My body shakes with nervous excitement as I press the buzzer to grant me entrance into these hallowed halls.

"Hello, Beatrice?"

"Yes." I offer my hand.

She ushers me in and the amount of fabric, thread, and notions are overwhelming. Floor to ceiling rolls of fabric create a labyrinth of fiber. She escorts me back to an open workspace and offers me a seat near a larger-than-life monitor. On the screen is the dress, sans Jody Foster.

"Oh, there she is, my precious," I say, looking up at the display without care for my inner dork making an appearance.

"I'm happy that you appreciate my work."

"My friend Matthew and I are both in the wedding and he is SOOO jealous."

"That wouldn't be your client, then."

"No, I am a personal assistant to Ihsan Zorlu. He's an actor from Turkey, I mean Türkiye that will be in an upcoming movie. You should check out his Instagram, he's a former model and foot- I mean soccer player. He has some fun posts if I do say so myself."

But he's an asshat today.

"I will! Ok, let's see what we can do. I have a pattern that is very similar to the skirt part of the dress. The bodice is where we might run into trouble."

"I figured; these ladies are not the easiest to deal with."

"Let me take some measurements, I can come up with a mockup and we can go from there."

"The other bridesmaids won't be such a pain as I will. Welcome to my life."

"There are different challenges to full figured dresses."

She is very nice about this whole thing, but that stings a bit.

She walks around me with a measuring tape, measuring several different places on my body. The more she measures, the more self-conscious I am. She is speaking all the measurements into an app so I can hear all the numbers. They're bigger numbers than I expected. I try to convince myself she's measuring in metric.

"Let's get an idea of breast size."

Oh, this is going to be the cherry on my self-conscious sundae.

She has me raise my arms and takes a few more measurements from all directions. Then does the same thing with my arms lowered.

"This is going to be a challenge. Do you have an idea of what kind of bra you'll wear? I could make it to hide the bra straps, but you'll have to have a bra with small straps. Doing a built in probably won't work but we can try. Shapewear will also help the line of the dress and how it falls. Are you sure you want to go sleeveless? We could do a sleeve of some sort."

Because I have thick arms? All of me is thick.

Her words don't seem encouraging. She does this for a living and probably doesn't do a lot of fittings or designs for girls my size.

"I'll let you know when I have a mockup ready and we can go from there. I think we can get pretty close to the look you want."

"Let me know what I owe you. Thank you so much for your time, I really can't tell you how much this means to me."

After leaving the shop, I call a car service to bring me back to the glass house. As soon as I get settled in the back seat, my eyes start to fill. All I wanted was that dress. All I wanted was to feel pretty for a couple of hours in a dress I've always wanted. I should have just looked in a stupid bridal magazine and found a dress that looked the least like a potato sack.

Ihsan: **Where did you go?**

Seventh circle of hell.

me: **Running an errand.**

Ihsan: **Will you be back for dinner?**

me: **I'm almost home.**

The car drops me off, the driver is kind enough to not talk to me on the way back. In my experience though, girls that look like me don't usually get concern from strangers.

If I walk quickly enough, I can avoid seeing Ihsan.

I open the door as quietly as I can, but Zeki sounds the alarm. I still attempt to get to my room without detection.

"Beatrice!" he calls out.

"I'm just dropping off my stuff," I answer. If I can just make it to my door, I'll be home free, but I feel his large hand around my elbow.

"Beatrice," he says quieter.

Maybe if I just stay turned around like in one of his dramas, he won't see my face.

"Hey."

He doesn't pull me around, but he is slick and walks around me to stick his nosey face in mine.

"What?" I stare at him defiantly.

"What's going on?"

"Nothing. What do you want?" I force myself to calm down. The fitting fiasco isn't his fault.

"I just wanted to apologize for earlier."

"Ok, apology accepted. I'd like to put my stuff away now."

He lets me pass and I pull my purse around over my head and as soon as I can see my bed, I throw it down. My shoes launch across the room, hitting the windows on the other side.

"Hey." I feel two hands on my shoulders as he pulls me back to his chest.

"What happened to you?"

I let my shoulders fall and my head drop to my chest.

"It was mortifying," I breathe out.

"It can't be that bad."

"For me it is. I really don't think you'll understand."

"Even if I don't understand, you might feel better if you talk about it."

I would tell this man anything. He is literally holding me up. I pull away from him and drop myself onto the edge of my bed.

"I don't think the dress is going to work out. Ihsan, it was humiliating. She was very nice, but she was taking all these measurements and suggesting alterations that I know she was just saying because this dress won't work on my body. I would have called Matthew, but he's just as excited as I am and I couldn't bear to tell him."

Ihsan moves me to my bed, sets me down and sits close to me, his large warm hand rubbing circles on my back.

"I've never dreamed of having a wedding dress, it's not going to happen for me. But this dress I could have. It was the one thing in this wedding that I could look forward to."

I rise slowly off the bed, pick up my shoes where they landed and walk down the hall toward the closet. "I just really wanted to feel pretty that day because I'm apparently a 12-year-old girl inside. Fuuuuuuuuck!" I yell when I reach my closet. "And sorry I was a bitch earlier."

"All is forgiven," he yells back.

I'm giving up today. Today can go fuck itself. I want to call Sarah and tell her I'm not going to be in her wedding but that would be me just being dramatic and it would hurt her and by the transitive property of equality, it would hurt Brandon as well.

Ihsan waits patiently on my bed, being the perfect listener. I stop at the top of the two stairs and lean my shoulder against the wall. My eyes have dried up a little and I can feel myself calming down.

"I really was sincere. I am sorry. I just wanted to make sure I said it before I went down an emotional spiral," I say laughing a little.

"I'm sorry, too." Ihsan's face brightens slightly.

"You don't have anything to apologize for. You came running when you thought I was bleeding out and it was nothing."

"I was rude."

"You had the right to be."

"No, I .... I have a hard time with Gül sometimes."

Walking down the stairs and slowly to the bed, I stop a few feet from him. I didn't realize what I said could hurt him. He hasn't given me a lot of details about his divorce and I haven't dug any further than what he told me from the beginning.

"And there I go telling you how wonderful she is."

He stands up slowly, still in his workout gear, and draws me into his arms.

"We are a fine pair, aren't we?" I laugh into his chest.

His hold around me is tight, in fact it's getting tighter, uncomfortably tight.

"Um, Fezzik...I'm cracking," I laugh trying to wriggle away. He isn't letting me go.

"No laugh, no go." His voice is unnaturally deep to go along with my "Princess Bride" reference.

"Come on, you're covering me with your man sweat and not in a good way. Ha...ha...ha." I say mockingly.

"That doesn't count." Then I feel his fingertips starting to dig into my side.

"AHHH...that's not fair. You have all those damn muscles." I continue trying to escape.

"Come on, you've got muscles too," he laughs at me.

"This is the worst workout I've ever had." Then I remember that he's ticklish too.

Reaching up to his ribs, I dig my fingers in his hard sides. His hold around me loosens as his body crumples and he lets out a loud manly scream.

"My muscles are up here," I point to the sides of my skull as I back away from him.

He smiles that beautiful gleaming smile and I wish I hadn't put up a fight. He grabs my shoulders and turns me toward the main part of the house.

"*Hadi*, let's have dinner," he says, holding my shoulders away from him at arm's length and marches me down the hall.

"So, I can eat my feelings?" I laugh at myself.

"I'm not leaving you alone, all you'll eat is Doritos and Jerry."

"Don't forget Ben, can't leave him out," I correct him as we enter the familiar kitchen space.

He pulls out a stool for me, and I reluctantly climb onto it. I cross my hands on the flat cool counter for a soft place for my head to land.

"I now know what 'been judged and found wanting' means," I say in my best regency voice.

"Hey, you always figure something out," he says, opening the refrigerator.

"My figure is the problem," I say into my hands.

"So, that is what you fix."

"Errrrrr." A low rumbling growl escapes into my hands.

"Ok, I'll back off."

In a most melodramatic movement, I throw myself back into the chair, my hair flying, and my arms draped down by my side as if they are dangling by the tendons under the skin.

"I'm sorry, you've caught me in a really shitty mood and as always you are stupid nice and supportive and crap. Can't you just let me have my Oreo medicine and take it to my bed?"

He places a bowl of strawberries in front of me and a small jar with a fancy label. As he drizzles a small spoonful of amber liquid over the bowl, he laughs at my woe is me act.

"This is not what I ordered," I say, staring down at the red speckled jewels.

"Just sit and eat with me."

I reluctantly grab a strawberry, inspecting this new preparation technique and sink my teeth slowly into the glossy flesh, savoring the fancy honey Ihsan decided to share. It is so sweet and juicy that it feels like it washes away some of the sting of today.

Smiling at Ihsan as I chew, his mouth curls upward, returning the sentiment.

"See, it's good," he says, trying to convince me.

"I like strawberries, I need Oreos," I say, finishing the fruit in my mouth.

His chest expands swiftly, and he braces his forearms on the counter as he leans over, his eyes stern yet sultry which I'm sure he didn't mean to do. It's probably his default.

"Look, I have trainers and you can use the gym downstairs. I won't help you unless you ask."

"Oh, I see. I really don't feel like being the Galatea to your Pygmalion." Pygmalion falls in love with Galatea, so my reference falls flat.

I stand up to leave but he appears in front of me without a sound or even a wisp of air. I don't understand how he moves so fluidly without detection.

"Listen," He lightly pushes me back onto the stool. "I'm only telling you because you look so miserable. If you want to feel good wearing the dress, this will help, I can help."

"God, I feel so pathetic." I look at him with my eyes starting to water.

"There is nothing pathetic about wanting something better for yourself. Am I pathetic for coming here?"

"Nobody looks at you as pathetic," I say, losing patience.

"Just let me know what you want."

Really? This could go south fast.

"I want time to think." I attempt to slide off the stool a second time. "Hey, thanks for not making this about being skinny."

I really meant it. Finding my strength again is more important. Just so happens my in-home Hercules offered himself up as tribute. I walk to my room, not feeling like eating more of his pretty food, as if that will help.

"You're already perfect," he shouts to my back, my shoulders tense up to my ears as if someone scraped their nails down an old school chalkboard.

Asshole.

He should know better than to say crap like that.

"And so are you," I yell from my room. It's hard to hear something like that when you don't believe it.

IHSAN

Watching a friend in pain is hard, even harder when you are helpless to prevent it. Gül and Beatrice have bonded over this dress, and I dread the day when I tell her why Gül and I ended. The fact that Gül's name even comes out of her mouth makes me ill and I can't hide my disgust.

Unfortunately, Beatrice doesn't understand and takes my anger personally. When she returns from her fitting, the energy in the house immediately turns dark as she rushes to her room. She brushes off my apology and the sounds of something hitting the walls force me to hazard my fortunes.

Listening to her words crush her spirit with every breath is nothing less than heartbreaking. She shocks me with her admission that she doesn't see a wedding in her future. She doesn't see someone to love her to make a live with her. This dress is more than a dress for her, it is her change to feel seen. I didn't truly understand the concept of the revenge body until now. I know that is what Beatrice needs, revenge for everything Brandon has put her through.

After years of working out, I know that it isn't just your body that changes but your mental health as well. Luring her to the kitchen probably isn't the best idea with all the knives and her unnaturally accurate aim but we do need to eat dinner. To hear that she feels that she isn't enough, that she isn't worthy, drives a shard of glass in my side. There is an inherent risk of addressing such a personal topic but when she opens the door I decide it's worth the risk. If she only knew how she heated up my insides when her full, ripe lips wrap around the strawberry and she sucks off the glistening honey. Well, it would at least give her more ammunition to torment me.

> **me: Matthew, I need your particular set of skills.**

> **Matthew: Yay me!**

> **me: I offered to help Bee before the wedding. The fitting did not go well.**

> **Matthew: I didn't know you could sew.**

> **me: Working out. I offered to help her fit into the dress.**

> **Matthew: I'm driving to ATM and the church right now.**

me: Why?

Matthew: **It's going to look like the Hindenburg dropped on the altar by the time I'm done lighting all the candles.**

me: **What?**

Matthew: **I'll be praying very hard for you. What else do you need from me?**

me: **Don't enable her.**

Matthew: *Moi?*

me: **Just keep her food options safe and no more drive by ice-creamings.**

Matthew: **I know. I need to take *Mobile Lunch Lady* off my contacts list.**

me: **You can come workout with us too if you want.**

me: **Matthew?**

Matthew: **Sorry they had to resuscitate me.**

me: **Just tell me you'll help me keep her on track.**

Matthew: **I'm in after she makes it out of withdrawal.**

me: **Deal.** *Sou.*

Matthew: **What?!**

me: **Thank you.**

Chapter 26

B EATRICE

Laying on my bed after my meal of strawberries and eye candy, I try to reconcile my emotions with my thoughts.

What do I want? I want to feel good at the wedding.

Why do you want to feel good? Because I am tired of Brandon and Sarah making me feel miserable.

Why do they make you feel miserable? Because I'm jealous.

What are you jealous of? I'm jealous of their relationship.

Are you jealous of their relationship or jealous that they have a relationship?

This question causes me to pause.

I let these questions whirl around in my head for a long while, but only more questions and internal negativity seem to add instead of subtracting from the confusion.

Brandon was the only person I ever allowed myself to have romantic feelings for and when it wasn't reciprocated, I was crushed. Carl just filled a space.

Going over all these questions in my mind made me think if it was really Brandon and Sarah's relationship making me miserable or if I am doing it to myself. Ihsan is offering me a real remedy for my curse, both the physical and mental malediction, and I'm running out of excuses not to accept. The universe is throwing me a tall, dark, seductively accented lifesaver and if I don't grab it, I don't deserve another offer. If I allow Ihsan to help me, he's really going to see the worst of me, but I guess we'll see if he can stomach that. I curl myself upwards and push myself off the bed.

Dragging myself down the hall, I try to muster all the bits of bravery I've summoned in my life for one last charge into the unknown. It's time for a new me.

That's right bitches, I'm doing this!

"Ihsan?" I call out.

Now that I'm motivated, however sluggishly, he ditches me?

Wow, Ihsan.

"Ihsan?" I call out again, using my diaphragm for breath support but trying not to sound panicky in case he does another Tom Cruise impression.

I walk up the stairs to his room and knock. Nothing, and Zeki is gone too. I didn't hear the front door open or close. He was in workout gear so it would only make sense that he is downstairs in this other dimension called "the gym."

UGH!

The word feels like sand in my mouth.

Passing the floral aroma of the laundry room and dumbwaiter closet, I reach the door that I ignored when I got the first tour. Unfamiliar music blasts from the hall, assaulting my ear drums. Opening the door slowly, I wince at the volume level vibrating off the walls. There is a set of free weights, a few medicine balls of different sizes, a treadmill with a TV, floor mats and on the far side a heavy bag suspended from the ceiling in front of a mirrored wall. I might as well be a witch that just got sprayed with a hose, melting into the floor when I see all those mirrors. Ihsan walks from around the corner wrapping his wrists, attaching boxing gloves.

Sweet Mary, Mother of God.

Both my hands grab onto the sides of the door frame to hold me upright. That scene when the vampire sparkles, it's real. Science would suggest it's from the lights reflecting off the sweat sliding down Ihsan's skin, but I prefer to think that he has some magical hotness glitter seeping out his pores. Science, however, cannot explain how all the bones in my body have just evaporated. A few dark locks fall on his forehead as his face shines from well-earned perspiration. The ropey veins in his arms and neck plump further down his shoulders and disappear into his tight bare muscled chest. His back is taut and thick with tanned sculpted tissue drawing my eyes to the intricate tattoo down his bicep that I'm doing everything in my power not to lick.

Feeling like I'm invading his sanctuary, I stay silent so as not to disturb him and halt the show. With the door jamb still holding me upright, my eyes target his back as he punches the bag like it just insulted his mother.

Our eyes meet as he spots me in the mirror and I crane my neck overhead and to the walls as if I was looking to change the light bulbs as part of my house manager duties. He smiles that panty wetting smile as he steadies the bag. I spot a white towel rack and take one from the top of the pile. Walking over to him, I lift my feet an extra inch so as to not trip on the floor mat, because that is exactly what would happen. Extending my arm toward him in a towel offering, I force my eyes to stay on his face and not journey south.

"*Teşekkürler*. Have you been down here before?" he asks, wiping the sweat the best he can while holding the towel with his boxing gloves.

"Bless you. I mean, you're welcome. And yeah, hours and hours," I say sarcastically.

After a few glances around the room, I decide to jump off the very deep cliff.

"Obama arms."

"*Neh*?"

"You asked me what I want. I want Michelle Obama's arms."

His torso shakes at my curtness.

"Anything else?"

Are you on the menu?

"That's all I could think of. Can we start there?"

"Yes, do you have anything to workout in?"

"Only if we are doing naked hot yoga."

Did I forget to pack my filter today?

"Weeell..." Ihsan raises his thick eyebrows.

"In your dreams, Superboy. I'll go see what I can order. After today's debacle, I don't think I can stomach trying on any workout clothes."

Turning to walk away, I feel a jolt to my shoulder causing my feet to falter.

"Did you just punch your employee?"

"You aren't technically my employee."

"You are literally punching me while I'm down. Why do you want to start a fight with me?"

Pulling me toward the bag with those ridiculously oversized gloves, he coaxes me forward.

"Here, stand here, like this." He stands next to me with his left foot forward and his right foot about a foot and half apart, facing a forty-five-degree angle from center.

"We're starting now, are we? Okay, Popeye."

"Bring your arms up like this." He bends his elbows with his fists near his face, well, giant gloves near his face. "Hold on."

He walks over to the corner and bites the tape around his wrist and unwraps his gloves.

"Bow chicka bow wow," flies out of my mouth. I don't think he appreciates my poor attempt at imitating stripper music as he continues ripping the tape with his teeth without even a flinch.

"Take it all off, baby. You know, if this acting thing doesn't work out, I'm sure we can get you a gig at Chippendales."

"Filter not functioning today?"

"It's on the fritz." Another word to add to his Turkish/English word spreadsheet. "It means it's temporarily not working,"

He nods in understanding, he's getting a lot of practice at that.

"Ok, back to where you were."

He stands facing me and I obey.

"Put your fists up to your face."

I ball up my hands, shove them in my cheeks and bat my eyelashes at him with anime eyes. He may grow tired of all the eye rolling, but today is not that day.

Pulling my hands away from my face, he puts my hands in his and moves my thumbs to the front of my fingers. He moves my right hand near the right of my chin and the left in front of my face.

I am totally counting this as hand holding.

"Bend your knees a little and put your weight equally on both legs." Patting his thighs, he demonstrates the way his knees bend.

He steps back and assesses my stance. I don't know how comfortable I am with a technicolor judging my first attempt at athletic activity. He circles behind me and puts his hands along the sides of my hips. My ass cheeks clench without any command from my brain.

"Twist your hips toward the bag."

As he gives me instructions, I feel him pushing my right hip away and pulling my left toward him. We repeat this movement a few times to set up a rhythm in my body.

"Just so you know, I'm counting this as first base."

I can see his face in the mirror waiting for me to explain.

"Matthew will have to explain that one to you."

"Should I be nervous?"

"Probably."

He returns to my front and grabs my right fist in his. His palm presses the flat part of my fist.

"This is where you hit the bag. Your wrist should line up with your fist. Keep your elbow in and twist your wrist right before you hit the bag," he says, laying his rather large hand over my wrist to force it straight and move my arm the way he described.

"Do I get to punch now, Coach?" I say in my best little kid voice. I'm still unsure if he appreciates my humor, his face providing zero clues.

"Twist your hips and use that power to push your fist through the bag. Try a couple times, slowly."

I review what he taught me and punch a few times in slow motion while he watches me.

"Ok, now use some power but through your hips," he says, twisting his body.

"Better stand back," I laugh as I prepare myself to mutilate the hanging bag.

The more I make contact with the bag, the less tension I feel in my body. The bag starts to swing so Ihsan moves to the other side and holds it against his body. I punch a few more times and stand back to relax.

"Float like a butterfly, sting like a...me," I smile at one of the only jokes I have ever made using my nickname.

"Good job!" he says, releasing the bag and walking around toward me. I'm not tired but my breath seems to carry the negativity out of my body.

"We can put pictures on this bag, right?" I ask Ihsan. "Because I can't afford to smash your gorgeous mug."

He pushes his fist against my cheek with a big smile and wraps his sweaty elbow around my neck as we walk toward the door.

"You are so disgusting!" I mock protest his strong arm around me to which he makes the grip around my neck stronger. As much as I languish in the physical contact from Ihsan, I know it doesn't come from a place of real affection. This still feels dishonest.

I wrap my arm around his waist and dig my fingers into his rib and he reacts exactly as I need him to. He lets out a yelp and releases his arm from around my neck.

I realize that I'm going to let Ihsan see me, really see me. I've never let anyone in this close. I've never been this vulnerable. The consequence of rejection, of losing something so important to me is almost more than I can bear. I want to run but I know Ihsan will find me and there's a comfort in that. He needs me too much and I need him possibly more. I just wish we needed the same thing from each other. If wishes were horses, beggars would ride.

ISHAN

I notice Beatrice watching me in the doorway after I spent the last twenty minutes working the bag. She did a very poor job hiding it from me, but she never apologizes for admiring me, in fact she usually uses it as fodder for her jabs. I feel honored that she is allowing me to help her change possibly her life. Antagonizing her seems to be the best way to eventually get what I want and when I shove her shoulder she doesn't disappoint. She lets me hold her hips and maneuver them in proper striking formation and in true Beatrice fashion she uses humor to deflect. It doesn't stop me from enjoying holding her, even if it is in this limited fashion. I have a feeling my right hand will get in an extra workout tonight. She doesn't pull away under my touch as she often does and when she allows me to move her body, I feel in some way humbled. I won't let her do this alone and I won't let her quit. I just hope she has as much confidence in herself as I have in her.

It is beyond improper to think of her the way I sometimes do at night. She is the only woman I have constant contact with besides Charlotte and the hair and make-up crew, so it isn't entirely my fault. She's the first person I see in the morning and often the last person I see at night. What attracts me initially to most women isn't always their physical traits. I have often been attracted to women who exude confidence, but that is most likely due to their own feeling of attractiveness. Beatrice's confidence comes from somewhere else, somewhere more genuine and a bit mischievous. Almost as if she knows she is the cleverest one in the room but is lying in wait for the next person to fall victim to her innocent seduction.

After our first impromptu boxing lesson, I make it halfway up the stairs before I realize that I had forgotten to let Beatrice know that she could start tomorrow morning with yoga. My feet quickly turn on the middle stair and head back down to the main floor. When I reach her room, I hear her familiar voice laugh at herself and then continue to talk. I lean in trying to figure out if she is talking to herself or someone on the phone. One of those would cause me great concern. Which one? I'm not sure.

"Mom, I'm starting something new tomorrow. Ihsan is letting me join his workouts to help me get in shape for Brandon's wedding. I'm scared mom. I can't fail at this. I can't live if I'm not actually living. I don't have any excuses. Even if I did, Ihsan has this ridiculous talent of running me out of them. I wish you could have met him when you were yourself. He's a special kind of man."

What does that mean?

"He'd probably be a good candidate for the cover of those romance novels you used to read. But that isn't what makes him special. He takes care of me mom, even when he doesn't have to. You'd be proud, I even let him. I gotta go mom, a new me starts tomorrow." A silence falls in the hallway outside her room, and I wait to hear rustling in her bed before I step away.

When she is video chatting with her mom, she talks as if she is talking to one of my children but this voice memo, this is Beatrice talking to her mom from years ago.

Chapter 27

BEATRICE

Every morning since the second week, Ihsan and one of his army of trainers workout either down in the gym or outside. When I started this job, I made it a point to schedule my wake-up time around the time they finish in the gym. Watching Ihsan all sweaty should be listed as one of the benefits of this job when I'm finished. Maybe under supervision? If you really think about it, it's a safety issue. He could accidentally fall in the hallway and his clothes could catch on something and be ripped off suddenly. I'm just being thorough. That is what I will tell HR anyway if it ever comes up.

Returning from my first boxing session, I decide that not only do I need workout outfits but I also need workout shoes. I spend the next morning looking online for athletic clothing, which turns out not to be as bad as I thought. Reading reviews from actual plus sized athletes, I didn't even know there were such people, is extremely helpful. I find some cute workout capris, large dry fit t-shirts, and even large dry fit tank tops. I was surprised how many options there were.

The biggest thing, literally and figuratively, I'm worried about is a bra. I have to dig deep into the webosphere to find what would be able to contain and support the ladies. I know that cute does not mean effective. That goes for life as well. I suspect that they used a size two model with size F breasts to demonstrate the best technique to clasp this badass bra.

Puuuullllease.

The garment is the bullet proof vest of braziers. I make my best guess for sizing and pick whatever fun colors and patterns are available and take the plunge. What surprised me was that you could send it back for repairs as if it was an engine part. That is some serious hardware.

Shoes were a whole other matter. I really didn't want to go into a sporting goods store and be waited on by a waif. My feet are only slightly wide so finding shoes that work can be tricky. That is why Vans are always my go-to. I'm going to have to ask someone for help and the only one available is God's gift to fitness sitting in the living room reading scripts. Maybe there's a hotline. I bite the bullet, shut my laptop, tuck it under my armpit, peel myself off the leather and head over to Ihsan's office annex.

Seeing him sit there so focused on reading, his highlighter in his mouth, in his sweats with one bare foot on the coffee table and the other across his lap could have been a Norman Rockwell plate hanging in my mom's kitchen. Walking quietly around the backside of the couch I plop down hard next to him and stare at his concentration face.

"Whatcha doin'?" I ask with a bit of a little kid tone.

"Killing aliens," he replies.

"*Neh*?" I ask.

He turns a script toward me and shows me the highlighted lines and doodles in the margins.

"Oh, I'm excited about that one! Pick that one, pick that one!" I say with adolescent excitement.

He puts the script down and pretends to be irritated.

"Did you need something?"

"Shoes."

"*Neh*?"

"If I'm going to do this workout thing, I'm going to need the proper equipment for whatever way you have chosen to break me. I know me and if I hurt myself, I'm done. So, what is your preferred form of torture?"

Ihsan dog ears the script, sets it on the coffee table and takes my laptop from me as if I don't have any business purchasing workout gear on my own.

"You're going to do everything."

"Brilliant plan, Pinky. Oh no, wait. What if we want a plan that works?"

When he looks over to me as if my face grew Brussel sprouts, I realize he isn't the audience for my very specific quote.

"I don't suppose you grew up watching 'Pinky and the Brain'?"

He clears his throat to indicate he is about to resume listing off the ways in which he will inflict pain.

"As I was saying, you will be joining me on all my workouts."

"Because killing your personal assistant sounds fun to you."

"Most days, it does." He smiles, staring at the screen. "Different sport, different shoes."

"You're so high maintenance." I purse my lips in frustration.

"Ok, ok. Let me think about this. So, yoga and swimming, no shoes." His head tilts upwards as if asking Allah for advice. Then he adds, "Martial arts and boxing can use the same shoe as well as running and strength training."

He spends the next couple of minutes clicking and closing websites. For someone who has issues with words, he has no problem cruising through these websites. I suppose when you workout as much as he does, the sites are familiar.

"What size shoe do you wear?"

"Nine and a half wide-ish." That would be a pretty good descriptor of me if the shoe size were lower.

"For the future, order a size larger in athletic shoes."

"Oh, you're so cute thinking there is a future for me in this. The whole shredding for the wedding doesn't go past December unless I go..." I stop too late.

"Go?"

The deepest fear of all is about to rear its ugly head. Ihsan wears down the protective wall and the beast is busting through.

"Unless I go back to teaching."

"*Neh*?" he says turning to me with a combination of hurt and confusion.

I take a deep breath and stare at the coffee table.

"When I was huddled on the floor of my room it became very obvious that this body wouldn't be able to protect my kids. I sat there thinking of what I was strong enough to lift and throw. If I could carry a kid if they were hurt. If I could even save myself. It's not that I don't think I'm qualified to teach them, I'm not qualified to save them. Maybe if I get my act together, I'll feel comfortable in the classroom again," I pause as the words darken the air. "They really should offer action hero training in credentialing programs."

Ihsan clears his throat a little too loud.

I poke his elbow with mine. "If this acting thing doesn't pan out..."

A grin threatens to overtake his face.

"Beatrice, I've been the target of your throwing arm. You've got that down."

"And don't you forget it."

"You might actually like working out, you never know."

He clicks the pull-down menus and chooses the size.

"Color?"

"Black is slimming," I say jokingly.

"Oh sorry, this is running shoes you have no choice."

He turns the laptop a little and shows me the most obnoxious orange I have ever seen.

"I'm not directing cars in a construction zone, those are hideous!"

"That is the only option. These shoes are easy on your feet and joints."

"So, I'm ordering orthopedic traffic cones? If I'm going to suffer through this I should at least have attractive outfits."

I sit back on the couch hard in frustration.

"Just put them in the cart. Don't pay for them. I am on to you and Gül's game," I say accusingly. "If I pay for all of it, I'm less likely to quit."

"Yes, but if I pay, you'll feel guilty if you quit." He looks at me, smiles and presses a button.

"Well, I already ordered clothes and a bra," I say, shaking my head sideways as if I pulled one over on him.

"You ordered a bra without me?" he feigns disappointment.

"Please tell me what valuable insight you could have provided when finding an athletic bra for a chest that is fifty times the size of yours," I say, motioning my hands over the large ladies.

I didn't mean for this gesture to call attention to them and I just gave him permission to look at my breasts with analytical interest.

"Fifty? I would have thought maybe thirty-five times," his accent is somehow thicker when saying this.

Does he know that laying it on like that immediately disarms me?

"I'm calling HR and reporting you."

"We should have them on speed dial."

"*Sus,*" I say using his language against him.

"I will contact all the trainers. You can start sessions once you have everything. But until then..."

"*Neh?*" I say, incorporating a bit more Turkish.

An evil smile spreads across his face. "We can do ab work on the floor of the gym and swim."

"I think it is safer to work with a professional," I protest.

He pulls up his shirt exposing the ripples of tanned muscles where a normal person's pooch should be.

"I think I know what I'm doing."

"Ew gross. Put those away," I say, pulling his shirt down as he smacks my hands away. "Do I have to swim?"

"*Evet.*"

"Do burkas come in bathing suit material?"

"You whine so much."

"If you had to do something you loathed every day for six months you'd whine too."

"I see your face every day," he smiles, quite happy with his quick response.

"I'm putting Ex-Lax in your protein shake. Just know that."

"Ex-Lax?"

"Oh, you'll figure it out."

He pulls the laptop to himself and types some things into the search bar, and his eyes get big.

"You wouldn't!" He turns to me with a tinge of fear in his eye.

"Wouldn't I? 'Hell, hath no fury like a woman scorned,' my boy," I say, tapping his knee as patronizingly as I can.

"I will have a conversation with Millie about meals."

"Dang, you're going balls deep," I knew the second I pronounced that last "p" sound that not only is he going to look at me confused but I'm also going to have to explain this to him too. But thinking more about it, I will not allow him to look that up on the internet.

"*Neh?*" he says as expected.

"Means going all in," I say.

Not only did that not help but it made my secret joke even funnier.

"I mean, really committing to something, really focusing on it."

Nice recovery.

Ihsan likes to use colloquialisms and idioms he learns in casual conversations as much as possible. I pray I am there when he uses this one.

"Then, I am. Are you 'going balls deep'?"

This is a gift that keeps on giving.

"Yep, sure am!" I say trying to hold back the eruption of hysterics that I would normally let go. I don't want to dissuade him from using it in casual conversation, that would be depriving someone of a good hearty laugh. I can't do that, it wouldn't be right.

Please universe, let me be there when he tries this one out in public.

"Give it to me straight, doc." I should just carve out a day to do English lessons with him. "It means give me the bad news and don't try to make it sound better."

"I think I get it. Millie is going to prepare all your meals and snacks to the instructions I give her."

"This is where I find out how you really feel about me."

"If you have a question or want to eat something not prepared for you, you have to text me. I'll put you on the same program I did to get in shape for 'The Web'. There's a lot of research and I can suggest some books if you want. I'll do it too."

"You do realize how much power I'm giving up, right? If I get hangry, hungry and angry at the same time, I'm going to book you a prostate exam at a learning college."

Watching his belly laugh is like a birthday present.

"Alright, you did look amazing in that show."

"Did I?" His eyes expand and an impish smile spreads across his face. "Oh, I have gift!"

It's so cute when he forgets articles of speech.

After putting down the laptop, he reminds me of his ridiculous physical prowess by jumping over the back of the couch and running up the stairs three at a time. He disappears into his bedroom then speeds down the stairs and jumps over all the pillows on the couch with a perfect landing, a rectangular box tucked in his elbow pit.

"I didn't wrap it, but here." His smile is so big as if he made the gift personally.

I see a picture of an insulated water bottle on the side of the inner box.

"Oh, that's great. Thank you."

"Open it."

Carefully, I release the tab on the top and grab the plastic lid on the top and pull. It is a black metal water bottle with a silver design etched into it. Ihsan's smile is way too big, I must be missing something. I turn the bottle around and suddenly notice the silver rose decal etched into the black bottle.

Really? When the hell did he have time to do this?

I could react one of two ways. I know how he wants me to react, but I will not give him that satisfaction.

"Oh, nice. It's pretty," I smile as earnestly as I can without giving him a clue that I see the scrolling roses.

"Do you see it, look." He turns the water bottle around again.

"Yeah, the silver filigree is cool. Thanks. I guess I better get used to having this attached to my hip," I say while slowly moving my hand along the couch to the nearest pillow.

"No, look closer." He leans in trying to show me on the bottle the rose that I can so clearly see.

He suddenly falls backward as I hit him as hard as I can in his smug mug with a couch pillow. While he is recovering from the shock of the first blow, I take the opportunity to grab another pillow, jump at him, push him down on the couch, and get in as many hits as I can. I brace one leg on the floor to make sure he can't just buck me off. Brandon and Matthew gave me plenty of training for situations such as these.

His hands flail as he attempts to grasp on my wrists as I pummel him relentlessly.

"You suck so much! You are the king of suckage! And the Oscar in the category of suck goes to Ihsan Zorlu," I yell at him as my ineffective weapons make contact.

"*Dosz, dosz, dosz,*" he keeps repeating, not being able to capture my hands and dodge my swings at the same time.

"I don't understand you! What was that you said? Keep hitting you? Oh ok, I can do that!"

He manages to get a grip on a pillow and pulls it away but drops it on the floor. I pull another pillow from the couch.

"Stop, stop, stop!"

"But you said to keep hitting you! I'm so confused. Your English is so bad. I don't understand anything you say. You should really work on that."

I realize that this is taking a lot of energy, thinking of clever things to say, dodging his hands and strategizing my attack.

"You have to tell me I win for this to stop." I pause briefly, slightly out of breath and then I swing again.

"What if I like it?" he says between swings.

"What?!" I stop with both hands cocked and loaded.

"What if I like it?" He takes this opportunity to swiftly snatch my wrists.

"That's really low, distracting someone in a pillow fight with innuendo."

"Inn..."

"Innuendo...sexual suggestion. Am I really explaining innuendo while sitting on your..." I look down and am drawing a blank coming up with a word to accurately describe where I am sitting.

"*Neh?*" he laughs. "Can't you say it?"

"I can feel it, why do I need to say it?" I say knowing damn well nothing is happening under me.

There, teach him.

"The body does what the body does," he says casually.

"Damn you and your hot confidence. Let me go!" I continue with fake disgust and try to loosen his grip.

"You have to tell me I win for this to stop," he says in a mocking voice.

"Fine! You win!" He releases my arms. I quickly realize that in order to get out of this situation I have to lean forward so my leg that is stuck in the couch can move freely. This would bring my boobs right in his face.

Damnit.

There is really no way to avoid his face's visit with the ladies.

Oh, dear God, help me.

Unless I distract him with something else.

I push my palms hard into his chest while I lean forward and move as quickly as I can. He lets out a loud groan and curls his body up as soon as my leg crosses over his.

"Oh, did that hurt your perfectly sculpted abs? Drama Queen."

Ihsan always laughs at my mocking tone.

"You're strong," he says, sitting up and acting like he's still in pain.

"You need a lot of muscle to move all this..." I make a sweeping gesture across my body, "hotness."

I grab my water bottle and step around the couch.

"Pick up all this crap," I say waving to the half destroyed living room once I'm far enough away in case of retaliation. "You really are a pig."

And as expected, he attempts to grab me by jumping over the couch.

"Your attempts to flirt with me are fruitless!" I say, running down the hall into my room.

IHSAN

When Beatrice suddenly appears next to me grinning at me like the Cheshire cat, I know I have to give her my undivided attention. I appreciate how she states the obvious so she can get right to the point. Even if she spent ten years under Brandon's spell, she doesn't seem to waste time in any other part of her life. I wonder how Brandon would have reacted if Beatrice had confronted him with how she felt about him. If she had, she wouldn't be sitting next to me right now, looking adorable and asking for my help.

She knocks the air out of my lungs describing what went through her head the last day of teaching. I know she still isn't ready to deal with everything that happened that day so this morsel of information out of the blue is to say the least, shocking. My country has not been immune to warfare on its own turf. Even though America hasn't had real fighting on its own land in modern times, it seems that the battlefield is their schools. Beatrice was thrown into a situation she wasn't emotionally or physically prepared for and even worse, she took on a soldier's burden. I doubt any of her classes to become a teacher covered that in their syllabus.

For someone as plump-ish like Beatrice, she certainly is spry. The water bottle idea had come to me while I caught myself watching her drink, chug really, in our office. Sometimes her actions reflect her "I could give a flying fuck" attitude and when I see her take down those sixteen ounces without care of it dripping down her chin and shirt, I knew she needed something with a large straw or she was going to ruin something important.

When I present her with the etched metal jug, I know her reaction would be strong, I had no clue she would jump me and beat me with couch cushions. The view from my angle gives me a unique perspective. I'm trying to attribute the rush of heat I feel surge through my muscles to the fact that I've had a long dry spell not to the fact that Beatrice's breasts are bobbing back and forth very close to my face. Because of this, I can't help but call attention to where she is sitting.

She may not know that I fake ignorance with some English words just so I can watch her squirm trying to explain them to me. As an actor, of course I know what innuendo means.

"*Hallo, abi*!" My sister explains. Her excitement to hear from me fills my heart.

"*Abla*!"

"How are you?"

"I am good. I need your help though."

"*Tamam*. I'm afraid to ask."

"It's nothing I'll regret but I want to make sure that I'm not breaking laws."

"Oh, Isa. What happened?" That disappointment in her voice still feels like salt in a cut you thought had long healed.

"It isn't about me, really. I need you to look into if Beatrice has anything in her contract about the termination of her employment."

"Are you going to fire her?"

"*Yok*. I just want to make sure she has something in her contract that gives her some kind of compensation if she no longer works for me or the agency."

"What is this about?"

"I just want to know if she is allowed to work for someone else or if she is specifically hired for me and if she cuts ties with me, if that means she can no longer work for the agency."

"What is this really about?" she asks again.

"She wants to train with me and I'm afraid it might be too much and she'll quit training and quit her job."

Farah's laugh fills my ear.

"Come on, *abi*. She's not going to quit over training. You wouldn't do something so cruel that she would leave you completely."

"I just want to make sure that if she does, she will be ok."

"*Abi*, that is sweet. I'll take a look but maybe you should think about going easy on her."

"I can't, she'll suspect something. Besides, I think she wants me to push her."

"From what you've told me, she wouldn't like you to win so her quitting probably won't happen."

"You're right."

"Just don't break her. It isn't like we can find spare parts to put her back together."

"I'll make sure we have plenty of ice packs on hand."

"*Abi!*"

"I meant for me."

Chapter 28

B EATRICE

Flipping through the channels on the TV with my bowl of cotton candy grapes and tiny carrots on my lap, Zeki climbs one straggly leg at a time beside me and my new fancy water bottle. I only have a few minutes left to enjoy my "treat" before the food czar sends me a reminder text to shut my snack hole.

With Ihsan's growing popularity, he is out almost every night with the number of invitations to exclusively technicolor events I RSVP to on his behalf. Several times a week we juggle his social schedule with his shooting schedule. He was even offered to be the face of a popular cologne brand, one I had actually heard of. Everything we've worked so hard for is coming true. With all of the parties he attends, his face appears in exponentially more American social media posts. His requests for me to vet his dates are becoming more frequent. He calls it networking, I call it prowling. I didn't foresee his popularity with women to blossom so quickly, but I'm not surprised. As a way of practicing my photo editing skills and sending him pictures of my snacks, I find several pornographic images to splice the food images onto and send them to him while he is out with one of his ladies I've approved. This activity may be on the passive aggressive side.

I hear the frequent sound of his casual dress shoes on the floating staircase. This time he jumps with both feet when he reaches the bottom. I can see him in the large glass windows as he finishes buttoning his shirt cuffs under a suit jacket he must have had left over from a modeling shoot. He straightens out his collar in the same glass windows I am spying through, and I quickly look down in the bowl for the perfect mini carrot.

This has become our routine. I get comfortable on the couch, he comes down to leave. I remind him to take lots of pictures. If a party is on the evening agenda, he asks me if I'm sure about not going and I come up with a clever retort. He says his goodbye and I'm left alone with Zeki. Why can't I be left alone with Ben and Jerry?

Aaaand action!

"How do I look?" he asks

"You look fantastic," I say robotically.

"You didn't even turn around."

"You could wear a burlap sack with a necklace of spoiled sausages and you would still be hotter than every cover of People Magazine's sexiest man of the year."

That might have been a little much.

"You should really come, I can be a little late," he says, grabbing his keys and wallet off the kitchen counter, clearly not listening to my best response yet.

"They wouldn't even let me park the cars," I retort.

"One of these days..." he says, checking out his hair in the windows.

One of these days, what? I'll suddenly be worthy of your technicolor crowd?

"Get out of here, Tomcat. Zeki is getting anxious for some snuggle time," I say, scratching his giant head on my lap.

He bends down over the back of the couch, grabs my head with both hands and kisses the hair on my crown.

"Ewwww," I swat my arms above my head, hoping to make at least one contact. "We don't have a vaccine for Turkish cooties."

"One of these days..." he shouts back as he makes his exit with confident slightly bow-legged strides.

"Have fun storming the castle!" I yell back with my familiar send off, then sigh quietly to myself, "One of these days."

I pick up the remote and resume my search for a distraction. As of late I've been preparing to torture him by watching an early series of his, a sort of Turkish version of Dynasty. I'm finding I can learn better conversational Turkish if I watch and read at the same time. The series is not as bad as I thought but Ihsan's character cries so much that I have to fast forward through it. Actors' eyes are always so red when they cry that they must use some irritating eye drops. I wouldn't need the drops for as easy as it is for me to shed a few tears these days.

Initially, I thought that I would watch a couple of episodes and that would provide me with enough ammunition to give him a boatload of shit.

That plan was thwarted when I couldn't drag myself away from the screen. Most of the actors in it are good but the production value is terrible. No second takes in this show, but I admire the actors' ability to work with the set pieces and dressings when they don't work as expected. If your hair is caught in your lipstick, you find a way to casually drag your hand across your face relocating the stranded lock. I'm starting to think this would make a good drinking game.

Tonight I decide to binge until I fall asleep. After watching two episodes of my current Ihsan series, I finally reach the one where the two main characters get married. It has been quite the investment in time, each episode is around two hours and I'm on episode thirty-two. Ihsan shows a huge range of emotion through this series and everything he does looks so natural. Usually, I fast forward through the montages but the wedding montage of all the suffering that these two have gone through to this point is irresistible. Her wedding dress is terrible but like Ihsan, she would still be beautiful in a burlap sack. Her hair is gorgeous in a poofy braided style and her make up, flawless. He is dressed in a tuxedo that is clearly too big as the sleeves fall down to his knuckles. I feel the tears streaming down my face but let them fall onto the blanket. The scene where they enter the wedding reception and walk through the greenery arch is blanket clutching worthy. He stands back on his heels and reaches his hand out casually to ask her to dance. The big ball lights hanging in the background add to the enchantment and I find myself holding my breath. He leads her to the grassy dance area and the camera focuses on their hands bathed in a soft light. Simply beautiful. I've always loved hand holding. The physical act of being loved and loving at the same time. A flash of memory strikes my inside as I remember the last time my mom took my hand in hers.

"*Vay.*"

An unexpected low voice behind me jolts me back to reality. Losing all control of my arms and legs, my ass slides off the couch and slams to the floor with a distinctive meaty thud. The laugh that bellows from his body is alarming as if he has little care for my safety.

"Hail to the reigning King of Suck. What the hell, Ihsan!" I yell as Zeki barks as angrily as I do.

"Are you watching another one of my shows?" He asks, wanting me to admit it out loud.

"Yes, I am." I lift myself back onto the couch and wipe off my wet face.

He leans over the couch to look at me and a genuine look of surprise develops on his face.

"You are...weeping."

Finally righting myself with Zeki back at my side, I explain.

"They've gone through so much to get to this point. The kidnapping, the miscarriage, the abusive father, the social norms of Turkish culture and look, they made it."

I can't help but cry harder and harder with each sentence, my ugly cry dial on the highest setting. His face looks mildly confused as he doesn't know if he should laugh at me or console me.

"I have a bone to pick with you. What were you thinking, getting married for money when you love her!" I say pointing to the other gorgeous woman on the screen and I turn my anger on him. "I would have stabbed you too!"

His look of confusion intensifies as he sits down next to me and takes the remote, pausing his face on the screen.

"It isn't me, Beatrice."

"I know, but it really seems like you," I say, wiping my face off, calming my mood.

"We're acting," he says a little condescendingly.

"I know you're acting. But damn, Ihsan. You are so good. When you talk to her about how much you love her...it looks so real."

"Um..." he stammers a bit and looks uncomfortable.

The way his muscles contort on his face confuses me for a second and then it clicks.

"Did you date the actress?" I ask in astonishment. "Well, I don't blame you. She's gorgeous. I'd date her. Wait, how many of your female co-stars have you been involved with?"

"Um..." he rings his fists together as his discomfort becomes more obvious.

"Ihsan! How many women are we talking?" He remains silent, looking away.

"You know I can easily look it up on Google and I will use a translator if I have to."

I sit staring at the side of his head.

"Is it seriously too many to count that you can't answer? *Vaaaaaaay*," I exhale the air left in my lungs as I stare forward.

He doesn't seem in the mood to discuss this as we sit in uncomfortable silence.

"And with that, I am going to go to bed, assuming I can lower my heart rate from you scaring me out of my pants. "

Pressing the power button on the remote, I leave Ihsan sitting on the couch. The slapping of my bare feet on the tile is the only sound in the house as I walk to my bedroom. I take care to slowly shut the door, dampening the clicking sound.

Why did I think Gül was the only relationship he had? My naivety is shockingly staggering. How did I expect a man this other worldly hot to not get as much action as possible? What do you expect a virile young man to do when surrounded by beautiful women? I thought guys were proud of that. Did I just slut shame him? How does frumpy ol' me make a hot guy feel guilty?

Twilight Zone, it must be.

Pulling the covers back, I climb into my bed, cover my legs, and remain upright. I feel like if I lay down I am going to drown in guilt. This weird glass house really is the freaking *Twilight Zone.* How many times can I be an ass? He probably had a great time tonight and I ruined it.

A quiet knock pushes me out of the whirlwind of voices arguing in my head. I can neither open my mouth nor get out of bed to open the door.

Another quiet knock. "Beatrice?" The way he says my name with that velvety smooth accent. I wish I could hear that every night.

"Come in," I say, shaking the impossibilities out of my head.

He opens the door and I can't bring myself to look up at him. I am so ashamed of what I said to him. I don't even have alcohol to blame.

"*Merhaba,*" he says quietly.

"Hey, look I'm sorry. I have no right to judge your..."

"*Sus,*" he stops me. He sits down near where my legs cross under the covers. He's removed his suit jacket and I can see a dried sweat ring on his shirt collar, a telltale sign of a significant amount of physical activity. He did have fun, until he came home.

"I have dated a lot of the actresses I work with. You believed what you saw because it was real."

I am such an asshole. I deserved that gut punch. He owes me a few more.

"You don't owe me an explanation," I say, barely able to keep the disgust out of my voice. "It's your job. I shouldn't be judging how you do it."

"It is a compliment that you believed what you saw. I loved Zeynep. I really care about all the women I act with," he says looking down at the floor. "It's what happens when you do the work I do. I got attached and then the project ended. Everyone moved on. I had a harder time moving on than others and didn't handle it very well."

"I believe you," I smile knowingly. "Giving you a hard time has become a habit and I think I took it too far. I'm sorry if I made-"

"It's fine. I saw your face. You were a maniac."

"I thought because you're ...all this," I say waving my hand over his body, "that you fool around with a lot of women. Not cool of me."

He nods his head quietly and we sit in the wordless room.

"Remember when I told you that I didn't have anything to be ashamed of?"

"Vaguely."

"That isn't exactly true. That is a time in my life I'm not proud of. I've tried to do better, be a better man to make up for it."

"I hadn't read anything like that," I say slightly shocked. There was no stone left unturned in all my late night trawlings. At least I thought so.

"When I married Gül and we found out we were pregnant, I didn't want my children to read about the man I was so-"

"You balanced the scale," I finish.

"I wanted to weigh it down so it never tipped again. By the time they were old enough to read, all my stupid behavior would be buried."

"Frontload your good deeds. Not a bad idea." I nod in approval, but my curiosity is starting to nibble. "How bad are we talking?"

"I bribed a lot of police to look the other way."

"Drugs, women, guns, baby tropical birds?"

"*Neh*?"

"Sorry, YouTube rabbit hole."

"Everything but guns and bird smuggling. I was not an addict, am not an addict. I just had too much freedom and no responsibilities."

"You clearly had a lot of fun tonight," I say, touching his shirt collar.

"A lot of dancing," he smiles. "But just dancing."

"I'm glad you had a good time." I start to gather the duvet around me. Everything he just revealed is not easy to digest. This living god sitting in front of me is just a man. He is fallible.

"I would like you to come to these parties with me."

"My chaperoning days are over and I don't make a very good third wheel or wingman, my standards are too high." I pull the covers over my shoulders and lay my head down on my fluffy pillow. I know he has an ulterior motive, but I choose to focus on the babysitting aspect of going out with him. Thanks to years spent on Brandon, the eligibility pool of possible love interests is more like a puddle.

"We have yoga in Satan's armpit tomorrow, so I'd like to get some sleep."

"Fine," he says, giving up. He pushes off my bed using the big lump which happens to be my butt.

"It was nice to see your 'love-struck' face but I'm going to have to report you to HR for touching my ass," I say muffled under the covers.

"They are tired of hearing from us," he says as he walks out the door and closes it quickly.

So that is what he looks like when he's in love. No wonder I couldn't stop the tears.

IHSAN

I am a little suspicious that Beatrice is trying to get rid of me night after night. She has me attending every gathering outside the set she can get me invited to, often with a blind date. I do like hanging out with all the new people I meet but the need to have her with me is verging on codependency. That little ball of witty cynicism and pluck has needled her way under my skin. No matter where I go, I find reminders of her, from a story I want to share to a simple comment that only she would understand the context. It would be good for her to get out of the house as her Zeki dates are a poor excuse for being a shut in. She needs to see what is out here, experience life outside the house. From what I gather, her partying years were spent swooning over Brandon and not actually partying. I want to see her have fun, enjoy more than just my company. But I want her to enjoy my company the most.

I thrive around people as if I'm using their energy as fuel. There is something almost tangible enjoying each other's company so much you don't want it to end. Tonight was one of those nights where the music is as hot as the women. If I were young Ihsan I would have a girl halfway to her car by now. With Beatrice at the house, I would have to be very particular about who I invite back to my place. I can feel my torso tighten when I think of the look in her eye if I let another woman into our sanctuary. I would be fulfilling all her playboy actor stereotypes and I'm not that man anymore.

As soon as I open the door, my heart rate rises as I hear her crying from the living room couch. I let out a sigh of relief when I see she is reacting to a show on the TV. One of my shows. Her cheeks are red and puffy and soaking with tears. She is so focused on the screen that she doesn't hear my footfalls behind her. Her animated reactions are not only entertaining but they also simply bring me joy. Watching her flop to the floor, white tissues flying in the air like dandelion puffs, I can't help but hold my chest attempting to stifle my amusement. This moment is etched in my memory. Her flushed face looking up at me in anger is delightful and surprisingly sexy as hell.

As she explains how she got lost in the story, I can see the machinations behind her eyes sorting out her words to answer her own questions. She is a keen woman and when her mind sorts everything out and after the rapid change of expression, she immediately becomes stoic. I don't seem to have the words to explain to her that it is difficult for me to get in the right frame of mind for the romantic scenes in my projects without developing a relationship with my co-stars. Many times, that working relationship became more. That is how the industry works. Give and take from both sides, that way both sides benefit. She didn't have to make those kinds of intimate connections with her co-workers. Maybe that is why I find it so easy to create relationships with so many people while Beatrice seems to avoid new casual contacts, at least since she left Texas. Unfortunately, not everyone's motives are forthright, and I have been crushed several times. But in my case, the opportunity to move on is usually a social event away. Beatrice has put herself in hibernation and doesn't see the merit in socializing, especially in Los Angeles. Since my divorce I am also finding it difficult to start all over, but Beatrice's instincts are good, so I trust her judgment on any woman she puts on my arm.

The truth about everything I was before Gül is better coming from me than in some gossip paper not fit to wipe your ass. It is easy to sum up, I was a young man with limitless money and limitless opportunity. Memories of nights I can barely stitch together take hold every so often and my stomach tightens, making me slightly sick. If Beatrice had met me back then...actually I never would have given her the time of day. I would have scouted around for her friends and never looked at her twice. I was a superficial ass but that was my crowd: shallow, drunk and horny. Combine that with celebrity and a fat bank account and I was easy pickings for the press. Gül's sophisticated life forced me to rethink my behavior but it wasn't until I saw the black and white glob on that flimsy paper in the doctor's office that I fundamentally changed. That memory is burned into my soul and when I start to feel myself getting out of control, I call upon it to right my sails. I've been wrestling with personal disappointment for a decade, and I've come to terms with most of those gnawing feelings.

What I don't understand is the feeling that radiates down my neck, through my spine to settle between my legs when her fingertip brushes the skin above my collar. Before she uses her sharper than normal human observational skills to discover what effect she's having on me, I push the large bump under her blankets to hopefully return the favor. If she knew what I intended to do upstairs, the nickname she bestowed upon me as the "One-take Wonder" would be the "One Hand Wonder," and that one would undoubtedly stick, and I don't think that would sit well with HR.

Chapter 29

B EATRICE

I'm in a whole different world, Ihsan's world. Everything that is normal to Ihsan is completely foreign to me. His arrival habits as we drive up to the studio in the mornings have become his new routine. He greets everyone by name, the guard posted at the gate, the craft service table staff, wardrobe, hair and makeup artists. He is the "Norm" on this set. I, on the other hand, am one of the customers at a table in the background. Until I find my place in this setting, where I know my way around like the back of my hand, I only communicate with Ihsan and those I am directed to. He does his best to include me, but all these people are just so damn pretty that I tend to pull back, fade away into a large plant or piece of furniture. But this cannot be me anymore, for Ihsan's sake or mine.

Today, I'm going to put words into action. I force my butterfly to emerge from its chrysalis and with every new interaction I have, I consciously summon my inner Dolly Parton and sprinkle delight wherever I go, even at the risk of being accused of pervasive flirtation. So far, the reception of my new extrovertedness has been positive but I haven't made any other solid friendships yet. Baby steps.

Ihsan's schedule settles down and the routine of filming on set is a welcome relief. What used to be a daily lesson on life on the set is now second nature. He is on set for a few hours every morning consistently and after a few weeks I find myself enjoying getting to know the crew and discovering their roles in the production. I'm learning the ins and outs of random jobs essential to getting this project finished. When he is busy filming, I try to stay out of everyone's way while finding myself a perch to observe all the activity. If I know he's filming on the sound stage, I take a little time to get some kind of mini workout in. Sometimes it's a walk along the outside of the building, doing stairs or even the dreaded tricep dip. No matter what, I'm always five minutes away like a good PA should be. That's what I tell myself anyways.

During down time, he usually socializes with his cast members: eating, laughing, and telling stories. He's so at ease with them, like they're all part of his family. I miss this comradery from my former life. Even though everyone on set is nice and helpful, it feels like they have their own secret society, so I sit in his trailer eating alone. Again, baby steps. I tell him I'm working but really I'm avoiding his natural habitat. I can only perform in short bursts and sustained socializing is saved for Ihsan.

Today's scheduled morning filming had to be delayed due to weather since the scene was set to be outside. Apparently, Ihsan can't shine without the sun. Instead of going back to their trailers, Ihsan's co-stars decide to wait on set to get going as soon as the sky allows. I busy myself walking around and returning emails and texting other support staff for help on silly things I should probably know how to do. Matthew is a great resource, but he doesn't know everything. I've been working on an addendum to his bible.

IHSAN

"Ihsan, you have to give me names of your social media team."

"Team?"

"Since I started following your Instagram, I've had to tell my people to step up their game," Charlotte says, sitting down delicately in the tall director's chair.

"It's just my assistant, Beatrice. She'll be happy to hear."

"Wait, your assistant takes care of all your personal stuff, your house and your social media?"

"I've seen her fall asleep on her laptop. She couldn't make it to her room," I say, feeling slightly guilty that I allowed that to happen. But it wasn't like I could stop her, she was on a mission that night.

"She lives with you, too?" Devon chimes in with a bit of innuendo that seems to ignite a spark of hostility.

"My agent thought it was best when I first came here. She's also great with my kids."

"A nanny too?" Chris adds from across the circle.

"*Yok.* I mean no. They just have visited. She, like me, is new to LA and Hollywood and she's just a bit well focused on me."

How do I tell my co-stars that Beatrice is heartbroken and traumatized and needed a break from the world and to do that she dove headfirst into my life?

I see her bird's nest poof bob over giant crates and call her over. She will do a much better job explaining her position than I have. When I see her stomp over to the group, I realize my mistake. Beatrice, unfiltered, could be dangerous to my reputation. As I suspected, she did not disappoint and brought the whole group under her spell as if she waved her arm and they were all unsuspectingly entranced. I don't mind if she uses me as the focus of her barbs, in fact I enjoy it. I'm always a little nervous she'll cross the line but that's the excitement I feel every time she opens her mouth.

"Ihsan, please fire her," Devon smiles and I return the smile, but I feel my teeth clenching together at the prospect of Devon Hazlet employing Beatrice.

"I don't know, Devon, she'd probably have you crying in the corner after the first day."

Thank you, Charlotte.

"Bee!" I shout. "Bee!"

She looks up from her email and I wave her over. The goofy smile on my face is probably giving her a clue that I might be up to something. She walks over to me, rolling her eyes so big I'm afraid that she will dislocate her skull from the atlas holding her altogether. The look on her face as she approaches us shows a glimmer of recognition when her eyes glance over my fellow co-stars.

"This is Beatrice Fredricks, my...."

"Personal assistant. He stumbles because he abuses his power and makes me do things way out of the job description, like extract his ingrown back hair," she interrupts.

The group erupts into laughter and I run my palm down my face.

I'm learning that Beatrice defaults to slightly juvenile and charming in casual in-person situations such as this impromptu gathering. We'll have to develop a hand signal for her to turn on "Pro-Bee" as Matthew deemed her if I feel she is going too far. We're both still learning but I trust her teacher instinct will kick in when appropriate. At least, I hope it will. Trust and hope are two different things.

"Now, are you going to distract me from my duties again?" she asks me curtly.

"*Vay,*" I say, not being able to hide my exasperation.

I introduce her to the idyllic individuals seated in a semi-circle but when I see the snarky spark in her eyes , I brace for impact.

"You'll forgive me for not shaking hands. I'm not a germaphobe but if I get him sick it will just be another thing he can blame me for and my list already has a table of contents. I can't deal with this baby if he gets sick."

They laugh again, turning to each other to share the fun.

"You're fired." I stare at her seriously.

"Yes!" She pumps her fist in the air. "Any of you have any job openings. Here, let me send you my resume."

She pretends to pull up email on her phone.

"*Hayir, hayir, hayir.*" I wave them off and block their physical access to her. "I can't live without her."

"That's right and it's best you remember," she says using that adorable Texas accent then jabbing her elbow into my side. Just like her, sweet and sour.

"I called you over because we were talking about my Instagram page and I wanted them to meet you."

"I remember you from the table read. It's very impressive, Beatrice." Charlotte turns to Beatrice with her celebrity smile.

Beatrice's eyes widen slightly which I believe is her starstruck look.

"Thank you. I'm very proud of it. It's easy when your subject has a smile that will drop panties from a mile away."

Kyle Ryan spit takes and wraps his arm around her shoulders. "Oh, yes, I'm giving her my card." The blood rushes up to the surface of my skin as I see Kyle touch Beatrice. A feeling I only got with Gül.

This is not working out the way I thought it would. She was just supposed to visit for a second and now she's casting her magic over my colleagues.

"Do you schedule all his appearances, too?" Devon asks.

"Most. I'm taking on some extra duties to gain more experience. So far, the big boss seems to be happy. Expand my horizons and all. Ihsan's been behaving but if he steps out of line, I'm booking him a geriatric reality dating show."

Beatrice's brand of humor resonates well from the appreciative reactions of my co-stars. I'm sure if it had fallen flat, her next lines would have been more polite. At least I hope so.

Devon glances down to his phone, his thumb waving over the screen.

"Have you seen Zeki's page?" he asks the group.

"I know right, I'm only staying in this relationship for the dog," she smiles at me with a cocky grin. "If I'm around and you need something, please don't hesitate to ask assuming Lord of the DILF's over here doesn't have me plucking gray hairs. Again."

I look at her curiously as the group erupts in laughter. Sometimes she says things and I know I should be worried but I'm not sure what to be worried about.

"DILF...Dads I'd Like to... " she leans in and pulls my jacket down to whisper into my ear. "You can fill in the blank. You're also called a TILF. Turk I'd..."

I put up a hand, indicating I don't need her to explain further. She can barely explain through her own laughter at my expression.

"*Allah*," I put my hands on my hips and look to the horizon.

"Ihsan, you really need to read your own feed," she says pulling away. "Fire me again, I dare you." She glares at me with an evil grin. "And with that, I'm going to get back to work. Someone has to schedule his goat yoga."

I point to my trailer. "*Almak, almak.*"

"Just so you all know, he's cussing at me in Turkish." Speed walking away, her voice fades as she gets in one last word. "Please feel free to take a peek at my resume."

Oh, she will be punished. I see a lot of burpees in her future. I smile to myself, thinking of Beatrice complaining about her most hated exercise and another feeling starts bubbling up as images of her body falling down onto the mat, all sweaty and bouncy.

BEATRICE

Ihsan introduces me to his co-stars and I have a mild freakout in my head and act as if these are regular people and nod. I already knew their names but in my mind their names are Gorgeous, Beautiful, Stunning, and Damn Handsome. I calm my nerves enough to give Ihsan the hard time he earned by not only distracting me but also thrusting me in front of Hollywood elite without more than a thirty second warning. I avoid shaking their hands because I just don't want to have to meet everyone in their eyes and touch them. That would be crossing a line into technicolor territory.

I do my best to not pee my pants as the group asks me questions and my mind races to compose funny responses. After hearing the oh so familiar "Allah" in his deep voice, I am satisfied that he is thoroughly embarrassed, and I can go on my way.

When I reach the trailer I can't wait to "tell" my mom what just happened to me. Opening the video app, I take a deep breath.

"Hey Mom. I'm hanging out with big movie stars now. I had an actual conversation. You'd be proud, nothing came out of my nose, and I didn't pass out. Ihsan is doing well and I'm having a great time. I'll be back soon for Brandon and Sarah's wedding. I think you'd really like these Turkish shows I'm watching. We can watch one then. I miss you, Mom."

Another message off to Travis. He can sometimes get her to send a brief 'hi' message back, but I don't hold my breath.

Charlotte aka "Stunning" and I find ourselves at the craft table during afternoon lunch break a few days later. She is always very nice, but we never have a conversation of more than two or three sentences before Ihsan formally introduced us. I feel more a part of this makeshift family now. Before, all I really paid attention to when they were shooting was Ihsan. Now that I'm getting to know them better, I feel myself watching all of them with the same admiration.

"Hey, Beatrice," Charlotte greets me in a black skintight latex suit with silver streak accents accentuating the lines of her muscles.

"Oh, hey," I say, grabbing a banana and a couple of plums. I look down and snicker to myself at the fruit version of male genitalia.

"I was checking out Ihsan's Instagram. I wanted to put a link to his in mine. Anyway, I well.... I got curious about you."

"Okay," I say suspiciously.

"You just don't seem like a typical assistant, and I had a couple of minutes of downtime."

"That sounds dangerous. Have you tried knitting?" I interrupt.

"I found out you were a teacher in San Antonio." Her face drops.

I stare down at my fruit, not looking as funny as before.

"So, you saw where I worked?"

"Yeah."

She puts her perfectly manicured hand on my arm in comfort. I can feel my heart rate rise as it beats more forcefully through my ribcage.

"Do you mind keeping it to yourself? I moved out here to get away from all that."

"Of course. Just wanted you to know the reason I looked is because you kick ass and I'd like for us to be friends."

"Ha! You're the one I want in a back alley with me," a slightly nervous laugh escapes my mouth. "Friends, like calling about a shoe sale friends?"

"Yes, that kind. Without the kissing up and backstabbing," she says with a little giggle.

"I can do that. You might be my first girlfriend I have here," I admit trying to redirect my rising anxious energy.

"Really?"

"I don't get out much. Ihsan keeps me pretty busy and only lets me out to pee. Is it cool to call you just to bitch?"

"Anytime," she smiles and returns to the set.

I close my eyes and breathe in as much air as I can through my nose and exhale through my mouth like Jordan, the yogi, taught me. It seems to help but I have the intense instinct to get to the trailer as soon as possible. Walking across the set, I can't see or hear anyone. I'm in a dimly lit tunnel. I just know I need to get somewhere safe. When I finally reach the trailer, I fumble with the pull handle, it won't open no matter what I try. Suddenly it swings open with Ihsan on the other side. I rush past him up the rickety stairs, thankful they are still holding up. Crashing on the couch opposite the door, Ihsan shuts the door and turns to me. Zeki immediately sits his large body across my feet, leaning on my legs.

"What's going on?" He says, placing his arm around my shoulder and his hand on my knee.

"I'm not quite sure. Ummm. Stunning, I mean Charlotte, looked me up and found out about Round Rock."

"Okay..."

"I just feel...weird. I just..." I take a long breath again.

Ihsan's large hand rotates across my back as I try to work things through, but it feels impossible to unjumble my thoughts. A few minutes pass while I concentrate on slowing down my breathing.

I gently pat Ihsan's knee.

"I'm good, I probably just need to eat something."

He pulls me sideways into his chest, my forehead resting at the base of his neck. He always knows how I need comforting, I just wish it was in a different package. A few silent minutes pass while he matches his breathing to mine. When the back rub slows, the end of a banana creeps its way up to my nose. Pulling my head away, I take the banana from Ihsan and peel the yellow casing back to take a few bites.

"Just so you know," I say, chewing my last bite, "I'm telling people you offered me your banana."

With half the banana untouched, I wrap the peel around it.

"Make sure you tell them it was too big to finish."

I give him a giant smile and nod at him in approval. He slaps my raised palm for a well deserved high five without missing a beat. I love the familiarity we have with each other, it makes me feel like I belong to something, to someone.

"Okay, let's go, you're going to be late, then they'll fire you and I'll be out of a job. You will go back to Türkiye ashamed and humiliated, and I'll be homeless on the street with only a coat full of feral kittens to keep me warm."

I attempt to stand, feeling almost back to normal. Offering both his hands, he overemphasizes the effort it takes to pull me off the couch by several loud grunts and moans.

"Come on, tight ass," I say walking down the steps.

"Doesn't that mean frugal?" he says following me out the trailer door.

"Or it means you have a tight ass."

If he thinks there are residual effects of my little breathing tantrum, he won't be able to work and what would my purpose here be? Stopping before all the mess of wires and cords, I give Ihsan's ass a full palm smack just so he knows I am really back to my old self. But when did I start smacking his ass?

I blame the banana.

"Go get 'em, hot stuff."

He jumps a little in surprise and looks back at me in shock.

"We need to review the sexual harassment clause in your contract," he smiles and points his finger at me.

"Stop being so sexy, and I won't harass you," I raise my voice at him as he walks over to his makeup stand.

I hear laughing from behind the large movie cameras.

"That was perfectly consensual! He has low self-esteem so I have to stroke his ego every once in a while. You know, make him feel pretty," I say with a wink at the tall cameraman nearest our trailer.

Watching Ihsan and his co-stars shoot the scene a few times, I'm reminded of why he's here, why he's on this set and why I'm here. Yep, this could actually work for me.

Chapter 30

B EATRICE

Ihsan is one of the hottest people I've ever seen, much less personally known. Now that he's on set with American costars, they are tagging him in their photos too. He's getting a lot more free press than I thought was possible. The duties of organizing his social media have settled down now that I know how to do it more efficiently. This gives me time to sneak other activities into my time on the set. It was going to be a boring day for me so taking Zeki for a walk was going to keep me out of the trailer and give me an opportunity to get a workout in. When I got back to the trailer, Ihsan was climbing down the steps.

"How was the party?" he asks, using a saying I taught him for mundane activities.

"Zeki had too much to drink and was making a fool of himself. We look pretty worse for wear, huh?"

"Well, it looks like you got in a good workout."

"I bet we smell like it, too."

He pulls out his phone from his pocket and raises his arm.

"Let's take a picture to document your progress. You'll be thankful later, I swear."

Looking at myself in the reflection of the window of his trailer door, I pull out the bun on top of my head and my hair falls down in pretty waves past my shoulders and down my arms. The sweat won't show up too bad. I'm not half as hideous as I think.

"I think this is quite unfair. You've been through hair and makeup and Zeki hasn't even brushed his fur. He's going to look ridiculous," I say, hoping he realizes I'm really talking about me.

"Come here."

He puts his head between Zeki's big muzzle and my red, sweaty cheeks. Reaching his long arm over my head, he takes a few pictures. Zeki has a different agenda and is a bit wriggly but finally we get a shot of his good side.

Scrolling through the shots, he lets me look over his shoulder for approval. My make-up free face looks a little red but passable. For so long I avoided viewing my appearance from a critical lens, but I'm actually satisfied with how I look. My face is symmetrical with my vibrant hazel eyes. My smile is straight, without the need for braces. My full lips contribute to my "not as bad as I thought" face and my nose comes in with an average rating. I've even been blessed with little to no acne.

"Can I post one of these?"

"Yeah sure," I respond with the few brain cells I have left functioning after a hard workout.

He posts it on all his social media like I've taught him with the caption "out with my two best friends."

After taking a break from Zeki's workout, I make the mistake of checking the comments on his post. Most were pretty standard, but I read the comment by the guy who made the mistake of trolling the Turk.

"I didn't know he had two dogs."

I take a deep breath to calm my nerves like I've been taught in sexy stretching class. I know the internet can be cruel which is why I rarely post to my personal social media. I've been pretty adept at deflecting negative comments but this one has made it through my armor. Before I made an effort with myself, I would have ignored this kind of comment completely. Now that I've been working so hard, it feels as if someone took a giant shit in my running shoes.

I don't know how often Ihsan reads the comments, but I pray he doesn't have any time to read this one. He opens the trailer door more forcefully than usual, confirming my fear. The tiny fridge is close to me so I open it, take out a beer that has been sitting in there for a month, twist the cap and offer it to him. This is not something I see from him very often, this raw anger. He rarely loses his cool. The scowl on his face is only familiar to me from the TV screen.

IHSAN

"Ihsan, I need to talk to you for a second."

"*Tamam*, Charlotte."

Charlotte stops me before I return to the trailer to relax until my next call.

"I was just checking my posts and I saw this."

She hands me her large phone where she has scrolled to a comment just below the picture of me, Beatrice and Zeki.

Immediately my fists clench and my forearms pump, ready to punch a hole in something, someone. The protector slash father slash friend instinct kicks in harder than it has in a long time.

"What the fuck is this?"

"Ihsan, I know. I wanted you to see it before Beatrice did."

After I hand Charlotte's phone back to her, I trudge toward the trailer trying to figure out how to tell her, how to be there for her, how to deal with the oxygen thief that hides behind their tiny little screen.

When I find her sitting at her office annex, I notice her hesitancy and I pray she hasn't seen those words. I want to keep her safe from the world she has convinced herself doesn't want her in it. This asshole just confirmed exactly what she has been trying to tell me.

I couldn't cool down. She said it didn't bother her but how could it not? I've had plenty of experience with assholes in the press not to mention critics of my work, but Beatrice is off limits. Maybe she has learned to build a wall around herself, but she knows why the wall is there and when you are reminded to reinforce it, it can bring up painful memories. I know how badly she wants this change, even if she complains throughout every workout. I can't have some feeble-minded piece of shit knocking her down.

Nothing I can think of will satisfy what I really want to do, which is find this person and show him how we treat those who disrespect our family back home. I pump out some push-ups to keep myself from punching a hole in the thin trailer wall, then make up an excuse to leave the trailer. I have to do something.

"Ihsan...Ihsan...IHSAN!"

"*Beni affet*...sorry. I'm having a hard time." I turn to face Charlotte whose sympathetic face is trying to search mine for clues on how I'm feeling.

"Is Bee ok? Are you ok?"

"I don't know what to do. She says she is ok, but I can't believe this doesn't bother her."

"Because it does." Charlotte's fingers wrap around my bicep.

"Could you help me?"

"What do you need?"

"Here, just hold my phone and press record when I nod."

I didn't rehearse, I didn't think, I just spoke what I wanted everyone to know about her. Charlotte's smile behind my phone kept me from doubting what I was saying and when it started to change more to a cringe, I stop.

Beatrice is morphing into a better version of herself, and I want the world to know. It isn't just her physique that I notice changing. She is scheduling more in-person meetings and I notice she has been dressing herself with clothes that actually fit her instead of clothes that hide her. The bun is still her preferred hairstyle but she's wearing necklaces that drape between her breasts and the blouses she chooses don't seem to button all the way up her neck. And her breasts, damn her breasts. She must have found the perfect bra because when she wears certain outfits, her breasts look nothing but magnificent. The way she now leans into a handshake when she is meeting someone for the first time is one of the subtle differences I notice. She walks more astride the other person rather than letting them take the lead no matter how miniscule the distance. I'm also noticing how others respond to her. Her smile and facial expressions have always been radiant but recently, I've found myself pushing my fingers into my palm when I see how other men respond to her casual touch on the arm or witty comment. The LGBTQ+ charity auction coming up will be good for her and I look forward to seeing how her confidence looks in a dress. Blaine and I were right, she does flirt and the only way I feel comfortable with it is that I know she is doing it for me.

"Well, Ihsan, I see why she calls you the 'One Shot Wonder'."

I try to crack a smile at Charlotte but until I see Beatrice, it's just too hard to make my face look happy, even with all my acting experience.

Beatrice has an amazing ability to hold herself together in public and let her hair down at the house. But when I return to the trailer after our final shot of the day, no sooner had I stepped inside did she wrap her arms around me and place her face on my chest. We stood for a moment listening to the crew packing the set outside. Laying my cheek on her head must have been too much because as soon as my face touched her hair, she pushed me away and climbed down the stairs. An unwelcome, familiar feeling of longing climbs up my arms. She belongs in my arms not fleeing from them.

BEATRICE

"Is there anything I can help you with?" I ask, already knowing why he's in a mood.

"I don't know. I don't know what to do. I don't know if I should do anything," he says, pacing a half step back and forth as that is all the trailer will allow.

"Something happened on set?"

"*Yok.*"

"What's going on?"

"I don't know if I should tell you."

"Ihsan, I've seen it already. I'm okay, there's always going to be trolls and assholes. They just don't have the courtesy to say it to my face," I say trying to convince him that I believe in the sticks and stones saying.

He slams his fist on the Formica countertop, causing everything to jump.

"Hey, I'm okay. It wasn't that bad. I appreciate your support but really, I am okay." I put my hands up on his shoulder.

"I am not okay," he continues. "I just can't believe my fans would say something like that."

"Just don't do anything."

"It just makes me so angry," he says through gritted teeth. His older brother side has been awakened and I struggle to find a way to calm him.

"Posting pictures can be risky. You just hardly ever get negative comments. But occasionally an asshole decides to be brave."

"That isn't bravery. That's cowardice."

"I can take it. Please find it in yourself to let it go, for me. I don't want to have to clean up a mess. I don't know what you could do that would make this better, so I say we ignore it."

"I just can't sit by and do nothing."

"Sometimes the fans moderate themselves, it's called natural consequences."

After seeing him a little calmer, I hand him another beer. I sit back in the little built-in dinette I have made into my mobile office and attempt to distract myself with the charity basketball event Ihsan is attending. He chucks the empty bottle into the makeshift recycling bin and starts to unbutton his shirt. Both of which rattle me slightly. I've been perfecting my shady skin spying skills, so I look like I'm working by typing vigorously but in reality I'm typing random thoughts, looking over the top of the laptop screen periodically, pretending to think. My covert way of eye-balling my client with lusty inappropriate for the workplace fantasies.

I should add that to the PA's Bible.

Ihsan hangs his shirt neatly in the closet and drops to the floor of the trailer. He seems to like to blow off steam by physical activity and doing push ups is about the only exercise the trailer can accommodate. I thought maybe he would do ten but at some point, I lost count after listening to his forced breaths for more than three minutes. I figure this is a healthy way of dealing with his anger, so I keep my snarky comments inside and let him work through it. When he wears himself out, he goes into the tiny bathroom, wipes down his chest and armpits, washes his hands and blots the sweat off his face, being careful not to ruin his make-up. He stands in the living area, buttoning his white long sleeve shirt but his face is still a scowl as he tucks his shirt back into his trousers.

"I'm going to run lines with Riley," he says as he steps down the trailer steps and opens the door in one move, only slightly slamming the flimsy door. I wish rehearsing with Riley made me feel better.

After moving around a few appointments and confirming reservations, and gossiping with my normal contacts, my phone rings on the tabletop. Matthew's name appears on the screen along with a picture of what I hope is his butt. Rolling my eyes, I answer.

"Hey Matthew, what's up?" I ask in a cheerful voice.

"Sooooooo, have you checked Ihsan's Instagram?"

"Not in the last hour."

"Did you see the comments?"

"Yes, I saw that comment. I'm okay."

"So, you haven't seen the video?"

"Nooooo."

I open Instagram and find the latest post.

Oh no oh no no no he didn't oh please let it be not what I think it is.

As soon as I click on his icon, Ihsan's irate face appears on the tiny screen. We've got to change that thumbnail.

"I know I show a lot of fun things for you to see my experience in America. But I guess this is something else that I get to experience, too. Now I understand why they call people trolls. But this is worse than I could imagine. Someone made a terrible comment about one of my dearest friends. Her name is Beatrice. None of this," he waves his arm around him, "would happen if I didn't have her. Everything I do here in America she has organized. She is my personal assistant and one of my best friends. She is funny, smart, kind and by all standards that matter, she is beautiful. I would hope that those of you who would make a comment like this would unfollow me. I don't want you on my page. I don't want to hear from you. You are not my people, Beatrice is my people."

Not today, troll.

Suddenly, I come down with a case of lockjaw. I can't believe he just went on the internet and called somebody out. He is always very positive online. It wasn't lost on me that he called me beautiful. Even if it was with a caveat, I'll take it. He is always thankful and kind no matter how much shit I give him, but this was more than I could've asked for. It's not very often when you are complimented publicly. Especially for me. Even as a teacher, they only choose the teacher of the year once. I know the exact sound bite I will extract when I'm feeling down. As soon as I figure out how to do that. No one has ever stood up for me like he just did.

"Matthew, I don't know what to say. He told me he wasn't going to do anything. What he said was ... amazing. I'm really hoping that he doesn't get any backlash from it. I'm almost speechless."

"Have you seen how many views?"

"I didn't even think of that."

"They are skyrocketing, and it's only been up for 20 minutes."

How can I be mad at him? I may be uncomfortable that my boss went on the interwebs to defend me but that is how we grow, right? I just have to sit and marinate on it for a while.

My bottom lip starts to quiver as my eyes fill and when I hear the janky handle clank against the trailer door, I quickly wipe my hands across my face and attempt to keep my composure. No one at any job I've ever had has ever seen me break down. I save that for home. Today, Ihsan might have broken me.

He climbs the stairs and the light from the industrial lamps shine from behind him and just like the first day I met him, it's as if he was sent just for me. His thick eyebrows soften his expression as he sees the relieved state I am in. As soon as his feet land on the main floor, I stand up and take a few steps toward him. If I look at his face, I'll lose it, so I slide my arms under his and wrap them around his back, keeping my cheek on his heart. My grip around him is soft and without pressure, I just need to thank him and move on. I can feel the continuous acts of kindness and generosity mend my insides, but they are also tearing me up. I'm praying that while he is building me up, he's making me strong enough to leave. It took me ten years to walk away from Brandon, and I won't make that mistake again.

Chapter 31

B EATRICE

I wish I had thought about filming some of my workouts early on in this journey. My favorite scenes in movies are when the main character does some kind of transformation sequence to a great song, throwing out all the old boyfriend crap or a training montage. It would be great to have something like that so when I'm down I can show myself that yes, I really did run on a treadmill, kick the shit out of a heavy bag and do a damn butterfly stroke even though it feels more like two seals battling over my head. My weekly video visits with my mom have become all about how I bested Ihsan that week and one of these days, I will beat him at something in the gym. So far the only thing I've been able to brag about is that I use more workout towels than he does. I usually let Ihsan pick the music in the gym since I pick the music in every other situation, especially when Bobby is there.

Oh Bobby, the nicest trainer in Hollywood. Ihsan sings along to some Turkish rage music which sounds exactly like American rage music, so I find myself shouting along. Bobby does his best to referee when Ihsan and I decide to work out together, but I fear he's going to start charging a squabbling fine. I see him cringe when Ihsan chastises me for not doing an extra anything whether it be another rep, a higher weight, or another set of combination punches. I wonder if Hollywood trainers have some kind of Facebook bitch account where they share stories of terrible clients. We have to be somewhere near the top of that list and if we aren't I'm going to try my darndest to get there.

"I swear to God, Ihsan. If you touch the incline one more time, I will haunt you," I say, attempting to simultaneously smack his hand away and keep the pace up on the ridiculous incline percentage the treadmill is already set at. "Not the cute flashy light, cool breeze kind of haunts either. I'm talking full blown poltergeist, pea soup possession."

He seems to have made a game out of pulling his hand away before I can make contact like the slap game I used to play when I was in elementary school. Apparently, it was training me for moments such as this.

"You are only at ten," he says, trying to sneak his hand back over the console.

"Just because it goes to eleven doesn't mean it should," I say, attempting my best Spinal Tap reference between heaving breaths.

If I could think right now, I'd make a note that we should watch that classic.

"Just for thirty seconds," he says, finally making contact with the up arrow.

I instinctively grab for the arm holds next to me.

"Hands off!"

My hands rebound as if they had just touched a hot stove, narrowly missing his smack back.

If Ihsan had a horse whip, my knuckles would be raw. I don't understand how it's cheating if I hold on for my life. My legs are still moving at an uncomfortable pace and an uncomfortable incline.

"Bobby, Ihsan's yelling at me again!"

"What's your heart rate, Bee?" Bobby asks as I see a tunnel of light in the distance.

"Mostly dead."

"Mostly dead is slightly alive," Ihsan smiles at me.

"Awww...you remembered, now get me off this hamster wheel," I gasp, watching the display reach the thirty seconds after Ihsan messed with it.

He presses the stop button which cues the machine to slow down and lower to sea level, counting down a five-minute cooldown.

"You didn't even know you were doing it."

I look down at my "smarter than me" activity tracker on my wrist and check my heart rate now that my feet don't look like they are propelling a Flintstones car.

"Is 'don't try that again' a real result or is my watch giving me shit?"

In exasperation, Ihsan grabs my wrist and presses the buttons to display my heart rate.

"One sixty-eight...niiice."

"So, waterboarding next?" I ask, putting my hands on my hips trying to catch my breath and not blind myself with the sweat streaking down my forehead.

"I'm out you two, keep up the good work. I want to see both of you alive next week."

"No promises!" I yell over the never-ending track.

Bobby grabs Ihsan's outstretched hand and they do the sweaty man chest bump kind of hug maneuver as I barely lift my arm to wave.

"Seriously, the treadmill is going to start to smoke if you keep doing shit like that."

"Beatrice, the treadmill is not going to smoke, the weights won't rip your arms out of their sockets, you are not going to dry drown and for the last time you aren't going to get stuck in lizard pose and have to pee in a bucket."

His recollection of my whining excuses during Turkish PE impresses me. He never engages or gives me any indication that he is listening, probably thinking I will stop if he doesn't give it attention. As the treadmill comes to a complete stop, I grab my sweat towel, sit on the deck, and wipe the sweat back into my hair. I can see Ihsan's shoes, no show socks, and strikingly defined calves in my eyeline a few feet from my toes.

"Now that we're all warmed up..."

He deftly hops out of the way of the snapping end of my towel.

I look up and he pulls his t-shirt up to dry the sweat off his face exposing his defined abs, as if walking two more steps to one of Thomas' neat piles of towels was just too much work. I think I have seen this pose before as my mind quickly flashes to a memory of Ihsan's gleaming muscle ripped chest from one of his dramas. But this time it was live, right in my face. He must have shaved his chest recently because the sweat didn't catch on any hair as a few drops slide down his six pack.

As much as I appreciate his visual stimulation, I must address the auditory assault he uses during our workouts.

"We need to talk about something." I shake my head attempting to clear away the lust filled forbidden thoughts. Finally, I found Ihsan's one attribute that proves he is human, his flaw.

"*Tamam.*"

"I don't know how much longer I can do this with you," I state as professionally as I can.

"What? Drop by drop makes a lake. You are doing great, don't give up," he says, sitting next to me on the treadmill foot grips.

"I'm not talking about giving up. I'm talking about not pushing a pillow in your face until you stop moving."

"*Neh*?" his eyebrows squish to the middle of his face and his lips press firmly together.

"Ihsan, you make so much noise when you work out. I'm sure our neighbors think we are holding animal sacrifices."

His face transforms from an expression of hurt to a wide mouth guffaw.

"Breathing is important."

"I think what you are doing might require a CPAP machine."

"It's a way of keeping up the rhythm of the activity so you don't slow down."

"I'm pretty sure they ban guys like you from the gym. What did your soccer buddies do when you made those noises?"

"Got better headphones," he says, grabbing the fluff ball on top of my head and using it to help himself up.

"I can't concentrate on what I'm doing when you're in the room."

"You can't concentrate when I'm in the room anyway," he smiles evilly as he turns his back to me to refill his water bottle from the giant blue translucent plastic tank.

Can confirm.

I remove my sweaty shoe and cock my arm back, sending it flying toward his tight ass, hitting his left butt cheek a little harder than I meant to by the sound it made hitting his glute. It's his fault for turning his back on me. The look on his face when he turned around verged on bizarro Superman, his features darkened with the veil of evil shading his eyes and cheekbones.

IHSAN

Beatrice is a pain in the ass. But she is an entertaining pain in the ass. I know it is a deflection strategy to distract me from watching her form or really watching her at all. I've been on some workout regimen my whole life with a variety of trainers, some for my projects and some for the sake of my sanity. Beatrice would cause any one of them to question their life choices. The more time we spend in the gym together, the more I am starting to think her delightful grievances are a way to distract herself. I don't believe she loathes sweating as much as she claims. In fact, I see her covertly sneak a smile at herself in the mirror every so often when she finishes a hard set.

To say that it warms my heart to see her react this way would be a considerable understatement. She pushes herself hard. It is possible that I may have something to do with that as I have a difficult time controlling my instincts to antagonize her. I declared to her months ago that she wouldn't be alone, I am showing her that I really meant it. She may not understand that now, but I'm hoping when she sees how her commitment to herself manifests into a body she earned, she will remember I was there to keep pushing her and all her buttons.

The way she leans against various surfaces in the house, I can see the way her t-shirt drapes down her stomach instead of getting caught on her midsection. Her arms filling out less of the sleeves and the muscles along her biceps more defined as she reaches out for items in the kitchen. If she were Farah, I would reach out, grasp her arm and run my finger over the new visible muscle tissue but it's Beatrice and she is picking up martial arts more quickly than the other exercises, so I keep my hands to myself. Her hips have narrowed as well but keeping that adorable ass has been a secret priority of mine. I've been "helping" Bobby "encourage" Beatrice to use the treadmill on the highest incline setting when she power walks to lift her ass. I'll surely need to spend more time in the make-up chair getting my eye retouched if Beatrice ever finds out about my subterfuge.

Sometimes finding the most beneficial time to have a hard conversation with Beatrice takes some finesse. I have to be delicate and astute, but most of all I have to pick a moment where she has nowhere to run. Her apprehension and avoidance of the subject of finding a therapist worries me. Broaching the topic when she can barely stand seems to be serendipitous.

"Hey, you asked for it."

Picking up the shoe off the floor, I turn it with the foot hole toward her, threatening to shove the stinky side in her face.

"Please, don't. I'm sorry. You know I can't control myself."

I glide next to her in two large strides and return to my seat, flipping her shoe in my hand as if it is a dagger.

"How are you doing?" I ask.

"What do you mean by that?" She leans away from me, slightly suspicious of my question.

"Did you get a therapist?"

She leans over and liquifies down to the floor and I swear I hear the electrical downward decent sound used in many sci fi movies as her body powers down. I can't stop my annoyed moan over her melodramatics.

I quickly move to the floor and slide her feet down to straighten out her legs and plop myself down on her pelvis. This was a move I perfected on Farah and Nadir growing up.

"What the hell?" she says in shock.

"I needed to get your attention, and this seems to work."

I put most of my weight on my legs so as not to crush her or at least give her something else to complain about. Staring down at her, I cross my arms celebrating her defeat.

"You know this is bullying. I took a test on it and everything. Got a hundred percent on the first try."

I continue my unimpressed glare and then tap her gently on the forehead.

"Really?" she says her growing impatience raising her voice.

My finger then finds different targets all over her torso, taking care not to poke her boobs. This is not the way they should be touched. With every poke she swats my hand in protest until she stops altogether so as not to react.

"Nothing?"

"Just your butt sweat on my coochie. I'm ignoring you. You want a reaction out of me."

I tip my head slightly, taking her remark as a challenge.

"Ouch!" she yelps as I pinch a small bit of skin below her elbow. "What the hell was that for?"

"Like you said, I wanted a reaction."

"Come on Ihsan, get off."

The pinches become more frequent but at least they weren't worse so she again stops reacting and holds back her yelps. In return, I pinch harder.

"Ok, now that really hurts."

"Fight back, then."

"I didn't realize you like it this rough."

My last pinch is extra hard and she smacks me hard on the cheek and I ...smile. Her feistiness is not only gratifying but a complete turn on and in this position, it's even more so. Grabbing both of her hands and pinning them next to her ears, my shocked face looms a foot over her face. Her teeth bite down on her lip in fear of what is to come next.

"Beatrice, you have to fight back. Therapy is fighting back. You didn't fight back when I poked you, you just tried to ignore it, so it got worse. Then when I pinched you, you did the same thing. Just because you ignore something doesn't mean it isn't doing damage. You can't let it get to the point where you just accept the pain and let it happen to you."

"You're right, you are a big giant pain."

I lower my face further, so close I can smell her sweat mixed with yesterday's shampoo.

"You need to take care of yourself," I say just above a whisper. This is not how I thought this intervention was going to go.

"Isn't that what I'm doing?"

"I need you, Beatrice. I can't lose you."

The light reflects off the glossiness pooling at the corners of her eyes. She tries to blink them back, but I've already seen them. I went too far. If I free her hands I wouldn't stop her from smacking me again.

"Sitting on me until I get therapy is so juvenile. At least you didn't spit and suck it up before it hits my face."

"I wouldn't."

"Good to know. As much as staring up into your dreamy eyes is hotter than hell, it isn't going to motivate me any faster."

"What more do I have to do then?" I smile down into her multi-colored eyes with a wicked spark. I had to turn this into something else to take away the sting of what I just said.

"Oh my God, this is so weird!" she half shouts and wiggles her hips in an attempt to free them.

I push up off her wrists and let them go, returning to my original sitting position.

"I'm going to call Sarah and Matthew."

"Ihsan, I swear I've looked into it." she says continuing our conversation in the weirdest seating arrangement to date. "The ones that I got references for are not taking patients and now I'm trying other avenues. I thought in this town that therapists would be on every street corner, next to a Starbucks."

"This is all a waste if you don't take care of your heart."

"I'm actually feeling mentally a lot better, you are right."

"What?" I clutch my chest in a dramatic overwhelming fashion. "I don't think I heard you."

Rolling her eyes, I see her considering what kind of damage it would do to our relationship if she admits it again.

"You...are...right. I know, I am in shock too," she says, almost gagging.

I crawl off her torso and lay down next to her with my knees bent parallel to hers.

"I'm not saying it again," she stares at the ceiling.

"I'm proud of you that you even repeated it."

"I won't make that mistake again."

"Since we are down here..."

"Naptime?"

"Ab time."

"I hate you."

"You love me," I say, plopping my shoe on her stomach as I start raising my arms and legs in a giant "V" shape with an obnoxiously loud groan.

Chapter 32

B EATRICE

Ihsan is out on another date so that means I am holding down the fort. Tonight's young lady is a movie producer's daughter he met at a club. She is of course beautiful, stylish, rich, connected and probably charitable as shit. In vetting her, I discovered her online presence isn't obnoxious, she has been out with only one other celebrity, at least that she posted about, and she likes art, especially art in fashion. Matthew said that he hadn't heard anything negative about her. This date will be good for him, I hope she's a keeper. Maybe I should remember her name.

Zeki and I have our own date to watch yet another one of Ihsan's Turkish dramas. In this particular show, he is a dashing rogue police officer with a mysterious past. Unfortunately, this one does not have English subtitles, so his past is extra mysterious to me. I read the episode synopsis so I wouldn't be totally lost, and I decide to make it even more fun by creating the dialogue myself. Two hours an episode is brutal; it makes it hard to binge and hard to not eat something I'm not supposed to. The snack of choice is a giant bowl of cut strawberries with Ihsan's super fancy honey drizzled on top. His six pm rule for no more food doesn't count when he is out on a date, Ihsan doesn't know that though. Zeki seems to be entertained by my word choices, his ears perking up and doing that adorable curious dog head cock.

Throughout the episode I see all these little choices that Ihsan makes when he is on screen. He tugs at his eyebrow when he is uncomfortable, he scratches the upper right side of his head with his middle and ring finger when he is thinking. He hasn't made these character choices in other shows, but it makes this character so much more endearing and real. This is also the first time I've seen him do a maniacal laugh which catches me off guard. I'm very glad I have his coattails to ride.

My train of thought is interrupted by lights shining into the living room and the sound of a car parking. The difference in this instance is that I can hear a woman's voice.

Oh sh..it, shit, shit.

Quickly pressing the power button on the remote, I grab the strawberry bowl and water bottle and sprint toward the foyer and then take a hard right into the hallway to my bedroom door. It's like those spy movies, as my bedroom door closes, the front door opens. Zeki gives them an obnoxious greeting and I plop on my bed, relieved to be safe. Since we have never discussed the protocol for bringing someone back to the house, I figured staying out of sight is probably the safest bet.

Would it be appropriate to sit by the door with my ear pressed against it? He is my charge so...yes, it is.

I hear the mumblings of conversation, a little laughter here and there but nothing interesting enough to continue straining to hear. Are they making out? Did he take her to his room? I need a distraction before curiosity eats me alive and I do something stupid and embarrass myself. I resign to abandon my twelve-year-old self to tend to my bedtime routine as my evening activities have been thwarted by "Hot Boss." After my dental routine is complete and my teeth are shiny like dentist commercial animations, I climb into my bed and stare up at the smooth ceiling, my eyes as wide as hockey pucks.

How would I know it is safe to go out of my room? Should I expect someone else for breakfast?

The suspense is making my brain ache. I'm pretty sure this is not the reaction a roommate or a work colleague would typically have. Suddenly I hear footsteps and the voices of soft goodbyes as the front door closes. The tension in my shoulders releases as I feel the relief of being able to leave my room or maybe it was knowing that the population of the house did not increase by one. Ihsan's guest didn't stay as long as I would think any hanky panky would take. To my surprise, this also helps my mood. There is no reason I can't leave my room now. I really do need some ice water and since I currently do not have an ice machine in my bedroom, it makes a good excuse to go to the kitchen.

Ihsan must still be awake and wandering around as the lights are bright in the main floor of the house. The sight of Zeki rolling around in the kitchen on his back, kicking out his legs confirms this suspicion as Zeki always sleeps in Ihsan's room. The cool tile feels refreshing on my feet, but it is too loud when I try to silently sneak into the kitchen to return the bowl of strawberries to the refrigerator, as if the food cheating never happened. Once I see that he is nowhere to be seen, I feel like I can let some air into my lungs. Pulling my phone out of my pajama pocket, I look for some music. Clicking through several options, I decide on an eighties compilation that my mom and I used to bake cookies.

Every year during Thanksgiving, I would send home a tin of homemade cookies with every student for their family. My mom and I would spend the weekend before Thanksgiving break holding a "Bake-a-thon" in the kitchen, dining room, and living room. This time of year could be difficult for many students and even if the cookies never made it home, they at least had something in their belly that was made with love. We went through the whole eighties decade of music in one weekend.

IHSAN

Some find blind dates intimidating but I tend to think of them as an exercise in improvisation which make them quite exciting. The date with Madison doesn't exactly stretch my skills. Her tall stature and wispy movements give her an elegant air. The off-white sweater that criss-crosses across her chest is in stark contrast to her long dark wavy hair. With heels, I only have to bend my head slightly to meet her dark brown eyes. Beatrice's penchant for finding the most exclusive parties and club openings is second to none and with this woman on my arm, I'm noticing the attention is palpable. I spotted several phones capturing us while we drank and chatted. The conversation is light and almost artificial as I go through the typical motions of what everyone expects. Madison is like Gül in many ways and the reminder of her leaves a sour taste in my soul. Without Beatrice understanding the true reason for my divorce, she can only make her best guess on who I might make a connection with and Madison checks all the boxes. All the old boxes.

As the night winds down, I escort Madison to the large black SUV parked on the street waiting alongside the thick red rope. I planned on taking her home when she suggests that we take a drive. I've never been very good at refusing a request from a beautiful woman. We chit chat about who we knew at the party and what we like to do in our spare time. Her polite laugh feels dishonest and a bit condescending. Beatrice made me earn her appreciation. I keep driving, hoping at some point my interest would be piqued but she either didn't seem that interested or I am not that interested in her, at least not her personality. Now her body is a whole different story. The first time my eyes moved from her head to her toes, my cock twitched. But as the night went on, it relaxed with little hope of the excitement returning.

The familiar drive goes by my temporary house and I can fill up the time by explaining the landmarks along the way. As we drive past the location of the rose bush incident, I smile and giggle to myself thinking of how Beatrice flips the house the bird every time we leave or return home. One of these days the owner is going to see her and I will have to send over a fruit basket to keep the peace on the street. My *anne* was always about peace on the street. She also taught me to be a gentleman and when Madison expresses her discomfort, I offer to stop by the house. I am familiar with the bathroom ploy. I played the game more than I'd like to admit in my younger days. It is a seemingly innocuous way to gain entry into your escort's house without suspicion. As we approach the front door, I remember that Beatrice is home and probably at her post. Madison strolls past me which raises my suspicion that her desperation for a bathroom was exaggerated. I motion her toward the downstairs powder room and lean back to see the light under Beatrice's bedroom door, the shadows thwarting Beatrice's efforts to stay covert bring a slight smile to my face.

After making the excuse of an early morning call, I order Madison a ride from my phone. I make a conscious effort to convince myself to ask her to stay but nothing about spending more time with her seems appealing. Checking down my list of traits I want in a woman, she meets all the qualifications, but nothing sounds better than closing the door with her on the other side. She doesn't seem hurt or show any emotion really, so my expected feeling of guilt does not bubble up. We chit chat about the quirkiness of the house before her car arrives and after I escort her to her ride, I walk upstairs untying and unbuttoning everything I can. All I want is to change into soft comforting clothes and relax.

As I close the bedroom door behind me, I hear the familiar sound of Beatrice's favorite music but this time I get to hear her sing along. Clearing the ceiling as I step further down the staircase, I am knocked into a fit of quiet laughter as I watch Beatrice dance with reckless abandon. Her moves match up perfectly with the beat of the music and her enthusiasm lightens my heart. My glee starts to twinge with hints of lust. Her free spirit permeating my nerves and sending electric shocks to all parts of me. I don't want to scare her, even though it is extremely tempting, so I walk very slowly into the kitchen, giving her eyes time to catch me in the corner of her view.

BEATRICE

As I prepare my glass of ice water, I sing along to the lyrics without fear but not at top volume. If Ihsan was still awake, I didn't want him witnessing this blackmail worthy karaoke party I was hosting. The air here seems to be lighter and more energetic than my room and a little dancing feels appropriate. Usually during this time of night, I'm searching for something chocolatey but with Ihsan's strict rules the strawberries will have to suffice. Staring down at the bowl, I'm reminded that this is all for a good reason and to just suck it up. Popping a few more in my mouth I return the bowl to the giant silver ice box. Quickly realizing that a freshly brushed mouth makes everything taste gross and as I go to spit out the fruit into the garbage disposal, Ihsan strides into the kitchen with a bright smile smothering his face. I spin around to face the fridge again, chewing furiously what didn't make it into the sink and sipping my water to rinse away any evidence of my berry adultery.

"Looks like your evening was a success," I attempt to say, with the berries stuck in my cheeks.

"Yes, it was," he says with annoying positivity. "Yours as well?"

I swallow bigger chunks than I should have before speaking and attempt to keep the strained expression off my face.

"Yes, I successfully protected the house against a band of pirates, a plague of locusts and a troupe of dancing clowns," I say, leaning against the counter holding my phone to turn down the volume. "Don't go anywhere, I'll be back."

After returning to the kitchen with a small gossamer sack tied with a satin ribbon, I stand in front of him with a large smile on my face.

"This is to thank you for the nice things you said on the video and for all the other crap you put up with."

I present it to him with two open palms.

"Beatrice, you didn't..."

"*Sus*, I wanted to. Besides, I might have found something to occupy my hands so I don't succumb to snackage."

Ihsan pulls the tie on the small pouch and removes the finished product of my new favorite hobby.

"*Vay*," he lets out as he lays the braided leather cord cuff bracelet across his wrist.

"I'll clasp it for you."

As I turn it over, I make sure he sees the silver inset tubular beads with the blue evil eye delicately carved into each bead.

"I figured you needed protection from my mean vibes."

"Beatrice, it's fantastic. I've never seen anything like it."

"I made it," I say proudly. "Don't look too closely, the tension isn't consistent. The lady at the bead store taught me the weaving technique and helped me order the beads. I took a class with a bunch of old ladies who tried to set me up with their lonely grandsons. I practiced a bit and then put a Turkish spin on it. I can't afford something fancy, but I can be crafty when I put my mind to it."

"I love it, it is so cool," he says as he turns his wrist over admiring it as I sit admiring him wearing it. His wrist looks incredibly sexy with leather wrapped around his wrist bone and I can feel my skin warm up unexpectedly.

It was relaxing creating something beautiful doing a mindless activity. The old ladies seemed to enjoy having me around and I got a bit of maternal attention I didn't realize I was missing. Their back and forth reminded me of the five minutes before staff meetings where my co-conspirators could briefly catch up with each other and remind ourselves why we worked at that school. We were a family. It was the first school I ever worked at but many of my teacher friends said that it was the only school they had ever taught that anyone would drop everything to support you. From the front office staff to the food services lead that moonlighted as Santa during the holidays, you always felt as if you belonged, and someone had your back. Instead of saying "have a good weekend," my principal always said, "can't wait to see you on Monday," and best of all, he actually meant it. The ladies' geriatric bickering also kept my mind off Ihsan's dates which is why I returned to their beading circle several times. Recently, I realized I was on Ihsan overload and needed to give myself a break. It couldn't be healthy to be so focused on one person a thousand out of the fourteen hundred forty minutes in the day.

"So, you've never brought anyone back here before," I slip, my brain immediately chastising my heart for inquiring.

"Are you the gatekeeper?" he teases.

"No, I just would hate to interrupt a romantic dalliance. How embarrassing for you if I come out looking like this while you're...ummm, hosting. Wouldn't want to tarnish the silver."

"I was brought up with manners," he says, stealing my bowl of strawberries out of the refrigerator.

"Actually, I have a question about these manners of yours," I say matter of factly and plop myself on a stool.

"I've tried to google it but nothing I found gave me the answers I was looking for so I'm going to the source."

"*Tamam.*"

"In these Turkish dramas, there is hardly any kissing. You can get ten episodes deep and nothing. The women are dressed seductively, barely a handkerchief, but hand holding is a big deal?"

He laughs a little at the sincerity of my question.

"The media companies have to adhere to a standard of morality."

"So wait, the women can have their hoo haws out but kissing on the lips can only happen once every twenty episodes? I've never seen so much hugging and cheek kissing in my life. It's a good thing the plots are engaging. Although, when the guy grabs her by the elbow and leans into her cheek and talks real close in her ear, that is seriously hot. I have to watch with an ol' Louisiana fan. Oh and no one beats a Turkish actor in eye stares and jaw clenching," I say, doing my best to imitate what I've seen in almost every show.

Ihsan watches me with a combination of amusement and disgust.

"I won't be doing that in front of anyone ever by your reaction. When will they put up the rest of the season of The Web, I'm dying to find out who killed the sister."

Ihsan's face grew dark and sour. "There won't be any more episodes."

"What? They can't put that on Netflix and then not finish it."

"We decided to not finish it."

"Oh, you have to do better than that."

Ihsan places both hands on the counter and pushes himself back.

"You look serious, what happened?"

Ihsan's face looks pained. "The writers wrote a homosexual character, and the government wouldn't approve. The streaming service came to us and asked if we'd like to be censored or cancelled. The cast and crew decided that we would not continue."

"Woah, that's intense."

"There is a resurgence of anti-LGBT attitudes in Istanbul, actually all over Türkiye. Being gay isn't illegal but during Pride last June, the police arrested more than they ever have."

"Oh, that's terrible, I'm so sorry." My face drops and he leans back against the cabinets across from me, wrapping his arms over his chest.

"I told you I have a sister, but I also have a brother, Nadir."

"Oh?" realizing that there must be a reason he didn't tell me.

"My brother is gay. You know my uncle lived with us growing up. He had a difficult time accepting Nadir. My dad worked a lot at the shop and when my uncle drank too much, he would beat on Nadir. When I was strong enough, in order to protect him, I would make him sleep in my bed when my uncle drank. My uncle knew I would give him the same beating if he touched him, and I didn't give him a chance to get his hands on him. He's the reason I got into a lot of fights in school."

Ihsan's gaze didn't leave the countertop.

When something this significant is dropped in your lap, you have to treat it with great care. This isn't the time to ask questions even though I have so many.

"This movie isn't just an opportunity for me, I want to bring Nadir to America. He is a journalist and I want him to be able to live without fear."

"We have so much room here, he should move in now."

"My brother is very proud. He's been in a bit of trouble for what he writes, and he needs to have a job in order to stay."

"He can have mine," I volunteer. It would certainly be easier for me to find something than for Nadir.

"Your job is too ... flexible. He needs to have something solid, reliable and concrete."

"So, he's a bit of a maverick?"

"Nadir's political activities got him in hot water with the government and the fact that he is my brother frustrated officials as it publicized their hypocrisy."

"Oh yeah, I can see where that would piss some people off."

"I don't shy away from questions about him or what is going on but I don't want to make it worse for him because he sees me as not standing up for him. But I also have a family to protect. I wasn't as eloquent on my feet as he thought I should be. When Blaine and I connected, it seemed like the perfect solution even though I would be away from my children for a while. I figured if I can get some publicity in the US, that would give me political clout and fulfill a dream. I'm hoping my influence will help get his visa approved. I appreciate your generosity though."

"Wow that's a lot. Well, if anybody can write a document full of BS to satisfy the government, it's a teacher. I can help."

The stakes for his success are much higher than I knew. I can feel my heart fracture in my chest for Ihsan and his family. I can't even imagine having to fight the government just to be who I am. My mind flashes back to my most vulnerable students that felt like my room was a safe space, where they trusted me enough to be themselves or at least start to figure it out. Middle school sucks no matter where you land in the social hierarchy so it was always important to me to make it as less sucky as I could. I always thought that my quirkiness gained me a connection that other teachers didn't have. My students could see that someone could be happy being themselves, I just hope they didn't see through my mask.

There is no way I can leave until I see Ihsan's brother in the flesh. I slip off the stool and cover his crossed hand with mine. My touch seems to return him from a dark place as his muscles relax under my palms.

"You know, a man from a faraway land once said something to me that seemed wise beyond his years. He told me that I was not alone." I smile and squeeze his hand gently. "I believed him. I hope you believe me when I say that I will do anything I can to help you with Nadir."

"That's not part of your job," he says, trying to brush me off.

"No, but it is part of being your friend."

The contradiction of kindness and sadness in his eyes actually causes a sharp pain at the bottom of my stomach but I can't turn away. He told me I would not be alone; I want to show him that he isn't either. I will never be a mother, so those mama bear instincts need a focus, and that focus is Ihsan.

"Besides, you are helping me buff up for the wedding. It's the least I can do."

IHSAN

Beatrice is smart but I am smart about Beatrice. When she turns to me with her cheeks looking much like her cheeks did a few months ago, a bit puffy, I stifle a laugh. By not calling attention to her cheating, I let her think she got away with something. As long as when she opens her mouth, her teeth gleam instead of being covered in dark chocolate paste, I let it slide. When she rushes away to her room with that absurd bun bouncing atop her head, I note how more agile she has become. Her new body fits into who she really is, vibrant and a bit quirky. I can't wait to see her shine at the LGBTQ+ charity auction in a few weeks. Seeing her face light up with pride is not something I expected to bring me so much joy.

It has been a while since we've hung out at night and to be honest, many of the nights she has me out with Hollywood's most eligible bachelorette, I just want to be back at the house hanging out with Beatrice. Sure, the women she has me taking out on the town are beautiful but I'm tired of trying to get to know someone all over again. I swore off the days of casual hook-ups because they were unhealthy and because my mother would give me an earful if she saw even the slightest spark of interest. The tabloids were no help either. Out of the blue, my old soccer coach called me and told me exactly what my father should have told me. I was out of control and not being someone my mother could be proud of. He finally told me, "You aren't even proud of you right now." Nadir and Farah had all but disowned me. Gül entered my life at the perfect time. She was sophisticated, successful, and sexy; everything I needed to turn my life around. Suddenly, I was the settled down playboy and she was the right woman to tame me. At least, that is what the internet said. The daily voicemail rants from my mother ceased and Farah and Nadir started inviting Gül and I to family dinners where my mother doted on her as if she were sent from *Allah* himself.

Whenever Beatrice asks me about my home, it excites me to share with her everything I miss. Sometimes I catch her watching a cooking channel hosted by a famous Turkish television cook. I'll overhear Beatrice asking Millie to cook one of Ria's recipes and laughing to myself at how she imitates her accent. She doesn't know how much it means to me to have the food I grew up eating filling my belly. Or maybe she does. But along with the good comes the bad and finally coming clean about Nadir feels cathartic. When her shiny, hazel eyes tilt to look in mine and her warm palms settle on my skin I feel comforted.

The bracelet. This accessory represents hours of time and research and practice, and she did it for me. Not because I asked her, paid her or guilted her. My gift seems insignificant in comparison, a trinket I could buy on the internet if I searched hard enough. The leather on my wrist is the only one in existence, created for me out of...kindness. A visual representation of what this woman is willing to do for me. A piece of her is always touching me. Her touch lightens all the blackness of my world. When Beatrice is your friend, she is all in; no hesitation, no limit, and no doubt.

me: *Hallo!*

Farah: *Abi*, were your ears ringing? *Anne* and I were just talking about you.

me: oh?

Farah: It was mostly about Beatrice.

me: That's what I wanted to ask you about.

Farah: *Tamam.*

me: **I want to ask her to come to Istanbul when we shoot there.**

Farah: **What about Asli?**

me: **I'll explain it to her. She probably has a new PA job anyway. Do you think it is a good idea?**

Farah: **Is it for the best?**

me: **I think so. Do you think it is a good idea?**

Farah: **I think you wouldn't be able to work without her.**

me: ***Tamam. Sou.***

I don't think I'll be able to do anything without her.

Chapter 33

B EATRICE

Running up the stairs the best I can, I shout "EEE-SAAAHN!."

I knock vigorously and he slowly opens the door, rubbing his fingers over his eyes in only his boxer briefs, baby blue boxers with little white hearts. Not that I notice those things. The conflict within my body to laugh or to drool is real.

"Stop trying to seduce me, put your clothes on and come down," I half joke, mostly wishing.

He shakes his head slightly as his English to Turkish translator in his head gets an early morning jump start.

I carefully walk down the stairs and when I reach the bottom I run back into the office. I open the email from a casting agent for a YouTube series. I notice he only put on long gym shorts when he enters our shared workspace. I explicitly told him to stop trying to get me all riled up and there he goes walking in all tattooed and shirtless with his hair still halfway matted to one side of his head.

"Come, sit. Look what I did."

"I'm scared."

I push my laptop in front of him. He is struggling to read what is displayed on the screen.

"Let me help you out, old man," I say, enlarging the print to two hundred percent which of course gets the reaction I was looking for, his glorious scowl. I'm glad he knows I would never tease him because of his dyslexia, I have so many other ways to do it.

He takes a few moments to read the email.

"This is great!"

Getting up out of the chair I start to slowly chant "Isa's going on 'Get Fit'" repeatedly in various vocal music styles. To emphasize my happiness, I perform possibly the worst slo-mo touchdown dance that has ever emanated from someone's body. Ihsan sit's back in the chair, crosses his arms across his bare chest and enjoys the show. The vibrant expression of amusement on his already gorgeous face only encourages me to make even more exaggerated inappropriate moves, some involving office furniture. I take my bun out and spin my hair around. After finally tiring myself out, I sit back down in the chair and return my hair to its typical bun.

"Wheeew, oh man it is hard work making you uncomfortable. I should get a dancing bonus."

"Oh no, you were entertaining. I'm going to make that a job requirement."

I pick up a pencil and send it flying through the air.

"The producer of the series wanted to know some things about you. I sent him a few clips from your dramas and then some clips from that bromance cop show. I also mentioned to them that you liked to do your own stunts in your films. When they heard that, they were really interested. We were coordinating schedules, and they want to do it in like two weeks," I say between heavy breaths.

"Ok, that sounds good."

"You sure that's enough time? You're looking a little soft there," I say poking his rock-hard side with my pen.

"Neh?!" He grabs at his skin where I stabbed my pen.

"Hey, if you are going to walk around here 90% naked, I'm going to take advantage. Now, go shower. You're much hotter when you're clean."

He grabs my bun and gives it a little shake before giving me one of my favorite views, but this time in damn cute basketball shorts. I notice he's wearing the bracelet I made him, and I smile to myself. Every time I see the bracelet he gifted me, the joint in my jaw tightens and I wonder if his body reacts the same.

This amazing opportunity comes at the perfect time. The start of the school year is usually a stressful time, and this is the first time since I was five that I didn't have to worry about it. No lesson planning, online classroom set up, seating charts, or mad scramble to get to the copy machine before a newbie teacher breaks it. If it weren't for this fitness series, I wouldn't know what to do with myself. Every commercial or online store is advertising back to school campaigns and I find myself looking for the cheapest deal on bulk number two pencils. I got very close to adding some to my cart but then happily pressed the delete button and closed the tab a little too aggressively.

The host of the show, Tyler Lee, is a Korean-American of a slightly short stature and a favorite stand up comic of many. His recent venture into online content creation has been wildly successful. I cannot wait to see their interactions while attempting various physical feats. I've seen Ihsan in the gym, Ihsan on set, and Ihsan with his kids. Ihsan in the wild is something else entirely.

Ihsan takes my comment a little too seriously and steps up his workouts. He also takes his revenge by putting the treadmill on the maximum incline and not letting me off until I couldn't recite my full name. I feel bad body shaming him but really, who does this hurt? Certainly not me. When we finish our sessions with our trainer, he spends an extra twenty minutes doing targeted muscle exercises. I didn't know the body could move in those ways. I often stay to make sure he wouldn't "hurt himself."

The day before shooting I have a video call with the segment producer.

"I just want to let you know that Ihsan has a great sense of humor, so no holds barred. I've been toughening him up."

"That's great to hear. We'll meet at the park at 9 a.m. and then go over to the second location."

"What is the second location?"

"We like to keep that a secret, so we get authentic reactions."

"You think I would tell? You realize my whole reason for living is to torture this man."

Laughing on the other line, he says, "I think this is going to work out great."

"I'll see you tomorrow morning."

"EEE-SAAHN!" I yell across the house. My tone indicates that I need him but that it isn't an emergency.

Continuing to call out his name, I walk out into the living room. He comes to the top of the stairs with his phone against his ear, trying to shush me.

"Just a second," he says on the phone and covers the receiver.

"What?! Hot date?" I say louder than I need hoping to sabotage his conversation.

"I'm trying...*sus!*" He waves me off and walks back into his room.

Oh, he is getting shit for this.

I walk up the stairs, trying to take two at a time and only did four steps till I decided Ihsan is a showoff and continued with singles.

Knocking on the door repeatedly, I say his name in a super loud whisper until it opens to his glaring face.

"You are fired."

Pushing my way into his room, I give him "the hand" and "*sus*" him back.

"We need to pick out something for you to wear for tomorrow," I say, going behind his bed into the hallway that leads to his closet. I rarely come up here, so I look around and notice he is neater than I am, a lot neater.

"Geez, you live like a pig. Have some self-respect."

"I wasn't expecting guests," he says walking in behind me.

"Didn't mean to invade your fortress of solitude," I say apologetically. I motion around the room. "So, what are you wearing?"

He opens a few drawers, picks up a few items and then places them back in the drawer.

"I'm not the fashion police, just pull something out."

He removes a small-ish black dry fit t-shirt and black basketball shorts.

"I think your muscles might be intimidating. Let's keep this one just in case. Maybe we should take a couple of outfits. We don't know what you'll be doing," I say, secretly hoping he wears the tiny black t-shirt.

"Go grab an overnight bag and we'll pack it up."

He grabs a brown leather bag from the top of the closet, and I notice the LV all over pattern.

"Gift from Gül?" I ask.

"Yes. How did you know?"

"There is no way you would buy this on your own. You're not this fancy. This is Gül."

"I thought I'd gotten rid of it."

I sit on the floor, open the bag, stick my head inside and suck in deeply.

"What are you doing?"

"I like the way new things smell," I say, like it is perfectly acceptable and wiggle my eyebrows at him hoping he knows I was referring to him as well.

"You are so strange."

"Whatever, you're Turkish," I retort.

"*Neh?*" His tone fake, offended.

"You heard me," I say, still checking out the bag.

Suddenly, I'm knocked on my side. He grabs my hands, moves my hips under his and pins my arms on the floor.

"Take that back!" he commands down at me.

"Not this again. You called me strange!" I shout up at him struggling to get him off me.

"You called me Turkish."

"You are Turkish."

"You are strange."

I stop struggling and he stares down at me.

"What is the magic word in American?"

"It's English! Get off before I open a can of whoop-ass," I threaten him.

"No, that isn't it."

"Ugh...Please."

"No, that isn't it," he looks up quizzically.

"Ugh...I don't know the Turkish word for please yet and you're crushing my intestines."

"I'll let you up, but you have to do something for me."

"Oh, my spleeeeen. Isn't it my turn to be on top?" I fake pain. "What do you want?"

"You have to play something for me. On the piano."

"Seriously, out of everything you could ask for?"

Taking in as big of a breath as I can to buy me some thinking time, I decide to give in. He didn't specify it had to be difficult. I'm going to enjoy playing variations of the classic "Mary Had a Little Lamb."

"Fine!"

He leans back and stands up in one move then offers to help me stand. Taking his hand, I pull myself up.

"Revenge is mine," I say glaring at his face. "You won't see it coming."

He walks over to his drawers and takes a clump of clothes and shoves it in his bag.

"There, packed."

"Actually, not a bad idea," I say, shrugging my shoulders. "My work here is done."

He starts to walk down the hallway when he turns and smiles at me evilly "Now, let's pick out your outfit."

I start to run after him and decide that taking him down will be a better option, so I launch myself onto his back. To my surprise, I made it halfway up his body. Ihsan yelled but then grabbed my legs and lifted me up the rest of the way.

Damn this guy is strong.

"Don't you dare!" I scream in his ear as he continues to walk with me clinging to his back.

"Stay away from the drawers in my drawers!" I say smacking his head.

"Ok, ok, ok..." he walks over to the bed and drops us both onto the mattress.

Releasing my grip on his shoulder, I try to push his mammoth body.

"You're hard to get into bed," he says, pushing my legs away.

"That's the rumor,"

"Ok, I'll let you get your beauty rest," I say trying to brush off all the physical contact. "You probably have some kind of skin ritual with gopher placenta or something."

"*Allah, Allah*. Wait, I need to ask you something."

"Ok."

"You noticed on the shooting schedule that we will eventually be shooting in Istanbul. I want you to come. I'll need you there."

"Seriously? Wow. Are you sure? You think they'll let me in?"

"I may have to bribe some people," he smiles proudly. "Let's get you a passport. I can't wait to show you around."

"I'm in!" I say without thinking.

Oh, crap. What did I just agree to?

As I close the door I hear my favorite lyrics. "Wicked Games" for sure.

The morning comes and I decide that I might as well wear something comfortable and find my favorite black capri workout pants, straight jacket bra, a too big for me light blue v neck t-shirt and my running shoes.

I wake up extra early to pack some snacks and fill our water bottles, but I have too much time on my hands, so I plot my revenge. Quietly, I creep up the stairs to his room. I told him to be out the door by seven thirty am. I check my watch, six forty-five. The doorknob turns easily, and the latch pulls back with barely a click. I can hardly contain my glee for how this plan is working out so far. My shoes are quiet on his tile floor, and I tip toe over to the bed where he lies peacefully sleeping, the flat sheet only covering half of his body and Zeki sprawled out over the other half. He's lying on his stomach with his perfectly ripped back exposed. It's times like these that I remind myself to get Matthew something really good for Christmas.

I carefully step onto the mattress near the headboard of his bed. He sleeps diagonally and I want to make sure I don't mark his face up before his big gig.

"Time to get up, time to get up, time to get up!" I scream at the top of my lungs, jumping up and down on top of the fluffy mattress.

All I see is an arm, leg, and sheet tornado. This is one of my best shenanigans yet. Zeki, raises his head quickly and then lays it back down as if I'm not worth getting worked up over. I slide down the headboard holding my stomach from bursting out of my body. He sits up holding his torso, his chest heaving and surprised rage in his eyes. This just makes me laugh harder. Pillows suddenly hit my face. I accept his reaction as it is absolutely understandable since I am almost literally rolling on the floor laughing.

"I told you that you wouldn't see it coming," I barely sputter through the laughter.

"I'm going to let Zeki out...oh, God. Best...revenge...ever," I say walking out with Zeki in tow, feeling another pillow smacking against my back.

"*Allah*..." I hear him say as I close the door.

We decided that Zeki needs an outing and the producer said that it would actually be a great idea to bring him since his Instagram following is so huge. As I'm gathering up our stuff, I hear Ihsan coming down the stairs mumbling something in Turkish. I wish he would talk louder. He reaches the bottom and drops the overnight bag on the floor.

"Goonie island, hot stuff."

"*Kovuldun*," he mumbles without even a glance in my direction or reaction to another one of my mutilations of the Turkish language.

You're fired, possibly?

He opens the refrigerator and pulls out one of his protein drinks. He looks at the seal wearily as I have threatened to spike it with laxatives in the past.

"I see you're going with the classy hobo look," I comment at his gray hoodie with black basketball shorts. He has pulled his hood over his head so I can't see his expression very well.

I grab the backpack and Zeki's head harness. Zeki waits at the double doors for us wagging his big butt excitedly. The ding of a text from the show producer provides us with the first location.

"Ready yet?" I shout too close to his face.

"*Evet*," he says in a rough quiet rumble as he walks by.

"Oh, come on, that was hilarious," I say to the back of his head as he walks to the car.

He pops the back to let Zeki up into his crate and turns to look at me.

"Your face is hilarious," he says with a giant smile on his face.

"Aw...you do have a sense of humor."

I notice the leather cuff on his wrist.

"Just so you know, I don't expect you to wear the bracelet every day."

"I know, I really like it."

Oh, all the feels happening right now.

He takes the keys, and we head out on what we hope to be a fun morning. In a lot of his movies, he prefers to do the stunt driving himself. The speed at which he operates his vehicle is a little fast for my taste, as usual. He is probably doing it on purpose to get back at me. Because of this there is a permanent impression of my fingers on the "oh shit" handle above me. Listening to my favorite 80's music distracts me and calms my nerves.

"Do we always have to listen to your music?"

"I don't understand Turkish, and it is really hard to sing along even if I faked the words, so yes. But, how about something a little different?"

Searching on my music app, I finally find the song that sparks one of my happiest memories.

"Ihsan, this song...oh, you just gotta hear it."

"What is it?"

"Something Stupid."

"Then why are we listening to it?"

"No, it's called 'Something Stupid' by Frank Sinatra. Mr. D introduced me to this song. He just broke out dancing one afternoon and we sang it over and over. He's the best."

The Latin beat plays through the car speakers and I start weaving my head and playing the rhythm of the drums on the dashboard. When Frank and his daughter start to sing in their close harmony, I join in. A sweet smile starts to move across his face as I start to exaggerate my movements and sing a little louder. And when the chorus pipes in, I have a moment of spontaneous bravery and turn to him and sing the chorus, choreographing to the lyrics.

Belting out the chorus line, I end with the final seven words that hit too close to home and end it with the punchline, "I love you."

I wish there was a pause button in life where you can just stop a moment and live in it just a few seconds longer. His face is pure delight. Why did the lyric have to end in those three words? There is a tiny spot of light in the corner of his eye that blinks in and out and his lips have stretched across his teeth turning into one of the most beautiful smiles I have ever seen. A smile that brings my breath to a halt as if I just saw one of the seven wonders of the world.

Oh...shit.

While I was goofing around, did I just accidentally tell him I loved him? Is he smiling because I'm making an ass out of myself or because he thought I told him I loved him.

Double shit.

How do I get out of this?

I do what a musician put on the spot often does, I double down and sing louder.

Not only do I sing louder but then I make my previous dance moves even more exaggerated and start singing to the people in the next car that I love them too. One driver even gave me the finger heart and a smile through the window. Pretty good for LA, I would say. As the song fades out with continuous "I love yous", I pray I played it off as just trying to entertain him.

"Mr. D does this fun little dance walk thing and spreads his arms out wide and would sing that at the top of his lungs in the middle of the choir room. He never cared what anyone thought, he just did what he loved, and he loved dancing like a fool to that song," I explain as I sit back into my seat staring at the music app to pause it.

"That is where you get your dance moves then?"

"For sure."

"No lessons?"

"Don't get any ideas for a new workout routine. That would be the end for both of us."

When we finally arrive at the location, I am thankful to see the production van parked in the lot next to a basketball court. No need to linger on this complete disaster of a drive any longer. I'm slightly disappointed they went with something so predictable, but it isn't my show.

I climb down from the seat, grab my backpack and proceed to the back of the SUV to release Zeki but Ihsan beats me to him. He seems to enjoy showing off his long legs compared to mine. With that little defeat, I walk toward the production van hoping it is for us.

"Hey, are you with 'Get Fit'?"

"Yes, I'm Bradley. You must be Beatrice."

Ihsan walks over with Zeki and offers his hand. Bradley's demeanor seemed a little nervous about Zeki, so I introduce them to set him at ease. Zeki doesn't need any bad press.

"This is Ihsan and Zeki," I motion respectfully.

"Ty will be here in a few minutes. Let's head out to the court. There are a few balls out there already."

"Ok, we'll head over."

Walking over to the "seen better days" basketball court, I notice there are some benches inside the chain link court. Ihsan hands Zeki to me and we take up our assigned seats. Zeki leans back and puts his butt on the bench with his front paws holding his body, making himself comfortable. His eye level is far higher than mine.

Ihsan grabs a ball and starts doing some dribbling tricks through his legs and around his back. He trots closer to the basket and shoots around, making bank shots off the backboard and short shots around the key, all of them go through with ease.

"Wait, I thought you played soccer- oh sorry 'futball'," I say as every American is annoyed with that.

"You think I'm only good at one sport?"

"Are you freaking kidding me?"

He continues his ball handling maneuvers as he makes his way back to me and Zeki on the bench.

"You know, I've never seen you play," I tell him.

"You said you did research," he says back to me, shooting at the hoop. Unlike other males I know, he doesn't react to the swish sound the basketball makes as it falls quietly through the net.

Show off.

A couple of cameramen come into the court and set up at the opposite side of us. I can hear Tyler's distinct voice saying hi to Bradley and watch him walk along the short side of the court. He raises his hand at Ihsan in a fun greeting.

"Heeeeyyyy...now, this is something I can do. Basketball, that's what I'm talk...What the fuck is that?" He jumps at the sight of Zeki and I sitting on the bench together, Zeki's long legs splaying out. He points and laughs but Zeki could care less as he shifts his eyebrows back to Ihsan.

"Such a good boy." I pet the back of his neck.

Tyler's mouth is wide open, laughing both with humor and nervousness.

"We ain't playing no polo," he walks back and forth on the court not quite knowing what to do.

Now I understand why Great Dane owners get sick of equine references.

Ihsan can't control his laughter either and Tyler finally walks cautiously over to Ihsan and puts out his hand, side eye-ing Zeki.

"Is that yours?" he asks.

"Yes, this is Zeki. He is very nice," Ihsan replies with a bit of a snicker in his voice, making his accent thicker.

"Nice...nice?! He's got Hannibal Lector headgear on. That's not nice, man."

Ihsan laughs some more which of course forces me to giggle. "He will sometimes pull when you walk and he's so big that you can't stop him. That's why he wears a head harness."

Do I love him?

Shut up, Beatrice!

"Is she his handler? You need like Ronda Rousey to hold that guy back," he says.

"No, this is Beatrice, my personal assistant."

I wave at Tyler because I have a feeling he isn't going to come over to shake my hand.

"Zeki, not a snack," I say and point to Tyler.

"Did she say, 'not a snack'? Ah, naw!" he says as his eyes grow twice as big in his sockets.

"We can sit somewhere else," I say, moving off the bench with Zeki standing next to me.

"Holy shit... are you sure that is a dog? That is a big ass," he says when he sees Zeki's back stands taller than my waist. "Oh, my gaw!"

"You are talking about Zeki, right?" I say, glaring at him as if he really did insult my backside.

Ihsan continues to laugh as Tyler tries to reconcile his preconceived ideas of canines.

"Yeah, the dog, the dog. I don't piss off PAs," he waves his hand in defense. I flash my eyes, showing him I didn't take offense.

"No, you can sit here where I can see him. I want to know where that dog is at all times. That dog shits my dog," he says as he walks further onto the court, keeping one eye focused on Zeki and I.

"Ok, let's get this going," Tyler commands after finally calming down. He offers his hand to Ihsan again. "Nice to meet you, Ihsan. I'm Ty. So, you are the Turkish delight, I hear."

Ihsan can't hide his large toothy smile as Ty measures himself against him.

"You can call me Isa."

No, this feels different. This is infatuation, not love.

Shut up, Beatrice.

"Ok, Isa...we gonna play some basketball?"

Ty struts around with a basketball dribbling like he knows what he is doing, bouncing the ball behind his back and between his legs, quite a bit less adeptly as Ihsan. He's followed by a man with a large camera strapped to his body. He dribbles closer to the hoop and makes a few shots, whooping and hollering every time he makes a basket. Ihsan watches with a basketball on his hip, letting Ty have his moment. I take my phone out and start taking pictures.

"So, you do this for fun, hobby?" Ty asks.

"I played a lot when I was younger." Ihsan starts to dribble.

"Oh yeah? High school, college?"

"Yeah, those and pro ball in Turkey," Ihsan replies and does a few tricks.

"You got me out here with a pro-baller? That's some buuuuullshit," Ty complains to the producer off to the side.

While Ty complains, Ihsan dribbles through some of his own ball handling tricks.

"Oh, ok. You got skills. Alright, let's see what else you got."

Ihsan puts the ball down on the court and starts to take off his hoodie. He pulls it over his head inadvertently raising the tank top with it, exposing his incredibly ripped abs. It still causes me a quick breath when they come out and play.

Daaayuuuum.

Absolutely infatuation. But does infatuation make all your woman parts flare up?

Not a good time, Beatrice.

I didn't realize my mouth was open until Ty points to me and laughs his signature loud rhythmic laugh, causing me to blush.

"What the fuck are those?" he asks Ihsan in disbelief as he walks over to him and pulls up his tank top to expose his abs to the cameraman.

"Turkish delight is right!" he shouts, pointing at Ihsan's torso. He walks away, turns on his heel and walks back. "Holy shit!"

Ihsan watches Ty's reaction, giggling slightly to himself.

I pull out my carrot sticks to watch the show, feeling like I need a snack. Biting off half of the orange stick, I stick the other half through Zeki's head strap.

"Did you just give him a carrot? Horses eat carrots. You can't tell me that's a dog when you just gave him a carrot."

"You don't want to see him when he's hungry."

Ty's mouth and eyes both grow large at my comment.

"Give that dog some fava beans, too."

I wink and point to Ty in appreciation of his movie reference.

"Don't worry, I'll explain it to Ihsan later."

"Alright let's get this game started," Ty shouts enthusiastically as he passes Ihsan the ball.

Ihsan squares up his body, dribbles twice and shoots from where he stands, well beyond the three-point line and yet again, swish.

IHSAN

Did Beatrice just declare that she loved me in a song? That would be a Beatrice thing to do. That is how she would do it, I'm sure. She wouldn't be able to handle the seriousness of the situation and so she would do something to distract herself from actually doing the deed.

This is bad. How am I supposed to concentrate on this YouTube program with that hanging in the air? There is no way she just picked that random song, right? I have no idea how Beatrice would tell someone she loved them, who am I kidding?

Allah, give me a sign.

Every shot I attempt at the hoop sinks through the net without a sound. There is no way this is the sign. Or is it? I've grown up playing all sorts of sports but <u>futball</u> was my main focus. Basketball was a game I would play in the neighborhood in random pick-up games. I was usually one of the best players on the court, even into adulthood with other pro athletes so it doesn't surprise me that I'm making all the shots. So, when Ty needs a demonstration of my skills, I test this theory of mine and try an absolutely impossible shot from the corner of Beatrice's bench.

Swish.

No...way.

I stare at the hoop until Zeki barks at Ty and disrupts my love thoughts about Beatrice. I shake out the possibility that her teasing, ranting, and thinly veiled insults are her way of getting my attention, a different kind of attention. I turn to see Beatrice's mouth and eyes wide open at my long shot. She is just as shocked as I am. I'm not one for superstition but that was divine intervention.

BEATRICE

As the ball bounces back over to us, Ty picks it up and throws the ball to the opposite side of the court.

"Yeah, we ain't doing that!" he says, clearly upset at the disproportionate skill set of the man the producers booked for this episode.

"By the way, Isa meant professional soccer, not basketball," I say as Ty decides whether to continue.

He turns to Ihsan and with an astonished look on his face yells, "FUCK!"

As he frustratedly struts out of the chain link gate, he inadvertently walks by Zeki and as if this dog is perfectly trained for the movies, Zeki barks loud and deep at him in protest.

"Jesus H. Christ," he screams as he kicks out a leg and arm in a pseudo martial arts maneuver.

Ihsan bends over laughing, not being able to hold it inside any longer. Ty exit's the court, his cussing diminishing the further he is. I hear something about setting him up with a pro football player with an enormous dog showing off his basketball skills. The poor guy was blindsided. As we gather outside the court, Bradley and Ty discuss the activities for the next location as they both keep an eye on Zeki.

"I know you won't believe me," I interrupt, "but Zeki is actually really kind."

"Suuuure."

"Well, I'd prefer to sleep with him in my bed than Ihsan."

"Oh damn!" Ty covers his mouth with his fist.

"Are you really doing this here?" Ihsan asks.

"Look, Ty just showed off that ridiculous ripped washboard of yours. If I don't say stuff like that your head won't fit in the car door. We'll have to put you in the back with Zeki."

Zeki's head moves back and forth between us as if he understands every word.

"Look at this guy!" Ty points to Zeki.

"Oh yeah, Zeki is a character. He even has his own Instagram."

"Naw...really?"

I pull it up on my phone and push the screen toward Ty. He takes the phone out of my hand and reviews Zeki's posts.

"He almost has as many followers as I do!" He hands my phone back and feigns hurt feelings as he walks away.

Turning to Zeki, I pet his head.

"It's ok Zeki, he'll learn to love you as we do."

Ihsan follows Ty with his bag in hand and Zeki and I close behind. Bradley musters up the nerve to walk next to me to explain that the next location where they have set up is an adult obstacle course. I smile knowing that Ihsan will be in his element with some indoor parkour.

"Bradley, I could kiss you. Ihsan is going to love this." I trot forward a few steps. "Ihsan, come here. Let's put that black t-shirt on, I think this will work better for what you are about to do."

Ihsan strips his tank and hoodie off and quickly puts on the tight black shirt that shows the ripples of his abs beneath the fabric. I wish it was always that easy to get a hot man to strip for me on command.

I'm doing it again. No, I'm not. Yes, I am.

SHUT UP, BEATRICE!

Walking up to the side of the building, the camera crew sets up outside the door. I saw another camera crew go in earlier, so I know he's going to have some great reaction footage.

As soon as Ty sees Ihsan, his infectious laugh starts all over again.

"What is this? Is this even allowed?" Ihsan stands with his hands on his hips like a superhero.

"I can't stop looking at his stomach. Sorry if I make you uncomfortable, man."

"No, it's fine. She does it all the time." Ihsan points to me.

"You be careful, she'll feed you to that dog."

Ihsan makes eye contact with me and flashes a crooked smile, knowing that Ty's warning holds merit. The rare imperfect smile just for me makes my heart skip a beat.

"So, I hear you're in this new action movie and you do a lot of your own stunts," Ty starts an impromptu casual interview.

"Yes, I really like all the physical stuff."

"Clearly." Ty points to his abs again. "With that in mind, we are going to see what they have set up for us in there."

As we walk in, I admire all the effort the team took to put this setup together. Different angled thick matts, trampolines, platforms of all sizes, poles, ropes for swinging and rope bridges fill the entire warehouse. The next hour the boys play as if no one is watching. I have almost as much fun watching as they do jumping around. Ihsan is perfectly charming while showing off all his physical prowess.

"Hey Bradley," I say from my perch on the wide catwalk with Zeki just as interested. "Ask Ihsan to Superman punch Ty. It's freaking amazing."

"Yeah! Should we tell Ty?"

"I don't know but you gotta see him do it. Shirt off, it's absolutely worth it."

Yep, totally infatuated. No love here. Just a simple immeasurable carnal desire to caress every inch of his skin with my nipples.

Beatrice! Are you made of spare parts or something?

Bradley calls Ty over and updates him on the plans for the next shot.

"What? Ah hell no, this fool is telling me you're going to take your shirt off and I'm supposed to stand perfectly still."

Ihsan looks over to me knowing I planned this.

"That never ends well for me," Ty says.

"It's worth it, Ty. I would totally stand there with a half-naked man getting physical with me but it's your show," I yell down to him.

"Yeah, you just keep holding onto that big ass dog. I got this. I got this," he says trying to convince himself he will be safe.

Ihsan stands sweaty and breathing slightly heavy as I mouth to him one word, "Superman."

He nods his head in understanding and turns to Ty.

"Do you trust me?" he asks.

"Hell no, I just met you."

"I would never ruin my chances for a buddy film with you."

Ty wags his finger at him and gives him a knowing smile.

"Oh, I see what you did."

"I'll make you a deal. You let me do this and I'll teach you how and then you can do it to me."

"I said that very same thing to many girls in high school."

It takes Ihsan a moment for the light to click in his head and laughs up at me as I shake my head down at him.

"Ok, ok, ok...just do it," Ty says, trying to pump himself with bravery.

"Don't close your eyes."

Ihsan moves Ty into position and counts the paces to figure out how much room he needs. I get my phone out and ready for what might possibly be content for the best post of all time.

"You ready?" Ihsan calls over to Ty.

"No," he says nervously.

"Keep your arms down."

Ihsan sets his feet to take two giant steps and then leaps into the air toward Ty with a wide scissor kick as he pulls his fist behind his shoulder and brings it down to strike at him, his fist a millimeter from Ty's nose as he lands on the soft mat, slightly behind him.

"Oooooo.....daaaaaaaamm!" Ty's smile was as large as his eyes. "That was awesome!"

Of course, Ihsan's execution was perfect.

They spend the next ten minutes going over the steps and rhythm of the move. Ihsan's teaching skills are impressive. I wasn't exactly concentrating on his pedagogy when he was teaching me how to box. But then his instruction quickly morphs into little boys playing at recess again.

"Bee...we're ready!" Ihsan shouts at me.

I turn on my camera again for Ty's turn.

Ihsan takes a boxer's stance and Ty runs after him which looks hilarious considering their size difference.

Ty works out the footwork a few times just to make sure he looks as good as Ihsan did and they go for it.

As soon as Ty comes down at Ihsan, Ihsan acts like he got hit by his fist and slams himself to the soft ground, pretending to be knocked out.

"Ooooohhhhh, did you see that?" Ty jumps around excitedly then pretends to continue hitting Ihsan with Ihsan's body responding in kind. It's like watching Brandon and Matthew from back in the day.

After the man boys finally finish their testosterone play, Ihsan takes a moment to make his traditional rounds of thanking everyone that helped with the production, charming everyone as usual. Walking out of the building, I see Ty and Ihsan huddled together, talking as if they have been friends forever.

"Hey Ty, would you be willing to take a picture for Ihsan's Instagram?"

"Oh yeah, sure. For mine too," he answers as he and Ihsan take it upon themselves to do as many dorky poses as I will allow.

"I'll send them to Bradley."

"Nah, send them to me," he takes my phone and adds his number into my contacts. Then does the same with Ihsan's phone. "Isa, brother, give me a call anytime."

"Since you are in such good spirit's, mind getting a photo with Zeki?" I ask with trepidation.

Ty looks at me like I just grew horns.

"We'll be right here with you," I say reassuringly.

I take Zeki's face harness off and hand Ihsan the leash. Being brave, I take Ty's hand and walk him over to Zeki, reassuring him with every step. Ihsan wait's, already on his knee holding Zeki.

"See, he's soft." I demonstrate by rubbing his ears.

Zeki is distracted by Ihsan giving him kisses.

"Feel his ears, they are my favorite."

Ty carefully sets his palm on Zeki's ear.

"Ok, just get on your knees, or bend over and put your arm around him. Ihsan will protect you."

"Sadly, I don't have to bend over," Ty observes.

"Did you use that line on girls too?" I ask.

Ihsan and Ty look at me with as much shock at my words as I feel, then burst into laughter. I sigh in relief that my joke was appreciated.

I quickly take a few steps back and click as many times as I possibly can before Ty loses his cool.

"Are you good if we post these on his site? I'll wait for the show to come out to post the action shots."

"Oh yeah, I'll post some too," he replies as I do an invisible fist pump. "No one is going to believe me."

Ihsan puts the head harness back on and stands up to move Zeki away from the nervous A-lister.

"Good job. I hope you and Zeki become fast friends."

"Don't you mean Ihsan?"

"No, screw him... Zeki is way better looking."

"Beatrice...*gerçekten*?" Ihsan's mock annoyance has become routine.

"You three need an internet show or something."

What I really need is a firehose to spray me down.

"Don't give her ideas," Ihsan moans.

We leave the outdoor set with a sense of accomplishment and a new friendship.

"Nice job! You've got a little buddy," I pat him on the back patronizingly and realize that I probably should have used a different word.

"Why do you always have to make it weird?"

"I'm regretting teaching you that phrase."

"Seems like you got yourself a new buddy, too."

"That makes my grand total of celebrity friends to two."

"*Neh?*"

"Charlotte and Ty."

"What about me?"

"I'm paid to like you."

"Doesn't that make you a..."

"Please finish that sentence. I need an excuse to kick your ass in public."

"Ah, you'd risk public embarrassment just for me?"

"Listen, I may seem like an irate squirrel to you, but I will bite."

"Promise?"

A deluge of hot red blood rushes to the top of my body causing my face to burst into giant red blotches as images of biting on Ihsan's lower lip flood my brain.

"Beatrice? Are you alright?"

"Just flushed from all the hard work today," I say, quickening my pace to the parking lot.

"You sat on a bench."

"Shut it."

Chapter 34

BEATRICE

Ihsan and Zeki bound into the kitchen while I prepare my evening snack of red, yellow, and orange bell peppers with some hippie hummus. I've got freshly washed sweatpants with an enormous sweatshirt to cuddle in to watch "10 Things I Hate About You" all ready to be worn and loved.

RIP Heath.

"I got you a new shirt for tonight. It's hanging in your closet next to the dark blue suit and gray vest. I just hope your big fat biceps fit into the sleeves," I say, squishing Ihsan's firm biceps through his soft cotton t-shirt.

"Hey, not so hard." He flinches away.

"Oh yeah, poor Hercules." Sarcasm drips from my words. "You posted a lot, and you need something new tonight."

"What are you wearing?"

"Tonight, I will be modeling the latest in single woman wear, fuzzy socks, fuzzy pants, fuzzy shirt."

"*Yok, yok, yok...*you are coming tonight." He stands up with alarm.

"*Yok, yok, yok...*I am staying here tonight."

"It's the auction. You put it on the schedule for both of us."

"No, I didn't. You have a date."

"Yes, you did...right here." Ihsan pushes his scheduling app into my face. The word 'auction', bold in purple text.

Shit.

"That is clearly a mistake...duh."

"I need your help," he says in a slightly whining tone.

"I refuse to participate in this tricycle fantasy of yours." I wave him off as I walk to my bedroom to change into my soft cotton cocoon.

"*Neh?*" He follows.

"A third wheel. You have a date and so do I. Isn't that right, my big handsome boy," I say, rubbing the soft fur under Zeki's saggy mouth.

Walking into my closet, I head for the corner where I have set aside a special spot for my movie watching gear. From behind me, I hear human feet, an unfamiliar sound in my sanctum sanctorum.

"Hey, you entered sacred ground here. You can't just waltz into a girl's closet without a special invitation."

"You are coming." He pushes hangers aside looking at my clothes critically.

"Stop, stop, stop..." I stand between his chest and all the hangers. "Why on earth would I have agreed to this?"

"It's a charity auction. I clearly remember you saying, 'that might be fun'." His expression conveys that I should remember, and he continues thumbing through my clothes, using his height to his advantage.

I really should watch what I say when I'm around this man. His retention of auditory information is second to none. And without clarification or follow up, he took my flippant remark seriously.

"Ugh, you have a date...you don't need me. I must have put it in purple by mistake," I explain, pushing him away from my hanging clothes.

"I thought you wanted to actually go and help me. You know, post photos of the event."

Giving him my most snarled annoyed stare à la Shakespeare's Katherina, I take a moment for all the conflicting conversations in my brain to come to a consensus.

"UGH! I'm not dressing up then, just work clothes. This is after hours so I'm charging you triple for my valuable time."

"Movie with a dog date is valuable?"

"Wow, ouch."

"You know what I meant."

"Just get out." I push him toward the doorway, irritated that he went through my clothes.

I don't let people peruse my clothes, as if they wouldn't be aware of my plumpness if they didn't see the size of clothes I wear. Pulling out my phone, I select the link I had attached to the title of the charity in the calendar.

"It's a cocktail party, oy... I'll figure it out, please go, Ihsan." Annoyed with the whole situation, I rack my brain about what Gül found that would work.

Not only did Gül overbuy that day on the patio but because I'm shrinking, I'm often finding that the outfit I pick out could have been mistaken for a tent found in the sporting goods .

After a few minutes of cussing at articles of clothing that really didn't deserve it, I find what I'm looking for, a notched neck sleeveless jacquard dress in light blue. Pulling the hanger up to my chin, I push it close to my waist as I look in the mirror. This will have to do. I'm not looking to impress; I just don't want to be turned away at the door. The tan wedge sandals should work, as well as the off-white knitted bolero.

I hang my outfit in the bathroom as I assess the hair and make-up situation in the mirror. Today was just an in-home workday so showering and a quick leg shave was all I took time to do. I love the feeling of freshly shaved legs in soft pants. At least it won't completely go to waste. My go-to performance hair is two Dutch braids on either side of my head with the end of the braid twisted around itself in the back to make an intricate bun. It was quick, no chance of burning myself on an iron, and in the end, looks very pretty. After struggling with the shapewear and zipper on the back of the dress, I put on the wedge sandals and add the bolero. The silver hoops, evil eye bracelet and neutral make-up with mascara to highlight my eyelashes in a serious way, finish off the ensemble. I attempt to wipe away my grumpy face but that seems to be the most difficult task out of everything I had to do this evening.

Before I leave the room, I open a car app and select my ride. Twelve minutes away seems a reasonable amount of time considering how far we are from the city. With one more glance in the mirror, I'm satisfied I won't embarrass myself or more importantly, Ihsan. I've unveiled an hourglass figure and my calves are showing off all the work I've been doing. I grab a pink glitter wristlet, stuff it with essentials and make my way to the foyer.

Ihsan waits in the hall wearing his new light blue shirt with a dark grey vest under his dark blue suit and a matching tie. The pair of pointy brown dress shoes matches his belt, as if I manifested him right out of a catalog.

Oh, the fashion gods never cease to amaze me with their sorcery. I hear his lungs suck in a quick breath as I approach.

"*Vay!* You look..."

"Stop there. I'm still annoyed and will only lash out," I warn him.

"Ok, let's go." He motions with his head to the front door.

"I ordered myself a car," I say, glancing down at the app to check the ETA.

"What? I've already called one. Come with us," he says casually.

"There is no way I am getting in a car with you and Hollywood Barbie. I'd look like the little sister you were forced to take." I scowl at him.

"That's ridiculous. Come on." He puts his hand on my back and pushes me toward the door.

"Stop!" I jerk my body away from him, pushing his arm off my back.

This whole situation catches me off guard. I'm angry that he doesn't understand why I don't want to be in a car with him and his date. Telling me that it is ridiculous just makes it hurt more.

Ridiculous is watching your boss make googly eyes at a beautiful woman in front of you.

Ridiculous is spending time in a place where no one will see you.

Ridiculous is constantly being reminded that you don't measure up.

Ridiculous is following said boss and Miss Beauty Before Brains around an event to take pictures.

Ridiculous is suffering all night because he asked you to.

Ihsan takes a step back, his face showing me he realizes this is not a fight he should be picking at this moment. I am thankful my response is understood. I'm a little embarrassed by the volume I used, there's a lot of emotion that has been on the verge of boiling over and sometimes the vent gets inadvertently pressed. Looking in my wristlet for something to diffuse the situation, I come up with an excuse to wait in my room.

"I forgot my lip stuff," I grumble, turning to walk down the glass walkway. "I'll see you there."

Sitting on the edge of my bed with the door slightly ajar, I wait to hear the glass latch open and shut. The universe hears my silent plea, and I am left alone in the house.

This night is going to be excruciating. I must be getting lazy at reading the calendar, how could I have screwed this up? The charity is for The Taylor Project, a cause that is close to both of us and I have no clue why I blanked it.

Giving it my best toddler tantrum walk, I head to the front door and wait to see headlights come down the driveway. Damn driver is right on time. I could sprain my ankle in these shoes walking down the steps, but he would know I was lying or had done it on purpose. I can't think of a reasonable way to get out of this without Ihsan knowing I ditched the auction. Someone could make millions for an "I don't give a shit" pill that doesn't get you high. I get into the little black Nissan and put my head back on the headrest and turn to watch the scenery.

"Do you feel okay?" the older man asked.

"I'm dressed up for a charity auction where I get to follow my gorgeous boss around with his gorgeous date, drinking gorgeous cocktails, eating gorgeous food none of which I'm allowed to touch. No, I'm not okay but I won't throw up if that is what you're worried about," my mouth blurts out.

"At least you got that out before we arrive," he says.

"The worst part is that he is smart and yet he still doesn't understand." I blink back tears. "He doesn't really need me there; he's doing it to make some kind of point."

"And what point is that?"

"The one he wants to make is I need to get out more. The point he actually makes is that I don't belong out there." I throw my arm out toward all the evening lights.

"Ah," he says knowingly.

"I'm just going to focus on my job and get home as soon as possible," I reiterate to myself.

The kind man nods and lets me stew in my frustration and anger for the rest of the drive.

The Hyatt-Regency radiates in all its glowing grandeur as I stand by a pillar waiting for Ihsan to respond to my text that I am at the entrance. My last thought to get out of this was that it was too late to get an extra ticket, which was foiled by Ihsan immediately. He had called before he left the house tonight. After waiting a few minutes without a message, I decide to wander into the hotel without an escort. I don't know why I thought I would have an arm to hold.

Every movie where the poor girl walks into a stately manor looks just like I do right now. The deep red with gold highlights everywhere gives the air of royalty and importance, clearly wanting me to turn on my heel and run off the property. The grand entrance is busy with patrons arm in arm gliding their way to different destinations, all looking as they are discussing critical topics. The marble-topped tables are decorated with tall, full flower arrangements of white and green. A placard indicating The Taylor Project auction points to the left hallway, thwarting my plan to feign getting lost.

Determined to finish my task as soon as possible, I quicken my pace to the double doored ballroom. The man standing behind a tall thin podium at the entrance seems busy checking and rechecking items on his tablet. I approach him and clear my throat. He meets my gaze and gives me a large smile. I suspect greeting people with such a sweet gesture is part of his job but something about him seems more honest than that.

"Hello, I'm supposed to be on the list for Ihsan Zorlu. I don't know if they've arrived yet."

"Let me see, what is your name?" he says, readying his tablet.

"Beatrice Fredricks," I answer.

"Last minute addition, I see. Glad to see you made it."

"Thank you, I guess?" I say with slight confusion. I'm pretty sure I don't know this man, but his demeanor seems to indicate otherwise.

"You aren't excited for tonight?"

Should I do a repeat performance?

"I'm here against my will but it's for a good cause so I'm trying to make the best of it."

"Well, if it's not up to your standards, let me know," he says with a wink of his blue eyes. His radiant blue eyes. They picked a rather fine young man to stand guard. He's a few inches shorter than Ishan with a stalkier build.

"Oh, I will. But you better be prepared for painfully honest feedback."

"I'm not really into pain."

"That's good to know. Ok, to go in now?"

"Or we could stand out here and flirt some more."

Wait what?

"I better get in there. Boss will dock my pay."

What just happened?

"You know where I'll be."

The room is full of sparkly dresses and busy drink waiters as I enter and seek out a lighted tree to hide behind and text my last message before I high tail it to the exit.

> me: **Ok, I'm here. Ten-minute warning. No text, I'm leaving.**

I type hard on the screen thinking in some way that it will convey my mood when Ihsan reads it. Even though the man at the door diluted my vinegary attitude I'm still full of piss. I should have said five minutes.

The only thing worse about being at a fancy event like this is being alone at a fancy event like this. I attempt to busy myself with taking a few pictures of the beautiful decorations and table settings on the tall cocktail tables. There are a few tables with chairs but those seem to be reserved for the older guests. I see the auction tables and realize it is a silent auction.

Shit...oh so much shit. How did I miss that?

A silent auction means it will go on a lot longer than I expected. Just when I sarcastically say to myself how great this night is turning out for me I hear a low, exotically accented voice sending an electrical shock to all my nerve endings.

Damn him.

"Beatrice."

"Ihsan," I say through gritted teeth as if he is a super villain and I turn around with an obnoxiously wide smile that doesn't reach my eyes.

"This is Lila," he motions to the beautifully blah fit woman standing beside him.

There is nothing significant about her; long brown straight hair, long straight teeth, long straight facial features, and somehow all that normal-ness makes her beautiful. Her floor length black satin spaghetti strap maxi dress doesn't even stand out. No bra for that dress, of course. She offers her hand and I take it, deciding if I want to break all the metacarpal bones or just a few. Her handshake is a lot like her, blah.

Why did I agree to go to Istanbul?

"Nice to meet you. I'm sure Ihsan has told you I'm here to just take a few pictures. If I get in the way, just kick me to the side."

She laughs slightly as she cozies up to Ihsan, staking her claim to him as if I was any threat at all. My smile could not be less sincere. Ihsan has been practicing his scowl on me a lot today and he's really kicked it up a notch tonight as he volleys my expression with one of his own.

"Let's go take a look at what all the one-percenters want for Christmas." The sarcasm valve is fully open this evening.

Slithering my way through the crowd of obvious wealth, I reach the auction tables. Several of the items are vacations in fabulous locations as well as bottles of wine which from the bids already submitted, were worth more than my monthly teacher salary. Companies donated jewelry, small sculptures, rare coins, paintings, and lessons of several different types. Hoping the pair had followed me to the tables, I turn to see them eyeing a colorful glass sculpture. With my phone camera at the ready, I snap a few shots of the two of them bidding on different items. They totally fit together, laughing, and smiling at each other. She's so boring, how could she make him laugh?

Somehow a pen from the bidding sheet next to me ends up in my hand and my arm cocks at my shoulder. This is what I used to do when students were on my last nerve. I never threw it, but the act of prepping seemed to alleviate some of the frustration. In this instance, I could throw it and behave as if I have no idea where it came from and Ihsan and the blow-up model doll would never be the wiser. I quickly put the pen down and continue to watch them be boring all over each other. She's good at flirting, finding every reason to touch him in small seemingly insignificant ways. I've seen enough Turkish dramas to know that is how it is done. It is definitely more uncomfortable watching this live than on one of his shows, but dramas often put those little moves into slow motion. I find myself rolling my eyes so often, I can feel the ocular muscles fatigue.

Their pace is excruciatingly slow as they read and discuss every auction item in great detail. I try to bob and weave around the guests as they try to look around me to investigate the auction items on the tables. Some not even acknowledging my existence, bump into me without turning to apologize. Photographers try to capture moments without being in the moment and my invisibility function at this event is working perfectly.

When they get to the sailing item, I decide I've had enough. Scrolling through the photos I've already taken, I select the one where they are smiling at each other over the glass sculpture and one of them standing together in front of the giant black "T" logo for the LGBTQ+ youth charity. I post those onto all his socials and try to come up with clever captions without the bitchy undertone I've had tonight.

The need to get away from these two overwhelms me. This is part of the job, I know, but the sick feeling in my stomach is permeating into the rest of my body. The intense focus on him and his date having fun is chipping away at me. When I'm at home alone, I at least have Zeki and a classic movie to distract me but here, everyone is on that same technicolor level and I'm still a grayscaler on a visitor pass. Watching Ihsan in the crowd talking with various people, he is clearly even above that. If I bail on him now, he'll attempt to make me stay and he'll make a scene of it. I don't have the energy or the temperament for that this evening and he doesn't need that kind of publicity.

IHSAN

As Beatrice lifts her face and our eyes meet, I am caught with my mouth open. Her soft cheeks are framed by an intricate updo I had not seen before. Her eyes radiate with what is most likely anger that shoots a tiny bolt of lightning down my spine, making the hair on my arms stand at attention. The dress pulls in at her waist and outlines her curves which she's been hiding under workout wear and blankets. The seam of the dress calls attention to the newly visible collar bones and the elegant sweep of her neck. The defined muscles in her calves peek out from under the hem and the shoes she chose highlight the lines of the strong tissue. I blink back my surprise because if she gets an inkling that I am shocked she won't see it as a compliment. As much as I've been trying to raise the baseline of her self-image, she always seems to return to her lowest point. At least she doesn't do it as often as she used to. In my heart I know she is beautiful, but this time my eyes see it too.

When she refuses to ride with my date, I realize where I had gone wrong. She has explained how she sees the world several times and it is stupid of me to think she would want to sit and stare at us in an enclosed space. I imagine her needing an air sickness bag just to get through the car ride.

I find Beatrice standing alone on the edge of the room with her eyes searching the crowd desperately looking for someone she recognizes. She really didn't need to be here, but I thought this would be the perfect casual event where others could see her the way I do, fun, clever, passionate, and my most recent realization, gorgeous. God, those eyes. The ones that see through me to the cellular level. They are almost hypnotic when she's in the right mood. The hazel raindrops that have crushed and carried me the past few months scour the room, looking for me. I realize I haven't taken a breath when Lila sidles up to me and I finally call out Beatrice's name.

BEATRICE

> me: **I'm going to the toilet.**

Screw pleasantries.

> Ihsan: *Tamam.*

I'm glad he could find the time to type five letters to me. Even Turkish texting is hot.

Now how do I find a bathroom on the other side of the hotel?

Walking out of the ballroom, I'm met by the charity gate keeper. His smile seems more genuine this time, as if he's actually happy to see me again.

"Excuse me, is there a public restroom I can use?" I ask the bored concierge.

"Is the one inside not to your liking?" he asks, standing up straighter as if a butler on a Brit sitcom.

"The bathroom is too crowded for me. I get anxious when there are too many people in a closed space," I lie.

"Well, miss. Allow me to guide you to a more secluded loo."

"That sounds like the last words a woman hears before she is never seen again."

His laugh is deep, heavy, and loud and warms the cockles of my heart.

"I just thought you might want some company. You look like you are beyond miserable in there."

"And now you sound like a creeper."

"I can see that," he says, then pinches his lips together as if disappointed in himself.

"My name is Scott. You know, so you have a name for the police report."

"Hello, Scott," I say, putting my hand out.

He takes my hand in his and shakes it gently accompanied by another sweet smile.

"I'm Beatrice. You know for your serial killer trophy scrapbook."

"I'm not really sure but is this a meet cute?" he asks, pointing his finger back and forth between us.

"More like a convocation ugly," I say as I squint. "Ok, that didn't work. Sometimes words are hard."

I could get used to his smile. It's sweet and genuine and I...believe it. He has no reason to talk to me. He could just as easily ignore me or give me verbal directions but he's offering to escort me. Since I'm not getting villain vibes, I might just let this man walk me to the powder room.

"Come on, I'll show you to the secret passageway."

"Thanks. There are cameras around here right?" I say pointing to the far corners of the tall lobby.

"You are a suspicious one, aren't you?"

"My instincts have been less than reliable so better to be safe than sorry."

"Now we're getting somewhere."

"We've walked fifteen feet."

"I mean, information about you."

"Yeah, why did I say that?

"Because I'm charming."

"And confident it seems. What number am I? At least fifty women checked in before I got here."

"Sixty-seven but you're the first one worth my witty repartee."

Now I know that flush is short for flash blush. Not only did my skin heat up but my lips go rogue and spread into a smile all on their own.

"That's oddly accurate."

"I like numbers."

Be still my beating heart.

"You might have just redeemed yourself," I smile back at him as we reach the opposite side of the large lobby.

"Scott!" A voice from behind him stops him in his tracks.

"I'll be right there, Mr. Haynes. I was just showing ...Beatrice the lower conference room restrooms."

Well, at least someone will know where to find the body.

He waves off the older gentlemen and turns toward me.

"If you go down the stairs, there is a long hallway. It's at the end. That is the least used restroom in the hotel," he smiles at me.

"Thank you, Scott. I appreciate your assistance across the hall. I wouldn't have made it on my own."

"Hope you make it back," he says, winking again as he turns to walk away. I then realize I am the only woman that entered the auction without a date, so I am the one available. Sounds about right, should have known better.

Navigating the stairs in wedges was a bit tricky and Scott didn't mention how many flights down the bathroom is. From the looks of the décor on the basement level, I wouldn't be surprised to find a sex cult. I listen to too much true crime during workouts, but it does give me ideas on where to hide Ihsan's body. The temperature drops slightly, and the smell is stale, but it is quiet, and I can get my head right as I walk down the long burgundy carpeted hallway.

The restroom has its own seating lounge and since I don't really need to use the facility, I plop down on the Elizabethan style fainting couch. The whole place is eerily quiet. A few deep breaths to clean out all the images of Ihsan and whatever her name is. I close my eyes and my shoulders drop; my chest relaxes. The feeling of inadequacy is draining, especially when you follow a pair of flirty technicolors. Working has always been important, and I put everything I have into what I'm doing. That is what I want to be judged on. That is what matters. How did I get here? Why am I promoting exactly what I don't believe in?

Click.

"Hello? Scott?" I shout, rushing to the door and pulling on the handle.

No. No. No.

"HELLO?" I shout louder into the wood door panel as if my voice will permeate the thickness of the slab.

Awesome. Fucking awesome.

I quickly press the contact button on the screen to look up the phone number of the hotel.

No connection.

FUCK!

Walking through every square foot of the bathroom, even on top of toilet bowls, I search desperately for a signal. Feeling defeated, I swallow my pride and lay down on the old-style couch, preparing to bite the proverbial bullet.

> **me: I'm locked in a bathroom in the basement on the other side of the hotel. Send help.**

The blue bar across the screen halts in the middle.

No. No. No.

"Message not sent" appears in red under my text.

The fear that I'm going to be stuck in this dank dungeon all night boils my blood. I click on the text bubble again and click "send as a text message." I have no idea why this is different, but it shows up in green. There is no indication if it was delivered or not. The wells of my eyes are starting to fill as I see the battery of my phone drain. I can feel the path of the tears down my cheeks.

Of course, this happens to me.

I just wanted to get away for a little bit, but the universe wants to teach me a lesson. Wish I could just figure out what I'm supposed to learn by getting myself locked up in a hotel basement. A consequence for running away from whatever makes me feel uncomfortable seems to be the most logical reason for this calamity. Who gets themselves locked in a stinky basement trying to avoid their boss? I do. I'm all for a good story but even the thought of retelling this harrowing tale is embarrassing.

I stomp my feet down hard on the floor and walk into the bathroom area raising and dropping my phone searching for a signal. After all avenues are explored, I decide that I may have to try the last place I want to go, the skinny stall. Without any indication of reception from anywhere around my five foot four-ish stature, I suck in my lips and accept the inevitable. I pull my skirt up and brace myself on the sides of the stall. With one motion I step and launch myself onto the sides of the toilet bowl. My left foot loses purchase and plunges toward the water. Luckily, I'm nimbler than I used to be and just my toes break the surface of the toilet water. With a sigh of relief, I relax just enough for my grip to loosen and my phone to slide down my arm, bounce from boob to boob then glide down my stomach between my legs and into the poop trap at the very bottom of the bowl. With reckless abandon I jump down, straddling the toilet bowl between my legs and reach for my phone without thought of where my arm is diving into.

Standing there for a moment, I drip dry my phone and shake off the toilet water from my arm. When I'm old and gray this will be a pretty funny story but right now my ego has been pummeled with a meat tenderizer. Grabbing the end of the single ply toilet roll I pull hard to gather a giant fist worth of tissue. Leaving the stall, my wet toe slips and I suddenly lunge forward as my heel snags the tile and I stumble toward the sink. Catching myself on the porcelain edge of the basin, almost face planting, I shout at the bathroom fixture.

Useless. No one can hear me scream.

"Stupid shoes, in this stupid place," I shout. Holding myself against the sink, I rip off the shoes and throw them into the lounge, careful to grip my phone tightly.

I look at my face in the mirror and let out another soul cleansing scream.

"Stupid hair!" I scream ripping out bobby pins, tearing off elastics from the end of the braids and unraveling the ropes around my head with no care for knots or tangles.

"Stupid face!"

I take a few paper towels and squirt hand soap on the stack and wet the soap to make a lather. I keep my eyes tight wiping the wet soapy bundle over my lids and scrubbing across my face. With the faucet running, I cup my hands and push the water up and over my cheeks. Trying to keep the drips off my dress, I lean over the sink. As I look up in the mirror, I see how much the soap and water did not wipe off my face. The extra mascara I used made me mas-scary when my attempt to remove it fails. Istanbul may not let me in if I keep this up.

"Hello?"

Oh, fuck no.

I hadn't realized that I had taken all of the paper towels when making my DIY make-up remover. I furiously look around for a dry paper towel and all I could find was the clump of toilet paper, already half wet from extraneous sink spray.

"Oh!" Ihsan says in shock at the state of me.

"No, no, no, no!" I say with increasing volume.

"What happened?"

"Another epic meltdown, aren't you tired of them by now?" I snap, scurrying around the lounge picking up my purse and looking for my hastily discarded wedges.

"Just help me find my stupid shoes," I plead with him.

"How did you lose them?"

"I threw them in here...duh, how else do you think it happened?" The teenager in me making her debut.

"Why did you throw them?" he says leaning over the back of the couch resurfacing with a wedge in his hand.

"Because I was tired of wearing all this crap," I say, swiping the footwear from his hand.

After finding the other shoe under a chair, I quickly stack the purse and shoes in my hands and power walk past him, fling the door open and storm down the hall.

"Hey," he calls out, pulling me back by my arm, a classic Turkish drama move.

I stare angrily at him.

"Tell me what happened." His annoyed voice raises my boiling point even more.

"Brutal honesty?" I say, challenging him to accept.

He nods and I pull my arm out of his firm grasp and lean against the hallway wall to hold me up.

"I needed to escape, and the bathroom is usually a good place to do it. The concierge told me about this one and I came in and someone locked it. I tried calling the hotel, but it wouldn't go through. I got frustrated, my phone fell in the toilet, I cried and had a tantrum," I say, matter of factly.

"Escape from what?"

You.

"All of it upstairs. Do you know not one person said anything to me besides you and Lila the Loser? She can barely tolerate my existence," I cringe at my uncontrolled bitter comment. "One can only handle being invisible for so long. But I was just there to take pictures, right?"

"I'm sorry, Beatrice," he says looking down at the floor.

"It's the way of the world, Ihsan. Don't apologize for things you can't change."

I push myself off the wall and continue the fast-paced walk down the hall. When I reach the staircase, I wish I had saved my energy. Taking a deep breath, I start to climb the shorter than normal steps. Each one angers me more than the last, which turns into more of stomping up the stairs instead of climbing them. By the time I reach the top of the second flight, the tears have collected in my eyes again. Wiping them away I'm determined to not let these stairs defeat me.

"Beatrice," I hear him come up quickly behind me. "Beatrice!"

When I finally reach the top of the staircase my bare feet are screaming from the rough carpet.

"Yes?" I turn to him slowly and answer with an exhausted sigh.

"Are you leaving?"

"I look like the worst walk of shame without the fun part. So yes, I'm leaving," I huff, knowing he didn't know what I was talking about but too tired to explain.

"Is there anything else I can do for you?" I ask patronizingly with a large fake smile pinned to my face which I can only imagine came out of a bad horror movie with my make-up melting down my face.

Before he can answer I turn on my heels and walk down the hall to the grand lobby trying to hold my head high. His long legs don't take much to surpass me, and he blocks my way.

"Please, Beatrice."

"What more do you want from me tonight? I've done my job. I'm done."

I try to hold back the hurt I feel from the embarrassment of the evening.

"Calm down and stay. You're still upset." He takes my shoulders and square them with his.

Did he really just tell me to calm down?

"Of course, I'm still upset. I feel humiliated. Can I please just go? No one wants a crying fat girl in their lobby. It's bad for business," I say, pushing his hand off my shoulder.

Sometimes the words fly out of my mouth like bats out of a cave. You try to stop them, but they just keep coming out of a dark, dark place.

"Look, don't worry about me. You were having such a good time. Lila is probably wondering where you are. I'll see you at the house." I take care not to call it a home. As much as I want it to be, I know not to fly too close to the sun. I've been burned before, and this situation will surely cause the third-degree kind.

Pulling out the phone from my sparkly wristlet I realize that I shouldn't attempt to call a car until my phone has recovered.

"Beatrice?" Scott's newly recognizable voice fills my ears.

Please, sir, can I have some more?

I didn't think my shoulders could drop even further.

"Are you ok? Did this man attack you? Let me call security," he says, putting his arm around my shoulder while taking his phone out of his pocket.

"No, Scott. I happened to me."

"Did I attack her?" Ihsan asks as if he has been accused of stealing the Peace Diamond.

"Calm down, Ihsan. Go back to Lila. Scott, this is my boss. Scott will call me a car."

"I'm not leaving you with a stranger."

"We aren't strangers," I say, putting my arm through Scott's bicep.

Ihsan's face tips back as if he is examining my new friendship for flaws.

"Scott, I dropped my phone in the toilet. Do you mind getting someone to take me home?"

"I'm off in an hour," he says smiling.

"What?" Ihsan raises his voice at my new friend.

"Chill. I was kidding. I'll call her a car," Scott says as he takes a small step backward and raises his hands in the international sign "my hands are off your property."

"Ihsan, I'll be fine. Just go back."

Scott reaches for his phone and presses a few icons.

"I'll need a destination for the app."

I outstretch my hand in front of Scott. "Phone."

"Yes, miss."

I take Scott's phone before Ihsan can rip it out of his hand and throw it across the room. After putting in the address, I click on all the subsequent prompts, order the car and open another app.

Ihsan remains, resting his hands on his hips as if waiting for something else from me.

"Let me know how much I owe you," I say, putting my number into his contacts.

"I guess that saves me the ask," Scott says smiling while Ihsan stands annoyed and irritated, not his best look. "They will meet you out front by the sign. I gotta get back. Are you sure you're ok with this guy?"

"Yes. I know he's a bit much but I'm okay."

"I'll give you a call."

"Thanks for your help, Scott."

He smiles as he waves and walks away, and I miss enjoying the whole experience because Ihsan loomed over us the whole time.

"Why are you still here?"

"I'm waiting with you until you get in the car."

"I'm a grown-up, I can handle this."

"Are you?" he says with a little more attitude than I'm used to.

"Am I what?"

"Are you a grown-up? Do you handle things like an adult?" he asks with annoyance.

"I'm not doing this here." My eyes widen at his rather curt question.

That urge to run is surging through my body, but I take a slower pace toward the front entry to the lobby where all the fancy cars are left to the valets. I can hear the loud footfalls of his shoes behind me. The area for car app reservations is off to the side of the valet station and I am determined to make it there without exchanging another word with Ihsan but with my short legs and his lengthy ones, it is a fruitless venture.

Staring expectantly at the dark space for a pair of headlights of a small four door sedan, Ihsan posts himself with his face perpendicular to mine.

My eyes avoiding his glance, I ask, "Are you complaining about how I do my job?"

"No."

"Then let me be. I'm off the clock."

"You're right. I'm just your job." His eyes bore a tiny hole into my temple.

Oh, he's good.

"You know that isn't what I meant." I turn to him. "I'm not needed here anymore and all I want to do is be home...I mean at the house."

Crap.

"I thought you might want to stay for some fun."

"This," I wave obnoxiously toward the interior of the building, "is your kind of fun, not mine."

"Fine. Thank you for helping tonight." He unexpectedly leans over and presses his lips onto my cheek. My eyelids half close involuntarily as his soft gentle lips press into my skin.

God, he smells amazing. Damn him!

"Here's my car," I say, more nervous than I intended and push his face off mine. No matter how gentle he kisses my cheek, it's brutally painful.

Chapter 35

IHSAN

Lila's company is tolerable at best. Every auction item we pass she either knows the artist, has a piece already or it isn't up to her standards. I really wish there was a way to tell Beatrice to stop doing her job because I don't want any footage of Lila and me together but after all the effort it took to get her here, I dare not. I like my balls where they are. I put on a masquerade, so the photos are decent.

Beatrice escapes my eyeline for a few minutes and my phone chimes with a message that she has found a way to avoid me for a few minutes. I'm not sure if I should tell her that Lila might as well be peeling my skin away from my fingernails. After a few minutes of watching the exit to the woman's restroom, I realize that I look a bit suspect. A small pang sets in my stomach as I would never forgive myself if something happened to Beatrice after my insistence on her attendance. When I finish the second lap around the perimeter of the room, the pang morphs into panic. Lila didn't even realize I had left, which was a small thing to be grateful for in my frustration. After a bit of investigation with the help of the front desk, I discover a woman matching Beatrice's description was sent to the hotel's catacombs.

A young staff member accompanies me to the distant bathroom in the catacombs of the hotel. After hearing rustling inside, she unlocks it and lets me enter to check on my friend. It wouldn't have surprised me to hear a hiss come from the scraggly haired, bloodshot eyed creature that slightly resembles my assistant standing before me. After Beatrice tells me her harrowing story, the panic in my gut turns into a heavy brick of ugly guilt. I had such high hopes for her this evening, especially when she walked out of her bedroom looking the way she did. Her Hermione hair framing her face only to be outdone by her horror movie eye make-up explains exactly how the last thirty minutes have been for her and it's my fault.

None of her answers to my questions relieve the anguish I feel for her. Lashing out at her was the wrong move and I bend down and kiss her cheek, hoping I can take away some of her pain.

Returning to the party, I see Lila across the room and realize that this is not where I belong. After pseudo explaining a minor emergency, I leave Lila at the party to torture some other poor unsuspecting soul and call a car to take me to Beatrice.

BEATRICE

When the car I summoned comes to a complete stop, Ihsan walks me to the rear door and when I reach for the door pull, his hand appears and opens the door.

"I got it, thanks." I slide into the back seat with my hands full of the night's shrapnel. When the door closes, I give him a small wave and half smile. The young woman in the driver seat smiles at me in the rear-view mirror.

"Rough night?"

"Don't worry, I'm sober," I answer.

"You're sober and you left that guy watching you drive away?"

"That's my boss and he's just making sure you aren't an axe murderer."

"You must have a great job."

"Not tonight," I say wryly. "If you don't mind, I just need to decompress."

"No problem."

As usual my brain has selected the perfected theme music for my mood. The first verse of Radiohead's "Creep" could not be closer to the truth.

"Wow, what job affords a house like this?" The driver saves me from continuing down the melancholic pop music chasm.

"I'm a live-in PA. It isn't my house."

"Damn, girl, you live with that guy?" She says in amazement.

"Believe me, it isn't all it's cracked up to be."

"Oh, he's an ogre?" she asks, her sympathetic tone cutting me.

"No, actually he's the opposite."

She sits quietly as I gather my things and look over the seats for anything I might have missed. After I shut the rear door of the compact car, I step carefully across the pavement of the small lot to the front door. Punching in the code I enter the silent house and enjoy the cold bold tile on my bare feet as I walk to my open bedroom, Zeki's padded feet following my path.

I figure even if I screwed up everything about my appearance, I could at least make sure the dress is hung up correctly. Robotically, I place my shoes in the correct slot of the shoe organizer, remove all constricting garments and change into my original outfit for tonight. I stare at the counter while removing my make-up from my face, continuing to rub until nothing appears on the cotton ball. I have already looked at my reflection too much tonight. I drag my fingers through my hair trying to tame what I had done earlier in the night. Before I turn in for the night, I walk to the kitchen for some ice water to cool me inside and out. My phone also needs a rice bath to recover from the dunk in the toilet. I search the depths of the pantry for the last remaining remnant of a carb filled life and find a bag of rice in the lower corner. This should work, I mean everything on the internet is true, right? As I stand against the kitchen island drinking the cold liquid and burying my phone in the rice kernels, my eyes wander around the room. They settle on the beautiful baby grand resting quietly in its fabric nook.

This is the therapy I need right now.

I ditch the glass of water on the counter as an invisible force pushes me toward the safety of the tufted bench. Pulling back the small seat, I slide onto it and open the keyboard lid. Looking across the shiny black surface I decide to lift the lid of the main body of the piano. I raise it to its fully open position, pull up the large peg, and set the lid down. Pianos are their most beautiful when they are completely open. As my eyes follow the length of the strings down the lateral harp, my hands settle on the keys as I sit again. Sometimes I just start where my hands naturally lay. This time, they positioned themselves over a B flat-major chord. Immediately, I hear it. Some pop songs just stick with you, and Adele's remake of Bob Dylan's "Make You Feel My Love" had been a staple at the height of my infatuation with Brandon. The piano part is easy enough and it was just me so who cares if it was on time or even if I played wrong notes. The words creep into my throat and then out my mouth. When singing to myself I usually keep the volume a little over the piano, but I feel a little more resigned and keep mostly quiet. When I finish, I leave my bare foot on the pedal letting the sound bounce off the tile and ring into the ether.

I didn't feel quite done and my fingers found their place on the keys again. A wash of relief flows through my body as I savor this place, in front of the piano where I've always felt welcome. E-flat major finds its way under my fingers. Coldplay's "Fix You" is another Beatrice classic when the mood is somber. The version I mostly listen to is *a Capella*, so I play the voicings I remember, the chords in a rhythm that feels right. The lyrics in the beginning are sweet and tender but then when I get to the chorus the words, volume and rhythm become loud and more powerful. The timing of the pedal and rhythmic chord changes creates a full deep sound filling the ground level of the house. After I finish the last word, I stretch my left hand to press the lowest E-flat. I close my eyes and let the sound dissipate. Not realizing how much my eyes were holding back, I wipe the drops across my cheeks. I sit for a moment just letting the music absorb into my skin and contemplate why those were the two songs that came to mind.

A low pitched *"Veeeey"* sounds from the other side of the piano lid.

Can't I have this one thing?

Ihsan's inky hair appears over the top of the black slant as he walks slowly over to me. Luckily, I'm in a much better mood, even as uncomfortable as I am with an audience. He leans where the sheet music bracket is usually propped up with that sweet, beautiful smile that simultaneously kills and cures me. He has intruded into my safe haven, and I don't have the emotional calories to kick him out.

"I thought you'd be home later. All that fun, et cetera." I look up at him passively.

"And miss the show?"

That sparkling smile is on a different level tonight.

"I don't put on a show." I push myself away from the bench and lean to stand toward him.

"Wait, wait." His strong hand pushes my shoulder down back onto the seat.

"You can count that as me playing for you. Debt paid." I look up at him pleading for him to release me.

"Beatrice, I've never heard you sing, at least not like that."

"No one is meant to hear me sing like that." My eyes avert his gaze at all costs.

"Why?" He leans further into my space.

"Because it's just for me."

"But—"

"The last time I shared that with someone, I thought I might have meant something to them, and I didn't," I blurt out and try to make the anger dry up the tears that are threatening to reappear.

"Brandon," he said quietly.

Damn, hearing that name hurts.

But it was a special kind of hurt coming from Ihsan's lips.

"It's the same old shit song," I exhale.

"I'm happy you shared it with me."

"I didn't, you stole it," I snap, my tone accusatory as if he physically did steal it.

I get up from the bench quickly and try to escape him and the conversation.

"So, you aren't going to open up to anyone, put yourself out there?"

"Like tonight when I was literally the invisible woman?" I throw my hands in the air.

"You weren't trying tonight."

"You don't have to try, why should I?" I ask, finally losing my patience.

"But you open up to me," he tries to counter, and a loud laugh erupts from my face.

"Ihsan, you don't count. You are a freaking movie star. You have multiple fan pages from all over the world. Women salivate when you appear on the screen. I might as well be confessing all my problems to the Almighty herself," I say, my tone straight and matter of fact. "Listen, you met me when I was at my lowest. I'm normally not...this. I swear I am outgoing and fun to be around but that is as far as anything ever goes. I get too attached, then I get hurt, repeat. This inability to hold all this pain back is new. For some reason, I've lost my power of indifference. It's exhausting."

"I know you are all that," he says quietly.

"This night needs to be over." I shuffle my feet to the kitchen, place my glass in the sink and pick up the phone rice bowl.

"Beatrice—"

"Good night, Ihsan. Don't worry I'll find a therapist in the morning, for real this time." My bucket of sarcasm is clearly not empty. The decrescendo clacking of his fancy shoes on the hard stairs saddens me as I walk down the hall. I told him people walk away from me. Deep down in the abyss of my being is a tiny speck of hope that he wouldn't be one of them.

"Good night, Beatrice," he says pensively.

IHSAN

Beatrice's smooth voice floods my ears as I open the front door. She doesn't notice I've entered the house and after dropping my coat quietly on the couch, I step slowly and silently to the far side of the piano. It's as if I'm watching some kind of musical homage and I don't want to break her train of thought. I can almost see the sound vibrations emanating from her body like gasoline evaporating off pavement. The timbre and energy changes in the second song and I can feel my own pulse quicken as I understand exactly why she picked this particular pop ballad. The poignant lyrics knocks the wind out of my lungs harder than any time it had happened on the pitch. Her gorgeous voice singing such sorrowful lyrics seems wrong. I don't know if Beatrice never gave up on Brandon or if she accepted living in steady repudiation or if she avoided the herculean task of healing from heartbreak.

I've never wanted to punch someone in the face so much as I do Brandon right now.

Beatrice's ability to open up and shut down in record time is almost admirable. How do I tell her she wasn't invisible to me, that she will never be invisible to me? She seems to be growing a thicker skin and I feel I don't have to watch my words around her as much. But she constantly puts me on a pedestal as if nothing phases me and I wouldn't understand heartbreak. My relationship disaster may not have lasted almost ten years, but it cuts just as deep. As expected, she shuts me down and escapes but at least this time she commits to getting help from someone.

I retreat up the stairs and call my all knowing sister.

"*Abla*?"

"*Abi*, everything okay?"

"*Evet. Hayir.* I don't fucking know."

"Tell me."

"*Abla*, I've screwed up."

"Do you need a lawyer?"

"*Yok*, it's not like that."

"Ok, Isa start from the beginning."

"I don't know when it began. I don't know if it is real. I don't know if she will even believe me."

"That's not helpful."

"It's Beatrice."

"What happened?" Farah's tone changes from caring to accusatory.

"I don't know if it is because I'm on a very long rebound from Gül or..."

"Isa, you better not do or say anything to her."

"I'm supposed to live with her feeling this way? And..." I hesitate, mentioning the silly mind game I played with myself a few weeks ago.

"And?"

"She might have told me she loved me. Actually, she sang it to me."

"*Neh*?" her voice raises in shock.

"She wanted me to listen to this song and then she started to sing along. Then there was basketball."

"She sang it while holding a basketball?"

"*Yok*. Nevermind that. The way she looked at me. It was...uh. But then she told half the highway she loved them too."

"Oh, *abi*."

"I didn't think about her that way until that drive."

"Think of her as if she is in rehab for addiction. She needs your friendship but that is it. If you break her heart, she won't recover."

"I don't even know what this is."

"And that is why you don't tell her anything."

A few quiet seconds pass before my beautiful oracle speaks again. "Who is the first person you think about when you wake up?"

"Beatrice."

The silence on the line is deafening.

"But that is because I'm trying to catch her spiking my morning smoothie."

I hear her snicker before her tone returns back to counseling me.

"Isa, you've told me she doesn't believe you when you give her a compliment. What do you think she will say if you tell her how you feel, especially when you can't even tell me?"

"She won't ever trust me again."

"I get it. Beatrice's whole focus is you right now. Gül's wasn't and that really messed you up. Are you sure you aren't confusing everything she does for you as more than her job?"

"I'm not sure. You're right."

"From what you have told me, if you tell her you feel something more than friendship for her, she's either going to be yours forever or you'll never see her again. It's not good for either of you."

"My insides feel raw."

"*Aşk sandığın kadar değil, yandığın kadardır.*" Love is not as much as you think, it's as much as you are burnt.

"She's lived that already, Farah."

"So have you."

"Why does this feel so different?"

"Because Isa, she is the first woman you've had to work for."

"*Neh?*"

"She's a challenge."

I do love a challenge. Beatrice loves one too. All her effort to get where she wants to be for this wedding is not her only challenge. She wants to be free of Brandon and free of everything that cuts her inside. I want that for her almost as much as she does. She doesn't deserve it; she is owed it.

"Thanks, *abla*, I'm going to try to sleep."

"*İyi şanslar, abi.*" Good luck, brother.

I pick up my phone and start the speech to text and then decide against it. She deserves better. Besides writing the Bee's name on the name placard at the table read and my signature, the closest I've done to writing since I've been here is holding a highlighter in my hand. The house is uncomfortably quiet as I walk down the staircase. Turning toward the guest wing, I pass Bee's room and walk into the office and look for the remaining handmade cards from Bee's first surge at charming Hollywood. The photograph her father took of the flower sits on her desktop. I laugh to myself thinking how much she is like that plant; not typically beautiful but if you wait long enough, a stunning bloom will emerge that captures your attention. I practice what I want to say on a scratch piece of paper, but nothing seems right, and I've never been good at writing. I decide short and sweet works best and when I'm satisfied, I tuck in the flap of the envelope over the card. Standing outside her room, I take a deep breath and I give it a little push under the door.

BEATRICE
As crappy as I feel, I should have had a few drinks last night. The sun isn't quite up but my body needs me to walk to the restroom. The moon is my favorite night light as I walk slowly across the floor. The light on my phone catches my eye. It's a small relief to find my phone operational after the demolition to my ego from the night before. I turn my back on the mirror and lean against the counter.

> unknown: **I hope your phone made a full recovery. It's Scott by the way.**

He adds a link to his Instagram with a goofy picture of him hanging out the window of a mud-covered truck.

It's either super early or super late but I decide to answer Scott's text because I hate loose ends.

> me: **It seems to be off life support.**

My phone tings almost immediately.

> unknown: **Good.**

Scott's quick response brings a small grin to my face.

Ok, maybe the night wasn't a complete behind a crappy fast food restaurant dumpster fire.

> **unknown: Why are you still up?**

me: Full bladder and you?

> **unknown: Just got home. Thought I would check on you. You seemed distraught.**

me: Thank you. I'm fine. What do I owe you?

> **unknown: Dinner.**

A loud "HA" escapes as if it is the funniest joke I'd ever heard but then realize that there is a possibility that this is, in fact, a real offer. It's too early in the morning to contemplate what is happening.

> **unknown: Hello?**

me: Would you accept a rain check?

> **unknown: How do you know you can't make it?**

me: It's not a good time. You saw.

> **unknown: I choose to think of you as the before picture.**

me: **Well, thank you. I'll get back to you. Since you know where I live, I'm warning you I have a big dog and you saw my boss on his lowest setting.**

unknown: **I'll just hold out for the rain check.**

me: **I'm impressed you've lasted this long.**

unknown: **Good night, Beatrice.**

me: **Good night, Scott.**

What the hell just happened? I was just asked out on a date, and I said no. Wait, no. I said later. Why would I wait? Why couldn't I say yes?

I turn back toward my reflection and brush my hair away from my face. I missed how much my body has changed last night while I was getting dressed. I was a raging Miss Pissy Pants. In fact, I haven't really looked at myself critically for a while. My hands spread across my stomach, noticing that they cover a lot more than they used to. I turn halfway in the mirror noticing my shape is more hourglass than brandy snifter.

Some random guy pursued a conversation with me, got my number, contacted me, and asked me to dinner. No one set me up. I did it all on my own. I turn back to the mirror and put my hands on my hips. I smile to myself thinking of the prom scene in Pretty in Pink where Ducky is stared down by a cool girl. Maybe being Ducky isn't so bad.

Good on you, Queen Bee.

Thinking back on the conversation with Ihsan, I was still right. Technically, the only person who noticed my existence was outside of the room. I pick up my phone again and tap on his Instagram profile and dig around looking for creeper or stalker vibes. Nothing pops out until a little note at the end of his profile. "Bi."

Well, that's that.

I'm not comfortable in my own sexuality so Scott's bisexuality is a deal breaker. At least for now. Someday I may be brave or confident or drunk enough to pay back my debt to him, but this Beatrice cannot stomach another Carl. But for all I know, this Beatrice was asked out over everyone else at the party. I will take that every day of the week.

It's a little disappointing that my gut reacted so strongly to discovering Scott's preference. He was not only in my league, but we could also have hung out in the dugout together. But upstairs is my shining star, and my personal Tartarus. He will always be out of reach, and I torture myself by thinking of him in tiny increments throughout the day as anything other than a close friend. I can't even enjoy a little attention from a stranger because Ihsan hasn't left any room for anyone else. How did I find myself another Brandon? How did I let myself be Brandoned again? How can he allow himself to be the next Brandon? Because Ihsan is a job, and I don't do any job halfway no matter what. It isn't his fault. What was he going to do? Fire his whole support staff because I developed a crush he didn't reciprocate? He needs me like Brandon did and I have a nasty habit of forming one sided attachments.

I shove my face in the palm of my hands and drag my fingers down my skin. I'm not going to solve this tonight and Scott's messages didn't negate the fiasco that was the charity auction and Lila's dumbass face. My bed calls and I'm helpless to those fake fur covered pillows.

My toe snags on something as I slowly stroll across the room, and I look down to find a light-colored envelope laying in the middle of the room. I rack my brain trying to think of anything it would have fallen off or out of. Nothing comes to mind, so I pick it up and turn it over. A large letter 'B' adorns the front, so I slip the flap open and pull out the card. Opening the pressed flowered front, I recognize writing I've seen very few times. After reading the handwritten text I do what so many women in movies do, I lay it across my heart. Now I know why.

"I will always see you, Beatrice. Yours, Ihsan."

TO BE CONTINUED...

SNEAK PEAK of Queen Bee and the Turk: Take 2

Pronunciation Guide

The following pronunciations are approximations only.

Names
Ihsan (ee-sahn) benevolence, charity
Farah (fehr-ah) happiness
Gül (goohl) rose
Nadir (nah-dizh) rare
Selim (say-lim) perfect
Tariq (tah-rik) morning star
Zeki (zeh-keh) clever
Zeyva (zeh-vah) temple

Turkish words or phrases
abi (ah-bee) brother
abla (ah-blah) sister
Allah (ah-lah) God
anne (ah-neh) mother
baklava (bah-klah-vah) phyllo pastry filled with nuts and soaked in honey.
    beni affet (behn-nee ah-feht) forgive me
bey (bay) sir-used at the end of a male name
evet (eh-vehy) yes
gelmek (geh-mek) to come
gerçekten (gehr-chehk-tehn) really
git (git) go
gitme (git-meh) stay
hadi (hah-dih) come om
hallo (hah-low) hello
hayir (hi-earzh) no
hoşçakal (hohsh-cheh-kahl) good bye
igrencsin (ear-reh-sis-in) you're disgusting
iyi şanslar (ee shahn-shlash) Good luck
kalın (kah-lin)....thick
kara sevda (Kah-rah sehv-dah) black love
kitap (kih-tahp) book
kovuldun (koh-vuhl-duhn) you are fired
merhaba (merh-hah-bah) hello
neh (neh) what

oturmak (oh-toor-mahk) sit
sus (soohs) shush, be quiet
tamam (tah-mam) okay
teşekkürler (teh-shehk-kew-lahzh) Thank you
üzgünüm (oohz-goohn-oohm) Sorry
vay (veye) wow
yok (yohk)

Music Titles

Bolero
Composed by Maurice Ravel

U Can't Touch This
Performed by MC Hammer

Danse Macabre
Composed by Camille Saint-Saens

Every Rose Has Its Thorn
Performed by Poison

Eye of the Tiger
Performed by Survivor

Fix You
Performed by Straight No Chaser

I'm Too Sexy
Performed by Right Said Fred

If You Leave
Performed by Orchestral Manoeuvres in the Dark

Kiss from a Rose
Performed by Seal

Legs
Performed by ZZ Top

Make You Feel My Love
Performed by Adele

Mars
Composed by Gustav Holst

Peel Me a Grape
Performed by Diana Krall

Ride of the Valkyries
Composed by Richard Wagner

School's Out
Performed by Alice Cooper

Short People
Performed by Randy Newman

Wicked Games
Performed by Chris Izaak

Wonderful Tonight
Performed by Eric Clapton

Movie Titles
10 Things I Hate About You
A League of Their Own
Bull Durham
Contact
Crocodile Dundee
Divergent
Don Quixote
Field of Dreams
Ghost
His Girl Friday
Little Shop of Horrors
Moneyball
Nanny McPhee
National Lampoon's Christmas Vacation
Pee-wee's Big Adventure
Pretty in Pink
Risky Business
Some Kind of Wonderful.
The Addams Family
The Princess Bride
Unbreakable

Television Show Titles
Cheers
Dr. Who
Pinky and the Brain
Twilight Zone

About the Author

Daphne MacLeod embarks on her literary adventures with a rich tapestry of experiences woven from her upbringing in the picturesque landscape of the far north and now finds herself nestled in the tranquil beauty of California's central valley. Originally trained as an instrumental and vocal teacher, Daphne transitioned her passions for education to become a teacher, specializing in students with learning disabilities where she channels her passion for teaching into powering young minds to overcome challenges and reach their full potential.

At home, she shares her life with her husband and two gentle but challenging giant Newfoundland/Standard Poodle mixes who add a touch of joy but mostly chaos to their household. With their two adult children carving their own paths in New York City and Northern California, her home is a sanctuary of love, laughter and shared dreams.

In her moments of respite, Daphne tends to her indoor plant sanctuary, and spends hours on her latest craft project. From beading to sewing to paper crafts to book binding to DIY construction projects, nothing is safe from repurposing.

Amidst her myriad of interests, Daphne harbors a guilty pleasure-a profound addiction to Turkish dramas. Enthralled by captivating narratives and rich cultural landscapes, she finds herself transported to distant lands and swept away by tales of love, intrigue and redemption. It's a passion that fuels her imagination and kindles a desire to explore the vibrant streets and ancient landmarks of Türkiye —a dream she holds close to her heart waiting to be fulfilled.

Through her writing, Daphne invites readers on a journey of exploration and self-discovery, weaving tales that reflect the depth of human emotion and the beauty of life's complexities. With each story she tells, she leaves an indelible mark on the hearts and minds of her readers, inspiring them to embrace their own passions and pursue their dreams with unwavering passion, never forgetting to find the humor and an 80's song lyric in everything.

If you would like to receive her newsletter for information on upcoming releases and giveaways, visit daphnemacleodauthor.com and follow me, daphnemacleodauthor, on Facebook, Instagram, X, Pinterest, and Threads and TikTok.

If you would like to contact me, please email me at daphne@daphnem acleodauthor.com or daphnemacleodauthor@gmail.com

www.ingramcontent.com/pod-product-compliance
Lightning Source LLC
Chambersburg PA
CBHW072338020726
47506CB00004B/927

9 7 9 8 9 9 0 2 9 9 5 0 4